NAZILAND

PETER KELLY

TAMAR

First published in the UK in 2026 by Tamar Publishing

Cataloguing in Publication Data is available from the British Library

ISBN: 978-1-9193550-0-9
also available as an e-book

Book design by ArtofComms Creative
www.book-design.co.uk

Tamar Publishing
Penzance, Cornwall

www.peterkellywriter.com

DEDICATION

For Winston, without whom this might not have been fiction.

The World of 2024

Eighty years after the War in Europe

NAZILAND

New York – August 2024

CHAPTER ONE

The journey to Israel always unsettled him. Only twenty minutes on the subway from downtown Manhattan but it was a different world – one where Richard Johnson, like so many of his contemporaries, knew he didn't belong.

The streets had a completely alien feel, but Richard sensed that he was the alien. As he walked past, people stopped and stared without making any pretence. His slim, six-foot frame, blond hair and bright blue eyes seemed to have the effect of something from one of those freak shows of the olden days. The thought crossed his mind that he might be able to charge admission for those who wanted to look at him. Many years ago he had briefly toyed with the idea that he might make a living from his good looks. The movies seemed to beckon, but the couple of auditions his grandmother sent him to quickly confirmed that looks alone were not the key to Hollywood, and the modicum of acting talent required lay well beyond his capabilities.

The thought of his grandmother awakened that pang of guilt that he was usually able to suppress. He knew she always went to great lengths to compensate for his lack of parents. She never mentioned it, but he guessed she had always felt out of place wherever young boys were accompanied by a mother, father, or both. The hours of baseball practice and Little League matches she endured must have been as difficult for her as the embarrassment was for him. There were only a few occasions when the two of them were invited round by his teammates. He had resented her for it, then later resented himself for feeling that way.

He dragged his thoughts back to the reason for today's visit. He was intrigued and irritated in equal measure. Why did one of the most significant figures in the Jewish community want to see him, and why couldn't he just be left in peace? Richard was having a hard enough time of it: his grandmother had died last month; his girlfriend had dumped him last week, and his career at the *Eastern Times* was going nowhere. Fast.

He turned into an elegant street and had to sidestep a beggar straddling the heavy winter coat his life would depend on a few months from now. The age-worn hat, resting on its crown, propped up the unheeded notice to passers-by. Richard often felt guilty at not reading these cardboard inscriptions, so this one being in an extremely neat Hebrew script provided a comforting excuse.

He spotted the house easily. One of those four-storey brownstones which hardly ever came on the open market in New York generally, and certainly never here in what used to be known as Harlem. Richard checked his watch – ten minutes early, but he was in no mood to give any hint of desperation by turning up ahead of time.

He crossed the street to browse the window display of an electrical retailer. He had been on the lookout for the FS90. Usually indifferent to new-fangled gadgets and gizmos, this latest innovation from the relentless production lines of Nazi Germany had somehow captured his imagination. Enough people considered an extra hundred dollars a price worth paying for the luxury of not having to get off the sofa to change the TV channel that all the major outlets had sold out their allocation on launch day. He had been out of town chasing a red herring, so had only caught Flash Kurt's press conference on his own clapped-out set on that evening's late news bulletin.

One of his colleagues had run a piece the next day speculating that 'the television with the red eye' was actually a sophisticated spying device, transmitting the secrets of America's living rooms back to the sinister black building on the outskirts of Berlin where the Gestapo kept tabs on those parts of the world still outside its direct control. From what Richard knew of America's living rooms, they were welcome to waste their time on such a futile undertaking.

It only took him a minute to establish that there was no sign of the FS90. All the brands on offer were domestic or Brazilian. Obvious really. There was no way a store with this address would ever be supplied with goods from the German

Empire, even if it wanted them.

Richard had bumped into 'Flash' Kurt von Papen once in the bar of the Plaza Hotel. The chief executive of the German Trade Mission worked out of an office next door, far enough from his country's embassy in Washington DC to grant him an unusual level of autonomy, and close enough to the centre of New York society to allow him unfettered access to the models, actresses and heiresses who tended to fall for him and did not look out of place in the city's most prestigious hotel. For Americans he represented everything that was positive about the Germans. His good looks, unquestionable charm and edgy sense of humour, combined with his success in persuading his government to authorise the export of new technologies and fast cars out of its empire, made him a popular figure it was difficult not to admire.

Richard crossed back to the other side of the street. The city was holding the hot, thick air prisoner as he mounted the steps and rang the bell. A silent, shuffling housemaid led him halfway down a dark, deserted hallway and motioned him through the door on the right. The room was ghostly, gloomy and oppressively hot. The familiar New York background hum of air conditioning was conspicuous by its absence – the power crisis triggered by the hottest summer on record must have struck again while he was en route, making a mockery of the scientists' predictions of an impending ice age. His suit, tie and hat, the ubiquitous uniform of America's office classes, were not helping, and as he fingered his collar, the feeling of strangulation only got worse.

The seven shimmering flames on the menorah, sucking the little remaining oxygen out of the dense air, created an intimidating, waxy atmosphere. He caught flickers of a bookcase, a heavy armchair and a variety of religious paraphernalia, with the occasional flash of gold as the candlelight chanced upon the spine of an ancient holy book. Though they had always been in the background since he was a child, Richard felt he would never get used to the strange smells and sounds; and there was something disquieting about the appearance of the Orthodox Jews, in the heat and the twenty-first century, with their formal black clothes, ringlets, beards and skullcaps.

Richard personally had nothing against the Jews, and he had never even visited Alaska or Nevada, where huge numbers had been deposited in the 1940s. Comedians often called these states the 'Lands of Milk and Honey', an ironic reference to the biblical description of the Jews' Promised Land. But snow being the colour of milk and desert sand the colour of honey was as far as the comparison stretched.

"I apologise for keeping you waiting, Mr Johnson." A heavy door to his right had opened wide enough to let in a short, stout figure, dressed in formal black with ringlets, beard and skullcap. Richard had just enough time to detect the signs of bustling family life on the other side of the door: the mother supervising lunch while giving instructions to the maid; the two laughing boys. A bright, wholesome world very like the one featured in television dramas, but still different. The distinctive accents that were American yet weren't.

Richard's eyes had adjusted sufficiently to make out the chair the maid had indicated. He heard the air conditioning start up in the kitchen as his host closed the door and swayed over to take up position behind his desk, switching on the small lamp. The white bulb, dull, but in starkly bright contrast to the candlelight, was directed subtly towards the visitor, leaving the other side of the desk in shadow. Richard could see the outline of the head peering at him, but he couldn't make out any features beyond the silhouette dominated by curls. He had never met the man before, but like every reporter in the city, he had heard of him.

Samuel Levy was one of the leaders of the Jewish community, not just in New York, but in the United States as a whole. While the public faces of Jewish politicians were becoming daily more familiar to American viewers through their television sets, the real power still lay in rooms like this one.

Richard received the telephone call yesterday evening. His colleague Dan Adams worked on the political desk of the *Eastern Times*. They were acquaintances rather than friends and occasionally passed each other tips when their worlds of politics and crime coincided. Dan always took great pains not to appear overtly Jewish and lived in the south of Manhattan, comfortably far from Israel in the north. He was able to move effortlessly within and between the Jewish and non-Jewish worlds of New York, and as the election campaign ground on, this was significantly benefiting his standing on the paper. Apparently, Samuel Levy had asked to see Richard urgently. Dan didn't know what it was about, or if he did, wasn't telling. Nor did he say why Richard had been singled out. But a meeting with such a figure was something no journalist would turn down – provided enough people knew exactly who you were visiting, when and where.

The Jewish elder sat down opposite him. "What do you know about Jimmy Sullivan?"

So, this was going to be a brief meeting, no opening pleasantries: *'Isn't it hot for the time of year?' 'Would you like a drink?' 'Gefilte fish bagel?'*

"The man who was found dead in Cuba yesterday?" Richard took the slight movement of the ringlets in the shadows as affirmation and continued. "It seems there was some kind of accident in the MicroWorld theme park. A tourist strayed into an area of Naziland where he shouldn't have been and managed to get himself killed."

Richard stopped. He had been in the game long enough to know that silence was a powerful tool. You have one mouth and two ears for a reason, his grandmother had always told him, and he tried to use them in that ratio. Many of his colleagues considered him taciturn. He preferred to think of it as careful, a good listener. It's to his readers that a journalist speaks. The rest of the time his job is about listening, and possibly there was something worth hearing in this big dark house on West 124th Street.

"You might want to take a closer look, Mr Johnson. Our sources think he may have found out something and that his death may not have been an accident." Richard chose not to fill the hiatus in the conversation. "Of course, we could be completely mistaken." The large hands emphasised the point as expressively as the deep, steady voice. "On the other hand, there may be a big story in it for you."

It was now Levy's turn to use the silence tactic. The air conditioning in the study clicked back on, sending the candle flames into renewed activity.

"What do I tell my editor, Mr Levy? Sounds a bit thin to me. And dangerous."

"Don't worry about your editor – that has been taken care of. As for the danger, I thought that was the kind of story you relished."

So that was why he had been approached. The Ginnelli organised-crime case eight years ago had brought Richard his brief moment of fame, and the bullet he took in the shoulder had done wonders for the *Eastern Times*' circulation, as well as putting a final stop to his baseball days. The royalties from the follow-up book also provided a nice nest egg which would supplement the newspaper's less-than-generous retirement plan. If he could just live long enough to enjoy it.

"I don't think so, Mr Levy. Not unless you give me a lot more to go on. How do I know this will be worth my while? I don't even know who Jimmy Sullivan was."

Even with its unbearable aspects – the weather, the over-crowding, the violence – New York was home and where Richard felt safest and most comfortable. He was settled – some would call it a rut, but not one he was in a particular hurry to trade for a wild goose chase.

"I'm sorry you feel that way, Mr Johnson. I thought this would be something you might welcome. I will just ask you to think it over." Richard was surprised that his brush-off hadn't provoked more of a counter. There must have been a buzzer underneath the desk – the door to the kitchen opened precisely on cue as Richard was dismissed.

"Martha, please show the gentleman out."

The door had opened further this time to admit the maid's considerable bulk. Behind her Richard could now also see the end of the kitchen table where a young girl with a mass of brown curly hair was sitting in a wheelchair. Her pale face lit up into a beaming smile, which echoed the curve of the oxygen line under her nose.

"Grandpappy!"

Richard turned and caught a glimpse of the corresponding smile on the face of the old man. In the light he looked almost benign.

The shuffling housemaid closed the front door behind Richard, extinguishing the hallway's supply of coolness. He hesitated on the top step, feeling he had been transported back into the depths of a raging furnace. The burning air was held in place by the tall buildings, which prevented even the traffic fumes from escaping. As he undid the top button of his collar, Richard started to have doubts. Had he been right to turn down an opportunity which his gut was now telling him could be as big as anything he had tackled in recent years? Still, he had never been one for backing down. He slung his jacket casually over his shoulder before descending to the street.

Walking towards the subway station, Richard felt the foreignness encircling him – the bustle as the vendors of kosher fast food tried to clear the last of their sour-smelling stock at the end of the lunch period, the informal mixture of vaguely familiar Yiddish and a strangely un-American English. In most of New York the Jews made an effort not to appear distinct from their Gentile countrymen and these sights, sounds and smells were virtually absent from the Diamond District and the area around Wall Street.

He reached the station and dropped his token into the turnstile. His mind was still lagging some way behind as Richard's body slumped onto a bench in the middle of the platform, eyes closed, his face upturned towards the hazy sun. When he again paid attention to his surroundings, he was staring into the cartoon face of a smiling soldier of indeterminate race. *Adventure. Comradeship. Riches. Join the Africa Corps!* Richard stood up and moved along the platform until the poster no longer contaminated his field of vision. It was three years since his best friend had been killed over there. Three years in which the borders of the American West African Federation had shifted several times, expanding and contracting as relentlessly as a tide, while the pointless skirmishes continued. The young Americans, Germans and Japanese, enticed by their governments into this military game, were sacrificed at an alarming rate. In this out-of-the-way place tactics, weapons and discipline could be tested and honed, in preparation for the real war, which everyone hoped would never come.

He sat down further along the platform of 125th Street

station, where the face of Josef Goldberg beamed down at him from an election billboard. Richard found the economics of political campaigning mind-boggling – the millions of dollars which even the longest of long shots was prepared to devote to the American dream of a four-year stint in the White House. At the start of the year he had asked Dan Adams about the Nevada senator's chances. The informed view at that time was that Goldberg would be lucky to achieve third place in most of the primaries. While his stance on the position of Jews in America appealed to many of the younger radicals within his own community, he was not expected to generate widespread support. However, things had turned out differently – the two leading Republican candidates got embroiled in a row which put them both out of the running. Goldberg was the sole beneficiary of this debacle and in July, virtually by default, he received his party's nomination. In the fallout the huge lead the Republicans enjoyed in earlier opinion polls was dramatically reduced, but they were still ahead of their Democrat rivals, who few expected to retain the presidency in November.

His thoughts were interrupted by the arrival of the train. In the stifling heat of the rickety Red Line carriage Richard again wondered about the rumours that the *Eastern Times* was ultimately controlled by Jewish interests. All businesses in America were required to declare their level of Jewish ownership, and the official documents filed for *ET* clearly showed this as zero. But there were probably many ways of circumventing the official procedures.

Richard cursed himself. Why had he turned down the opportunity for a change? New York may be home, but what was there here for him? Oppressive heat, which showed no sign of breaking. Okay, so Cuba was even hotter, but the breeze off the sea apparently made it much more bearable. And a dead-end job which he used to love, but the last few years had been a procession of not-quite scoops, and every internal reshuffle brought a couple of weeks of nervousness before his position had been confirmed in the new organisation, even if it was a desk or two further away from the subeditor's office. Things hadn't been the same since his grandmother died. Her illness kept him on track for the two years it took the cancer to finish her off, giving his life a structure of hospital appointments and evenings spent cooking and reading for her. *Moby Dick* had been her favourite. He was halfway through the third reading when she finally passed away. The book was one of the few things he kept, even though he knew he would never open it again.

He loosened his tie a bit more and let his body slump into the seat, determined to relax for the final quarter hour of the journey back to the office.

The subway rattled into his stop. He got off the train and crossed to the opposite platform. Two trains screeched and screamed in and out of the station as he toyed with the idea of returning to Mr Levy to tell him that he had reconsidered. But that was something his pride would never let him do. No, he just had to trust to luck that something would come along. If not, there was always that novel he'd been promising he'd write for the past decade.

CHAPTER TWO

"Come in, Tom."

The curtains were now open, and Samuel Levy's study was particularly welcoming in the bright summer sun. The mementoes of a long, happy life and the ancient religious artefacts perfectly reflected the character of Tom's oldest friend.

Tom Monroe was a head taller than his client, and his silver hair was a sharp contrast to the pure black of Levy's ringlets. They were the same age, though different in every other respect. Since meeting on their first day at Yale fifty-six years earlier, they had remained the closest of friends and as inseparable as their different cultures and divergent career paths allowed. There had been occasional conflicts of interest in their professional relationship, but these had been relatively minor and quickly resolved.

Tom's legal services were compensated on a retainer basis these days, but it was in his capacity of friend that he had agreed to carry out Samuel Levy's wishes. There was clearly no question of Samuel, or any of his family or Jewish acquaintances, undertaking a trip across the Atlantic. The risks were something Tom chose not to think about. Had his wife not died three years ago, and his two children not become independent long since in ways more than the merely financial, he might have thought twice. Nor were other clients a consideration, because Samuel had been his sole professional obligation for the last five years.

"Is everything arranged?"

"Yes," said Tom. "We leave on Saturday. The German will be travelling with us." The arguments about the trustworthiness of Doctor Engels were past but not forgotten. His participation in the undertaking was not optional, so further discussion would have been moot. "What was the journalist doing here, Samuel?"

"It has nothing at all to do with our business, Tom. Just a small matter I have to sort out for the elders."

"Is he going to Europe as well? I assume that's why you asked me to find someone who could speak German."

"No. He's off to Cuba. The two trips are completely unrelated." The old man hesitated. "Tom, you know how much Rebecca means to us ..." His words trailed off as his voice cracked.

"I know, Samuel. I will do everything in my power for her."

"I know you will. Thank you. Travel safe."

CHAPTER THREE

"I heard Old Red was looking for you." Dan Adams was crossing the lobby towards the Fifth Avenue exit of the *Eastern Times* with his attractive and very un-Jewish new secretary, as Richard Johnson made for the elevator back to his office on the thirty-fifth floor. When she was sure her boss couldn't see, the blonde flashed Richard a broad smile. He was too preoccupied to return it – probably a good thing as office romances were always a source of complications. To avoid incurring the wrath of the editor, Richard punched the button for the fortieth floor instead, put the jacket back on and adjusted his tie. The receptionist who sat guard over the editorial suite looked up as the door pinged open.

"I believe Mr Donovan was looking for me?"

"He's not back from his lunch at the JBC yet. You're welcome to sit and wait, or I can call you when he gets in Mr ..."

"Johnson. Richard Johnson." The ping of the express elevator door removed the need for a decision.

"Ah, Johnson, there you are. So good of you to come up. Please step into my office."

This was a friendly, even courteous side to the editor-in-chief that Richard had not experienced often. 'Red' Donovan had earned his nickname from the excessive use of the pen with which he had made his mark, literally, as the youngest editor of the *New York Times*, before being poached by the *Eastern Times* ten years ago. The lunch at the Jewish Business Center must have been excellent to put him in this good a mood. It was somewhere Richard had always wanted to eat but never had the cash or the contacts. The attraction of the building had nothing to do with its Jewishness, and the restaurant's repertoire far exceeded the confines of the merely kosher. *King Kong* was one of his favourite films and he, like so many New Yorkers, could never quite shake the association with the iconic building which for so many years had been the tallest in the world, then the tallest outside Europe, and still remained unsurpassed within the United States today.

"Johnson, I've got an interesting project for you." The office door clicked shut behind them. "Crime isn't currently enjoying much interest, so I'm sure your department can spare you for a few days. By the time the Berlin Olympics have finished, I want a piece on the current state of entertainment in the old US of A. So, you're off down to the 'Pleasure State,' as they like to call themselves in Cuba. Take a look at the gambling joints, the cabarets in places like Sinatra's, and the theme parks. Go for a mix of the sleaze and the family angle – prostitution and the educational aspirations of the likes of MicroWorld. You've just got time to pick up a bag on your way to the airport. Jenny outside has your ticket and hotel reservation. Any questions?"

The editor moved behind his desk and picked up the phone. There were to be no more details, no explanations, and Jenny was already waiting in the doorway behind Richard, a brown envelope stuffed with travel documents in her expensively manicured hand, which she touched against his just a second longer than she needed to. He was curious to check whether the booking had been made before or after his visit to Samuel Levy.

"Good. Well, we'll see you in a week or so, then. And try not to enjoy yourself too much!" The laugh was forced, as was Richard's imitation. He wondered whether he had time to stop off on his own floor and make sure Barbara, the department's secretary, knew where he was going. He decided he would find a payphone and call her from the airport instead.

CHAPTER FOUR

"Come in, Isaiah. I'm terribly sorry to have kept you waiting."

Isaiah Horowitz took in his surroundings as he walked towards the plush leather armchair indicated by his host. The presidential suite of the Central Park Hilton had seen better days, and this was probably the closest it had ever come to having a real president in residence. The Nevada senator had a glass of what looked like whiskey on the table between them but made no move to offer his guest a drink.

"That's quite okay, Senator. I know how busy you are. I'm sorry to have to trouble you with my domestic problems."

"What are friends for, Isaiah? What are friends for? In any case, I wanted to talk to you about the fundraiser. It went rather well, I thought."

"It would have gone even better if Masters had turned up instead of sending his aide to Cuba to represent him. Doesn't he realise the damage that did? All the people I got there on the promise that they could meet both of you?"

"Yes, that was unfortunate. But I didn't get the impression people felt they'd been short-changed. And it means they had more time for the girls!" The Jewish senator laughed.

"Well, they're not going to say that to you, sir, are they! You don't go whining to the next president of the United States. You complain to his fundraiser." The businessman hesitated as his host took a sip of his drink. "I think we should do the next one in Texas. Steaks and cowgirls on his ranch. Then we can be sure he'll turn up."

"Now, now, Isaiah. I know you don't like the man. But we need him. With Masters on the ticket, it's not just a Jewish vote. He gets big business on board, and he's a lot more acceptable to the Bible Belt than a Jew or a couple of Catholics."

"The fact that I don't like the man is neither here nor there. I'm sure he feels the same about me. The problem, Josef, is that I don't *trust* him. He came out of nowhere. Before the convention he hadn't shown any interest in the election. Then, up he pops, the answer to our prayers. The candidate able to heal the rift in the party and broaden our appeal at a stroke. He's too good to be true. And he's happy to go along with all your policies. Doesn't even try to negotiate. I don't get it. It's like he's happy to be vice president. No one is ever happy to be VP. They want more. Except Masters."

"I know what you mean, Isaiah. But you know what they say about gift horses."

"I also know what they say about gifts from Greeks, Senator."

"Well, none of that's going to change now. We must focus on winning the White House in November, then he can sink back into that oblivion specially created for vice presidents. Half the people in the country won't even remember his name. Anyway, what is it that brings you here?"

"It's my wife. She's started talking about a divorce."

"Oh. That's very unfortunate. But we can stop her doing anything before the election, can't we?"

"I need to stop her for longer than that, Josef. My financial affairs are a bit complicated at the moment. If this went ahead, she'd ruin me."

"Sorry, Isaiah, you've lost me there. Why does the timing affect the money side of things?"

"I needed to get a few assets revalued to underwrite a loan. It's a buyers' market at the moment, so I wouldn't realise anything like those values if I had to sell."

"Oh, I see. There's no risk of you being exposed for fraud, I hope."

"No. You have nothing to worry about on that score, Senator. I just wanted to ask if you could have a word with her? She respects you and wouldn't want to do the campaign any damage."

"I suppose she's got no shortage of evidence against you, Isaiah. You're not exactly discreet!"

"Less than you might think, Sir, in terms of what a court would want to establish culpability."

The presidential candidate swirled his drink, and the

ice cubes clinked. "Does she know we were at the villa last weekend?"

"Of course. She arranged the caterers."

"Good. I can call to thank her for her hospitality and discretion. Leave it with me, Isaiah."

CHAPTER FIVE

"You cut that fine, buddy."

The extra fifteen minutes allowed for business class passengers to check in, the lack of hold baggage, and his way with words, as effective with female airline staff as with the readers of the *Eastern Times*, had combined to ensure Richard was allowed on board long after the flight had officially closed. He ignored the safety briefing and the man beside him for as long as it took to drag the buckle end of the seatbelt from under his body. As they pushed back from gate twenty-four of Idlewild's main terminal, he experienced his customary panic that he had forgotten something vital. The reassuring feel of the Supalite typewriter in its case beneath his feet meant that he at least had the most vital tool of his trade. He always kept a small, packed bag on top of the closet in his apartment, but it was designed for trekking round underworld haunts, fast getaways and nights spent hiding in shrubbery. He hoped the requirements for Cuba would be a lot different and had wasted fifteen minutes establishing that he didn't own a suitable set of swimming trunks, before deciding that they, and anything else he might need, would be easily available in the world's entertainment capital.

The engines of the Boeing 760 were already at half judder by the time he turned to look at the man sitting next to him. He went through his usual game of guessing a person's characteristics based purely on their appearance. Medium height, as far as it was possible to tell in an all-swallowing business class seat, the black frames of his thick glasses matched the colour of his curly hair, which already showed signs of thinning at odds with his youthful face. Olive complexion: Mediterranean origin? Expensive suit, white shirt set off with an overly jazzy tie, at least to Richard's taste. Probably someone with artistic pretensions in a boring but well-paid job. Maybe Jewish, so could be an accountant. Heavy, expensive watch, but a domestic brand rather than a more fashionable German one, so probably Jewish. Richard decided to catch his breath rather than wasting it competing with the roar of the imminent take-off, and anyway his neighbour was already engrossed in the airline magazine. The *Pan-American Review* was generally considered the best of the in-flight publications, and it looked like Richard was in luck. This month's edition carried a feature on Cuba, celebrating its place at the top of the hospitality industry's league table – an article which seemed to be fascinating his travelling companion.

When the aircraft started to level off and the engine pitch dropped, Richard twisted towards the man in the window seat.

"First time in Cuba?"

"God, no!" The heavy glasses seemed to be locked on a point somewhere just above Richard's head. "At the moment I'm spending every other week there."

"So not a vacation then?"

"Far from it. You heard of AnimalWorld?"

"The theme park the Hughes group is building south of Havana?"

"That's the boy. I'm the architect."

"I thought it was all open space filled with wild animals. Is there much work for an architect?"

"No, not much. Just the hotels, the theatres, the animal pens, the retail outlets, the man-made lake, the infrastructure, the underground tunnels that supply the whole park."

"Okay, I get the picture," laughed Richard.

"What about you? Vacation or business?"

"I'm writing a piece on the entertainment industry."

"Ah, journalist. Take a free holiday, string all the postcards together, and call it an article. Nice job, if you can get it. Work for anything I'd know?"

"The *Eastern Times*. Richard Johnson."

"Aaron Selonof. Hughes Corporation." The two men shook hands just as the stewardess started to hover. "What do you have by way of whiskey, dear? American whiskey."

"Jack Daniels, Jim Beam," she said.

"Jack on the rocks, for me. What about you, Richard?"

The journalist directed his reply at the stewardess, the real source of the benevolence – not that one free drink on the back of a thousand-dollar air ticket exactly smacked of generosity.

"Gin and tonic, please."

"So, do you journos always get to travel business class?"

Richard shrugged. He had no desire to satisfy the scorn of the architect. The truth that he was only in the front of the plane because of the lateness of the booking would have highlighted the gulf between them in the meritocracy. And he guessed it probably wasn't the newspaper footing the bill this time. Still, he was grateful for the rare luxury of not having screaming children kicking the back of his seat or running their sticky paws through his hair.

After negotiating an extra ice cube, the other man pushed the magazine back in the seat pocket and Richard resigned himself to the long haul.

"How about you? Have you been to Cuba before?"

"No. Never had the pleasure, until now," Richard said.

"At this time of year, I wouldn't exactly call it a pleasure, Richard. Way too hot and sticky. Fine, if you're inside somewhere that the AC works, but out in the open it can be torture. And some of them don't even speak the lingo. You'll be all right since you'll only meet those in the service industries, but even some of the construction managers on our site only speak Spanish. You wouldn't think it had been part of the US for nearly seventy years. Still, it's better than when we were doing MicroWorld."

Richard started to take an interest. "How so?"

"Before 'fifty-five it was all plantations – tobacco and sugar. The only industries were cigars and rum. Today even the farms and factories that remain make more money from the tourists than they do from their products. Anyway, it started with the casinos. To compete with Las Vegas, they realised they would have to start speaking English. Then the hotels followed. And when the cartoon guy got into trouble with the tax man, Mr Hughes saw the opportunity and picked up the pieces." The architect rattled the ice cubes in his whiskey. "The park his studio had built in California was starting to make a profit, and it leaked that they were planning another in Florida. He was starting to buy up all the swamps there, but as soon as the word got out, the price of the land went through the roof. By then the old guy was very sick."

"And Howard Hughes was never slow to spot an opportunity!"

"We offered him a way out, and he jumped at it. Sold us the rights to the park design and gave up on Florida. Mr Hughes bought up all the plantations just inland from Havana. They were going for a song since all the farm staff were flocking to the new hotels on the coast where they could earn three times the money."

Richard was irritated by the implication that his fellow passenger had been personally involved in all this, when in reality, he hadn't even been born.

"So, what's MicroWorld actually like?"

"It's our second generation. The first was just a park with rides, FantasyWorld, the same as the original cartoon theme park in California. Well, not exactly the same because the cartoon characters weren't included in the deal." The architect drained the last of his drink before continuing. "So, we had to create our own set of characters in double-quick time. Luckily, Mr Hughes hadn't quite sold off the film studios, so that all worked out okay. Then he had the idea of branching out. He had all the casinos as well, of course, but wanted something different. That was when he came up with the idea of 'edutainment', as he called it."

"Understanding the culture of other lands through theme park rides," Richard offered.

"Actually, that idea only came along later. The first element was the scientific part. When they realised that wouldn't provide enough to keep people occupied for a whole day, they added the geography."

"So which bit did you work on, Aaron?"

"I got involved with Brazil. When they decided to put a restaurant inside the mountain with the statue on top of it. That was just over three years ago. Then there were some modifications to the USA section. Since then, I've been working on AnimalWorld. We should be open by 2026."

"Wasn't there a new restaurant in the Egypt area around the same time as the Brazil one?"

"Yeah, but I wasn't on that project. The Germans do it all in-house." The architect leant forward, grabbed the headphones from the seat pocket and proceeded to break open the plastic bag.

"Mind if I take a look at the magazine, Aaron? There doesn't seem to be one in this seat."

"Sure. There's an article on Cuba which might give you some info, seeing as it's your first trip."

As the architect tried to find a channel more entertaining than talking about projects he hadn't worked on, Richard got down to business. He liked to research his subject in advance – in the crime world it was the best way to stay alive – but the circumstances of the current story hadn't allowed him the time for that luxury.

Just as he finished reading the article, the main cabin lights were extinguished. He reached for the button to activate the individual reading light, then thought better of it and pushed the call button instead, letting the newspaper buy him a second gin and tonic.

It was obvious he was being used, but it was far from clear why or by whom. He was often accused of being politically naive, but even he could see that the old Jew knew far more than he was saying. Samuel Levy was clearly a man of great influence – if he could control the editor of the *Eastern Times*, who else did he have in his pocket? And why wasn't it just a simple police matter working out what had happened to Jimmy Sullivan? What did Levy think a journalist could achieve that they couldn't? And how much did the police know already? It was his priority on landing to find out how far their investigation had progressed. Having the commission to do a piece on the family entertainment angle was good cover, but he doubted that anyone would even care if the article never got written.

And was there a European dimension to it at all? Like most Americans, he had never been to Europe and never expected to. Visitors were very carefully vetted and had to pay substantially for the privilege. He only knew a couple of people who had been there privately, and a few more who had visited for work or in government service. The paper had its European correspondent, of course, but Wolfgang was a German national, who had been allocated to them by his own government, and he had only made it to New York twice in the last decade. Two of the top sports writers were currently in Berlin for the Olympics, having braved the extensive and invasive accreditation process, but their freedom of movement was tightly restricted, and they were herded from one competition venue or staged event to the next with the rest of the free world's press.

Richard's own background was part European, not that it set him apart. His grandmother had been born in Sweden in late 1942, in the brief hiatus between the war ending and her native land being absorbed into Germany's European empire. His great-grandmother had revoked her own and her baby daughter's Swedish-German nationality the moment they set off for the United States in the December of that year – not a condition of immigration into the USA, but a condition of emigration imposed by the victorious Nazis, who allowed this one remaining neutral state a six-month window for anyone who didn't want to participate in the glorious future of the thousand-year Reich. Richard's grandmother couldn't even speak Swedish, or German. By an accident of fate he, on the other hand, had started to learn German at school when the language had been briefly in vogue in the mid-2000s. His grandmother had been friendly with Frau Henkel, the old German teacher at his school and, after the language was removed from the official curriculum following a diplomatic row, she'd come to their apartment a couple of evenings a week to give him extra tuition.

There were lots of rumours about Frau Henkel. Some believed she was Jewish and had moved to the USA in the mass exodus of 1942, but that would have destined her for Nevada or Alaska, as she had no other family already in New York. Others claimed she was a Nazi spy. Richard had often wondered as a child what she could possibly have spied on, but her fearsome reputation for discipline ensured that the question had never been asked. On a couple of occasions, Frau Henkel had come to the apartment in the middle of the night. He shouldn't have been up, so he never asked about it, and his grandmother never mentioned the visits.

Cradling the drink, he closed his eyes and tipped the seat back to a more comfortable angle. On balance, Richard thought a German connection to the Cuban murder was unlikely and that the location of the dead body might just be a coincidence. But with the Germans, you could never know for sure. All his instincts told him this was a good lead. The route by which it had come to him had some similarities with the Ginnelli case, which had given him his big break eight years ago – an unknown informant singling him out, apparently at random, like a plumber in the *Yellow Pages*. If he was right, this was his big chance to get back on the career ladder. The Ginnellis had unwittingly turned him into the golden boy, but his inability to conjure up the next big story ensured his status was short-lived. Since then, he had watched a procession of young hopefuls file into the editor's office. Some went on to greater things, while the majority followed his own route of brief glory leading to disappointment and stagnation. Even a move to another paper was difficult: this was one profession where past achievements were very visibly in the public domain, and not a question of how much you dared to fabricate a résumé for a job application. The thought of still being in this rut at sixty was unbearable. Not that it often happened. For most journalists the alcohol usually made sure of that.

Berlin – May 1941

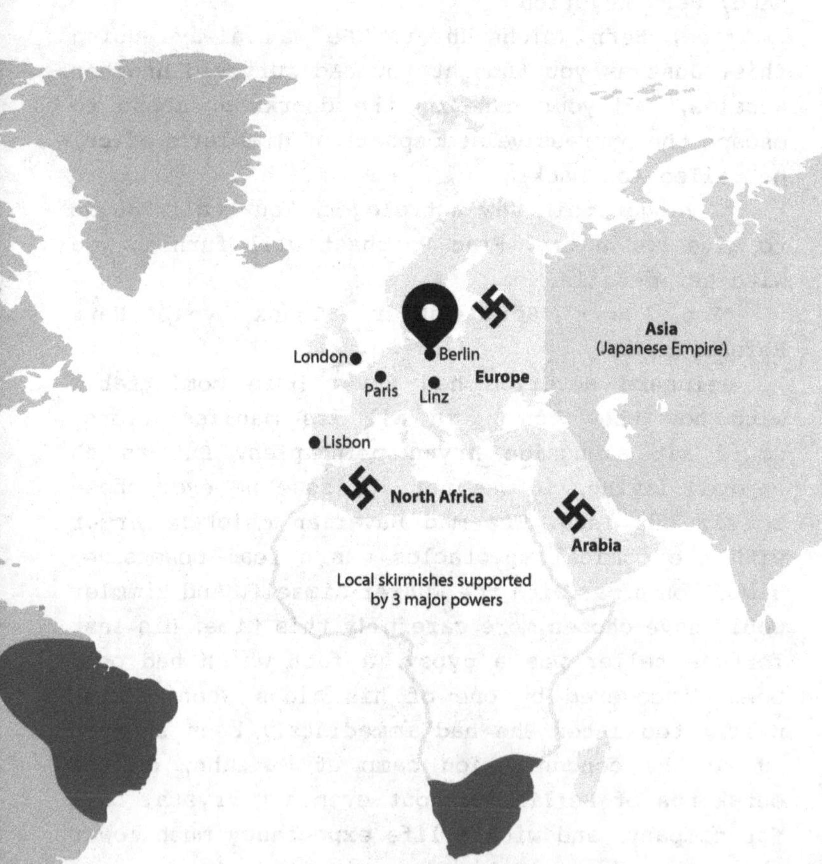

CHAPTER SIX

"And, Herr Heydrich."

"Yes, Herr Reichsführer?" He was always doing this. Just as you thought you had survived another session, had your hand on the doorknob, about to escape the oppressive atmosphere of Himmler's office, he called you back.

"I've got this new astrologer. You really ought to give her a try. Frau Potthast will furnish you with her details."

"Yes, Herr Reichsführer. Thank you, Herr Reichsführer."

Reinhard Heydrich had never been comfortable with how the occult, in all its manifestations, could sit alongside Aryan principles. But as he enjoyed living, it was not an issue he ever chose to air out loud. The mad Bavarian chicken farmer with the comical spectacles was a real obsessive, almost on a par with the Führer himself. And Himmler would have chosen more carefully this time. His last fortune teller was a gypsy, a fact which had only been discovered by one of his aides when it was nearly too late. She had immediately been shipped off to the concentration camp at Marzahn, on the outskirts of Berlin, without even her crystal ball for company, and with a life expectancy much lower than the political prisoners she would be joining. Heydrich wondered if she'd seen that coming.

He stepped towards Frau Potthast's desk. Without even looking up, she handed him a folded piece of cheap writing paper. Himmler was a stickler for bureaucracy: SS stationery for SS business; his personal Reichsführer stock for personal notes —

unless they were unofficial personal notes which he would not want traced. Those were scribbled out on this low-quality pad which his secretary kept in her bottom drawer. So, it had not been an afterthought. Himmler relished the psychological power he held over his staff, especially the most senior ones, manipulating their hopes and fears at every opportunity. God, he hated that man. Heydrich had quickly risen to head up most of the Third Reich's internal security services — the regular police, the dreaded Gestapo secret police and the sinister Sicherheitsdienst. The SD, as it was known, was responsible for spying on all enemies and potential enemies of the regime within Germany, and very few people escaped that particular net. Apart from Adolf Hitler himself, the only person able to intimidate Heydrich was his boss, Heinrich Himmler, who headed up the whole of the SS, which included its own armed branch, the Waffen-SS, as well as all Heydrich's policemen and spies. The SS was also one of Germany's major commercial enterprises, running the concentration camps to provide the Reich with forced labour for armament production and Himmler with almost unlimited access to wealth.

Heydrich glanced at the address — a poorer neighbourhood in the south of the city. Life was so much simpler if you humoured the boss on occasions like this. He would change out of his uniform and get his driver to drop him off a couple of blocks away that evening. If she was any good, it wouldn't matter that he wasn't going to make an appointment.

CHAPTER SEVEN

A rectangle of yellow light shot across his path. The voices of a whole platoon of drunks making the most of their leave were in the second verse of the *Horst Wessel Song*, doing for the eerie silence what the light was doing for the blackout. Heydrich skirted the group of three corporals who were about to collide with him. Normally he would have bawled them out, demanding their names, ruining their lives for the next month until they realised there wasn't going to be any follow-up. But tonight he wanted to remain inconspicuous. Let them enjoy Berlin while they could. They would be blissfully ignorant that their next heroic adventure was likely to be the Soviet Union, probably punishment enough for any indiscretion. As the door closed itself, returning the street to its pristine darkness, Heydrich passed through an invisible cloud of cigarette smoke. The unmistakeable sharp whiff of French tobacco almost made him rethink his leniency, except that it nearly masked the odour of sweat, against which the wartime soap was powerless. The house he wanted was three doors further along.

"Come in, Herr Obergruppenführer."

General Heydrich parted the bead curtain and stepped inside. Red wallpaper, red carpet, red lights illuminating a circular table covered with a red velvet tablecloth and dominated by a crystal ball. Behind it sat a small woman of about sixty. The lighting made it impossible to discern her complexion, but the strands of hair which had escaped from her predominantly red headscarf looked jet black.

"Frau Korsch?"

"Cross my palm with silver." She stretched out a soft pink hand towards the middle of the table. Heydrich hadn't been through this ritual before and was embarrassed not to have been prepared.

"I'll pay when there's something worth paying for."

"Oh! A touch of Jewish ancestry, maybe?"

The rumour that his grandfather was Jewish had plagued Heydrich's time in the National Socialist party. Now responsible for the enforcement of the Nuremberg laws on racial purity, any hint that he himself fell within their scope was hugely damaging. The Nazis' top genealogist had been hired to show beyond doubt that the story was completely unfounded, but any mention of it still disturbed Heydrich deeply. He thrust his hand into his trouser pocket. He rarely had need of cash in his day-to-day dealings and, in his hurry to change out of uniform, he had failed to move his wallet into his civilian outfit.

"Silver is a figurative term. I'll take any form of cash. But no cheques — the tax, you understand." She was grinning, enjoying his discomfort and displaying two large gold teeth. All he had was the hundred Reichsmark note he kept tucked into the pouch containing his identity papers, which was for absolute emergencies. It was as much as many families had to live off for two weeks.

"Your boss doesn't know about the homosexual encounter on that navy ship, does he?"

He picked the banknote out from its hiding place and slapped it into her still outstretched palm. He noticed that his fingers were trembling.

"Clearly no Jewish descent there. A true Aryan, if ever I saw one." She pocketed the note deftly under the table, returning both hands to the classic pose, framing the crystal ball into which she now peered. Heydrich sat down and managed to drag his eyes from her face and look into the glass. He thought he could see a white fog swirling within it and wondered how she created that effect.

"You are thinking how you can kill me." She looked into his eyes, but he was staring, transfixed, into the crystal ball. "But we needn't worry about that. Herr Himmler has secrets of his own. For a start there's that secretary of his. But there are others which don't appear on your colour-coded file cards — not even the ones you keep hidden under your daughter's bed." She paused again, but still Heydrich didn't flinch. "And don't be thinking you can put me in one of those camps, like he did with Edith. Not only was she a gypsy, she was a fraud. You're not going to take me by surprise like that. Anyway, you want me alive. I'm the only one who can help you avoid the slow, painful death whose shadow is currently hanging over you. Come to see me again before you go to Prague."

Heydrich looked up as she paused again, but the woman was staring into the depths of her crystal ball. Alone among everything she had said, the reference to Prague made no sense to him.

"Wait. There's something else." Heydrich watched her face as she frowned. "You will receive an important message from the grave." The doubt and hesitation in her voice would have been clear even to someone whose main role in life was not to identify lies and falsification.

"And just what is that supposed to mean?"

"I have no idea, Herr Heydrich. I really have no idea."

She placed the palms of her hands on the tablecloth either side of the crystal ball, and her head tipped forward over them. She was completely still, and he couldn't even make out any sign of breathing. Was this the time he should leave? He could never remember feeling so ill at ease. He felt compelled to get up but was rooted to the chair and couldn't move a muscle.

"Go now. Your driver will be on the opposite side of the road, about fifty metres from where you left him."

Heydrich was in a cold sweat as he climbed the steps from the basement. It had started to drizzle, so he absent-mindedly turned up the collar of his coat, stuffed his hands into his pockets and walked hunched towards the street where he had left the car. He had his head down and was concentrating on the dull white of the kerb edges which barely managed to stay visible through the pervasive darkness of the blackout.

He caught the driver completely unawares. Max was watching for his boss to come down the other side of the road and was anxious not to let him walk past, towards where the car had originally been.

"Sorry, sir, but there were two men watching the car, so I thought it best to move. As soon as I drove off, they disappeared, but when I went round the block, the space had been taken, so I had to park here."

Still completely lost in his thoughts, the driver's words hardly registered.

"Take me home."

CHAPTER EIGHT

"Good morning, Herr Obergruppenführer."

"Good morning, Frau Schmidt. What's in the diary for today?"

This morning routine played itself out in the office on Prinz-Albrecht-Strasse shortly before eight on every working day when Heydrich was in Berlin. The security chief was typically at his desk in this converted palace by seven in the morning, which gave him the opportunity to prepare his notes for all the day's routine sessions before the distractions of office life set in: the seemingly endless round of meetings that it took to maintain control over the combined SD Security Service, the Police and Gestapo; the constant looking over the shoulder to avoid getting caught out by the machinations of the Reichsführer-SS; the telephone calls that Frau Schmidt couldn't shield him from; the management of the Nazi party's internal power struggles, encouraged by the Führer himself, which made the apparatus of government very cumbersome and inefficient. And if there was one thing that Reinhard Heydrich hated, it was inefficiency. That had been a bonus for his boss. Himmler had been attracted to the man's intellect, visible ambition and dedication to the cause. Heydrich famously designed what was now the SD, the Nazi party's main intelligence-gathering operation inside Germany, as the answer to an interview question Himmler asked from his sickbed all those years ago.

Heydrich's days were typically a round of committee meetings and briefings given or received, but with a large degree of flexibility built in. If

Himmler called for him, which happened on most days, he had to make the trip across the courtyard to the Wilhelmstrasse building within minutes. Of course, any summons from the Führer required an even quicker response, but those tended not to be so frequent. He was scheduled to spend the weekend at the Berghof, Hitler's mountain retreat, so such a call was unlikely today. This flexibility, rather than being a burden, afforded Heydrich the opportunity to drop in on his colleagues unannounced, thus maintaining his reputation for unpredictability, intensifying the dread most members of the hierarchy, even the most senior, felt when they received a visit from him.

"And Herr Himmler wants to see you at midday. His secretary said it was something to do with Prague, but I don't think she knew any more than that."

Prague. What was it the old woman had said? 'Come and see me again before you go to Prague.' And something about a slow, painful death. Coincidence? A lucky guess?

"And what about the rest of the department, Frau Schmidt?"

"Oberst Stengel is still in Warsaw until tomorrow. Hauptmann Lindemann is in the office all day. Apart from his meetings with you, he is seeing a lieutenant from the Abwehr this morning, and he has a briefing with the head of the Hanover office later this afternoon."

"What does the Abwehr want with us, Frau Schmidt?"

The Abwehr was Germany's external intelligence-gathering service, and its head, Admiral Wilhelm Canaris, was a major antagonist of Heydrich's.

"The lieutenant asked for an urgent meeting and didn't say what it was about. I applied the standard policy and didn't probe further." The standard policy was designed to ensure that access to the SD was never denied to someone who might want to shed light on their own department's motivations and machinations. And that was particularly true of departments seen as rivals. Frau Schmidt opened the grey folder in her lap. "It is a Leutnant von Graber. He joined the Abwehr a few months ago after being invalided out of active service in the navy."

Heydrich tried to conceal his feeling of shock. Von Graber. Grab was the German for grave. Could this be what the fortune teller had meant last night — an important message from the grave?

"What time is the lieutenant coming here, Frau Schmidt?"

"At ten a.m., Herr Heydrich, so Hauptmann Lindemann can see him when your Intelligence Review meeting finishes."

"No, I think I will see him myself. Postpone my ten o'clock meeting for half an hour."

"Very good, Herr Obergruppenführer."

Their initial business of the day concluded, Frau Schmidt returned to her desk outside Heydrich's office. She phoned Hauptmann Lindemann on the internal line to tell him that he had an unexpected free half hour to catch up on his paperwork.

CHAPTER NINE

Lieutenant Alois von Graber had never been so nervous in his life - a life that had already included pitched battles against the British Royal Navy, fought in violent winter storms in the far North Atlantic. Even when the battleship *Scharnhorst* had been damaged in action and the shrapnel from a torpedo had ripped into his leg, his fear had come nowhere near to what he felt now.

On his arrival he was shocked to hear that the meeting he had requested with Germany's internal security service would be with its head, the 'Blond Beast' himself. Von Graber's family were delighted that his war wound had not only brought further honour to add to their proud tradition of service to both the Prussian and German nations, but that it also transported him from one of the most dangerous postings in Germany's all-conquering armed forces. Today he had a desk job where his linguistic skills and intelligence should ensure interesting work, far from any more hot flying metal. Now he had needlessly placed himself in a position of danger. A danger of a very different complexion from the simple kill or be killed of battle, but no less real. The office politics of the upper echelons of the Nazi party were the stuff of hushed gossip wherever junior officers congregated, and the wardroom of the *Scharnhorst* had been no exception. He had heard tales of Heydrich's efficient brutality, which could only have been exaggeration. And the rumours of rivalries and manoeuvrings between the complex power bases of the party and military apparatus were as closely studied as the football results had been before the war.

"The Obergruppenführer will see you now."

The secretary, behind whom a stream of senior uniforms representing a complete cross-section of Nazi military and police was now filing, had to repeat the instruction to bring the lieutenant back to reality. When von Graber stood, a shaft of pain shot up his left leg, as it always did when he had been sitting too long.

Heydrich was at his large mahogany desk, the sun streaming in through the window behind him. Its rays shimmered off his blond hair, giving the momentary impression of a halo. He was ordering the papers on his desk into three brown folders. As he handed the folders to his secretary, he looked up for the first time and indicated the visitor's chair.

"Leutnant von Graber. And what can the SD do for you?"

Heydrich's large palms lay flat on the desk, his fingers pointing towards the navy man, thumbs perpendicular, framing the single sheet of paper, to the top of which was clipped a white file index card. Von Graber opened his mouth, but nothing came out. He closed it then started again.

"Herr Obergruppenführer. I know this is highly irregular, but there is something which I believe I must bring to your attention. For the benefit of the Fatherland."

Heydrich didn't say a word. The blue eyes just continued to bore into von Graber's skull.

"On Sunday evening I attended a reception for Admiral Nomura, the Japanese naval attaché. I was sitting next to an officer in the Japanese navy at dinner, and he had clearly acquired a taste for Admiral Doenitz's schnapps. This captain was showing off, hinting that the Japanese were planning a major naval operation which would put our exploits into the shade. He clearly had some personal involvement in it." He looked into Heydrich's eyes, but the stare hadn't moved on. "We had already established that we both spoke German and Japanese and English, so I asked if he was talking of the USA. I have never seen a man sober up so fast, Herr Obergruppenführer. He had clearly overstepped the mark, so I made a joke of it and asked him where he had learned his German."

"So you reported your observations to your senior officer?"

"Of course, sir. As we were leaving, I told Admiral Bürkner what I have just told you. When he came into the office late the next morning, he was visibly angry. I had the opportunity to ask him about it later in the day. He had reported my conversation to Admiral Canaris in person. The admiral had dismissed the idea out of hand and showed no intention of pursuing it any further. That's when I decided I should talk to the SD, Herr Obergruppenführer."

"Does your boss know you are here?"

"No, sir."

"Well, we'll keep it that way, shall we? You still have a lot to learn about how intelligence works, Herr Leutnant. Perhaps we'll be able to give you an opportunity to do so. I am sure our esteemed colleague, Admiral Canaris, knows exactly what he is doing. He is hardly going to confirm what we know of Japan's plans to someone who does not need to know. However, you have my personal assurance that the Reich will be fully informed of what you heard and will take it into account appropriately. It is always better to be safe than sorry. How well do you speak Japanese?"

Von Graber explained that he had studied the language at university both in Heidelberg and Tokyo, and he left Heydrich's office a very relieved man.

Heydrich sat at his desk in silent reverie. He was twirling the handle of his SS dagger lightly between thumb and forefinger, as he often did when he was concentrating. He didn't hear his secretary come in and almost let the dagger fall as she coughed to make him aware of her presence.

"The Reichsführer wants to see you in his office in ten minutes. I have moved your ten thirty meeting back to twelve."

"Thank you, Frau Schmidt. Can you check for me if Admiral Canaris will be in his office this afternoon? He doesn't need to know I asked."

Cuba – August 2024

CHAPTER TEN

The Pan Am Boeing touched down at Havana's domestic airport, and Richard Johnson wondered what lay ahead. It was a brave man who crossed the German Empire, and a lucky one who survived. He was convinced there was something sinister behind the mysterious death he was really here to investigate, but he couldn't shake the feeling that the Jewish interest in this murder might prove to be more dangerous for him personally. Everyone knew the Nazi view on the Jews, and the rumours that up to half a million had disappeared during the war. There were now no Jews living in Europe, and while travel into the Germans' European empire was difficult for Americans, it was completely impossible for Jews. One of the many concessions made by the United States at the end of the war in 1942 had been the *Act of Registration*. The ruling that American identity documents had to include religion was not a decision which the United States Senate and Congress had taken of their own volition. Protests against it were not actually forbidden by the government, they were simply ignored. And with this documentary evidence always to hand, the US government wouldn't even forward European visa applications for those whose passports contained the 'J'.

"If you're staying at the Old Cuba Hotel, I can give you a ride." Now he was standing, the architect was a good six inches shorter than Richard's full six feet.

"Thanks, but I'm at the Raffles, and they're supposed to be sending a car."

"Okay for some. We obviously have to stay at the corporation's hotels. Still, have a good trip."

"Thanks, Aaron. You too."

When he deplaned, bypassing the luggage carousel, he scanned the line of drivers queued beyond the arrivals gate. Richard was first out, and seeing him come through the automatic doors, they all stood to attention, holding up their name signs. Those from the higher-class hotels straightened the caps and ties of their uniforms and put on their best smiles. Tips were a welcome supplement to their wages, and with fierce competition for jobs in the service industries, they couldn't afford to have any of their passengers complain. When the man in the burgundy uniform and cap with the narrow yellow piping realised he had been singled out, he smiled broadly, showing two rows of gleaming white teeth behind a dark mulatto complexion.

"Mr Johnson? May I extend the warmest welcome of the Raffles Hotel, sir. If you will follow me. May I take your bag? Is this all your luggage?"

Richard followed him out of the air-conditioned arrivals hall and, despite the darkness, he was immediately hit by the wall of stifling heat. Fortunately, the brand-new Mercedes sedan boasted the latest air-conditioning equipment, and he was whisked along the Cuban freeway in comfort.

The service at the hotel was as slick as would be expected at one of the world's top chains. Although it no longer possessed its iconic original establishment in Singapore, the Raffles group maintained the oriental feel of its heritage, starting with the lobby décor. Richard knew that this hotel was not on his paper's approved list and looked forward to enjoying a standard of comfort he wasn't permitted on business and could certainly never afford privately. He just had time for a quick shower before his first taste of the famous Cuban nightlife.

CHAPTER ELEVEN

"Richard, good to see you again. It's been a while." Jack Gordon stood and reached out his hand. He was a couple of inches shorter than the journalist, but a powerful frame stretched the tight-fitting colourful shirt which made him look like a tourist. They both sat at the table in the middle of the hotel's main bar.

"Sorry, Jack. You know how things are!"

"It is what it is, Richard. You call me when you need something and ignore me when you don't!"

"That and the little fact that you moved away from New York."

"Staying in New York became a little uncomfortable when word got out how I helped you with the Ginnelli family. And I prefer the climate down here."

The banter was like the second half of a conversation, with no hint that it was two years since they last met.

Richard called the waitress over and ordered a gin and tonic. "You want another?"

Jack Gordon shook his head, caressing his beer, and the waitress moved off.

"You know you're being tailed, Richard?"

"Am I? That was quick. Where?"

"The guy was sitting in the lobby reading a newspaper. Looked out of place. Big build, serious muscle, bulge under the left armpit. Not how the casino guards work. Cut of the suit isn't American. Followed you into the bar. Now sitting at the counter, trying very hard not to look over here. Drinking a gin and tonic, without the gin. Whoever he is, he's not paid for the brains. Tailing people isn't his usual gig."

"Does he know you're onto him?"

"Please! What do you take me for?"

Richard chuckled. Jack had made a good living as a private investigator, with a sideline as an informer for journalists, after retiring from the NYPD with one too many bullets in his body. He was one of the best, and very choosy about who he worked for. He had already managed to build up as good a range of contacts within both the Havana Police Department and the Cuba State Police as he ever had in New York. He was the only person Richard had time to call from Idlewild airport that afternoon.

"So, what do you have for me, Jack?"

"I saw the preliminary police report on the death of Jimmy Sullivan earlier this evening, but I couldn't get a copy. The guys are dead touchy 'cos of the German angle. Technically it took place on foreign soil." He took a sip of his beer.

The German Empire Experience at MicroWorld, known universally, but unofficially, as Naziland, had the status – normally reserved for embassies and consulates – of being the sovereign territory of its German owners, despite being inside the United States.

"The Germans are leaving it to the HPD, but keeping a very close eye," Jack continued. "There are rumours that the Nazis have a few of the Havana Police Department on their payroll, but personally I don't think that's the case. The Germans want to be seen to cooperate. They're desperate to distance themselves from any involvement. They're on the back foot because they screwed up initially by denying that anything had happened."

"So did the Germans have anything to do with it, or not?"

"Looks like they didn't, which is dead weird. The body was moved into Naziland after he was killed. The security there isn't great at night, but even so, that's one hell of a risk. Whoever put the body there was definitely trying to frame the Germans. But they made a bad job of it. It's clear as day he was killed somewhere else."

"Exactly where was the body found?"

"Do you know the German area of MicroWorld?"

"Only what I read on the plane coming over here."

Jack got his hands ready to use as props supporting his explanation, "There's an administrative block directly behind the Bierkeller – the big beer hall and restaurant where they hold the *Oktoberfest* every evening." He laid two beermats side by side on the table. "That's where all the paperwork happens, and where the staff changing rooms are. The body was right at the back, slumped against the door that leads into a corridor connecting another building." Jack put down a third beermat and cast a quick glance around the bar before leaning forward. "Now that third building is a completely different proposition. It's totally off limits. Word is it's a communications centre, with direct links back to Berlin. Big signs all over the place. Entry and everything else absolutely *verboten*. The Krauts get jumpy if anyone even talks about it. There was no way they were going to let the boys in blue in, and since it was so obvious that the body had been killed somewhere else – just dumped there – the police let it drop. That's why the Germans have been so cooperative."

"You mean someone was trying to get the police to investigate this building?" Richard asked.

"Looks like it. But that was for certain not going to happen. The Germans scream 'diplomatic territory' if you so much as look at the door."

"The newspaper reports I saw didn't say how he died."

"Blunt-force trauma. Someone hit him on the head, or he fell and banged it – not yet clear which. They'll be checking in the post-mortem in the morning."

"Anything else I should know?"

"He had no ID on him," Jack said.

"But the newspapers published his name immediately. How did that happen?"

"A complete fluke. One of the officers at the scene had talked to him on Monday. He was called to deal with a disturbance in a casino. The hotel manager mentioned they had a New York PI staying, and the cop had a quick word to find out why he was there. It all looked above board – a routine case – so he thought nothing more of it until the guy turned up dead. If it wasn't for that, it would have taken ages to work out who he was."

"No one said he was a private investigator. Did you ever come across him in your former life, then?"

"No. But in my line of work we tend to keep to ourselves. I can check if he was in the phone book."

"That's great, Jack. Let me know if anything else turns up."

"That's not all. He had the letters *J S* carved into his left hand. I saw the photo. Big and crude, probably with a penknife. He definitely wasn't writing himself a reminder."

"Any idea what *J S* means?"

"Apart from the dead obvious, no," Jack said.

"You mean Jimmy Sullivan?"

"Yup. But why would you remove someone's ID and then cut his initials into his hand? It makes no sense."

"But then none of this seems to make any sense. I'll go and check out the scene in the morning. Tell me where we can meet tomorrow afternoon and I'll make sure I lose the goon."

"Will do, Richard. But be careful. These guys don't mess around, and I don't want to lose a good source of income." He emptied the remnants of his beer. "So, are you going to tell me what your angle is on this? Why a big New York reporter treks the length of the country for a dead PI?"

"I needed a holiday." Richard finished the last of his gin and stood up.

"I'll take that as a 'no', then. Ready to hit the town?"

CHAPTER TWELVE

Jack's car was parked two blocks from the hotel – an old private investigator's trick which Richard would have resented because of the uncomfortable heat and humidity, if the man from the bar hadn't stood up and followed them out of the hotel. Richard had always considered himself to be good, but he was impressed with the ease with which his friend shook their tail.

"Where are we going?"

"I thought Sinatra's. I can be your friendly local guide. Which means you're paying!"

"Sounds good to me. Is it still controlled by the mob?"

"It's still *run* by the mob. It stayed in the family. Why change a winning formula! They use it to front a lot of the drug operation. It undermines the protection racket if they push the drugs through the other casinos. The threat of smashing the place up doesn't ring as true if it costs you two weeks' dope sales. So, they run Sinatra's and a couple of the smaller gambling joints themselves and just take their cut from all the other operators."

"What about the theme parks. What's their involvement there?"

"Not so much. They're not as profitable, and since they bring a lot of punters to the island, they don't want to scare people off by sabotaging the roller coasters. They just take a small cut. Except from MicroWorld, that is."

"How's that, Jack?"

"Word is Carluccio tried it on a few years ago. A week later all three of his sons washed up in Florida. At least they think they were his sons. They identified them by the tattoos."

"The Germans?"

"What do you think? Who else is going to scare Italians? Since then, it's all been peaceful and friendly. The police get two pay checks; the operators are allowed to make a profit; the punters are happy enough to come back year after year. The American dream!"

The car was a beat-up old BMW.

"No expense spared, I see."

Jack looked at his friend as he turned the ignition and put his foot to the floor for a fraction of a second. A cat snoozing under a car twenty yards away shot across the road like a pack of dogs was after it.

"Okay, I take it back. The investment's under the hood."

"Low profile works best. This can outrun anything on the island." Jack pulled away from the kerb. Three right turns later they were back on the Malecón coast road. The crowd outside Richard's hotel showed no interest as they drove past and joined the crawl of traffic towards the nightlife.

The giant neon smiling face topped with the fedora made the name sign over the door superfluous. The piercing light of the blue eyes sent a shudder down Richard's spine. Jack ignored the valet parking and stopped in a side street two blocks away.

Once they were inside, Sinatra's fulfilled all the stereotypes. The doormen were twice the size of the average Italian, and their suits were cut to emphasise rather than accommodate the thick arms and thighs which showed they spent most daylight hours in the gym. The price of the drinks made it easy to differentiate those on expense accounts or casino complimentaries from the punters paying out of their own pockets. Richard and Jack entered during a pause in the entertainment and the hostesses were taking the opportunity to drum up extra business. Eventually a bottle blonde in the compulsory bright red number, which left little to the imagination and did its best to cause a worldwide shortage of sequins, showed them to a booth three-quarters of the way back from the stage. The first bottle of champagne arrived unbidden. Their position gave them an uninterrupted view across to the toilets. The rapid flow of patrons in and out formed the impression that more business was being carried out behind the red velvet door than on this side of it.

"If you go over there for a leak, you'll be in a minority." Jack nodded subtly in the direction Richard was watching. Girls making their visits in pairs was so common it was a cliché, but the pattern here was similarly marked. The typical pairing was a white American, mostly pasty or with the red of over-exposure to the sun, with a local. The shirts created a counterpoint – the drug dealers neat in white, the holidaymakers conforming to the unwritten rule – garish, tasteless and a size too small.

The lights dimmed even further, and a spotlight shone onto the stage. The crooner had been a major star ten or fifteen years ago, but the make-up and lighting kept the wrinkles in check. To Richard's ear the voice sounded as good as it ever had. He knew all the songs, as Hank Riley had been one of his grandmother's favourites. The next act was a magician. After getting a couple of willing victims up on stage, he started his tour of the tables, sticking to those nearest the dance floor where he was still in sight of most of his audience.

"Do you still get to the Yankees as much as you used to?"

Totally engrossed in the show, it took Richard a while to register that he had been asked a question. He turned back towards his friend.

"No. It's been years since I went. Life has changed a lot since your day, Jack."

"You're not under the thumb of some woman, are you? That would be a turn-up!"

"Not any more." Richard's tone cooled noticeably.

"Oops! Sorry. Change the subject, Jack."

"Don't worry. It would never have worked out. I'm back to being young, free and single. Well, single at least. How about you?"

"Incompatible with the lifestyle. I occasionally hook up with a tourist, but then they go back home. This island may have the highest concentration of good-looking women outside Hollywood, but they're all here for a reason."

"Working girls?"

"Yeah, in one way or another. You heard of Isaiah Horowitz?"

"The dodgy businessman who keeps getting his picture in the paper with a couple of pretty girls at every social event?"

"That's him. Has a villa about five miles out of town. Last weekend he hired dozens of girls for a party. Places like this are half empty every time something like that happens."

"Didn't you get an invite?"

"Strictly A-list, mate. Rich corporate types. It was a fundraiser for the Republican Party."

"I didn't realise Horowitz was into politics."

"I think it's only since we got ourselves a serious Jewish candidate. But he owns a couple of the casinos, so he's probably always paid off both sides to make sure he keeps the licences. We can drive past his place, and you can judge for yourself whether crime pays."

"I need another drink, Jack, but not at these prices. Have we got time to see something at the other end of the spectrum? I fancy a seedy bar."

"Well, you sure came to the right town! Follow me."

It was almost three in the morning when Jack dropped Richard back at his hotel. He managed to stuff the receipts from the night's tour into an envelope and set the alarm clock before crashing out.

CHAPTER THIRTEEN

It was the first time Richard had visited a theme park. His work had previously brought him into contact with the casinos in Atlantic City, and he knew of their much less developed cousins in Las Vegas. However, he had always viewed the parks, and their rides of ever-increasing complexity and apparent danger, with something approaching contempt. But he knew that MicroWorld was different. There were rides, of course, but they were not the focal point of the attraction. They served to deflect attention away from the educational core of the park's mission, ensuring that young visitors would not be put off by an overly serious environment.

He arrived at around quarter past nine in a deliberate attempt to miss the queues which started to build up more than half an hour before opening. It had also given him time for a stack of pancakes with bacon, the best cure he knew for the morning-after headache. He had bought a single-day pass at the hotel, which saved not only the need to join a third queue to get into the park, but also reduced the complexity of his expenses claim, the real downside of one of these trips. If he'd wanted to be an accountant, he would have trained as one.

The cool breeze was in sharp contrast to the oppressive heat of last night, and the scent of the hibiscus was a million miles away from the pollution-laden air of New York City. The security checks at the entrance were superficial. The list of restricted items was focused more on commercial potential than criminal activity. The general rules restricting the carrying of guns and knives in public establishments were repeated, as was the ban on smoking, but the carrying of picnic hampers, and drinks other than bottled water, were also expressly forbidden. A separate notice reminded visitors that they would not be allowed into the German Empire exhibit without their passports or 'other official government-issued identification'.

The fact that this was to stop Jewish visitors didn't need to be explicitly stated.

The entry ticket had one of those new-fangled bar codes which was scanned by a laser at the turnstile. Most people had now come to terms with these machines and their thin beams of red light, which could already be found in many supermarkets, but some still believed there was a real risk of burning your fingers off if you weren't quick enough. One of the entrance lanes was for those who didn't want to expose themselves to this technology personally, where a park attendant would scan the ticket. Laser technology had only been declassified five years previously, after it became clear that little progress was going to be made with weapons applications. In a climate of reducing military budgets, the commercial world had been given free rein to make of the technology what it could.

The World in Miniature was located at the far end of MicroWorld. This ensured that visitors couldn't completely ignore the exhibits in ScienceWorld. The most direct route took you through Botany, Agrology and finally Meteorology. The more popular exhibits were Zoology and Cosmology, and these were located on opposite sides of the complex in an effort to manage the crowds during major vacation periods. The Engineering pavilion was currently being refurbished following the decision to remove the military hardware which had originally been its major draw. A separate Museum of Military History was being developed by the government on the other side of Havana. The rumour was that the ever-widening gulf between American and German military technology made the exhibition at best uninteresting and at worst embarrassing. The fact that America had not been involved in a serious conflict since 1918 had removed most of the impetus that drives military development. This, now combined with the economic downturn, had reduced the country's appetite for weapons beyond the merely personal.

As Richard passed out of Meteorology, he rounded a line of trees which had shielded the World in Miniature from view, making the science zone feel like a destination in its own right rather than merely a cut-through to the main attraction. He halted to take in the panoramic view of the countries of the world. Directly ahead, across the expanse of the artificial lake, lay the United States of America, dominated by the replica of the Capitol from Washington DC. He remembered reading on the plane how the technique of forced perspective had been used on these iconic monuments, and how the higher storeys were compressed to fool the eye into believing the buildings were taller.

A few steps down the gentle slope was Brazil. It was as if he could feel the joy and vibrancy of *Carnaval* coming to get him. Visitors were transported into the cheerful exuberance of Brazil, where, here in MicroWorld, every day was Mardi Gras. He found it easier to trail behind the procession of oversized papier mâché heads weaving their way through the crowds than to avoid it. Although the artificial beach looked inviting, it was strictly off limits to the public. It was currently being used for a demonstration of beach soccer. Gift shops and stalls sold everything the American tourist would associate with Brazil, from coffee beans to gold football shirts, and from maracas to cricket bats. The centrepiece of Brazil, surrounded by banners proclaiming *Brazil: friend to the world*, was a replica of the gigantic statue of Christ on top of Sugarloaf Mountain in Rio de Janeiro. The few who were aware of the poetic licence used to fuse Rio's two distinct features into this one attraction probably applauded its economy. The high-spirited queue for the elevator, which provided a brief visit to the head of the statue with its view of the world and beyond, snaked in good-natured confusion around makeshift barriers. Round the corner was the entrance to the Brazilian Copacabana restaurant, housed inside the concrete mountain itself.

The joy and frivolity of Brazil could not have been in sharper contrast to the dour self-consciousness of Japan. Richard quickly got the impression that this was not somewhere people chose to linger. The Japanese hosts were noticeably older than their Brazilian counterparts and seemed to hold back, not inviting contact from their 'guests'. The quick-food stalls were popular as sushi had developed a cult following across the United States over the last couple of years. The Shinto temples and drumming exhibitions, on the other hand, were completely alien to most of the visitors and attracted only a small, polite following. The fact that Japan had chosen not to include any wider representation from its empire meant that this unexciting display was the only experience of the Asian continent.

Fun returned to the agenda as the visitor left Japan by setting foot on the replica of the Sydney Harbour Bridge and passing between the rows of green and gold national flags into Australia. The miniature zoo with its collection of unique animals was the highlight of the whole day for most of MicroWorld's youngest visitors. Unless they had been to the major zoos in Los Angeles, Houston or Miami, they would never have seen kangaroos, wallabies and ostriches. Even New York could only boast stuffed specimens as Australia's strict animal-welfare laws meant these creatures had to be housed with access to the open air in a climate which would be familiar to them. The lakeside beach was given over to a summer Christmas barbecue. Here visitors were very welcome, with giant prawns, lamb and, of course, roast turkey topping the menu. Those who wanted to sample the culinary side of Australia's exotic animals were politely referred to the very expensive Ayers Rock restaurant further inland, which served kangaroo and ostrich shipped frozen from the mother country. Hourly demonstrations of cricket and Australian-rules football served only to confuse most American visitors. Australia chose to make greater reference than Brazil to its role as one of the Unaligned States. An exhibition explained the mechanics of the Unaligned Conference which met in one of the four independent countries every year to provide a forum for the peaceful resolution of disputes between the German Empire, the Japanese Empire and the Pan-American Bloc.

The sun-worshipping Australians bordered the snowbound Canadians. Here the emphasis was very definitely on vacation opportunities, since Canada and Mexico competed fiercely for those adventurous holidaymakers who considered escaping from the USA. The spectacular scenery was represented by a miniature Niagara Falls while the cultural aspect was showcased by a community of Eskimos in their whitewashed carbon fibre igloos.

The sophistication of Canada gave way to the primitive vibrancy of American West Africa. The gift shops in this United States colony did a brisk trade in miniature wooden face masks and spears, while the more affluent visitors could stock up on the full-sized versions and the exquisite bronze sculptures. The roughly built traditional tribal dwellings gave no indication of the wealth to be found under the ground of this region. Although the food attracted little interest from the public, the tribal dances were quite well attended by those who could keep their impatience in check for a few more minutes before reaching the climax of their visit and entering the park designers' carefully re-imagined representation of their native land.

The United States of America was larger than any other single country in MicroWorld and was itself segmented into zones. The first of these showcased a different state every week. The fifty-first week was allocated to the Unincorporated Territory of Hawaii, whose absorption into the United States proper had long been the aim both of its local government and Washington DC, but nervousness about the potential Japanese reaction had always prevented its final ratification. The fifty-second week was far less contentious, being given over to the celebration of Christmas. The current week was dedicated to Idaho, and hosts and hostesses dressed in giant potato costumes were trying to drum up interest in exhibitions on farming and demonstrations of recipes for Idaho's most famous crop. A short film promoting everything the state had to offer didn't attract large audiences. Most of the people milling around in Idaho were waiting to take their seats for the next showing of the re-enactment of the Civil War's Battle of Gettysburg, which took place on the stage of the main open-air theatre every two hours. Opposite this theatre was the re-creation of Washington DC's Capitol building, which contained the exhibition of the presidents. In keeping with MicroWorld's stance of political neutrality, the incumbent president always played a minor role in this presentation, but inevitably his family was very prominent, as Joseph Patrick Kennedy III was already its fourth member to hold the office. The final attraction in the United States was the skyscraper ride. What this roller coaster lacked in gut-wrenching thrills, it made up for in architectural ingenuity. It offered a high-speed journey through America's iconic structures including the Chrysler Building and JBC from New York, the Pyramid Tower of San Francisco, the Sears Building in Chicago and the Starbucks Needle in Seattle.

Richard purchased a donut and cola from the Burger Giant concession at the far end of the USA to give himself the opportunity of surveying the entrance to Naziland. This unofficial name was almost universally used despite, or perhaps because of, the irritation which it provoked among the Germans. They had long since stopped protesting, as their initial insistence on calling it the European Empire was too easily countered by the challenge that Egypt was not in Europe. Its official political title of 'The German Empire of Europe, North Africa and Arabia,' or GEENAA for short, was too much of a mouthful. The marketing expertise that had been applied to its attractions over the past ten years had been quite successful. It was generally known that a Madison Avenue advertising firm had been enlisted to address the problem that the majority of visitors to the World in Miniature reached the USA and then returned the way they had come. Quite how the Germans had managed to find a New York agency with no Jewish interests had been a popular topic among comedians for a while. The gentile agency had devised several promotional gimmicks including competitions, world-class art exhibitions – which continued to this day – and even free food to try to get visitor numbers up. A big barrier, quite literally, had been the entry formalities. These had not only been simplified, but they had been turned into an attraction in their own right. A helmeted soldier, his vintage rifle slung over his shoulder and stick mortars hanging from his belt, stood at the entrance. This was barred by a red-and-white-striped wooden pole of the type familiar to anyone who had seen the adventure films based on the European War. The historical feel was reinforced by trucks and tanks of the same era. Unlike the unchanging military uniform, these vehicles were in sharp contrast to the current models which were on display within the Germany exhibit. Unique among the roles played out in MicroWorld, this was no actor, foreign exchange student or offspring of a party bigwig, but a real serving soldier performing real checks. With US citizens his role was a simple one. The standard format passport had, since 1944, indicated the holder's religion, and in the late 'sixties this principle had been extended when photographic driving licences were first introduced. It was possible to decline to declare your religion and still have a passport or driving licence issued, but those with the 'X' for 'undeclared' were refused entry in exactly the same way anyone with the 'J' would have been. Although the vast majority of visitors were US citizens, there were other nationalities who sought entrance. Their passports were scanned by the sentry, while an array of miniature cameras captured a series of images of the individual. These pictures were instantaneously processed by a computerised system which judged whether the dimensions of the facial features indicated Jewish descent or not.

Richard felt in his pocket to check that his driving licence was to hand. This piece of plastic, the size of a credit card, doubled as a travel document within the Pan-American Bloc, and was sufficient for the current needs. Anyone wanting to visit a foreign country which required a visa, first needed a full passport. Richard, like most Americans, didn't have one.

He casually sauntered down the gentle slope towards the soldier guarding the red-and-white pole and joined the queue. When he reached the front, Richard felt rather than saw the cameras pointing at him as he approached the frontier and took the ID out of his pocket. The soldier took the card and studied the photograph briefly before staring into Richard's eyes from beneath the steel-grey helmet, holding the licence face down on the scanner – the only visible piece of equipment which didn't belong in the 1940s. Richard guessed that the passport scanner did its job much more quickly than seemed to be the case, and the delay was to give the eye monitors and body-heat sensors time to register any undue nervousness in the would-be visitors. Eventually the green light on the scanning machine lit at the same time as a faint beep was heard. The soldier handed back the card and pressed down on the counterbalanced end of the barrier pole to let Richard through.

"Welcome to the European Empire. Enjoy your visit."

Beyond the barrier the dense vegetation re-created a wood at the time of the Battle of France in 1940. This soon gave way to a golden sandy desert, dominated by the white glare of the sun reflecting off the polished limestone casing of a pyramid. Most of the Egyptian exhibit was taken up with representations of its ancient past, but one of the gift shops was a miniature replica of a typical mosque. Although religions formed no part of Nazi ideology, they were tolerated as long as they didn't encroach on German plans or ideals. Friday prayers were respected throughout the Arabian Zone of the empire (though not here in Naziland) but praying five times a day was restricted to the licensed religious officials and was not allowed to impede economic activity. The ancient culture of Egypt, with its unique imagery of animal-headed gods and its spectacular architecture, was a major attraction for visitors. The opportunity to visit Tutankhamen's re-created tomb and the roller coaster travelling through the perils of the Underworld had significantly increased visitor levels to the German Empire since their introduction three years earlier. The same could not be said of the food, which lacked appeal to the conservative tastes of the Americans, as did the strong coffee. Most of the visitors to the Egyptian Ramesses restaurant were attracted by the opportunity to boast that they had been inside a pharaoh's pyramid, rather than by the menu.

The antique splendour of Egypt bordered the quirky feel of England, where the emphasis was largely on the medieval. The court of Henry VIII contained the crown jewels of a later era, but this was realised by few, if any, of the visitors. As in many other locations throughout the World in Miniature, historical accuracy had been willingly sacrificed to enhance the appeal. The military presence here was restricted to the bright red costumes of the Beefeaters, who guarded the Tower of London as they had for centuries, though the white flag with its red cross and the swastika in the upper left quadrant had only flown there for the last eighty years. The soldiers of more recent times, who had beaten the Germans in the Great War of 1914-18 and run them so close in the European War a quarter of a century later, were nowhere to be seen. The English pub, the King's Arms, was the most frequented eating establishment on this side of the park, affording Americans the rare opportunity to sample the traditional dishes of their former colonial masters. The two countries were still tied by their common language, but the bonds, which had been damaged by the American Revolution of 1776, were permanently ruptured in 1941 when the German-American Pact had effectively ended the war.

Richard checked his watch. It was just after midday.

He intended to have a late lunch in the German Bierkeller restaurant, so he decided to skirt Germany for the moment and visit the two remaining components of Naziland. He made his way along the edge of the World Ocean, here converted into a scene from Germany's mythical Aryan past as immortalised by Wagner, until an ornate stone bridge, with gift stalls on either side, marked the passage into the Grand Canal of Venice.

Once again there was little of the contemporary to be found in Italy. A seventeenth-century regatta rubbed shoulders with a battle between human gladiators and animatronic lions in the Colosseum, while harlequins and jugglers provided medieval street entertainment in front of the reconstructed Roman Forum. For a while it had been possible to watch Julius Caesar being murdered there at three every afternoon, until someone had tried something similar in Berlin. The pizza restaurant in the Doge's Palace was another favourite with the Americans, its tables chaotically encroaching into the piazza with its painted backdrop of St Mark's cathedral.

The relaxed mood of Italy contrasted with the laboured splendour and sophistication of France, dominated by the Eiffel Tower, which contained the park's most expensive restaurant. Most of the shops were focused on food and wine, ranging from long baguettes and cheeses to frogs' legs and snails for the more curious or daring. Napoleon was the only non-German military leader to feature in the European Empire, as the exploits of Adolf Hitler's original role model had been safely eclipsed by the Führer. This was particularly true of his strategy for dealing with a Russian winter and capturing Moscow virtually intact during the chaos and power vacuum following the assassination of Stalin. The reconstructed Loire chateau provided the opportunity of wine tasting for those able to afford the supplementary tickets.

The smells of Parisian bakeries and cheese shops had worked their magic, and Richard was feeling hungry as he made his way back to the centrepiece of Naziland. The careful management of sightlines and backdrops meant that the towering edifice of the fairy-tale castle of Neuschwanstein was not visible until you reached the very edge of Italy. The original had been built in the nineteenth century by Ludwig II, the mad king of Bavaria.

The castle was flanked on the far side by a futuristic exhibition building and on this side by the miniature version of the Linz Art Museum. Linz had been one of Adolf Hitler's favourite personal projects. The city had played an important part in his youth and formed the backdrop to many of his early paintings. Following Austria's incorporation into Germany in 1938 it had been his ambition for Linz to house the world's greatest art collection, an achievement realised in time for the gallery's opening in 1945. It was the nominal owner of all major public art in Germany, and the hub of a network of key galleries throughout the empire which received rotating exhibitions. This MicroWorld branch of the Linz Art Museum was itself on the exhibition circuit, along with the Louvre in Paris, the Prado in Madrid, the Trafalgar Gallery in London and the Uffizi in Florence. Its size meant that the number of paintings which could be displayed was limited, but the quality of the works was only compromised by its quota of the Führer's own attempts. At the moment, Leonardo's *Mona Lisa* was the major attraction, as this iconic masterpiece was otherwise virtually inaccessible to Americans.

Richard turned left towards the lake, passing the model railway which combined steam, electric and magnetronic technologies in a ground-level display designed to provide photographers with uninterrupted sightlines. He skirted the substantial quick-service restaurant, with its large 'W' logo and the cartoon sausage with arms, legs, eyes and smile, which was such a common sight throughout the European empire but had only this single outlet in America.

Suffering from the heat, Richard entered the main gift shop, a miniature replica of Berlin's famous KaDeWe department store, complete with a rooftop café overlooking the lake. The shops displayed the usual array of typically German items. Most popular with the tourists were the alcoholic drinks, both beer and schnapps, and the wide selection of sausages. The models of military and space vehicles were popular with the younger visitors, while those of a more cultural bias took the opportunity to collect samples of European artistic heritage, ranging from inexpensive postcard sets to serious works of art history and criticism. A set of busts of all the chancellors of Germany was displayed on a prominent top shelf in the main gift shop. These bronze heads were carefully dusted every day to ensure there was no visible sign of their unpopularity. The double-sized figure of the Führer, Adolf Hitler, was flanked on either side by his successors in chronological order from left to right, the two Goebbels giving the display a certain symmetry, as Hitler's immediate successor headed the line-up which his recently deceased grandson brought to an end. Adolf Heydrich who, like his grandfather, had succeeded a Goebbels, didn't form part of the line-up, since his inauguration had not yet taken place, and the portrait bust would only then be officially released. The Germans' most popular hobby was also well represented with a small specialist shop of its own, but the shortage of stamp collectors in the USA meant this was poorly frequented.

On the inland side of the Germany exhibit, facing the department store, was the military pavilion. Outside stood the major players in the decisive Battle of Moscow in April 1942 – the Tiger II tank, the Stuka dive-bomber, a rocket artillery launcher and an over-life-size statue of a paratrooper in the heroic style of Hitler's favoured 'social realist' art. Richard didn't go inside the main building, which he knew from the airline magazine described the post-war development of jet and rocket aircraft and of the atomic bombs which had never been used in anger.

The final major exhibit, housed in the futuristic building alongside the castle centrepiece, showcased the German achievements in space exploration. The so-called 'Space Race' had been won in 1961 with the first manned lunar landing. Since then, the USA had restricted itself to missions in Earth orbit while Germany had continued to stretch the boundaries, putting men on Mars in 1972 and on Saturn's moon Titan in 1990. The benefits of further manned exploration didn't seem sufficient to justify any more such ventures, but the colony on Mars was generating significant scientific advances. The true value of space exploration had, however, shown itself in 2019 when an enormous asteroid heading straight for the Earth had been destroyed by the massive fire power which the Germans maintained in orbit for just such an eventuality.

Richard walked past this exhibition hall to make his way through the façade of the fairy-tale castle into the Bierkeller restaurant. It was the tail end of the lunchtime rush. Only the main floor of the restaurant was open because the raised platforms and balconies were reserved for the much more popular evening session – the spectacular nightly re-enactment of Munich's famous *Oktoberfest*. The interior of the hall was gaudily decorated with scenes from the classics of German mythology, where handsome heroes rescued feisty blonde maidens from the forces of evil. Richard ordered set meal number one – three different regional sausages with potato salad, followed by a cream-topped gateau from the extensive selection, and a half measure of Bavarian beer, which was still larger than the standard size available in the United States. He finished less than half of the food or the beer as he concentrated on the comings and goings of the serving staff. Dressed in their traditional *lederhosen* and *dirndls*, they passed in and out of a double swing door to the left of the stage where they would perform the thigh-slapping drinking songs that evening. As the Bierkeller was at the furthest point of Germany from the lake, Richard assumed that the administrative block lay behind the kitchen, with the mysterious communications centre behind that.

He paid and left through the only public entrance, then made his way round the side of the castle building. Consistent with the rest of MicroWorld, the limit of the public area was bounded with heavy vegetation, interrupted occasionally by tall wooden gates bearing signs which said, 'Staff only.' The opening between the castle and the art gallery was only for vehicles, as the small wicket gate set into many of these entrances throughout the park was absent here. Richard was in luck. As he stood pondering his next move, one of the small carts which patrolled the park ceaselessly, picking up any rubbish almost as soon as it was dropped, arrived to deposit the latest load contained in its trailer. It didn't slow down, in fact it accelerated as it trundled towards the gate, and Richard was convinced it was going to crash. Precisely on cue, the wooden gate swung open just wide enough for the cart to pass through, then closed behind it. This momentary glimpse of the inner workings of the park was enough for Richard to make out the low administrative block beyond the restaurant, and behind it a much more solid construction with a dark glass dome on the roof. Out of the corner of his eye Richard noticed a slight movement in the tall bushes to the side of the gate. Looking more closely, he could just make out the surveillance camera which had tracked the small vehicle's progress and was now returning to its resting position, from which it had an overview of everything approaching the gate from the park side. With his plan for the evening taking shape in his mind, Richard made his way back through Italy and France and bypassed the second border post, exiting the World in Miniature through the turnstile. At the main park exit he got the back of his hand stamped to allow him to return later in the day. Within twenty minutes he was back in his room at the hotel.

Berlin – May 1941

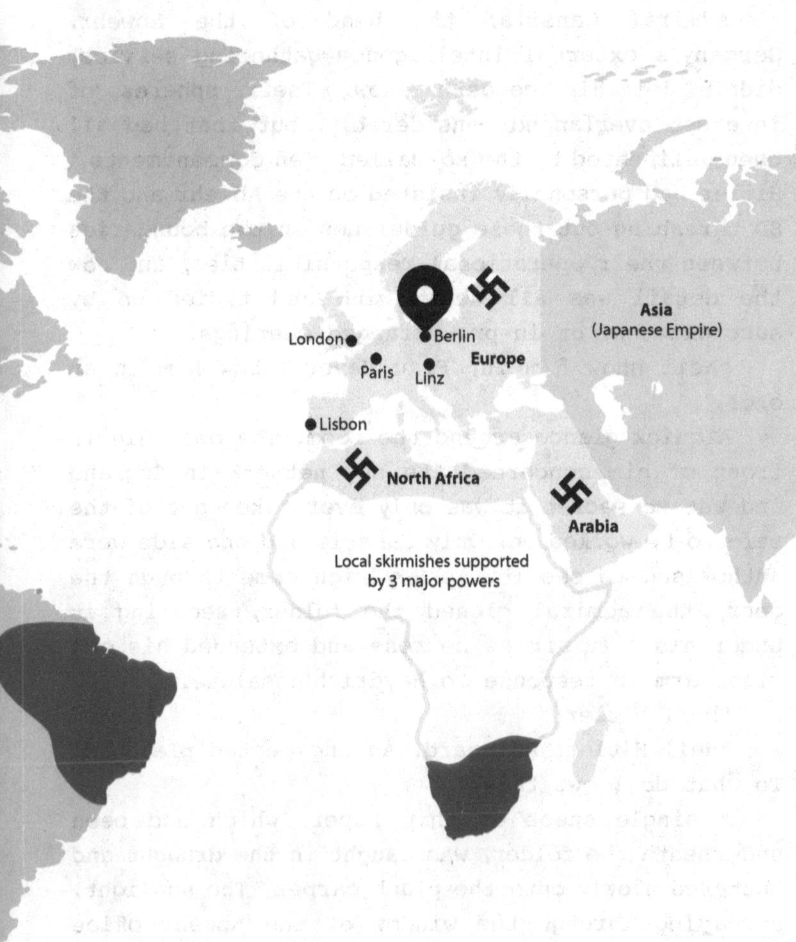

CHAPTER FOURTEEN

"Herr Admiral, Obergruppenführer Heydrich is here."

Admiral Canaris, the head of the Abwehr, Germany's external intelligence-gathering service, didn't let his concern show. Their spheres of interest overlapped considerably, but that had all been delineated by the so-called 'Ten Commandments.' Hitler had personally insisted on the Abwehr and the SD thrashing out these guidelines on the boundaries between their operational responsibilities, and now the detail was all dealt with and tidied up by subordinates, or in pre-arranged meetings.

"Well show him in, Frau Meyer. Show him in at once."

A quick glance around the room. The open file in front of him concerned the spy network in England and was so secret it was only ever taken out of the safe to be worked on. Only Canaris and one aide were authorised to see it. As Heydrich came through the door, the admiral closed the folder, securing it under his left arm as he rose and extended his own right arm in response to Heydrich's salute.

"Heil Hitler!"

"Heil Hitler! Reinhard. An unexpected pleasure. To what do I owe this?"

A single sheet of thin paper, which had been underneath the folder, was caught in the draught and fluttered slowly onto the plush carpet. The sunlight, streaming through the window of the Abwehr office on the Tirpitzufer, made the dust particles around it glitter.

"Do I need a reason to visit my old friend, Wilhelm?" The two men had first met many years previously, when their paths had crossed in the navy. Since then, they had managed to keep their competitive official relationship quite separate from the personal one, which was cemented by the strong social bonds of classical music and living in the same street.

Keeping his gaze firmly on Canaris's face, Heydrich crouched to pick the single sheet off the floor.

"Of course not, Reinhard. I would just be surprised if you had time to spare for a casual visit."

Heydrich didn't respond for a moment. His attention was now engrossed in the piece of paper — a sheet of flimsy used for typing when a carbon copy was produced. The top half of the page was in code. The bottom had the tickertape strips glued to it which were used in telegrams, and for deciphered messages.

"I don't recognise this code, Wilhelm. It's not another new navy variant of Enigma, is it?"

"No, nothing so sophisticated. This is a one-time-pad code, Reinhard. The message is from one of our agents in London. We could hardly let them have Enigma machines over there!"

"Of course not. How many agents do you have in London at the moment?"

Canaris looked at Heydrich in shock. "You can't be serious!"

"No, of course not. Forgive me." A strained silence of several seconds followed, allowing the distant rumble of Berlin's traffic into the office, and the chugging of a barge on the nearby canal. "I just wanted a quick word with you. Off the record, as it were. We have heard some rumours that our Japanese friends are showing an unhealthy interest in the United States navy. Provoking the Americans out of their neutrality is something we wouldn't want to happen, especially considering what else we have planned at the moment." Both men were on the 'need-to-know' list for Operation Barbarossa, and the wisdom of invading the Soviet Union at this stage of the war was something they had discussed privately.

"What is your source for that?"

"I would classify it as gossip at this stage, Wilhelm, which is why it's not going down on paper, just getting mentioned in an off-the-record chat between old friends. I'll leave you with that thought." In the uncomfortable silence that followed, Heydrich again stared intently at the message from London, before reaching across the desk to hand it back to Canaris.

"Actually, Reinhard, as we're talking off the record, there was something else."

"Yes, Wilhelm?"

"I've heard a few rumblings about the plans for Barbarossa. Most, if not all, of the generals believe there are serious flaws. For example, the plan to wage war on the Ukraine, when they would probably be very happy to fight on our side, the same as Finland will."

"That's a matter for the Führer, Wilhelm. They need to discuss it with him."

"They've tried, Reinhard. But, since all his military decisions have turned out to be correct so far, he refuses to listen to them. Some of us were wondering if your boss would have any more success. We would welcome your view on that."

"Himmler might be able to get involved, but he would absolutely insist on that being kept very secret. And we would need to know in detail what the generals think should be done instead."

"The best person to talk to about that would be General Jodl. He's in Berlin today. Should I ask him to speak to you?"

"Yes, Wilhelm. Do that. But keep Himmler out of it for the moment."

"Thank you, Reinhard. Is there any truth in the rumour that you're off to Prague?"

"I have no idea, Wilhelm. I am happy to serve the Führer in whatever capacity he sees fit."

"As are we all, Reinhard. As are we all."

As Heydrich left the office, Canaris took a long, hard look at the message from his English agent. Something in it had clearly caught the SD chief's attention.

Heydrich stopped beside the desk of Canaris's secretary to use the telephone on her desk.

"Frau Schmidt. If General Jodl calls, clear as much space in my diary for him as he wants. And cancel all my appointments this evening."

CHAPTER FIFTEEN

"Just can't keep away, can you, Herr Heydrich."

Frau Korsch was seated exactly as he had left her a little less than twenty-four hours earlier. Unbidden, he sat opposite her. This time he was determined to stay in control of their meeting. He had even brought silver.

"I want to know what you can see of the progress of the war."

"I don't do wars. Just people."

"Then tell me what the future has in store for the Führer."

She raised her eyes for the first time and stared into his.

"For that he would have to be sitting where you are now, Herr Heydrich. I need his aura."

"What would you be able to tell him?"

"He doesn't know you're here, does he? No one does. What exactly are you up to Herr Heydrich?"

The Obergruppenführer hesitated. He felt uncomfortable when he was not in his uniform, somehow exposed.

"Our Führer is a great man. A very wise man, with exceptional judgment. But he is about to make a very grave mistake."

"And no one dare tell him?"

"No. That's not it. There are enough people who will tell him, but he doesn't listen to them. His decisions have been so successful, up to now, that he believes he's infallible."

"And you think I can help you? What do you have in mind?"

It took Heydrich almost an hour to enlist Frau

Korsch's support. She was initially sceptical of both his motives and his judgment that the Führer was indeed about to make a catastrophic error. In the end his arguments proved sufficient to appeal to her deep-seated love of Germany. She would try what he was asking, for the sake of the Fatherland.

As he left the basement in one of the poorer parts of Berlin's Kreuzberg district, he was already planning the detail of his next step. The trickiest part had already been achieved. Convincing the fortune teller to play along had been the part of the plan where he saw the greatest risk of failure. Dealing with the Führer himself would be much easier in comparison, and this weekend's visit to the Berghof would provide the ideal opportunity. Heydrich had no faith in the magical powers of the old woman, so he was certain that she would convey precisely the message he had put into her head. But her talents of persuasion were clearly very real, and he had little doubt that she would be able to hold Hitler's interest.

CHAPTER SIXTEEN

"Herr Himmler, what does the Führer think of your astrologer?"

Heydrich felt his boss's eyes scanning his face and managed to banish all trace of smugness. The Reichsführer's earlier anger at being ambushed by Hitler asking why he had not himself recommended Frau Korsch, had subsided after Heydrich had explained how the Führer trapped him into revealing the details of the woman.

"I think it's fair to say he is genuinely impressed, Herr Heydrich. Over the last two weeks he has shown more trust in her than in some of his generals."

The decision not to delay the invasion of the Soviet Union because of a little local difficulty in Yugoslavia had come as a welcome surprise to those concerned about getting the conquest over before the winter set in, especially with the Führer's insistence that the invasion force must not be encumbered with the burden of winter equipment. And the change of heart about the Ukraine had been vindicated by the enthusiasm and effectiveness of the Ukrainians' efforts to undermine their oppressors in Moscow.

"In fact, that's the reason I wanted to talk to you," said Himmler.

"Do you wish me to stop consulting her, Herr Reichsführer?" Heydrich's concern was genuine, but for practical reasons, rather than through any need for mystical assistance.

"You're right, we need to be careful about that, Herr Heydrich. But there are more immediate matters to be dealt with. There was something Frau Korsch said on her first visit to the Führer. You will remember that he was still suffering from the betrayal of that idiot Hess, so he was not himself that day." Heydrich remembered very well. He had been in the sitting room at Hitler's Berghof mountain retreat when the Führer had been told that his deputy and old friend Rudolf Hess had taken it upon himself to fly to Scotland. Hitler had gone into one of his black rages. Heydrich hadn't personally witnessed one of these before, so he was surprised to learn, from some of the more regular weekend visitors to Bavaria, that this fury was not at its usual intensity. There was even some speculation that Hitler was only doing it for effect. But the Führer's immediate action had affected Heydrich directly. He had decided there was an urgent need to consult the 'wise woman', as he referred to her. Heydrich had had to telephone Colonel Stengel to get him to pick up the Korsch woman from her Kreuzberg basement and fly her to Berchtesgaden that evening. It was mid-afternoon on Sunday when Hitler finally met her. Their session lasted nearly two hours, much to the consternation of those responsible for getting the Führer back to Berlin. It was not until two days later, back in that basement, that Heydrich received first-hand confirmation that his plan had been executed to the letter.

"Well, Herr Heydrich. On that fateful weekend, the woman told the Führer of her vision. Red rain fell down from the sun on a large bird, killing it. At first, she had thought this was an eagle, but then it rose up from its own ashes, so it must have been a phoenix. The huge bird then flew straight into the sun and tore it to shreds. This vision troubled our Führer deeply, and as the woman's other predictions all came true, he worried about it more and more. During several visits he asked her to explain what it meant, but she insisted she had no idea. Then suddenly, yesterday, it came to him. The sun was Japan, and the bird was America. He asked the acting head of the Abwehr what information they had about Japan's plans. Admiral Bürkner went through Canaris's personal files and found intelligence of a Japanese plan to attack America." Himmler paused for effect and Heydrich tried to conjure up an appropriate look of shock and concern.

"So, what does this have to do with me, Herr Reichsführer?"

"Hitler has asked me to ensure that the Japanese do not carry out their intended attack on the United States," said Himmler. "So, you need to come back to me with a plan of how you're going to achieve that."

Cuba – August 2024

CHAPTER SEVENTEEN

This time Richard was already sitting in a booth in the bar of the Raffles Hotel when Jack Gordon arrived.

"Hi, Jack. Beer? You look like you need one."

"Thanks. Too warm for rushing round out there. How was your sightseeing?"

"Very educational. What do you have for me?"

Jack delayed his answer until the waitress had taken the order and disappeared.

"The police have now got lots of answers, but they don't make any sense. Sullivan was killed by a single blow to the back of the head. Some time late Monday. Something with a sharp corner. He probably fell on it, but they can't be sure."

"Monday?"

"Quite. The *J S* on his left hand was carved with a penknife after he died. They think the body was dumped just before midnight Tuesday, after the staff had left for the night. At one in the morning the Havana Police Department arrived at the back door of the Bierkeller restaurant via the service road, in response to a 911 call which they thought was from someone inside Naziland. Said they'd found a body. The night watchman, who apparently had been drinking, but that won't appear in any of the official reports, let them in without checking with his superiors. The cops found the body exactly where they were told."

"That means the body was dumped there after the night watchman's round and before the phone call at midnight."

"Looks that way. The night security is actually dead lax. They rely on their reputation. And there's no real reason to break in. No one knows if there's video surveillance. The Germans say not, but the cops assume there is. Anyway, if there is, it's classified. The police will never get to see it."

"Do they have any idea where he was actually killed?"

"Nope. They've checked out his hotel and a couple of bars he'd visited but found nothing. His rental car was in the hotel car park, and that was clean. Anyway, the investigation changed direction around two in the morning when the shit hit the fan."

"How so?"

"The security guard sobered up enough to call his superiors. At around three a.m. the state governor got a call from the German ambassador in Washington DC. Lodged an official complaint about the police violating diplomatic territory by forcing their way into the park. The two cops have been suspended until it all blows over to avoid an international incident. They claimed the gate at the end of the access road was open, which the Germans deny, of course, and that the security guard invited them into the building itself."

"And that's how the killer got the body into the park?"

"Looks that way, but that's one hell of a risk to take. The only possible reason I can think of is to embarrass the Germans. There are much easier places to get rid of a body in Cuba."

"So it's not to cover up the murder? The dumping of the body was the objective itself? Was Jimmy Sullivan just in the wrong place at the wrong time?"

"Could be, Richard. The final part of the jigsaw, so far anyway, is the phone call to the *Cuba Post* just after two in the morning, saying that the body of a tourist had been found in Naziland. Again, this call seemed to come from inside the park, so it was presumably made by the same person who called the police. The *Post* called the German consulate in Havana to confirm the story, but the duty officer issued the denial, which their embassy in Washington later had to retract." Jack chuckled and waited for the waitress delivering his beer to move away before continuing. "There must be a lot of unhappy Germans around at the moment. They aren't known for tolerating mistakes, so the security guard and the guy from the consulate are both for the high jump. The ambassador started with the moral high ground when he called up the governor, but since then he's had to do an embarrassing climb down. And to cap it all, they've allowed the local police to investigate the scene to try to build some bridges. And that has highlighted just how sensitive they are about the building next door to where the body was found.”

“So just what do the police think, Jack?”

“No one knows what’s going on. The facts are straightforward enough, but nothing adds up.”

“What do we know about *J S*?”

“Again, nothing. Unless it’s the victim’s name. But then why would you kill a guy with a blow to the head, dump him somewhere to embarrass the Germans, then write his own initials on his hand? Beats me. I’ve never come across anything quite this bizarre. It’s the sort of thing you associate with a student prank, except that it’s way too serious.” Jack took a sip of his beer before continuing. “Have you considered the possibility that it might be an elaborate attempt at misdirection?”

“Which part?”

“That’s just it. What if it’s both parts – the location of the body and the marks on the hand?”

“But what could they be hiding?”

“We may never know. If they’ve made a good enough job of it, no one is going to look any further.”

The pair sat in silence for a few minutes, trying, without success, to make sense of the jumble of facts.

Finally, without looking up from his beer, Richard asked, “Is there any hint of a Jewish connection?”

Jack frowned. “No. Not that I’ve heard. The Jews aren’t allowed in Naziland, and Jimmy Sullivan wasn’t Jewish, or it would have come up by now. Why do you ask?”

“No reason,” Richard lied, not wanting to explain what had brought him to Cuba. “Just thought it might explain the ‘J’ written on his hand.”

They both sipped their beers until the silence became too uncomfortable for Jack.

“What’s your next move?”

“I want to get a look at that communications building. Someone is going to a lot of trouble to point the finger at it, which tells me there’s something hidden that’s worth digging up.”

“Just be careful, Richard. The security will have tightened up since Tuesday, and someone might be expecting you.”

“I’ll be fine. But if it makes you feel any better, I’ll call you tomorrow before midday. If I don't, you can tell the police what I was doing. Okay?"

Richard signed the tab and left the bar to get a cab back to MicroWorld. Jack finished his beer and walked out three minutes later. The Hispanic man sitting on the opposite side of the bar threw the switch on the side of the fake cigarette packet which had been pointing at Richard's table since he had arrived. He hoped this would give the foreigner what he wanted. A few more paydays like this one would be very welcome.

CHAPTER EIGHTEEN

The firework display had been going for nearly ten minutes and, judging by the tempo and volume of the music, was now heading towards its climax. Most of the park lights had been switched off, with just a few glowing faintly at ground level to comply with safety requirements. Orange and white flashes briefly illuminated the faces looking up at the colourful explosions above the lake. All eyes were focused on the display, so Richard had no difficulty backing away unseen from the crowd towards the darkened buildings of the German area of MicroWorld. He had correctly guessed that the litter patrols wouldn't be allowed to move through the darkness during the display. He passed in front of the turrets and pinnacles of the fairy-tale castle, eerily ghostly in the firework flashes, and started to backtrack along the route he had observed earlier. After walking the length of the Linz gallery, he turned left past the shop which occupied its far corner. It was here that he spotted the cart on the grass verge at the side of the path, right up against the vegetation which formed the park boundary. The faint red glow as the driver drew on his illegal cigarette was enough for Richard to see that he was sitting at his steering wheel and that the cart had two of the small trailers hooked up behind it. The music was now even louder, so Richard was quite confident of walking past and then turning back on himself to creep up on the vehicle without being heard. Again, he was in luck. The second trailer was already nearly full, containing five or six tied rubbish sacks, while the front one had none. Richard took a final look around to check that everyone was still engrossed either by the firework display or the cigarette, and eased himself into the rear trailer, taking great care not to rock it. He lay down and gently nestled himself between the sacks, like a guinea pig preparing for sleep, ensuring as best he could in the near total darkness, that he was completely obscured from view. Satisfied with his covering, he lay silent and waited.

The muffled applause penetrated his hiding place as the display reached its climax and then fell silent. This was followed by the official announcement that the park was now closed. Richard was vaguely aware of the lights coming back on and he tensed, waiting for the jolt as he started to move. Nothing happened. The noise of the departing crowd subsided to a murmur, and then a whisper, but still there was no movement. He heard voices approaching from behind the cart and froze. It sounded like two men, but he couldn't make out the language they were speaking. Just as it seemed they had reached his hiding place, they became silent, and Richard resigned himself to the failure of his plan at the first hurdle. He heard splashing as if a tap had been turned on in the bushes a few inches from his head, and then another. After what seemed an age, the flow stopped and he heard the two men do up their zippers, before resuming their unintelligible chatter and continuing their way towards the exit. The jolt shocked him as he was still contemplating his near escape when the litter vehicle started up under the power of its silent electric motor. They had been going for less than a minute when the driver stopped and he heard the clicks of the parking brake being applied. Richard listened to the soft footsteps of the rubber-soled boots receding on the concrete pathway, followed by the quiet clatter of a bag being removed from one of the park's rubbish bins. The driver returned to the vehicle, and Richard heard the thud as the half-full sack was dumped into the first trailer. The vehicle was then driven for another minute, and the exercise was repeated twice more. One of the sacks was dumped into Richard's trailer, but he was mentally prepared for this and neither moved nor made a sound. Eventually the driver threw in one more sack and then drove off with a perceptibly different style and determination, racing along at around five miles an hour. When Richard felt the driver accelerate, he guessed this was the perverse behaviour he had spotted earlier in the day, where all the drivers sped up as they headed towards the closed gate, as if they were trying to catch out the electronic access-control system which allowed them into the service area. He had finally decided that this must be a security procedure to ensure that the gates remained open for the briefest possible period, to minimise the chance of any guests straying into the restricted area. Once through the gate, the vehicle slowed to a crawl. Richard knew he only had a few seconds to jump out of his hiding place. The camera would be swinging back to watch the outside of the gate, and he had to get out before the cart turned the corner beyond the Bierkeller. He hadn't been able to see past that corner from his vantage point inside the park that afternoon, but he knew that the brief stretch alongside the restaurant was not overlooked by any windows in the building. The other side of the road was bounded by the same dense bushes that marked the perimeter inside the park, which should provide him sufficient cover, especially at night.

He got to his feet, swaying as the vehicle started to corner and, taking great care not to dislodge any of the sacks, he jumped lightly onto the concrete roadway. The cart seemed to hesitate slightly, before continuing on its way as Richard ran on tiptoes into the bushes. He checked his watch. It was a few minutes before ten. The firework display finished at a quarter past nine in the summer months, and the park officially closed at that time, though it took at least half an hour for the last of the crowds to make their way to the exit. He guessed that the late shift probably finished no later than eleven, so he settled himself down in his hiding place to wait for another hour.

By half past ten the park was completely silent. As he was looking at his watch for the twentieth time, all the lights went out. He patted his pocket to check that the tiny but powerful flashlight was still there and was reassured by the feel of the cold metal. His eyes quickly accustomed themselves to the new level of darkness, and he could again make out the shapes of the buildings. In the dark they seemed much bigger, and the wooden gate which separated him from the public area looked impossibly high. His plan didn't involve getting back into the park, but it would have been reassuring to have an alternative escape route. By ten minutes to eleven he was suffering from cramp and cold, which he had not anticipated. He wanted to move to get the circulation back into his legs, but caution prevailed.

Knowing the methodical approach for which the Germans were renowned, he guessed that there would be some significance to the hour mark. He was not wrong. A few seconds after eleven the windowless door in the side wall of the Bierkeller restaurant building swung open, and a shaft of torchlight shone straight into Richard's face. His heart rate doubled, but he managed to stay still and silent, and the beam swung away as the guard turned round to close the door behind himself, before marching purposefully away from the gate into the depths of the service area. When he stopped to point his torch at the next doorway at the far end of the Bierkeller, Richard could see his silhouette outlined against the circular pool of yellow light. The guard moved off, passed the mysterious building without a second glance, and disappeared around the corner the litter cart had taken. The night was so silent that Richard could still hear his receding footsteps, stopping occasionally as they became ever fainter. He decided to follow the guard, since he was bound to pay special attention to anything the Germans considered particularly sensitive, but as he stepped out of the bushes, a thought occurred to him: the guard hadn't locked the door. That was probably because it had electronic access, but it was worth checking. Half crouching, he took the few steps towards the door. His eyes were now sufficiently acclimatised that he immediately saw it had a keyhole and no electronic keypad or card reader. He gripped the handle, took a deep breath, and twisted. The door opened easily and silently.

Richard listened for a second and, hearing absolutely nothing, he stepped inside. The emergency lighting was bright in contrast to the darkness outside, so he quickly closed the door behind him. He walked forwards a few feet, and on his left he recognised the large double swing door of the staff entrance to the restaurant. That meant that the kitchen was on the other side of the stage area, and that the body had been left on this side of the building, over to his right.

He crept forwards and soon found a passage off to the right. The doors on either side seemed to be offices on the left and storerooms on the right. The passage turned to the left, and after a few feet a short corridor led off it to the right. A heavy grey steel door with no visible handle stopped any further progress. The large, enamelled sign riveted to it stated in bold black letters on a white background 'No unauthorised admittance' and words to the same effect in German. Centred at the bottom of the sign, just inside the red border, was the German eagle with the circled swastika in its claws.

On the whitewashed concrete frame of the door Richard could make out the remnants of the blue and white crime scene tape which the local police had used to add their own additional access restriction. The floor just in front of the steel door seemed to have a slightly lighter patch. Richard took the flashlight out of his pocket to get a closer look. Whatever had stained the ground at this point had been taken care of so well that the floor here was much cleaner than elsewhere.

He retraced his steps and waited against the inside of the door by which he had entered. He listened hard, and when he was sure it was silent outside, he opened the door a crack and looked out. Again, there was no sign of life, so he closed the door behind him and skipped lightly across the path to within a step of the vegetation. He followed the direction the security guard had taken. A few yards from the corner, Richard could see the corridor which lay behind the steel door, joining the castle's admin area to a further building which also had no windows. Its only visible feature was a large dome on the top, which looked to be about five yards across and six to eight feet high, though it was difficult to judge scale on a building completely devoid of features. He was staring up at this, toying with the idea of using his flashlight on it to get a better idea of its purpose, when he heard footsteps. Richard had been careful to remain within three steps of the vegetation which ran along the side wall of the art gallery, and he quickly retreated into its cover as the security guard returned from his round. The beam of the guard's torch swayed across the ground as he approached the main path from the road which ran behind the mysterious building.

At the moment the shape of the guard appeared in the opening, Richard instinctively took a step backwards. The snap of the twig under his foot sounded like a gunshot in the silence of the night. The guard stopped and shone his torch in Richard's direction, moving the beam rapidly from side to side in a small arc until he located the clear outline of a man hiding in the bushes. Without a second thought, Richard leapt forward, homing in on the beam, and crashed into the guard, who seemed rooted to the spot. The large flashlight clattered to the floor and went out. The guard was still on his feet but bent double and clearly winded. Richard decided his only chance was to make a run for it before the guard could recover his composure or his torch.

He ran as fast as he could along the main concrete pathway. This was the only route he had seen wide enough for a vehicle and therefore must lead directly to the park's service access gate. He expected to hear gunshots or at least a whistle blast behind him, but the only sound was his own footsteps on the path.

Richard stopped his half-hearted zigzagging and stuck to the middle of the path, putting as much distance as possible between himself and the guard. The iron gate across the road loomed up in front of him much sooner than he had anticipated. Remembering the police patrol's version of the story, he pushed and pulled in the hope that it would simply open for him. The rattling of the pristine chain and padlock near Richard's hands confirmed that this was not going to happen.

He stopped for a moment to catch his breath. The gate was about ten feet high with a horizontal bar halfway up, reinforcing the vertical grill. As far as he could tell from its silhouette, the top was smooth and not enhanced by spikes or razor wire. He easily pulled himself up far enough to get a foot onto the central bar. From this elevated position he repeated the exercise. Gingerly he lowered his hand. The top of the gate was covered only in a layer of grime, so he pulled himself over and clambered down the other side.

Surprised at how easy this had been, Richard kept his handhold on two of the vertical bars and strained his eyes to peer back through the gate. He could make out neither movement nor sound. He turned round and jogged along the concrete road until it inclined slightly downwards and the low bushes to either side turned into tall grass.

Richard took a few steps away from the path and stood still and silent for several minutes. He could hear nothing. Now that his heart and breathing had stabilised, he set off along the path at a slow steady pace, to ensure he would hear any sounds of pursuit.

He had been walking for half an hour when a sharp turn brought him face to face with the main freeway which ran along the rear of MicroWorld. He crouched down on the verge, bent forwards, hands on his knees, trying to orient himself. He must be about four miles from his hotel which lay off to the left, so in the direction of the traffic on the opposite carriageway, not that much traffic was passing at this time. He jogged across the road, easily vaulting the safety barrier between the two carriageways, and decided to walk along the side of the road. If he got picked up by the police, he would spin some story about going out for a walk and getting lost. He set off purposefully, resigned to walking all the way back to his hotel, but looking over his shoulder every few seconds. Every time a car approached which didn't look like a police or other official vehicle, he half-heartedly stuck out his thumb. The few drivers on the road in the early hours of this Saturday morning showed even less enthusiasm. After about twenty minutes he saw what looked like the familiar outline of a taxi, and as it passed under a light, the yellow colour confirmed this. Even though its 'For Hire' light was out, Richard turned and put up his hand to hail it, just as he would have done in broad daylight on a New York sidewalk. To his amazement the cab pulled in from the fast lane and stopped on the verge a few feet away from him.

"Where to, buddy?"

"The Raffles Hotel."

"I doubt they'll let you in looking like that. It'll cost you twenty-five."

Richard decided not to argue that the official fare for this distance would have been about five dollars in daylight.

"Fine, as long as I get a receipt."

"No problem. Get in."

In less than ten minutes he was ringing the night bell of the hotel. Despite the twenty-four-hour gambling opportunities theoretically available, those who wanted to play the tables through the night usually chose to either do so in their own hotel or in the big casinos. The night porter came out from his cubby hole behind the reception desk and ambled towards the door, fingering the bunch of keys in his hand. As he looked up, he stalled at the sight that greeted him. Noticing the hesitation,

Richard fumbled in his pocket for his keycard and held it against the glass door. This seemed to pacify the porter, who continued his slow shuffle forwards and unlocked the door.

"Good evening, sir," he said, with as much good grace as he could muster.

"Good evening," replied Richard, curtly, and made for the elevator. Once inside his room he stood in front of the mirror. He had never seen a chimney sweep, but he guessed they were probably cleaner at the end of a shift. For a moment he considered getting into the shower fully dressed in his suit and tie but quickly thought better of it. The *Eastern Times* would just have to foot the extortionate bill five-star hotels charged for their express laundry services. He dropped all his clothes on the floor just inside the door, and tiptoed into the shower, trying not to shake any of the grime onto the carpet or bathroom floor. Five minutes of hot water, soap and shampoo left him unrecognisable from the vagrant who had entered the hotel less than a quarter of an hour earlier. He wrapped himself in the luxuriant towelling robe provided by the hotel – eighty dollars if you want to purchase one as a memento of your stay – and sat on the edge of his bed. The laundry service was surprised to receive a commission in the early hours of the morning but promised that the bag left outside his door would be returned before six. Richard lay on top of the bed and tried to unravel what had just happened, but within seconds he had slipped into a deep sleep.

CHAPTER NINETEEN

After the exertions of the previous night, Richard allowed himself the rare luxury of a lie-in. The laundry service was as good as its word, and while none of the dirt of his exploits remained, the suit was showing increasing signs of wear. He filed away until later the question of who he could charge for a replacement and strode past the Hispanic man sitting in the reception area apparently reading the morning newspaper. He arrived at the hotel's breakfast buffet a couple of minutes before the half past ten embargo.

The short-order chef at the egg station had almost finished clearing up the accoutrements of his morning shift and made a half-hearted attempt to disguise his frustration as Richard ordered two over easy. While he waited for them to be cooked, Richard piled his plate with bacon, sausages, hash browns and Boston baked beans. After persuading the one remaining waitress to provide him with coffee, he settled himself in at a corner table to review the *Cuba Post*. The front page was almost totally given over to the presidential election campaign, with reports on the latest speeches of the leading contenders for the Democrat Party nomination, both trying to distance themselves from the disastrous economic policy of their party's current leader. An editorial summary analysed the benefits each candidate claimed they would bring to Cuba and contrasted these with the policies of the Republican candidate, Senator Goldberg. The sports coverage focused on the island's major league baseball team and hardly mentioned the Olympic Games. With the business pages and the classified adverts, there was little space left for general news.

Richard was surprised that there was absolutely no mention of the body found in Naziland. Any newspaper would make sure it kept at least a trickle of the story going, so that when there were developments to be reported, there was a thread of continuity.

The complete death of a current story was usually an indicator of pressure being applied at a high level. The international page contained a couple of business and human-interest stories with a specific Cuban dimension. The only purely international article was a short profile of the new German chancellor who was to be installed in two weeks' time. The sudden death of Heinrich Goebbels, one week before the start of the Olympic Games, had clearly caused the German authorities a major dilemma. Berlin's hosting of the Games every twenty-four years provided one of few occasions when the government chose to showcase the country to the wider world. There was a clear irony that this public relations challenge was created by the death of the grandson of Hitler's propaganda minister. But he, and his grandfather, would surely have approved of the decision to carry on with the games, and defer the inauguration of the new head of state until later. The Germans were masters of symbolism, and the single national flag, flying at half-mast at the Olympic venues alongside all the other Nazi banners and flags of other nations flying normally, created a poignant sight. It even seemed to soften the views of the regime's harshest critics, as the nation fulfilled its international obligations despite its grief.

Richard was immune to the increasing attempts of the staff to hurry their one remaining guest out of breakfast. He left when he was ready, returning to his room where he managed to cause similar irritation to the chambermaid, who was halfway through cleaning up his mess. At these prices they could clean his room when it suited him, even if he was not paying personally. He phoned Jack Gordon, as he had promised. Jack was clearly agitated and frustrated that Richard hadn't received any of the several messages he had left that morning. There was something Jack didn't want to discuss over the phone, so they arranged to meet in the coffee shop of the Old Cuba Hotel a quarter of a mile along El Malecón. Richard grabbed his notepad, pen, credit card, room key and a twenty-dollar note, and left everything else behind, trying to smile at the maid he had thrown out less than five minutes earlier.

The hotel entrance doors slid open, and he walked into a wall of heat as the sun approached its highest point in the sky. Richard crossed the road to enjoy the benefit of the spray from the breakers which crashed against the sea wall. Only too late did he become aware of the large black vehicle pulling up a few yards behind him. It disgorged the two heavies who grabbed him, forced him inside and sped off. His arms and legs were pinned to the car seat as he felt the cloth squeezed over his face. The noxious smell of chloroform filled his nostrils.

New York – August 2024

CHAPTER TWENTY

"Tom. At last. How's it going?" Samuel Levy could now clearly hear the voice of his friend over the background buzz on the transatlantic telephone line.

"Everything's fine, Samuel. We are in Oxford, England, precisely as planned. Sorry for the delay, but there was a problem with the phones."

"How was the journey?"

"Long and complicated, but she coped very well. He made sure she slept most of the way."

"And when is it scheduled for?"

"Three days from now. They expect it will take between eight and ten hours. The preparations are almost complete. They were able to use the samples we provided without any difficulty. I've booked a call here at the hotel, so I can phone you after it's finished, and give you their initial view. But it will be three or four days more before they can do a proper assessment."

"I understand, Tom. Everyone here sends their love. Let her know."

"I will, Samuel. If you need to get in touch, I'm in room 315 at the Randolph Hotel. My time's up, I've got to go. I'll speak to you Saturday."

The line went dead. Samuel Levy sat motionless, the receiver still to his ear. The second click brought him back from his thoughts. He had assumed that someone might be taking an interest in the conversation, but the confirmation was still a cause for concern.

CHAPTER TWENTY-ONE

"Well, Tom. What's the news?"

"Very good, Samuel. It all went extremely well, and our friend is very pleased with the progress."

"Excellent. Thank you. How long before they know if she will fully recover?"

"They say they will have a very good idea on the basis of the next two to three days, so I will call you then. It's difficult to schedule calls more frequently."

"I understand, Tom." He hesitated. "Tom, has anything changed?"

"Like what, Samuel?"

"Oh, I don't know. Attitudes, for example?"

There was a hesitation. *Attitude* was not one of the code words they had agreed on.

"Not that I've noticed, Samuel. But I think there is something going on here, because the hotel has a few more guests in black leather coats than it did when I arrived."

"I understand. Take care of yourself, Tom, and ..."

The line went dead.

CHAPTER TWENTY-TWO

It took Samuel Levy two national call-clearing centres and more than thirty minutes to get his phone call connected through to England.

"Hello. Is that the Randolph Hotel in Oxford?"

"Yes, that's correct, sir."

"Can you put me through to Mr Monroe in room three-one-five, please?"

For thirty seconds the line crackled. Samuel Levy was about to hang up, assuming the connection had been lost.

"Hello, caller. Are you still there?" It was a different voice, with the slightest trace of a European accent.

"I'm still here. Can I speak with Mr Monroe, please?"

"Who is calling?"

"John Smith. I'm a business associate of Mr Monroe. It's very urgent that I speak with him."

"Mr Monroe, you said?"

"Yes, that's right. Tom Monroe."

"We do not have a guest under that name, Mr Smith."

"He is in room three hundred fifteen."

"No, sir. As I said, we do not have a guest under that name."

"Can you tell me when he checked out?"

"We have never had a guest under that name, Mr Smith. Perhaps you have the wrong hotel?"

This time it was Samuel Levy who broke off the connection.

CHAPTER TWENTY-THREE

"Hello, Mark. It's Samuel Levy."

"Hello, Mr Levy, sir. What can the FBI do for you?"

The old Jew hesitated. "This is rather awkward, Mark. My granddaughter is in Europe."

"What! Why? How?"

"I sent her there for an operation."

The line went silent for almost a whole minute.

"Are you sure you should be telling me this, Mr Levy?"

"I don't have any other options, Mark. She's gone missing. I need your help."

"This is one for my friends, Samuel, not the FBI."

"The CIA isn't going to help me, Mark. She left the United States on false papers, and it was all arranged by the German government. They have complete deniability. And there's no way the Germans are going to admit that they let a Jew into their precious Reich."

"I see what you mean, Samuel. I'll have a word with them anyway." He hesitated before continuing. "Look, Samuel. I'm going to get asked, so I have to ask you now. What persuaded the Nazis to give medical treatment to a Jew?"

"I'm really sorry, Mark, but I can't tell you that. If I must explain, it will have to be to our ambassador in Berlin."

"Okay, sir. I'll see what I can do. Is there anything else you can tell me?"

"She was taken to Europe by an old friend of mine, Tom Monroe. The last time I spoke with him he was staying at the Randolph Hotel in Oxford, room three hundred fifteen. Rebecca was in the hospital there and had already had her operation."

CHAPTER TWENTY-FOUR

"Mr Levy, sir, it's Mark Gibbs."

"Is there any news?"

"Nothing positive, Samuel. There's no trace of Tom Monroe, as we would expect. The record of him at the hotel has been eradicated. There have been no reported deaths of foreigners that could possibly relate to him. We know that their entry into the country was not recorded in the normal way, so we wouldn't be able to access that information anyway."

"What about Rebecca? Is there any trace of her?"

"Unfortunately, we haven't been able to find anything. There are medical records which show operations for people who are obviously using an alias, but none of them match her age or condition, so we have no way of following up." The line went quiet for an uncomfortably long time. "I'm very sorry, Samuel. I don't know what to suggest. Our people will check the records as often as they can, to see if anything crops up, but unless it does, she has just disappeared within the system."

Berlin – August 2024

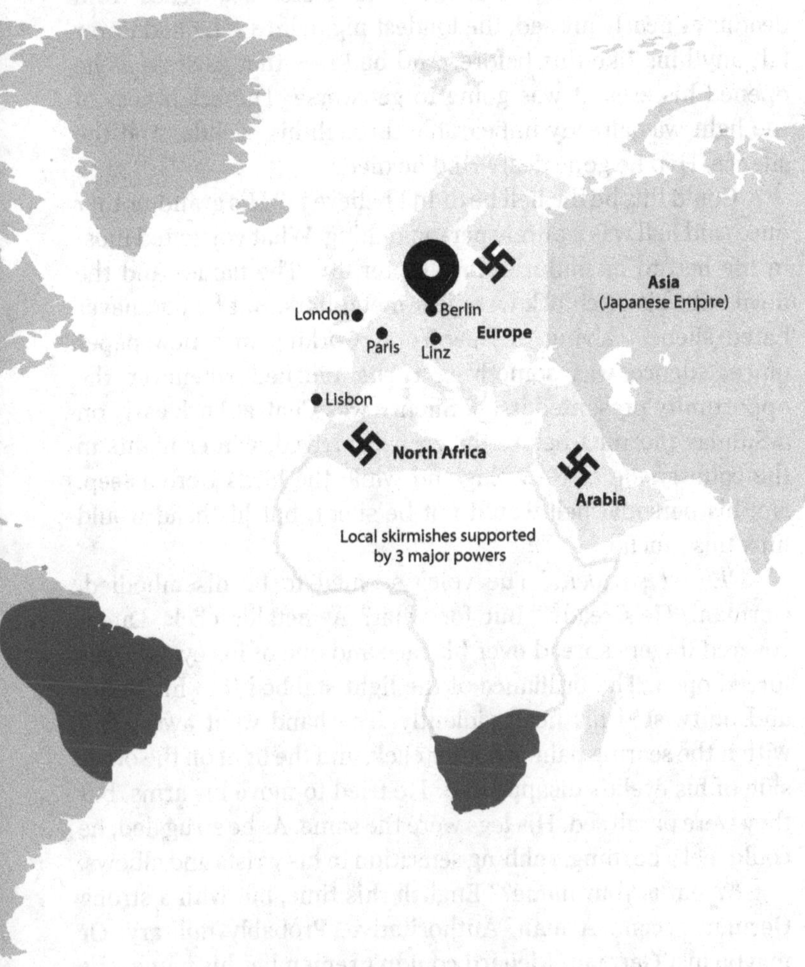

CHAPTER TWENTY-FIVE

His head hurt. All Richard knew was how much his head hurt. The worst hangovers, the worst stress headaches from deadlines nearly missed, the loudest nightclubs – he had never felt anything like this before. And he knew that as soon as he opened his eyes, it was going to get worse. The brightness of the light was already unbearable through his eyelids. And the silence. Had he gone deaf? Had he died?

Could this be the hell he didn't believe in? His grandmother once said hell was a purely personal thing. What you hated most in life had to be endured for all eternity. The flames and the devil with his pitchfork were just metaphors. But he had never hated silence. Living in New York, working in a newspaper office, silence was something to be relished whenever the opportunity presented itself. Silence was Central Park early on a Sunday morning before the crowds arrived; winter nights in the countryside of New England while the birds were asleep. No, his personal hell would not be silent, but his head would hurt this much.

"Er ist so weit." The voice seemed to be disembodied. German. 'He's ready.' But for what? A metallic click. Latex-covered fingers spread over his face and one of his eyelids was forced open. The brilliance of the light stabbed into his brain, and he twisted his head violently. The hand went away, and with it the searing pain. Another click, and the light on the other side of his eyelids disappeared. He tried to move his arms, but they were paralysed. His legs were the same. As he struggled, he could feel a burning, rubbing sensation in his wrists and elbows.

"What is your name?" English this time, but with a strong German accent. A man. Authoritative. Probably military. Or maybe just German. Richard couldn't remember his name. His head was throbbing. His mouth was parched.

"Water."

"It does not help if you lie. We will get the truth out of you. It is just a matter of time. And pain. What is your name?" The tone was soft but threatening. The vocal version of an iron fist in a velvet glove. And the questions came slowly and clearly, as if his interrogator was carefully weighing every word before speaking.

"Give me water." He heard a soft click and footsteps, then felt a plastic cup pushed to his lips and tipped. He managed to rescue a tiny trickle from it and licked his lips. Another click. "Richard Johnson."

"Now that is much better, Richard. I can see that this will be very fine, and you can get away from here very soon. You just have to answer our questions, honestly, and then you can go home. Where is home, Richard?"

"New York."

"Ah, New York. A great city. And what do you do in New York, Richard?"

"Journalist."

"Excellent. Are you working on a story at the moment?"

"Yes."

"And what sort of a story is that, Richard?"

"Murder."

"Oh, dear. You have lots of murders in your country, don't you, Richard? Not a safe country at all."

The pain in his head was now a dull ache and just about bearable, but he still didn't dare open his eyes. As the silence dragged on, he started to get agitated. The silence was not natural. There was no background noise at all. He frowned, and as the skin on his forehead formed into wrinkles, he felt a slight scratching. Stretching his fingers created the same effect. His head and hands were covered in sticking plasters. Was he wired up to a lie detector like the FBI used?

He heard a faint click preceding the next question. A second layer of fear gripped him, tightening the muscles in his throat, as he worked out that he was alone in a sealed room.

"So, who was murdered, Richard?"

"Jimmy Sullivan."

"Why was he killed?"

"I don't know."

"Come on, Richard. You were doing so well. You know you can't lie to us. Why was he murdered?"

"I really don't know."

"So, tell us what you do know. Who told you there was a murder?"

"My editor." Richard swallowed hard, and it hurt. The silence returned and he tensed, waiting to experience the reaction to this first lie, which their system must have picked up.

"Is your editor a Jew?" The question took Richard by surprise. He had expected to be punished for lying, or to be asked why he was in Cuba.

"No. I don't know."

"Which is it? No, or you don't know?"

"I don't think he's Jewish, but I'm not sure. It's never been important."

"Does he look Jewish?"

"I don't think so. But you can't always tell."

"That's very true, Richard."

Why did that make him feel guilty? The editor had powerful Jewish friends. And there were rumours of significant Jewish control over the newspaper, although that was not to be found in the official ownership declaration, so they had been able to send journalists to cover the Berlin Olympics.

"Who was your contact in Cuba?"

"I didn't have a contact in Cuba."

"Then who was it you met in the bar of the Raffles Hotel?"

"Just an old friend."

"What is his name?"

"Jack."

"Jack what?"

"I just know him as Jack."

"I admire your loyalty, Richard, but I've told you there is no point lying to us. What is his name?"

"Jack Gordon."

"That's better. That's enough for today, Richard. Get some rest. We'll chat some more tomorrow."

Richard opened his eyes, surprised that it was over. German interrogation techniques had a reputation for brutal effectiveness, but this had been a piece of cake. The room was very dimly lit. The wall opposite him emitted a faint glow. There was a sudden strip of light on his left, like a rapid sunrise, but vertical. The door opened and a silhouette came into the room. The light level was too low to distinguish anything beyond the rough outline of the person who was undoing the straps which had held him fast in the chair. He thought about overpowering this person, who looked to be quite small. When his bonds were untied, he strained to lift himself from the seat but managed about an inch before collapsing back into it, exhausted. The small man stepped out of sight behind him, and he felt the chair jolt backwards before being wheeled out through the door. He was pushed along well-lit corridors and then spun round to the left to face the open door of a prison cell. Richard felt the man come alongside him and pick him up, dragging him into the cell, where he expertly deposited him on his side onto the bed.

Immediately he fell into a deep sleep.

CHAPTER TWENTY-SIX

The shock was so sudden he awoke with a start. He had no idea what was happening. It was completely dark. He was freezing. The harsh white light from the bare bulb above his head flicked on, and his world came into focus. The uniformed soldier standing over him with the empty bucket. The white walls of the tiny cell. The wheelchair standing just inside the open door.

While the water continued to drip down Richard's face, the soldier hauled him to his feet. In the doorway a second soldier with a sub-machine gun did nothing to help, nor did the officer standing in the corner of the cell. He was dragged towards the wheelchair and manhandled roughly into it. The officer led the way out of the cell and turned right down the corridor he remembered vaguely from the previous evening – if it had been evening. If it had been yesterday. There were no windows and no clocks. There was nothing on the stark white walls of the corridor, or on the cell doors which interrupted them. He was pushed into a room on the right side. The lights were off, but he recognised it from the last session. As the wheelchair was spun round and manoeuvred into the slots in the floor, he could see the shadowy figures moving on the other side of the frosted observation window. A tall man in a white lab coat appeared in the doorway, a kidney-shaped metal dish in his hand. The steel-rimmed round spectacles seemed somehow at odds with the curls of red hair which gave the appearance of a very un-German anarchy. The man did not move until the soldier finished tightening the restraining straps around Richard's legs and arms. He came forward and picked up the full syringe. Richard looked down and realised he was now wearing hospital clothing – a green, short-sleeved smock which left his arms and legs exposed. The syringe looked like it was going to hurt a lot, and as it was forced into the soft skin of his elbow, he was proved correct. He gritted his teeth, something deep inside him refusing to give them the satisfaction of crying out in pain. He felt the electrical monitoring devices being attached back onto his forehead and also his upper chest, and a plastic crocodile clip was clamped on the index finger of each hand. Then they left him alone in the silence.

"What is your name?"

"Richard Johnson"

"Where do you live?"

"New York."

"Why did you travel to Cuba."

"My newspaper sent me. For a story."

"Do you love your mother?"

He hesitated. What was the point of the question? What relevance did it have to the current situation? How much did they really know about him if they thought his mother was still alive? Richard had no memory of her, as she and his father had died before his first birthday.

"I have no memory of my mother."

The jolt of pain started in his fingertip, but instantly gripped his whole body, sending it into spasm, forcing every limb against the restraining straps.

"Answer our questions immediately. Do you understand?"

He was not fully concentrating on the question, trying instead to cope with the pain and understand why it had been inflicted. The second jolt felt even more powerful than the first and seemed to last longer.

"Answer our questions immediately. Do you understand?"

"Yes. I understand." The words were painful to form as Richard struggled to catch his breath.

"Good. Who is Dan Adams?"

"He works on my newspaper."

"Is he your boss?"

"No. He works in a different department."

"Is he a Jew?"

"Yes."

"What is your relationship with him?"

"We are just colleagues." The technique was working. Richard was saying the first thing that came into his head to avoid the threat of another electric shock.

"Are you friends?"

"No. Not really."

"Who is your boss?"

"Mike Miller. A Jewish sub-editor." Richard heard his response as if he was a spectator of his own interrogation. Why had he said that? Was he just trying to pre-empt the next question? To get the ordeal over a few seconds earlier?

"Did he give you the assignment in Cuba?"

"No. It was Patrick Donovan, the editor."

"Why do you think that was?"

"I have no idea." Richard realised only after he had answered the question that this was not true, so he had not deliberately lied. He wondered how that would show up on their polygraph.

"Are you sure about that, Richard?"

"Yes. He just called me into his office and told me I was booked on a flight to Cuba that afternoon." Again, not a lie, just a deliberate attempt at misdirection. A sin of omission. Momentarily he was amused by his verbal dexterity at avoiding the truth while also avoiding a lie. But then he remembered that he had little experience of this game, and even without the brain monitors and the drugs, the people in the room next door were expert professionals - quite possibly the best in the world.

"Who was the dead man?"

"His name was Jimmy Sullivan."

"Why was he killed?"

"I have no idea. That's what I was trying to find out when your people brought me here."

"What does *J S* mean?"

Richard had heard that before, but he couldn't remember where. The fear rose in him. Delay would surely bring another shock, but he didn't know what to answer.

"I don't know."

"You don't seem too sure about that, Richard."

"I heard it mentioned in Cuba, but I can't remember why."

"Who mentioned it?"

"I can't remember." He could remember now but didn't want to implicate his friend. The third jolt was definitely more powerful and definitely longer. He squeezed his eyelids shut in a vain attempt to stop the stabbing tingling in his eyeballs.

Resistance was useless. He was no coward, but his pain threshold was not high and had already been exceeded.

"Jack Gordon mentioned it. But I honestly can't remember why." He could feel the cold sweat beading on his forehead as he waited for the next jolt.

"Jack Gordon. That would be the friend you met for a drink when you arrived in Cuba."

"Yes. That's right."

"Good, Richard. Go and get some rest. We will talk again later."

The light flicked back on, casting the matted observation window into darkness, and the door swung slowly open. Richard noticed that the soldier who came in to unfasten the monitoring equipment and restraints was unarmed. His belt sheath was neatly buttoned shut, with the knife conspicuous by its absence. His colleague, standing in the corridor immediately beyond the open door, was holding an automatic rifle across his chest, while his eyes focused on the activity inside the cell. The officer was standing alongside him, his right hand resting on top of the Lüger pistol in the unbuttoned holster at his hip. As the unarmed soldier moved behind the wheelchair to dislodge it from its floor mounting, the other two members of the detail moved to either side of the doorway. Richard was pushed out of the interrogation room, and the wheelchair retraced its earlier route as they followed the soldier with the rifle along the corridors.

The cell door was closed behind him, but this time the light remained on as he listened to the three men marching away. Richard looked at his hands. Apart from a slight swelling on the tips of his fingers, they looked quite normal. He swung his bare feet off the bed onto the floor. It felt cool, but rough. Gingerly, he tried to push himself up from the bed, to see if his legs could support his weight. As he stood, a little unsteadily, he heard a scraping noise to his left. Turning his head, he saw that a metal semi-circular compartment had appeared in his cell door. He tottered towards it and clumsily managed to retrieve the hunk of bread and tin beaker it contained. No sooner had his hands cleared the contraption than it snapped round and disappeared. He didn't feel hungry but gulped greedily at the liquid in the mug.

Cold water, but no less welcome for that. Despite the objection of his stomach, his head was telling him to eat. There was no way of knowing when he would next be fed, or even how long it had been since his last meal. The bread tasted as dry as it looked. He thought that, under the circumstances, his grandmother would forgive him and dipped the bread in the mug before taking the next bite. He managed another two mouthfuls before the nausea welled up from the pit of his stomach. He hadn't even made it to his knees when he vomited, collapsing into the corner of the cell. He lay on the floor, the temporary exuberance overcoming the discomfort and shame of the cold, lumpy liquid his cheek was lying in. The relief didn't last. The stomach cramps forced him into the foetal position, and he struggled to get onto his knees to avoid choking himself. The next five minutes seemed like an eternity as his empty stomach repeatedly tried to force more and more of itself onto the cell floor. He took deep breaths and eventually managed to reach his bed, collapsing into a relieved, smelly pile. He had slipped into unconsciousness long before the light was extinguished.

New York – August 2024

"Mr Levy, I have Mr Donovan for you."

"Thank you."

"Hello, Samuel. How are you?"

"Quite well, thank you, Patrick. What can I do for you?"

"Have you heard from Richard Johnson at all?"

"No, Patrick, I haven't. But nor was I expecting to. Why? Is something wrong?"

"He missed a meeting with one of his contacts out there, and he's not been seen at his hotel for five days. The guy rang to let me know. He said something about the Nazis being involved."

"I'm sorry, Patrick. I don't think I can help you. But I will be sure to let you know if I do hear from him."

The editor hesitated. "Samuel."

"Yes, Patrick?"

"Just what was Johnson doing in Cuba?"

"That's something I would rather not discuss on the phone. But I don't think it's anything that would have got him into difficulties. I guess he'll turn up very soon."

Samuel Levy replaced the receiver and ran his fingers through his beard for a couple of minutes before dialling the number of the FBI's New York field office.

"Mark Gibbs, please."

"Who shall I say is calling?"

"A friend."

"Putting you through." It was almost a minute before he heard the familiar voice announce itself at the other end of the line.

"Hello, Mark. It's Samuel.

"Hi, Mr Levy. I'm afraid there's nothing new to report yet, sir."

"I need to make you aware of something else which may have a bearing on the case. You need to call the editor of the

Eastern Times, Patrick Donovan, and offer to help him locate Richard Johnson. Say I asked you to call."

"Can't you be more explicit, Mr Levy?"

"Not over an open line, I can't. And Mark, check who's listening in, will you?"

CHAPTER TWENTY-EIGHT

"Mr Levy, it's Mark. About your friend in Cuba. The one you asked about yesterday."

"Yes?"

"Someone decided he had to cut short his holiday. And it was such a rush job they even used a private jet. Filed a flight plan from Havana to Houston, Texas, but they diverted en route. We're still working on where they ended up flying, but it looks like it might have been Europe. Is there anything more I should know, sir?"

"Not from this end. I haven't spoken to him since he was in New York."

"Do you have anything more solid to go on? We can't ask our foreign friends to help with no evidence that it's anything to do with them."

"I realise that, Mark. I'll see if I can come up with anything."

Samuel pressed down the cradle on the phone and released it after a few seconds before dialling the direct line of the editor of the *Eastern Times*.

"Patrick, it's Samuel Levy. Have you heard anything from Johnson yet?"

"No, nothing. What about you? Or your government friend?"

"Patrick, do you trust your man in Berlin?"

"As much as you ever can. Wolfgang clears everything through the Propaganda Ministry before passing it on to us, but he sails as close to the wind as he can. Why? What have you heard?"

"Well, it's only a rumour, but there is some talk on the grapevine that the Germans lifted an American journalist in Cuba and that he's now in Germany."

"Johnson?"

"As I said, it's only the vaguest of rumours, but it would

explain his sudden disappearance. And also his friend's comment about the Nazis."

"We can't go accusing the Germans of kidnapping a journalist without something more substantial to go on."

"No, Patrick. But your man in Berlin could ask around. And he wouldn't have to be too subtle about it."

"You mean embarrass them into releasing him?"

"Well, if the Germans are holding him, it would be difficult for them if the story got out. It's probably worth a try. But, of course, it has to be your decision. I'm just trying to help."

"Yes. Thank you, Samuel. I'll give it some thought."

CHAPTER TWENTY-NINE

"Samuel, it's Patrick. I thought you ought to know. It seems our mutual friend may be in Berlin."

"How did you work that out?"

"I got our man in Germany to start asking indiscreet questions. He asked if there were any unaccredited American journalists currently in Berlin. A couple of days later he got the response that the Gestapo were not currently holding any US citizens."

"Sorry, Patrick. You've lost me. How does that help us?"

"He never asked about the Gestapo, Samuel."

"Are you sure about this? It all sounds a bit far-fetched. The Gestapo are many things, but stupid isn't usually one of them."

"I know, I know. But this type of mistake has been seen before. And to confirm it, our man has now got increased surveillance on him."

"I see. It sounds like you're convinced. So, what do we do now?"

"Tomorrow our embassy in Berlin will make a formal request to the German Foreign Ministry for help in tracking down an American citizen who has gone missing. This is a standard procedure. We don't accuse the government of anything. We say we think he has been kidnapped by European criminals in a case of mistaken identity. It lets them know that we know they are holding him, so it's that much harder for them to make him just disappear."

"Do we have any idea why the Nazis are interested in Johnson?"

"I was going to ask you exactly the same question, Samuel."

Samuel clicked the cradle down before calling the FBI.

"Hello, Mark. It's Samuel."

"Hello, Mr Levy. I was just about to call you. There's been a development with your friend from Cuba."

“Have you found him?”

“Not exactly, Samuel. I’ve been talking to an old friend from university, and we are now acting on the basis that he is being held by the Gestapo in Berlin.”

“And you’re requesting the help of the German authorities in finding him.”

Mark was crest-fallen. “I thought we were supposed to be the intelligence agency. How did you find that out, if I may ask?”

“His editor just told me. But what about Rebecca? Have you made any progress there?”

There was a hesitation on the other end of the line. “Not yet, I’m afraid. But we’ve got everyone we can working on it.”

Berlin – October 2024

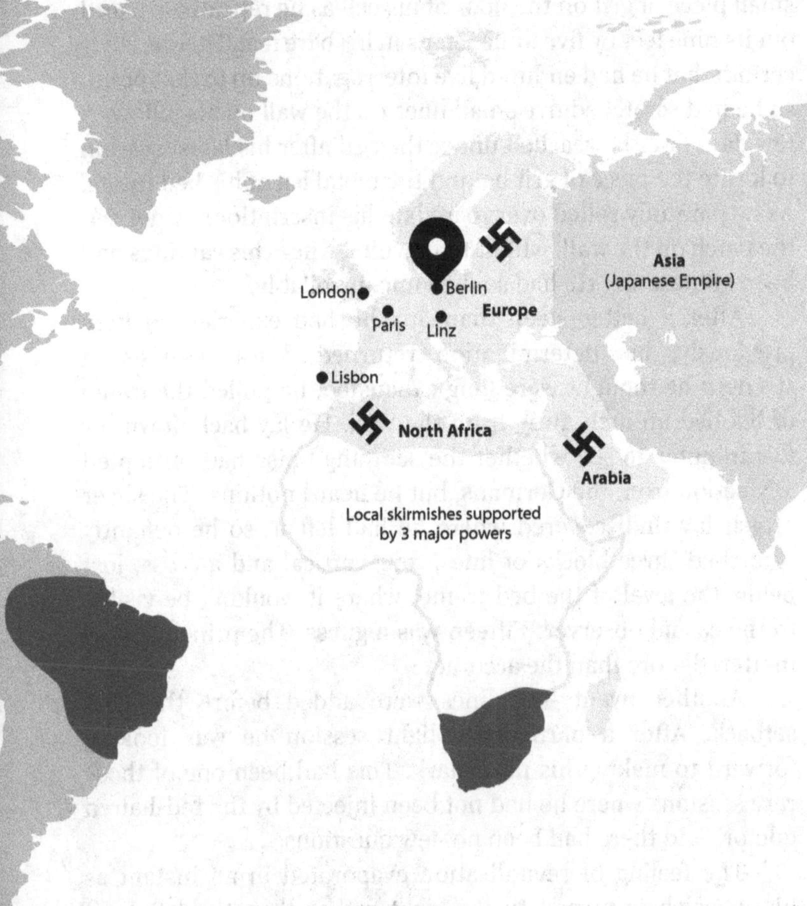

CHAPTER THIRTY

Richard had quickly given up trying to count the sessions in his head. After the first few interrogations he had discovered a small piece of grit on the floor of his cell as he repeatedly paced out its nine feet by five dimensions in his bare feet. He was fairly certain that he had endured five interrogations up to that point, so he had scratched five small lines on the wall by his pillow. A few days later he reached under the bed after his latest session to locate the piece of grit behind the metal leg of his bed frame. As he painfully rolled over to update his inscription, he noticed the patch on the wall, whiter than white, where his carvings had been obliterated. He had sobbed uncontrollably.

After a better sleep than any he had experienced here previously, his determination returned. With reserves of strength he thought were long exhausted, he pulled the frame of his bed an inch away from the wall. He lay back down for five minutes to see whether the scraping noise had prompted any action from the Germans, but he heard nothing. The sliver of grit lay undiscovered where he had left it, so he defiantly scratched three blocks of lines, four vertical and a cross, just below the level of the bed frame, where it wouldn't be visible to the casual observer. Fifteen was a guess. The principle now mattered more than the accuracy.

Another twenty-five lines were added before the next setback. After a particularly light session he was looking forward to making his next mark. This had been one of those rare sessions where he had not been injected by the red-haired doctor. And there had been no new questions.

The feeling of revitalisation evaporated in an instant as his wheelchair turned to the right rather than the left as it reached the corridor. He was about to point out the mistake to his guards, when he realised what was happening. The new cell was identical in every respect. Every respect except the wall inscription and the tiny stone secreted behind the leg of the bed.

He felt desperate. He had been telling the truth, divulging everything he knew, since day one. What more could he do to end it? As he lay, staring into the darkness, he wondered how long it would be before they returned him to a cell containing a length of rope. And how long he would resist using it.

That night he dreamed of police cars chasing bank robbers. It was a dream he had often enjoyed as a child, only then he had been in the police car. He opened his eyes, but the insistent clanging followed him into wakefulness. The bells sounded a long way off, but he knew from weeks of silence, only ever punctuated by boot steps, that no external noise ever penetrated to where he was. Richard froze as panic overtook him. He could hear boots running and distant shouts. Disorder. Chaos. Not the planned certainties and discipline by which the 'master race' liked to characterise itself. The footsteps were not getting any closer.

He jumped to his feet and took the two steps to the cell door. He thought he could smell smoke as the sound of the footsteps receded. He filled his lungs ready to shout but then hesitated. What should he shout? He felt suddenly overwhelmed by apathy. It was probably just another of their psychological tricks. And if not, at least this would put an end to the pain. He slowly walked back to his bed and crashed onto it, burying his face deep in the rough pillow.

The next morning he woke up but couldn't hear anything. He usually slept in the cell until the footsteps of the guards woke him – one set for food, three sets for interrogation. That whole day passed without activity. He alternately paced and slept until he could sleep no more. He even caught himself thinking that an interrogation would be preferable to the total nothingness of this day. Provided there was no injection.

Then normality returned: three sets of footsteps. He braced himself for the regular routine. Today's officer was the one in the Luftwaffe uniform. His right hand rested on top of the Lüger in the unbuttoned holster. His left hand was bandaged. The procession turned right out of the cell. It was a few seconds before the significance hit Richard. They always turned right. But following the previous session, he had been moved into a new cell, so they were going a different way. Or going somewhere else. His senses heightened. They turned left at the end of the corridor, then left again, and again. The wheelchair came to a halt outside the usual door and stopped. Richard glanced to his right. For the second before he was shoved into the interrogation room, he could make out what looked like scorch marks defacing the pristine white of the corridor walls.

London – October 2024

CHAPTER THIRTY-ONE

Victoria listened hard and stared into the middle distance, her bright, green eyes matching the smart jacket slung over the back of her chair. Below her a shaft of unseasonal sunshine glinted on the grey surface of the River Thames. Satisfied by the silence, she wiggled the connection at the back of her computer terminal. It took two attempts until the letters and numbers exploded into a scattering of dots, which slowly faded from view. She looked over her shoulder. Despite the bright light shining in through the windows on two sides of her, the twenty-first floor of the building was like a ghost ship. It was ironic that her reputation for working late had already resulted in a promotion. She picked up the small stack of green files and moved across the office. Tonight, she elected to sit at Sally's desk – not as the result of any carefully crafted plan to disguise the pattern of her evening activities, but just because, for once, it was the tidiest. Victoria threw her jacket over the back of Sally's chair and contorted herself to reach under the desk and push the button on the processor. She returned to the upright seated position, counted to ten, and flicked the switch on the screen, which was in every sense identical to the one on her own desk. Except that it had a different identity number, and the activity on it was logged in a separate file on the English Health Ministry's security system.

From memory she tapped in Sally's identity key and password. It would have been too dangerous to keep a written note of them all, but fortunately she had always had a good memory.

She typed in HHC, the code for the Heinrich Himmler hospital in Carlisle.

CARLISLE IS A SECURE FACILITY. LEVEL 2 CLEARANCE OR ABOVE REQUIRED. REFER TO YOUR SUPERVISOR.

Victoria stared at the screen in horror. Stupid mistake. Sally's security clearance was only level four. If she closed the session now, the system would record a failed attempt to access restricted files, so there was no alternative. She highlighted the on-screen button marked 'Supervisor Authorisation' and hit enter. In the spaces which now appeared, she typed in her own identity key and password, hesitating for a second before hitting enter again. After a few seconds the standard hospital enquiry screen appeared. She typed quickly, suppressing the slight trembling in her fingers.

`Surname — SCHMIDT, First Name — JOHANNA`

Leaving the rest of the form blank, Victoria again hit enter and waited for the response.

`Johanna Sarah Schmidt. Date of Birth`
`01.01.2012. Transfer IN scheduled for`
`16.10.2024. Current location: JMO-37-08.`
`Procedure: UD. Special note: UD.`

She had seen the reference 'UD' before but couldn't immediately recall what it stood for. It was not on the official list of medical acronyms pinned above every workstation in the ministry's administration centre. Victoria logged out of the system. The transfer was scheduled for five days' time, which meant she had to carry on this evening, despite the risks. No one had explained why, but since Victoria had identified the anomaly a week ago, she had been told of the importance of keeping this girl safe, which initially meant making sure she was not transferred to Carlisle.

This time without changing desks, she logged back into the system as Clive Ogden. His password was the name of his cat followed by the two digits of the current year. At the opening screen she typed in JMO, which brought up the general enquiry screen for the Josef Mengele hospital in Oxford. She again typed in JOHANNA SCHMIDT, which this time returned ten records. The first was for a patient undergoing treatment for an advanced brain tumour. The next three patients had all been discharged within the last three months. Victoria selected the fifth record.

`Johanna Sarah Schmidt. Date of Birth`
`01.01.2012.  Transfer OUT to HHC scheduled`
`for 16.10.2024. Location: 37-08. Procedure:`

It was the HLT(W) which had shown up on the report Victoria created as part of her responsibility for overseeing budget allocation. The heart and lung transplant operation was itself quite common, and selling the technology to citizens of the United States, for values well in excess of the hundred thousand Reichsmarks on the official pricelist, was accepted practice. But the technique of DNA washing had only recently been perfected. While this would in time become the standard procedure, it was currently restricted to the highest category of patients. DNA washing removed the need for a lifetime's supply of expensive anti-rejection drugs by conditioning the organs to the recipient's own blood before the operation. Whoever Johanna Schmidt might be, she was certainly not a senior party official. That the cost of half a million had been charged to the Foreign Ministry in Berlin was also extremely odd. And that anyone who had undergone such a procedure was being transferred to Carlisle made no sense at all. The discharge records for the hospital in Carlisle were not even available to someone with Victoria's administrative access rights on the computer system. She had heard the whispers about the HHC. While it was nominally run by the Health Ministry it was, in reality, a Gestapo facility. And there never were any discharges. The SS and its police forces didn't normally require medical facilities to dispose of its problems, but whenever they did, Carlisle was the location of choice. For those who developed mental illnesses or undesirable political views, Carlisle was often the final port of call. Undesirables. *UD.*

The out-of-key whistling of a Wagner overture jolted her back to the present reality. Victoria stood up and walked back towards her own desk, stretching her arms above her head to relieve the tension in her shoulders. She prayed that this was not one of the nights the burly guard would drop in for a chat, as her work was not yet complete. Victoria was in luck. A friendly wave and he was off, not to reappear for another hour. She returned to switch off Sally's computer and transferred the green files back onto her own desk. This time she did need to check for the login password, scattered in pencil marks across four pages of her desk diary. The politicians took computer security more seriously than the bureaucrats, but as the minister's personal assistant had only changed his password two weeks previously, she felt confident that she had the up-to-date version. Victoria wrote the code in pencil on a scrap of paper and moved into the office of her boss, the Director of Health Administration for England. His computer was a newer model than those in the open plan area, and it took noticeably less time for the log-in screen to appear above the shiny Siemens logo on the plastic housing. She typed in the identity key and password of Gerald Forsyth, the Health Minister's executive assistant, and hit enter. As the screen appeared, she popped the scrap of paper into her mouth and started to chew while typing TXF. The blank transfer form appeared, and her fingers moved quickly over the keys.

Transfer from? JMO
Name? JOHANNA SARAH SCHMIDT
Confirm: Johanna Sarah Schmidt, DOB
01.01.2012? YES
Transfer to?

Victoria hesitated. She needed somewhere out of the way. And preferably in the opposite direction to Carlisle. She typed Hampshire and waited for the options to appear, scanning the list for a few moments. The hospitals in Portsmouth were likely to be full of military because of the naval bases in the area. Southampton Central was a very busy hospital which acted as the hub for the whole south coast. Next on the list was the Magda Goebbels hospital in Southampton. Until recently that had been a children's hospital, but it had been reclassified in the last review, having narrowly escaped complete closure. She highlighted it on the screen and pressed enter. The transfer form reappeared with MGS filled in as the target institution. Within seconds a flashing box appeared on the screen.

TRANSFER TO HHC ALREADY SCHEDULED FOR 16.10.2024. CONFIRM OVERRIDE?

Victoria typed YES and the next question on the screen was highlighted:

Transfer date requested? To avoid a second notification being sent to the Oxford hospital, Victoria entered the same date as the originally scheduled transfer.

Expected duration of stay? 2 WEEKS

Reason for transfer? Victoria hit the enter key and started to scroll down the options. She stopped at POST-OPERATIVE RECUPERATION — NEAR RELATIVES and pressed enter, hoping the super-efficient system wouldn't ask for additional details.

Transfer confirmed. Reference 24-1534978JMO–MGS.

Transfer 24-1530887JMO–HHC Cancellation confirmed.

Please print now for your records.

Victoria stared at the computer and realised she was still holding her breath. She exited the transfer screen and landed back at the main page, where she typed in the code of the special facility in Carlisle, HHC. For the final time she typed in JOHANNA SCHMIDT.

Record not found.

She logged out of the system and turned off her boss's computer. Returning to her own desk, she pushed the cable firmly into the back of the screen and waited until it returned to life before logging off and killing the power to the screen and processor.

Outside it was still bright. She needed a drink, but the prospect of drinking alone at home didn't appeal. As she stepped into the elevator, Victoria tried to empty her mind of every thought except which of the local pubs would be least likely to contain any of her colleagues on a Friday evening.

Berlin – October 2024

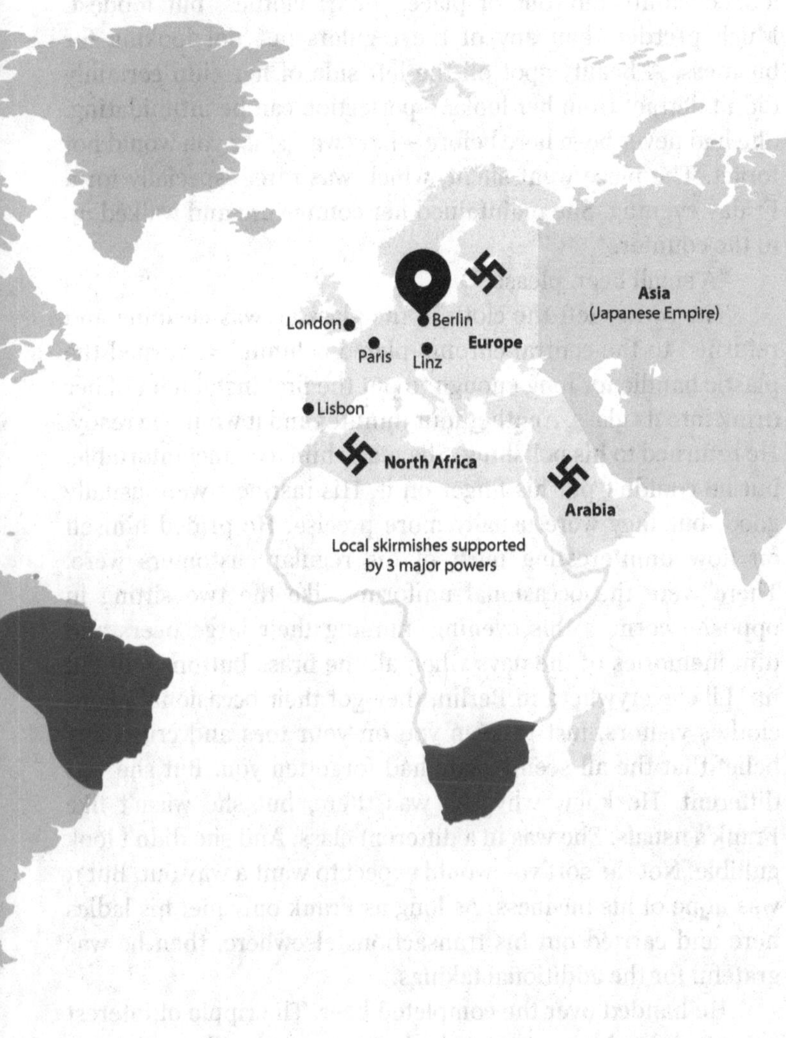

CHAPTER THIRTY-TWO

The blonde took her sunglasses off as she entered his bar. She looked completely out of place. Smart clothes, but modest. Much prettier than any of the regulars but not looking for business. A beauty spot on the left side of her chin certainly didn't detract from her looks – perfection can be intimidating. She had never been here before – hers was a face you would not forget. The place went silent, which was rare, especially for a Friday evening. She maintained her composure and walked up to the counter.

"A small beer, please."

The owner left the cloth in the glass he was cleaning and returned to the central chrome-plated column. He turned the plastic handle for long enough to put the first instalment of her drink into its glass. Another four minutes and it would be ready. He returned to his polishing. She made him feel uncomfortable, but he couldn't put his finger on it. His instincts were usually good, but they were usually more precise. He prided himself on how uninteresting most of his regular customers were. There were the occasional uniforms, like the two sitting in opposite corners this evening, nursing their large beers and dim memories of the days when all the brass buttons still did up. Like everywhere in Berlin, they got their occasional plain-clothes visitors, just to keep you on your toes and crush any belief that the all-seeing state had forgotten you. But she was different. He knew why she was there, but she wasn't like Frank's usuals. She was in a different class. And she didn't look gullible. Not the sort you would expect to want a way out. But it was none of his business. As long as Frank only met his ladies here and carried out his transactions elsewhere, then he was grateful for the additional takings.

He handed over the completed beer. The ripple of interest provoked by her entrance had petered out. She was now returning the compliment, scanning the room with blue eyes that looked like they knew what they were doing. He needed to be careful with this one. Hopefully, Frank would have a quick schnapps then take her somewhere else.

"Double corn, Bert." Frank slid onto the bar stool, appearing not even to notice the blonde sitting next to him, while he waited for the drink. He took a short sip before scanning the room, his head turning as far as it could to the left before snapping back into its starting position and completing the sweep to the right. The beads of sweat on the top lip, just below the Führer moustache, mingled with the second sip and disappeared as he wiped his sleeve across his mouth. His slight nod gained the desired acknowledgment from the blonde.

"Do you come here often?"

"No. It's my first time."

"I'm a regular. Not a bad place really. And Bert's a good sort." The jolt of his head in the direction of the barman was studiously ignored. Bert still remembered the first time he had heard the classic line, and he had been about to laugh out loud, when the girl Frank was sitting next to actually replied. Since then, it had been a regular occurrence. Always young women. Usually quite good-looking, but Frank had excelled himself this time. And they usually came back one more time, possibly twice. Perhaps they did somehow make it out of the country. He had certainly never seen any of them again, but then he had never seen any of them previously.

"I know a better place. A bit more lively. Fancy coming along?" Bert watched as Frank's hand moved off the bar to where her knee must be.

"Aren't your friends coming here?"

"Not tonight, they're not. They still need a bit more convincing." Frank slipped down from the stool and stood waiting. The blonde opened her bag and took out a mark piece which she set on the bar next to her half-empty glass. The man looked first at his own empty glass, then at the girl's bag. She took out another mark, which she placed beside the shot glass before following the man out into the Berlin evening.

CHAPTER THIRTY-THREE

Richard had conceded defeat on his graffiti attempts, and without the count of his interrogation sessions, he quickly lost all track of time. The conventional framework of markers everyone uses to orient themselves had been completely disrupted since day one. He couldn't remember when he had last seen daylight, and mealtimes were not just infrequent, but very erratic, so hunger was also no guide. He had convinced himself he was in Germany, based on a combination of the uniforms, the accents and the preponderance of sausages in his diet. His demands to see someone from the United States embassy had been laughed at when they were not completely ignored.

There was no discernible pattern to the interrogation sessions. Some days he got an injection, and some days he didn't. The injection was extremely potent. Almost instantly he experienced a momentary blurring of his vision, followed by the sensation that he was floating outside his body, looking down on himself. On these days he felt that he was not in control of his mind. Like a drunk, who can't get his body to do what he wants, or stop it doing what it wants, he seemed to have no power over what he was saying or even thinking. Sometimes he had bright lights shone into his eyes, but mostly he was in darkness. On a couple of occasions, he could sense there were one or more people in the room with him, but normally he was completely alone. Sometimes he got the electric shocks, and sometimes his fingers or toes were not wired up, although the monitoring electrodes were always there. There were sessions where he was wired up, but not shocked. He didn't think he had ever been shocked when he answered a question honestly and without hesitation, but surprisingly he had often escaped punishment for even obvious lies.

He was always escorted to and from these sessions by a team of three with strictly regimented roles, even though the faces changed. He also noticed that there was a repertoire of random questions, which were interspersed in the sessions: 'which city do you live in', 'what was your father's middle name?', 'how many homosexual encounters have you had?', 'how many Jews do you know?', 'what are eighteen sixes?' He assumed these were calibration questions for their monitoring equipment. He had long since given up trying to beat the system because he knew that would mean testing the boundaries, like a child seeing what level of disobedience results in punishment. His terror of the electric shocks ruled that out. The tough question was always about *J S*. This came up during virtually every session, and he had quickly concluded they were desperate about it. Their need to find out was even greater than their need to disguise just how desperate they were. Something he couldn't put his finger on made Richard think there was a link with the European War, but that made no sense. Of course, this could just be a deliberate misdirection, to take attention away from their real objective, which was being handled more subtly. During one of the drugged sessions he had remembered the context of the mention of *J S* by his Cuban friend. It had been cut into the hand of the dead man in Naziland.

His main source of hope was in the way he was being treated outside the interrogation room. He was never starved or beaten, and every two or three days he was shaved while strapped into his chair. In a word, he was presentable. There were no outward signs of physical abuse, so he could safely be turned over to the US authorities at any time, without provoking allegations of torture.

What really surprised Richard was that this was still going on. He could feel his mind passing out of his control whenever he was injected, and it would have been impossible for him to lie. Not that he really had any inclination to hide the truth. He didn't understand the real reasons behind his trip to Cuba, and he had told the story countless times, presumably consistently, as he made no attempt to resist. When asked about his two visits to Naziland he was surprised to hear himself describing details which he didn't realise he had remembered. He was not a coward, but he would do almost anything to avoid the prospect of pain, as he had demonstrated to his captors on several occasions. They must realise that they already had as much information out of him as they were ever going to get. No, he didn't know any Germans living in America. No, he had not met Samuel Levy before the fateful day he flew to Cuba. He didn't know the man who had been killed in Naziland and had only ever heard his name in the reports of his death. And no, he had no idea what the letters *J S* stood for.

CHAPTER THIRTY-FOUR

The blonde's second visit to his bar was a few days later, early in the afternoon. The liquid lunches had finished, and even the longest of evening sessions wouldn't start for another couple of hours. The only people in a Berlin bar at this time of the day were those who had nowhere else to go. Or those who desperately needed to get away. The man in the cap falling asleep over his beer at the bar was a Berlin stereotype. Retired, with no remaining purpose in life, he was either escaping a wife with a list of long-overdue chores or keeping a safe distance from one who realised the wisdom of doing them herself. The student with the dark curly hair and beard sitting against the wall was about thirty. His book looked anything but frivolous. Hard, pale green board covers with no dust jacket, it had as studious an air as a young man stuck inside on a warm day with a glass of water containing nothing but a single slice of lemon. He ought to be charging him rent.

The blonde ordered a beer and sat at the corner table next to the cigarette machine, a strategic point commanding a complete view of the establishment. She had to wait five minutes for the drink, then five more, nervously touching her sunglasses, moving them from table to pocket to bag and back again.

"Beer." The door hadn't yet settled back into its frame by the time Frank took his seat opposite the blonde. She looked expectantly into his face, and he stared back, defiantly.

"Are your friends coming?"

"No. Not today. To be honest, Hanna, they don't trust you. You're too much of a risk."

Her eyes dropped down to the table, and she started fidgeting with the white circle of paper round the stem of her beer glass. Their silence matched the rest of the surroundings until she straightened her shoulders and took a deep breath before looking straight into the man's eyes. "Then give me my money back. I'll find someone else."

"No one else is going to touch you."

"I want my money back."

"It's gone. Expenses. There were things I had to arrange. People I had to pay off. Most of it's gone."

"You really don't want to cross me. Do you? You should be careful where you make enemies."

"Look, there may be a chance. I know some other people. But it will take more money to ...." Frank stopped mid-sentence, as he noticed Hanna's face had turned upwards and was now looking over his head.

"Is this man bothering you?" The student towered over the seated Frank, the green book clasped in his left hand, closed around his index finger. The pointed beard and full moustache were reminiscent of a Bolshevik revolutionary leader.

"No. It's okay. Thank you." But Frank was already squirming his way out of the seat, his eyes glued to the book, as if it was a deadly weapon being aimed at him. The woman was still staring into the student's piercing green eyes as the door banged shut.

"It's Hanna, isn't it?" The surprise which registered on her face looked genuine.

"How do you ...?" Her question dried up.

"We should talk, Hanna. Do you have time for a walk? It's a lovely day. I'm Alex."

Bert watched as his two customers left the bar together. He really did not want to know what had just happened. He tipped the half-poured beer down the sluice.

CHAPTER THIRTY-FIVE

Richard awoke naturally. He only remembered that happening once before, and he didn't know what to do. He must have been sitting on the bed for five or ten minutes, his mind more or less blank, when the door to his cell was unlocked. A tall man he hadn't seen before stood in the doorway. His short silver hair could be seen as he carried his cap under his left arm. He was wearing rimless glasses, something rarely seen as an accessory to the black Gestapo uniform. He looked about sixty, around twenty years older than anyone else Richard had encountered during his enforced stay here.

"Follow me, please, Herr Johnson." The voice was firm, crisp and polite, which made it sound all the more threatening. As Richard got to his feet, he could distinguish the gold triple-oak-leaf rank insignia on the man's shoulders. Like every American schoolboy, he had collected bubble gum cards, and after the baseball and football series, the most popular had always been the sets with Nazi uniforms and insignia. This officer was a Gruppenführer, the equivalent of a two-star general in the USA. The guards were standing even more rigidly to attention than usual. The unarmed corporal beside the door was one of only three who had fulfilled that role during Richard's stay. He had three rows of medal ribbons across his chest and looked to be in his early thirties. The armed guard in the corridor was a sergeant who looked younger than the corporal. These two positions were always army men in the field grey uniform that had barely changed in decades. There was always an officer leading the guard. This role was more often than not filled by a very tall SS captain with regulation blond hair under his regulation black cap with its shiny peak. Sometimes it had been someone from the navy or the air force, and on a few occasions, there had been a junior officer from the *Wehrmacht*, like the two subordinates. But today it was again the blonde Gestapo captain who had accompanied him on the two previous occasions. She was the only woman he had seen during his captivity, and he remembered the shock he had registered when he had first set eyes on her two days ago. Her pale, blue eyes had seemed to burn right into his soul. Not wanting to display weakness, he had fixed his stare on the beauty spot on the left side of her chin rather than admit defeat.

The general turned on his heel and marched down the corridor, which Richard had passed along every day but had never previously set foot in. The corporal followed the general, and Richard knew his place was next in this cortege. He tried to detect the perfume of the officer he knew was marching behind him, simply to stop his mind racing to a thousand different conclusions of what had brought on this dramatic change. As the corporal was in line with the door of the interrogation room, they all stopped. Richard noticed that he was himself precisely in step with the Germans. The general turned to face him while the corporal opened the door. Unnecessarily, he motioned Richard to enter. The wheelchair was already in place. Richard took his seat without being asked, and waited to be strapped in. The general stood in the doorway until the corporal had finished, with the armed sergeant at the ready behind him. The monitors were attached with their sticking plasters, but today Richard was not wired into the electric-shock mechanism. Nor did the red-headed doctor appear with his syringe. The corporal stood to attention and saluted the general, who returned the salute and entered the room. The corporal left, closing the door behind him. Richard was aware of two shapes in the control room as usual. But in all his visits to this chamber, this was the first time he had come face to face with his questioner. He noticed that the general spoke much better English than any of his colleagues, and with much less of an accent.

"Now, Mr Johnson, there are a number of things I wish to clarify, if I may." The politeness sounded no less sinister than before. A man in his position never had to ask permission. The black uniform would strike terror into the heart of any citizen of the empire with the slightest guilt on his conscience and the fear of doubt into the completely innocent. And most would never have even seen a black uniform with gold rank insignia instead of the usual silver. "Why were you in Cuba?"

"I was working on a story for my newspaper. A body had been found in MicroWorld, and my editor must have thought there was something about it that would make a good story."

"And what might that have been, Mr Johnson?"

"He didn't tell me. As the newspaper's most experienced crime reporter, he probably felt he didn't need to tell me."

"Who helped you break into our facility in MicroWorld?"

"No one. I had visited earlier in the day and seen where the garbage was stored. I guessed that it would be picked up after the park closed, and that might provide me with a way in."

"What would you have done if you had been wrong?"

"I would have looked for another way in. It's an entertainment complex, so the security is all about stopping pickpockets and queue jumpers. They don't expect people to break in at night."

"I see. They clearly have a lot to learn. Who was the dead man – this Jimmy Sullivan?"

"I never found out. He was an American – from the mainland. There was a rumour he was a PI, but before I had the opportunity to check that out, I was overtaken by events."

As Richard expected, the sarcasm was ignored.

"A private investigator." This was not phrased as a question. Richard assumed it was for the benefit of the tape recorders, or those whose grasp of colloquial American was not as robust as the one asking the questions. "Yes, he was indeed a private investigator. From New York. Perhaps you knew him there?"

"New York is a big town. Was he Jewish?" The words just poured out of Richard's mouth. He surprised himself that he had said this. For weeks he had had random questions thrown at him to see how he responded, so something deep inside wanted to see how they liked it. It was an act of pure bravado, born of mounting frustration and the fact that today he was not wired into the mains. There was obviously a reason why such a senior officer had come in to see him. Richard sensed that a turning point had been reached. His sensible side knew that being deferential was the best way of staying out of trouble with the Nazis, but that self-destructive instinct, which had tailed him through most of his life, seemed to pick the most dangerous moments to show its true colours.

"No, he was not." The craggy face beneath the silver hair was frozen to avoid betraying any of the surprise or irritation caused by being on the receiving end of a question for once. It didn't work. "But the person he was working for certainly was. A Mrs Horowitz. Mrs Isaiah Horowitz." The German spoke slowly, laying great emphasis on the man's name. The cold eyes were staring, and Richard could feel them burning into a spot on the inside of his skull. He knew of Isaiah Horowitz. One of New York's richest and least-liked businessmen. There were lots of rumours about him, but if you knew what was good for you, you didn't repeat them. It was generally assumed that he was a major contributor to the New York Police Department's 'benevolent fund,' otherwise he would have been behind bars, or worse, a long time ago. Apart from the shady business deals and extortion, he was also known as a ladies' man. He had no problem appearing in the society pages of newspapers and magazines accompanied by glamorous women less than half his age, and never usually singly. He believed he managed to balance this with the appearance of a good Jewish family man, devoted to his two daughters and long-suffering wife. Richard hadn't given the man a second thought since Jack Gordon had driven them past his villa during their night out in Havana.

"Do you know Mrs Horowitz, Richard?" The use of his first name for the first time was in stark contrast to the harsh, sneering coldness of the voice.

"No."

"But you know who she is, don't you?"

"I know who her husband is."

"Have you met him?"

"No."

"Are you sure, Richard? I have heard he knows every important journalist in New York." The audible sneer was this time accompanied by a visible one.

"I'm a crime journalist. He wouldn't want to talk to me."

"I see. So why do you think his wife would need a private investigator?"

"I really have no idea. I'm afraid I can't help you there."

"That's a pity. We were really hoping you could." The voice was filled with mock regret. This was not going well. He had chosen the wrong person to antagonise.

"Does Isaiah Horowitz know Samuel Levy?"

"I don't know. I expect he does. Perhaps they go to the same synagogue."

"And does Senator Goldberg go to the same synagogue?"

"I doubt it. Senator Goldberg is from Nevada."

"What do you know about *J S*?"

"Only that you are very interested in it."

The general made a not-altogether-successful attempt to conceal his anger.

"We are interested in you, Herr Johnson. We want to understand how much of a threat you and your associates pose to the Reich."

"I keep telling you. I have no associates."

"So you say. Look, Mr Johnson. I want to help you resolve this, so that we can all get on with our lives. That is why I decided to talk to you myself. But I need your cooperation. We know when you are lying. We know when you are concealing something. We just don't know what it is that you are not telling us. And if you're going to such lengths to keep secrets from us, they must be important, and they must threaten our security, mustn't they?"

"I have told you everything I know. I have no secrets. I don't know anything about *J S*. I just want to go home." Richard hadn't wanted to sound quite so pathetic or desperate, but what harm could it do?

"I wish I could help you, Herr Johnson. I really do. I suggest that you think seriously about your situation and stop protecting your associates. That is all. *Das ist alles.*" The German translation of his final remark was the signal for his colleagues to spring into action. The figures in the control room started moving and the unarmed guard opened the door to the interrogation room and stood to attention as the general marched out. His shoulders had sagged slightly, giving the impression of a tired old man. Richard was in no doubt that this sign of resignation and weakness was for his benefit. He was equally sure that the clock was now really ticking. He was not going to be in this building very much longer. But would he be leaving in an unmarked car in the direction of the US embassy, or in a body bag?

CHAPTER THIRTY-SIX

The peephole in his cell door slid aside – always the immediate precursor to an interrogation session. But this was not the momentary glance from a soldier needing to establish that the prisoner was not hiding behind the door before he opened it. He recognised the cold blue eye on the other side of the door. They almost all had cold blue eyes, but only one used mascara.

The door opened and two male guards came in, each taking a shoulder, by which they lifted him off the bed and kept his feet from touching the ground. A third guard, one of the older sergeants, stood outside, weapon in hand, and the blonde Gestapo captain was clasping the butt of her Lüger pistol, which was still secure in its belt holster. The guards' faces were all familiar, but this was the first time there had been four of them. The blonde and the armed guard stepped away to the left of the cell door. That too was a novelty. From this cell he had always turned left for interrogation. The two armed guards had always gone to the right, out of his reach, as he exited the cell, and then followed behind him to the interrogation room. Sure enough, this time he was frog-marched to the right. Once past the row of cells, he started to pass offices – wooden doors with windows and nameplates.

The unarmed guards at his shoulders stopped, and when the complete party had come to a halt, the older of these two took a key from his pocket and inserted it into a wooden door with a frosted glass pane in its centre. The dull metal plate on the door identified this one as belonging to Dr S. Fürst, MBBS (Oxon), MD (Berlin). When the door opened, he could see a white coat hanging on a stand in the corner of the cluttered office. The desk against the far wall didn't give the impression of the ordered mind of a German man of science. It was piled with folders stuffed with papers, creating a random mountain of half-finished work, almost obscuring the telephone. The eerie silence struck Richard as he was pointed to the visitor's chair next to the round meeting table in the middle of the office.

The younger of the unarmed guards moved to the far corner of the office, facing the door where his armed colleague had taken up position. The fourth guard who had been on Richard's left shoulder was now dismissed. The woman Gestapo captain came in and was about to close the door behind her to start proceedings. He heard the sharp rapid clicks as a pair of military boots marched towards them down the corridor. Richard noticed as the two men exchanged nervous glances and the woman stopped mid-stride, her hand still on the door handle. The marching stopped. After a moment's hesitation there was a tentative knock on the door, which was still partly open. She pulled it back towards her and poked her head around.

"*Frau Kapitän, der General will mit Ihnen sprechen.*" He could clearly hear the Gestapo captain being summoned, presumably by the senior officer who had interviewed him the day before.

"*Passen Sie auf ihn auf. Ich bin gleich wieder da.*" The thought struck Richard that this was the first time he had overheard a conversation between those around him. Until now he had either been escorted in silence, or he had had questions directed at him, and always in English. Did they even realise he could speak German? Was he supposed to know that she had just told the two guards to keep an eye on him until she returned?

As he heard the two sets of footsteps recede down the corridor in perfect time, Richard took a longer look around the doctor's office. There was a small, locked cupboard on the wall above the desk, which he assumed contained controlled drugs, possibly including the liquid with which he was so familiar. On the wall he could make out a small collection of framed photographs including a military group picture and an informal shot of a happy couple out of uniform. The curly red hair looked longer and even more unruly than in real life, and the glasses were missing. Richard guessed the doctor had been in his early thirties, so the picture must have been taken about ten years ago. To the left was a tall steel filing cupboard, next to which stood a fire extinguisher.

"Have you ever done a firing squad before?"

Richard froze. He forced his eyes to look down at the table in front of him rather than make eye contact with either of the guards. So yesterday had been his last chance, and all he had worried about was irritating the most senior officer he had ever seen. A lifetime of insubordination was now going to be paid off in full.

"A couple of times. There's nothing to worry about. Focus on the target hanging round the neck and think of it as a shooting test. Just don't hesitate when they give the order."

"I need a piss."

"Fine. Take my gun with you and lock the door from the outside. I can take care of him on my own. But be quick about it. She's not going to be away long."

Richard glanced at the now unarmed guard as his partner locked them both into the office and rushed off down the corridor, his heavy boots echoing in the silence. The guard was now standing next to the doctor's desk, staring at a point above the door. Richard couldn't understand why he suddenly felt so calm. He had never set great store by the concept of closure, but perhaps he had been wrong. Random thoughts flitted into his mind. What would the paper print as his obituary? How would they find out about his death? Would the Germans offer him a last cigarette, even though they knew he didn't smoke? Was he actually in Germany or not? What was the date? This last one was the most pressing. He had the urgent need to know the date on which he was about to die.

Just as Richard became aware of the true depth of the silence surrounding him, the fire alarm started. The guard cursed under his breath, "*Scheisse*", and looked incongruously at his watch. He glanced nervously at his prisoner and took a single step forwards towards the desk. As the guard reached out for the phone, Richard heard a series of muffled clicks rattling towards them down the corridor. They were not footsteps. Apart from the alarm and these clicks there was not a sound to be heard. No rushing feet, no clamour, no shouting. The next click was in the room with them and Richard noticed the door move slightly as the fire management system automatically unlocked it.

He jumped to his feet and grabbed the red fire extinguisher

in his left hand. It was surprisingly light. He saw the look of shock and horror as the guard turned from the phone, alerted by the movement behind him. He raised his hands in front of his face in the classic defensive pose. Richard's blow sent him reeling. The look of dread on the soldier's face evaporated into unconsciousness as his body crashed against the desk stacked with untidy piles of files and documents. Richard was rooted to the spot and let the extinguisher slip from his fingers as the slow-motion avalanche of papers glided onto the floor. A photograph in a heavy glass frame, dislodged from its brass nail on the wall, was carried towards the edge.

Coming back to his senses, Richard leaned forward to catch the picture just as the cascade launched it into free fall. Holding the frame with both hands in front of his face, the image itself registered for the first time. His eye was drawn to the flash of a familiar redness, incongruous against the background of black uniforms. The doctor's unruly hair and steel-rimmed spectacles were identical to those on a very familiar but less fresh face, which now looked around twenty years older. Among the two rows of spectators at the scene frozen in time by the camera, the redhead alone managed to make the dress uniform of the Gestapo look less than immaculate. The photograph showed a medal ceremony. The face of the man making the award had recently featured in all the world's newspapers when his sudden death was announced. His brown uniform, a colour reserved for those of at least Reichsminister rank, was in sharp contrast to everyone else in the image. The photographer had somehow managed to capture the precise moment when the medal, swaying on the end of its red neck ribbon, was twisted slightly towards the viewer. Richard didn't recognise the large Maltese cross, its polished gold mostly coated in brilliant white enamel, with bird shaped smudges between each of the arms. The recipient was wearing a business suit, topped off with a fedora. The face was turned slightly away from the camera, as if it had something to hide. This, combined with the slight shadow, was why Richard hadn't instantly recognised the man. But now he couldn't take his eyes off him.

A groan from the floor reinstated Richard's panic. It was with trembling hands that he reached across the devastated desk to return the photograph to its hook, before grabbing the white coat from the stand. Something deep inside him stopped Richard kicking the soldier in the head. Instead, he put on the white coat and walked, as casually as he could manage, into the corridor, pulling the door closed behind him. He hesitated. He could still hear no footsteps or other sounds, except for the alarm itself. He couldn't remember any potential escape route the way he had come, so he opted to turn left, away from the direction in which all the military personnel had marched off.

As he started to run, the slip-on shoes felt increasingly insecure, and he considered ditching them, but thought better of it. Reaching the end of the corridor, he had a choice. To his left was another corridor, seemingly full of offices. Immediately in front of him was an emergency exit door with a plastic seal and a warning sign that opening the door would set off an alarm. He guessed the alarm wouldn't function now, but the fact that he had broken the seal would be immediately apparent to anyone pursuing him. He broke the door open and poked his head through. Behind was a narrow concrete corridor with emergency lighting which led off to the right. There was no end in sight. He pulled the door to and deliberately knocked the remnants of the yellow plastic seal onto the floor as he sped away from the exit along the second corridor of offices. That should at least gain him a couple of minutes' grace, and probably split any party sent to chase after him.

At the end of this corridor was an almost identical emergency exit. He gently prised the plastic seal apart and slipped through the doorway. The same emergency lighting showed him a staircase leading down a couple of flights, beyond which it turned out of sight. He reached back through the door and balanced the yellow plastic as carefully as he could before gently pushing the door shut behind him. The sound of the alarm was still audible but now muffled. He started to run down the stairs, holding the handrail to stop him slipping on the wrought iron steps. As he reached the bottom, he found himself at the start of a straight passage, with an arrow pointing in the only possible direction on a sign saying starkly *'Notausgang'* – emergency exit. He set off at a run, and then the lights went out.

Richard stopped and listened. Not a sound. He reached his

right hand out to touch the wall and started to run, cautiously at first, but building speed until he was going almost as quickly as before, scraping his fingertips along the wall for guidance and stability. A couple of times he stumbled, crashing to the floor, bruising his knees and elbows, but quickly stood up and continued.

In the distance he saw an orange flash, then another, but continued to run. The third one was much brighter, much closer, and lasted much longer. Richard stopped to catch his breath and could hear a faint rumbling in front of him, followed by a slight screech. Now he walked.

The tunnel turned slightly to the left and abruptly ended where it emerged into a wider one. As he stood, trying to decide which way to turn, a slow underground train clattered round the bend to his left. He jumped back into the shadows, hoping he hadn't been seen. A few moments later the rails in front of him start to rattle again. He wrestled himself out of the white doctor's coat, preferring to take his chances against the train lights in the olive green of the prison uniform. Once this one had passed, he set off along the side of the tracks, following in the train's wake. Several times he had to dive for cover as more trains passed.

After what felt like about a mile, Richard noticed a growth on the right side of the tunnel wall ahead of him. Getting nearer, he could distinguish the outline of a workmen's hut. He crept closer and pressed his ear to the wooden construction. He could hear nothing. Ready to barge the door, he gripped the knob to guide his aim in the nearly total darkness. It twisted ever so slightly in his hand. Not believing his luck, he pulled the unlocked door open towards him.

The very faint glow from one of the tunnel lights seeped in through the small window in the hut's side wall. As Richard heard another train approaching, he rushed inside, pulled the door closed behind him, and crouched on the floor below the level of the window. In the flickering light from the passing train, he could see to his left a low bench, stretching the length of the wall under the single window. On the opposite wall he could make out the vague shapes of oversized wrenches and spanners, with a hint of their orange paint and the reflective tape wrapped at strategic points around their handles. Against the far wall, opposite the door, was a row of ten coat hangers. From two of these hung coveralls – one short and bright orange with more reflective patches, the other a paler colour it was impossible to distinguish in this low level of light. Once the train had passed, he stepped over to the wall, crouched down and ran his hands along the floor underneath the coat hooks. Again, he was in luck. There were three pairs of workmen's boots, their laces neatly tied together. As the light from the next train flickered into the hut, Richard caught sight of three huge flashlights. He reached forward to pick one up but thought better of it – switching it on would make the hut glow like a lighthouse. He settled back onto the bench and stretched his hands to either side. His left hand brushed against the fluffy outline of a cloth, or perhaps even a towel. Richard felt as if all his Christmases had come at once. He tried on the light-coloured coverall for size. It was slightly too large, but not so big that anyone would notice, and crucially had no reflective patches on it. He was even more fortunate with the boots. Not only was the second pair a near perfect fit, but they even had socks rolled up inside them. He stuffed the towel into his pocket and, feeling pleased with himself, he put his hand on the doorknob.

He hesitated. This was Germany, land of logic and regimentation. A workmen's hut in the tunnels of the underground railway network would surely have a map on the wall showing the emergency assembly points and evacuation routes. He again reached for one of the flashlights and wrapped his towel around it. He pointed the torch towards the floor and twisted the end. The beam was a brilliant white, even filtered through the towel, but as he twisted it further, its intensity diminished. He played the beam quickly around the walls. What he was looking for was on the inside of the door. Underneath the German for 'Berlin Transport Network' was a simple diagram. He assumed the red dot showed his current location and studied the line running alongside it. Of the several marked exits Richard opted for the one marked *Fluchtweg*, as a designated escape route was less likely to be barricaded. According to the scale on the diagram, it must be about another two hundred metres in the direction he had been travelling, on the opposite side of the track.

He left the hut, and as his step count reached two hundred

and thirty, he started to wonder if he had missed the exit and contemplated going back. Rounding a slight curve, he noticed a dim yellow glow, which seemed to be coming from within the opposite wall.

He ducked down, out of the way of yet another train. When he was quite sure there was nothing coming, he clambered back up and picked his way gingerly across the track, taking great care to give as much clearance as possible to the raised central rail, which he could hear crackling as he passed over it.

He found himself standing framed in a brick archway, bathed in a pool of yellow light. A couple of yards away was the bottom of a spiral staircase with a cast-iron handrail. He set off up the steps. His boots gave off a resounding echo in the near silence, and he started to feel claustrophobic.

A sudden panic took hold of him, and he started to run, taking two steps at a time until his toecap crashed against the lip of a step, and he stumbled. He just managed to keep himself upright by the force of his grip on the handrail. Eventually the staircase finished, depositing him at a waist-high stainless-steel rail. Richard clambered over it into a wide corridor, which could have comfortably accommodated twenty people across, but was completely deserted and silent. A tiled sign on the wall opposite him seemed to be specifically for the benefit of those emerging from the spiral staircase, indicating the direction of the exit to his left.

Richard followed the sign. The echo of his boots was just as loud but now rang out a different note. After about a hundred yards, still without encountering any other sign of life, he found himself at the bottom of a short staircase. Richard hesitated and looked up. The bright blue patch in front of him was his first sight of the sky in who knows how long. He pulled the towel from his pocket and rubbed his hands and face as thoroughly as he could.

Set into the archway framing the staircase, the modernity of the electronic clock looked strangely out of place. Richard stared as it ticked through a whole minute, trying to process the implications of its display: Friday 25th October, 14:55. It was eleven weeks since his visits to the theme park in Cuba.

Paris – June 1941

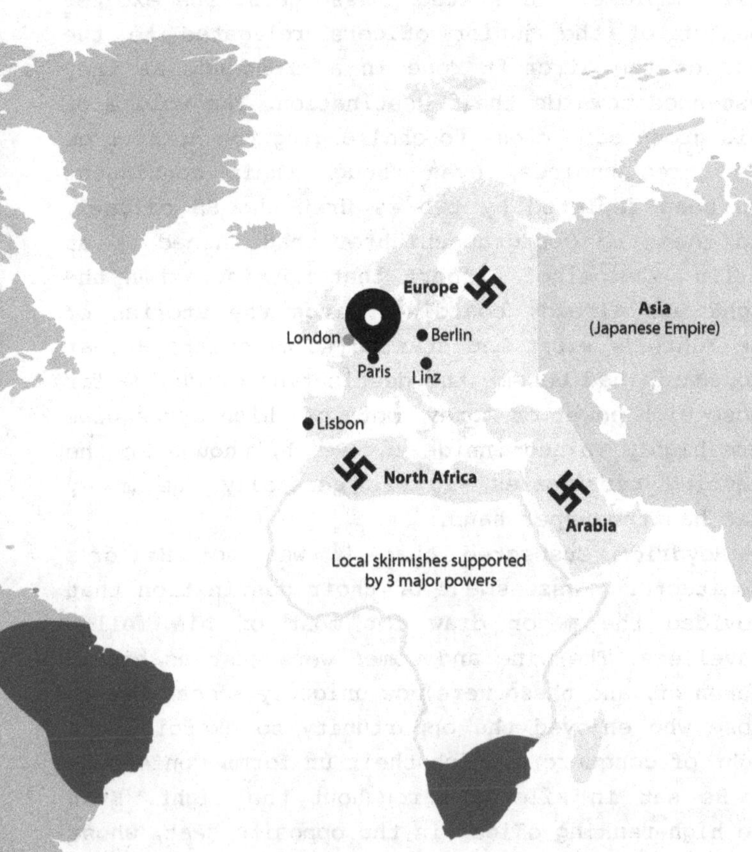

CHAPTER THIRTY-SEVEN

The Junkers Ju 52 transport was crowded with its full complement of sixteen passengers. The excited chatter of the junior officers relegated to the rear of the aircraft rose in a crescendo as they descended towards their destination. The volume of this group came close to challenging the noise from the three engines, even though their contingent had been depleted by two as first the SS colonel, and then the Obergruppenführer, had turned up at Berlin's Tempelhof airport that morning, when the flight was already boarding. Since the stories of the Führer's visit had started to circulate a year ago, Paris had become the destination of choice for those with power or money, both of which currencies were highly valued inside the Reich, though in the occupied territories, it was generally the money that had the upper hand.

Heydrich suspected that it was not Hitler's architectural assessment of their destination that provided the major draw for most of his fellow travellers. The wine and women were just as highly spoken of, and these were now uniquely accessible to those who enjoyed the opportunity to exercise the right of conquerors which their uniforms conferred.

He sat in silence throughout the flight. Even the high-ranking officer in the opposite seat, whose uniform bore the same silver runic flashes on its collar, knew better than to intrude on this self-imposed solitude. Heydrich assumed that all those on the aircraft recognised the famous and feared profile of the head of the security services, topped by its mop of pure Aryan gold, and most would have heard the rumours of his womanising. This irritating fiction for once served his current purpose, as the true nature of his visit had to remain a closely guarded secret. The unexpected need to travel on a scheduled flight, due to a mechanical problem with his personal aircraft, had already compromised that secrecy.

As they taxied to a halt next to the main building of Le Bourget airfield, everyone stayed rooted to their seats to avoid the risk, however slight, of incurring the wrath of the blond man, who would expect to be first off the flight. He stood, or rather stooped, as the Junkers was too compact to accommodate his full height, clamped the black leather briefcase under his arm and marched towards the door, without so much as a glance behind him, forcing a smile at the pretty girl in the Luftwaffe uniform who opened the door. As the other passengers descended the steps to the tarmac, they were relieved to see the black Mercedes, with its SS pennants, accelerating towards the airport gate. At least their ground transportation had not been hijacked.

"Where to, Herr Heydrich?"

"The Hotel George V." It was irritating to be forced into the French usage, especially when talking to a fellow countryman. He wondered how long it would be before it occurred to someone to change the name of Paris's landmark hotel from one which celebrated an English king in the French language. Such a detail was not something the Führer himself would expect to get involved in, or if he did, it would quickly end up as the Hotel Adolf Hitler. Heydrich made a mental note to send a reminder to General von Stülpnagel, the Military Governor of France, on his return to Berlin.

The lackey in the frock coat and top hat opened the door of the Mercedes as soon as it stopped outside the hotel's main entrance. He stood ramrod straight but declined to salute the German uniform which descended from the vehicle. Heydrich was surprised that the Frenchman had lasted this long. Similarly oiled efficiency opened the hotel's door which he strode through, scanning the bemedalled grey throng in front of him. He became aware of a determined movement from the left and breathed an inward sigh of relief that he wouldn't have to compete with his brother officers for the attention of the hotel's overworked staff during the evening rush hour. Heydrich's latest recruit was proving efficient and effective, combining the discipline of a navy man with the insight of an intelligence officer. His decision to reward the young man's bravery and loyalty to the cause seemed to have been justified.

"Follow me, sir." No name, no rank, as it appeared the Obergruppenführer's presence had not yet been noted by any of the other officers in the lobby. His visit could not conceivably be kept secret, but the fewer who noticed him, the better. As he marched two steps behind his subordinate, he had the impression that von Graber's limp, the after-effect of the injury which had ended his service in the *Kriegsmarine*, was becoming less pronounced. But his stiffness while climbing the stairs was still evident.

Heydrich was quietly impressed by his new man's methodical approach. The fact that his pedigree included both the German navy and the Abwehr also increased his personal satisfaction, as this went some way towards settling old scores. He confidently expected it would only be a matter of time before the Abwehr intelligence service fell within his own remit, once the execution of its traitorous former head, Admiral Canaris, had finally been scheduled. In his idle moments, of which there were not many, Heydrich wondered what would have happened if that piece of paper had not fluttered off the desk when he had paid a surprise visit to the admiral less than a month earlier. He still didn't know what instinct had prompted him to follow it up. The decoded text of the message from the agent in London had been concise, detailed and workmanlike. Not a word was wasted. Good tradecraft, as Canaris put it. If you were using a radio transmitter in enemy territory, you would be as brief as you could, to prevent anyone getting a bearing on your location. But not a single word? He had stopped pushing, needing to go away and check that his understanding, from all the spy novels he had read in earlier times, was an accurate reflection of current espionage practice. There would have to be a failsafe system in place. An agent sending a message from enemy territory would always have a failsafe. *If I have not been captured, you can tell by the inclusion of this word. If it isn't there, I have been taken. And the message is what they want me to send.* And since Canaris was the only one who saw the actual decrypts, providing his own summary and analysis to the rest of the top brass in Berlin, he was the only one who knew that the failsafe was not present. That the agent had been captured. That the message was what the British wanted them to read. Within an hour, Canaris had been summoned from his canal-side office to the Führer's huge study in the Reich Chancellery, to provide an update on the intelligence being gathered from England. Less than an hour later, he was under arrest. Within a week all the Reich's military codes had been changed.

Taking the elevator from the first floor rather than the lobby level avoided the unseemly crush in competition with the suitcases of those who were planning a long stay. The suite on the fifth floor precisely met the requirements Heydrich had stipulated. Impressive in its opulence, distracting in its splendid view towards Paris's most iconic landmark — a delicate lattice illuminated against the darkening sky — and provisioned with the best the hotel had to offer — the twin chilled delicacies of vintage champagne and black caviar, produce of one country already conquered, and one whose potential spoils were to be the subject of today's meeting.

"Tell me about today, von Graber."

Von Graber presented his report, detailing his activities as the vanguard to this operation, which had been as carefully planned as any military campaign. The materials employed had been exclusively culinary; the personnel exclusively female, beautiful and totally accommodating to any whim of those with sufficient money. All of the proceedings had been immortalised on film, both still and moving, by the technicians installed behind the false mirrors in the two connecting bedrooms on the hotel's third floor. The emperor's two special envoys would even now be nursing sore heads, but if reports of their stamina hadn't been exaggerated, they would be back on near top form within the hour. Von Graber had previously indicated to his boss the questionable benefit of collecting material for blackmail. Criticism would be the wrong word, as criticism of Heydrich was not good for the prospects. But as an expert in Japanese culture, he knew that coercion of high-ranking military officers through shame would always fail. Rather than betray their emperor and country as a consequence of their personal weakness, the victims would choose to fall on their swords. And in the case of Japanese officers, that meant literally. But the lieutenant had confirmed to his boss that the girls would definitely be a good idea, and the two he had managed to procure seemed impeccably qualified. Not only were they among the top earners in their profession — and with the current stakes, money was absolutely no object — but they were also ideologically sound. Born in Alsace shortly after the humiliation of Versailles, they both came from good German families which had proved themselves unwavering in their support of Hitler from the earliest days. One even went by the working name of Lorraine.

"How much did you tell them about what we want to discuss?"

"I told them we knew of their plans to attack the United States. They were visibly shocked. Foreigners think the Japanese are inscrutable, but you could read these two like a book. They looked at each other and there was real fear in their faces."

"So that is the confirmation we needed?"

"Absolutely, Herr Obergruppenführer. Then I said that we wanted to discuss with them an even greater opportunity. They got the message, so I didn't pursue the point."

"Good. Are they bringing an interpreter?"

"They turned up this morning with a military attaché from their embassy in Berlin. But I made sure our whole conversation was in Japanese, and when I mentioned the girls, the senior envoy told the interpreter his services would no longer be required."

"Excellent. How do you think they will react to our proposal?"

"My view has not changed, Herr Heydrich. In fact, since meeting the two gentlemen in question, it has been reinforced. Protocol dictates that they cannot speak on behalf of the emperor – how can mere mortals pre-judge the wisdom of a divine being – but the older one definitely has his ear. The emperor does not trust all of his military advisers, but we know from our people in Tokyo that General Hashimoto has huge credibility. If we can convince him, he can convince Emperor Hirohito."

"Good. Very good." He paused momentarily. "Have your photographers left?"

"They set off for Le Bourget a couple of hours ago. I have all the prints, negatives and films in my room. All the equipment has gone back with them. There are no spyholes in this room, and I checked it for listening devices myself just before you arrived. We won't be disturbed, and the only notes will be any you choose to make yourself, Herr Obergruppenführer."

"Good. Very good. Do they speak German at all?"

"Hashimoto knows enough to order beer and girls on his visits to Berlin. He speaks reasonable English. Yamamoshi is fluent in English, and we think he can understand German very well, but no one has ever heard him speak it."

"Isn't that odd?"

"Not at all, sir. It's all to do with their concept of face. It would be humiliating to make a fool of himself by making mistakes. So, I would advise that you don't put him in a position where he's expected to reply to you, but you should anticipate that he will understand everything you and I say."

"But you said he speaks English."

"He studied in Cambridge, so he is quite comfortable speaking English. You can talk to him in English, if you want."

"No. I don't think it will come to that." Heydrich looked at his watch. It was quarter to ten. "Get us both a coffee."

As von Graber strode over to the serving table, Heydrich opened his briefcase and pulled out a large single sheet of heavy paper, folded twice to obscure every aspect of its contents. He hadn't looked at it since leaving his office in the Prinz-Albrecht-Strasse the previous evening. He spread it out now for one final review. The Ukraine had already been hashed out as Reich territory, following the last-minute deal concluded the day before the initial German assault. The rest of the Soviet Union was severed by the thick red line which ran from Archangel, virtually at the top of the map, right down to Astrakhan at the bottom, straight except where overwhelming geographical features made that impractical. The Führer's view that the Japanese would happily settle for the larger part of the Soviet Union would soon be put to the test. The major cities and enough of the oil were on the European side of the Urals — itself a massive area, more than double that already absorbed into the Reich during the war. The rest was mostly uninhabitable and therefore worthless to the Reich as 'Lebensraum' — living space, either for settlement by ethnic Germans or for growing crops. Certainly much more trouble to manage than any value which it could deliver. The Japanese were welcome to it. No. The Germans desperately needed the Japanese to covet it. Hitler's ambition to smash the evil of Bolshevism was not matched by any desire to oversee the whole of the sprawling country of its birth. And the dreaded prospect of a war on two fronts, which he had focused on avoiding for the last few years, was now going to serve the Reich rather than threaten it.

"Good. Very good. Go and ask our honoured guests to join us, Herr Leutnant."

Berlin – October 2024

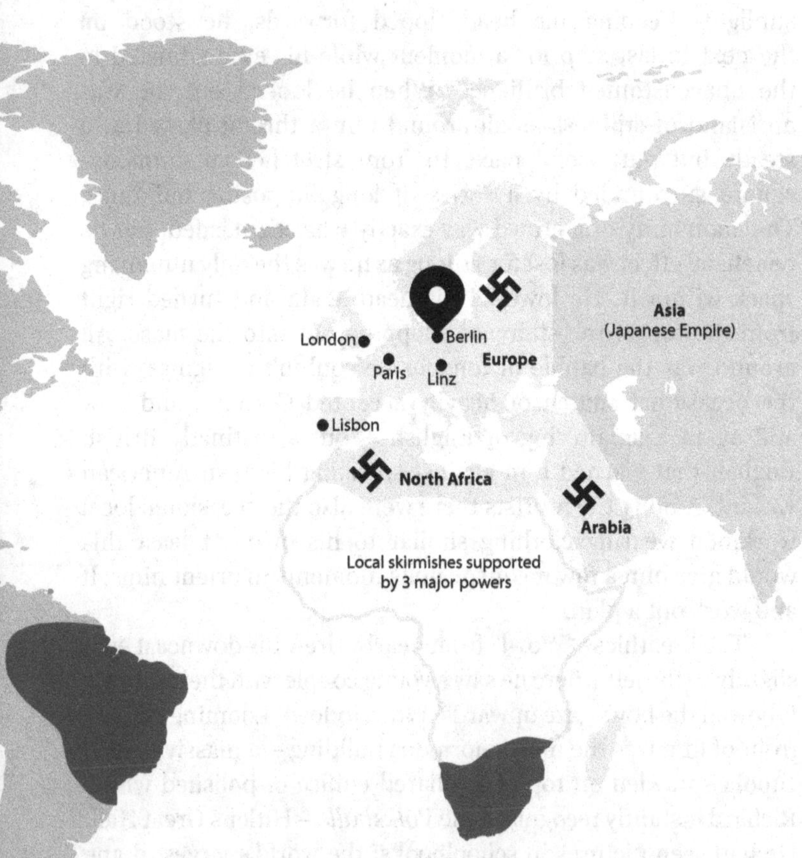

CHAPTER THIRTY-EIGHT

As Richard reached the top of the staircase he was in bright sunlight. Keeping his head tipped forwards, he stood on the next to last step for a moment while his eyes adjusted to the unaccustomed brilliance. When he looked out, he was an island of stillness as all around him a throng passed at a steady but purposeful pace. In front stretched an immense square surrounded by a series of long, imposing buildings. The anonymity of a crowd was exactly what he needed, but its beneficial effect was lost for as long as he was the only unmoving speck within it. He lowered his head again and turned right from the top of the staircase, stepping out into the mass. All around was the babble of tongues he couldn't recognise, with the occasional snatch of heavily accented German, and now and again a smattering of English – but a distinctly British English that warned him against speaking his own American variant. Among the tourists there were also the occasional local workmen wearing clothing similar to his own. At least this would give him a few inconspicuous moments to orient himself and work out a plan.

The breathless "Wow!" from nearby drew his downcast eyes slightly to the left where he saw a young couple with their son. He followed the boy's gaze upwards. Wow, indeed! Looming right in front of him was the most enormous building – a massive green cupola sprawled on top of a pillared edifice of polished white. Richard instantly recognised the *Volkshalle* – Hitler's Great Hall. He had seen pictures in schoolbooks: the world's largest dome on top of the world's largest covered space in the world's largest square. From the depths of his memory he recalled the statistic that this dome was sixteen times the size of the one on top of St Peter's in Rome and considered well beyond the construction technology available in the second half of the 1940s, when it had been completed. Every schoolboy knew the story of how it was so big that rain clouds had actually formed inside the dome when the hall was first filled to its capacity – just short of two hundred thousand – and the elegantly simple technology that had been used to prevent them. But no picture could begin to do justice to this huge shrine to National Socialism, which was literally breathtaking.

As if on cue he spotted a sign on a low lamppost which said, only in German, *Viewing of the Führer, Friday 2-4 p.m., no ticket required*. He knew his chances of remaining undetected in this ultimate police state, with the most advanced technology in the world, were slim at best, but this favour which fate had just done him was immensely heartening. Richard made the conscious decision that hiding in plain sight was his best chance, hoping that some opportunity would arise which showed him the next step on his quest to get back home.

The crowd started to slow, and some of those at its edges took the opportunity to purchase white roses, individually wrapped in cellophane adorned with simple black swastikas. As Richard looked over the heads of those in front, he saw the flaming torches funnelling the crowd into a single stream. A few minutes later he reached this narrowest point of the route, and an awed, respectful hush started to descend around him. Guided by the torches, the crowd turned as one to the left. The flames on either side rose slowly into the autumn sky as the crowd progressed down a long, gentle slope. He couldn't help thinking how much more spectacular this would look in winter, vividly reminiscent of the huge torch-lit rallies of the early years of Nazi rule in Germany. Those images, somehow even more dramatic in black and white, had aired regularly on television last year as a comparison with the events held to mark the ninetieth anniversary of the thousand-year Reich.

Richard looked up at the building they were about to enter. Immense, it was still dwarfed by the colossus now to his right. He could see the main entrance to his left – a narrow arch set into a deep arcade supported by huge pillars. They dwarfed the statues at either side of the entrance, even though these were twice the size of the SS guards standing in front of them. The archway was set into a portal of dark red stone, starkly bright against the pale grey of the rest of the building. Above it was a second arcade with a row of single red pillars and the largest bronze eagle Richard had ever seen. The top of the building consisted of a white marble centrepiece, so far above him that its size was impossible to gauge. This was decorated with a frieze carved into its polished side, which gave it the appearance of an imperial tomb, surmounted by more bronze eagles, their wings folded back to touch the ground, standing guard at each corner.

The crowd was completely hushed now as it passed into the building. He overheard an Englishman immediately to his left, whispering reverently.

"Son, this is the Führer's Palace."

"I know, Dad. We did all that at school." The hostility of those close enough to hear was almost tangible, and from that moment the silence was only interrupted by the shuffling of a thousand feet.

The guards, standing on raised platforms either side of the walkway, were resplendent in the grey and silver of their dress uniforms, the SS flashes on the collars flickering gold in the light of the torches. The unit designation around the sleeve cuffs was clearly visible - *Leibstandarte SS Adolf Hitler* – Adolf Hitler's personal bodyguard. All specimens of perfect Aryan manhood – tall, short-cropped blond hair, piercing blue eyes, no facial hair and not a dental filling between them, still protecting their adored leader – short, dark, mustachioed.

So intently was he watching these ceremonial guardians that Richard only at the very last moment noticed the polished railings separating the crowd into threads two or three wide. Those to his right started to rise as those to his left sank. Each of these ribbons of pilgrims was now on its own marble step, every staggered viewing platform a good head's height above and below its neighbours.

"Attention. Moving walkway ahead. Step on and stand still." The message repeated continuously, alternating a man's military voice in German, and a softer woman's voice in a foreign language. He heard Italian, English and Spanish before the carefully directed loudspeakers were behind him as he stepped onto the rubberised walkway, which now conveyed him gently upwards at its own pace.

As they passed into near darkness, he looked to his left. Less than ten yards away was the object of all this silent veneration and technology. He looked like an old man in a peaceful sleep. Covered from toe to chin in a grey blanket, only the head was visible with its unmistakeable moustache and mop of black hair. He looked younger than the eighty years at which he had made the journey to his current resting place over half a century ago. The glass case was an almost imperceptible barrier between the Führer and his adoring public. Nothing betrayed the temperature difference approaching three hundred degrees Celsius, and only the tubes visible underneath the head and foot of the container indicated the technology keeping Adolf Hitler in cryogenic suspension until the combination of medical advances and the needs of the Reich would result in his reanimation.

Beneath the glass case was the slightly larger polished steel box from which it was hydraulically raised every week. Richard noticed that this was aligned at the head end but protruded noticeably at the old leader's feet. He twisted his head to peer back in that direction. He had overlooked the much smaller case which contained what looked like a mass of brown and black fur. He remembered the story about how the pet dog Blondi, the fourth to carry that name, had been cryogenically stored immediately before his master – an act of sentimental devotion, or a final check of the technology, depending on your level of cynicism.

The light level started to rise, and Richard noticed the silhouetted shapes in front of him replacing their hats. After more multilingual warnings, the travelators disgorged their passengers into their ten terraced walkways which gradually merged back onto a single level and then into a single mass as the chrome-plated barriers came to an end. Some of the children had started chattering excitedly, but among the adults the hushed awe still generally prevailed as they were turned to the right into one of the palace's main corridors.

The viewing route deposited its throng at the building's northern exit, overlooking the grey river, with a choice of viewing the extensive formal gardens to the left, or returning to the main square and its over-towering dome to the right. Only a small minority of his fellows opted for the gardens, so the principle of remaining inconspicuous dictated that he should go right.

So, what was his next step going to be? He couldn't be closer to the heart of the Reich than he was at this moment, between the two most important centres of the Nazi cult. New York was four thousand miles and a whole world away, and most of the bridges had long since been cut. There was the daily rocket plane from Berlin's Tempelhof to New York's Idlewild airport, but this route was taken almost exclusively by diplomats and the senior executives who controlled the trade between the two countries. Ordinary citizens had no reason, and no opportunity, to leave the Reich, just as foreigners had very little chance to visit. Richard let himself be swept along by the crowd, hoping that inspiration would strike, or that at least he would find a street map.

He headed towards the massive dome of the Great Hall. He could see the out-of-towners in Adolf-Hitler-Platz being assailed by the vendors of flags and pennants of all sizes, and busts of Hitler in every imaginable material. Not wishing to attract the attention of any of these hawkers, he erred to his left.

He passed the open doors leading into the huge domed arena and could see in the far distance, above the three tiers of amphitheatre-like seating, the start of its upward curve. The matted metallic finish of the coffered interior contrasted starkly with the green outer skin. He had no desire to take a closer look inside the stark empty space, which turned the few who had chosen to enter into insignificant specks. Instead, he turned his back on the hall to review the options which the square presented from this higher vantage point.

His eye was drawn straight ahead, through the gap between the almost symmetrical buildings now facing him on the opposite side of the square. The road on the other side seemed to run, straight as an arrow, as far as the eye could see. In the distance was the dark outline of the Triumphal Arch, another example of Hitler's obsession with taking the best of Europe's monuments and expanding them to enormous proportions.

Looking back inside the square, he noticed the different architectural style of the building on his left, whose more modest dome clearly pre-dated the Nazi era. He could read the inscription 'Dem deutschen Volke' picked out in shining gold letters.

A small group of tourists brushed past him and turned left. He followed as they merged into a larger trickle of visitors disappearing into the ground beyond the wall of the Great Hall. The tunnel was well lit, but noticeably colder than the bracing autumn air out in the square. Eventually they all emerged into the bright glare of the setting sun and a slight rise in temperature, offset by a breeze he hadn't noticed before.

Even from this low viewpoint, Richard could see a slender pair of tall square free-standing pillars in the middle distance. As they climbed back to ground level, he was confronted by the huge rectangular expanse of water in front of him. Standing at the water's edge, just to his left, were a policeman and an army officer, apparently in casual conversation. Richard turned right and soon reached the corner of the artificial lake. He was still too close to the uniforms to risk raising suspicion by doubling back, so he turned left to continue walking beside the water. The bank on this side was home not just to ambling tourists and escapees from the Gestapo, but also to several groups who were starting or finishing their recreational activities. In the water immediately beside him he could see at least twenty swimmers, some of whom seemed intent on criss-crossing the width of the lake, which looked to be about a quarter of a mile. Beyond the line of orange floats, which segregated the swimmers from the main expanse of the water, was a veritable flotilla of craft, from small sailing dinghies to eight-man rowing boats. Closer to the shore were a few boys, under the watchful, perhaps envious gaze of their fathers, steering their radio-controlled battleships and hovercraft across the water's surface, perfecting the skills which the next generation of the Reich's navy would require. One child, standing some way apart from the others, was flying a model helicopter from a plastic contraption slung around his neck. His mother was a couple of paces behind him, the concentration etched on her face matching that of the boy.

Richard continued to walk along the length of the lake in the direction of the two pillars at its end. These towered over a building as wide as the lake, and he could make out trains departing from each end. He next turned his attention to the three buildings on the opposite bank, which between them took up its whole length. The central one was by far the most impressive of the three. Its major distinguishing feature was a pair of towers, flanking the higher middle section of the three-part construction. These clock towers brought to mind an inelegantly constructed square wedding cake, with segments of varying heights, topped by a golden orb. Each of the corners, at each of the levels, carried the same design of bronze eagle that he had seen on the top section of the palace occupied by the frozen Führer.

He turned again to look at the railway station, still about half a mile away. It was raised above the surrounding area, and being open at both ends it would be difficult to approach unobserved. But it gave Richard the start of an idea.

He returned the way he had come and marched purposefully towards the immense dome of the Great Hall, whose rippled reflection in the lake by his side was shattered by a rowing crew which was finishing its training session.

When he reached the corner of the lake, he kept to the path and continued underneath the elevated section of the local railway, and then through the shadow of the Great Hall. A minute later he reached the north bank of the river Spree and turned left. The dull grey of its surface was in sharp contrast to the blue-black of the artificial lake, as was the complete lack of water traffic. He was still confident that the number of fellow walkers, including a sprinkling of manual workers dressed similarly to himself, stopped him from being too conspicuous. However, his heart skipped a beat every time a police or army vehicle sped towards him on the road running parallel on his left. Off to the right, in the far distance, he could see the modern steel and glass edifices of the city's financial centre. He passed the brightly lit interior of a Wurstmann fast-food restaurant, whose logo of a cartoon sausage man and an enormous yellow 'W' he recognised from the park in Cuba. As he walked past its entrance, the smell of cooked pork wafted across his path, reminding him of his hunger.

A sudden gust of wind off the river caught him unawares, and he stopped in his tracks as his head started spinning. Did he even have any idea what he was doing? Cold, hungry, possessing only the stolen workman's clothes he was standing up in, here he was strolling casually through the capital of what his government occasionally referred to as the 'Evil Empire'. He thought he had known loneliness in his life, but this isolation was out of all proportion. There was probably not a soul he knew within several thousand miles, and any Americans would be locked safely away in the embassy compound. He shuddered and carried on walking.

After about half an hour, a slight bend in the river revealed an island crowded with old buildings. He stopped outside a mock Egyptian palace. The colours of its gaudily decorated twin pylons, which flanked the entrance stairway, seemed out of place among the drab uniformity of most of the other buildings. The clock on the very tall tower of the museum on the left showed it was just after half past five. His obvious course of action should be to find the United States embassy. The nagging doubt, which had plagued him since reaching the surface a couple of hours previously, was that this idea was too obvious. As the time had passed, with no indication that a major manhunt was underway for an escaped American, Richard had managed to convince himself that the Nazi forces would be concentrated around the embassy, waiting for him to run into their trap. The alternative plan forming in his mind required darkness and a railway station, so he probably still had an hour to kill.

CHAPTER THIRTY-NINE

Richard had been swept up by a group of about a dozen workers in a side street a few yards from the major city-centre boulevard Unter den Linden. At first, he had tried to resist the tide, but when he realised they were crowding into a bar, he let himself be carried into the warm. They stopped just inside the door to deposit their heavy coats on the rack of metal hooks. Richard stepped away from the group so the fact he had no coat on this chilly evening wouldn't make him stand out. This left him in front of the bar, with the owner about to catch his eye, so he moved away again towards the wall, and bent to fumble with his bootlace. The group of new arrivals was making its way to the bar as one, so he took his chance, backtracking towards the entrance, picking the largest coat he could see off the hanger, before slipping through the door as the next customer came in. Stopping on the pavement, he put on the coat, turned up the collar, thrust his hands in the pockets, and marched off with renewed determination.

Richard went round a corner. The woman was obviously lost in her thoughts, head down, as she walked straight into him. The mutual recognition was almost instantaneous. The last time they had seen each other, in the prison that morning, they had been in their respective uniforms. Her current clothes were a light shade of beige – no less smart and precise than the official black, but distinctly civilian. And he looked like a workman on his way home from tending streets or drains.

He felt absolute terror – a terror no mere uniform could have instilled in him. She must have been literally the last person he expected to walk into on the street. He could imagine the look on his own face. What he could not understand was the identical fear now visible in hers. The little colour in her face drained dramatically and she had to put a hand out onto the wall to steady herself. Richard's spirits dived even more as he saw she was leaning against a poster advertising the public execution of a murderer taking place this weekend. He was rooted to the spot, resigned to her blowing a whistle, or whatever they did, to bring every uniformed and plain clothes policeman from within a hundred yards rushing to their side.

"Are you alone?" Her voice was timid, not at all what he remembered from earlier that day. Perhaps it was because she was speaking English. He nodded dumbly. "Follow me." She took her eyes off him and walked past, hesitant at first, then with purpose. Following made no sense, but then what choice did he have? She could summon help at any moment, and he could hardly attack her in the street, with its evening strollers enjoying the final rays of an autumn sunset.

What could she be afraid of? Would she be held accountable for his escape? Perhaps she didn't have a whistle or a radio, or even one of those pocket telephone things which everyone else out on the streets seemed to possess. As they came to a crossing, the green man started to flash. Those around her speeded up to get across, but she stopped on the edge of the pavement and stood rigidly to attention. That afternoon Richard had already come to realise that the red man on pedestrian crossings was someone else the Germans obeyed unquestioningly.

Her opportunities to turn him in came and went, so he became calmer. She disappeared into a café. As he reached the window, he knelt down to attend to a bootlace, giving himself chance to look inside. He was sure the game was up as the streetlight directly above his head flickered into incandescence the moment his knee touched the ground. The blonde Gestapo officer was standing at the counter, already being served by a young red-haired girl, who seemed to take pride in making her uniform of black shirt and green apron look as untidy as possible. The blonde picked up the very unfeminine steaming mug of coffee, and a plate with a large pastry, and walked towards the other side of the café. She put the mug and plate down on a table for two and then sat on the opposite side. She forced a smile in the direction of the window, which Richard took as an invitation. He opened the door and walked inside. As he pulled out the chair to sit opposite her, she stood up. Brushing past him she whispered. "Stay here. I'll be as quick as

I can," and disappeared through the door he had just used.

The next hour was one of the longest of his life. His mind kept going over and over the pros and cons of sitting here. Wouldn't he be safer just making a run for it now, and going back to his original plan of somehow getting on a freight train? It was all too bizarre, but on balance, he decided, she must be his best chance.

His field of vision was restricted to the window on his right, which was almost completely filled by a bus stop. The only person who made eye contact was a young boy of about eight, his shock of golden hair, brown shirt and black shorts closely mirroring the recruitment poster for the *Afrika Korps* above his head. Richard risked a smile in response to his interested gaze. Quick as a flash, the boy's right hand shot into his pocket, emerging with a small pistol which he pointed straight at Richard's head. The boy's eyes filled with hate as his mother slapped her son across the face, without even looking in Richard's direction.

It was a long time, and twilight had turned to dusk, before Richard dared to raise his eyes again. Mother and son were long gone. His eye was drawn to the recruitment poster. He had never seen an advertisement before which boasted that a criminal record was no barrier to entry.

Every time the café door behind him opened, he tensed. Was it the police? Had she come back to turn him in? Had she come back to help him? He had no idea who had come in as he always managed to resist the temptation to turn round.

He desperately needed the toilet but didn't dare leave his seat at the café table. The point came where he could bear it no longer. The door to the unisex toilet was facing him tauntingly, about three yards away. He had felt increasingly strong twinges every time someone had gone in, but no relief as they came out again. It was empty at the moment. The combination of the huge mug of coffee and the adrenalin meant it had now reached the point where staying at his seat created a far greater risk than a quick visit. As he slid his chair back a couple of inches, a man started to pass him. He couldn't afford any more delay, so he rushed for the door and dashed inside. The relief was so intense it was initially painful, but soon settled to a warm glow. Richard felt his shoulders relax as the least, but most immediate of his problems flowed away.

When he opened the door, his heart sank. The man was not there, but someone was sitting at his table – a woman in a black leather jacket wearing a red headscarf. What was he to do now? He couldn't sit down at a different table without a drink, and he had already decided that his chances were better if he stayed in the café rather than leaving. As he approached the table, he noticed that his own cup was still there and glanced down. A lock of the blonde hair had escaped the headscarf and was lying over the side of the dark glasses.

"Just sit down." He seated himself as casually as he could and clasped the cold mug like a long-lost friend. He now took a long, hard look at the woman sitting opposite him. There was something comical about a senior member of the secret police looking for all the world like a badly disguised spy from a second-rate movie thriller, but he didn't laugh. She wouldn't have understood. The German sense of humour was notoriously different, and, reputedly, completely non-existent in the security forces.

"Someone is working on getting you out of Germany, but they can't do anything until the morning. You'll have to stay with me tonight." Richard strained to hear her whisper, and his brain went into overdrive. She could not be serious. But she was probably already past the point of no return, and if she couldn't get rid of him until the morning, what alternative would she have except to keep him safe herself? He certainly didn't have one. And if anyone was capable of evading the state's mechanisms for recapturing dangerous escaped foreigners, it must be the Gestapo. "We can't be seen together, so you'll have to follow me again. It's a fifteen-minute walk because we can't use the subway train. Stay close enough so that you can get through the door to my apartment block before it closes. Go up the stairs to the third floor. Got all that?" He nodded. This would make it look like he was tailing her, and not that she was leading him, giving her a glimmer of a chance if anything went wrong. And she could presumably ensure that he didn't survive to be interrogated if they were caught.

She stood up and walked straight to the door of the café. He kept a respectful distance, looking up every few moments to check that the red headscarf was still bobbing up and down on the street in front of him. At all other times he tried to keep his face down. He had noticed earlier that roughly every second lamppost was equipped with surveillance cameras. He remembered hearing that the Germans had developed facial-recognition systems which could automatically track an individual across the city. One of his colleagues on the newspaper had researched an article about the US government's attempt to buy this system from the Germans to enhance the security at Idlewild airport, but it fell into the category of restricted technology, which meant it was not authorised for use outside the German government. He wondered how effective they would be now darkness had fallen.

No one on the street seemed to pay him any attention. The population knew not to fall prey to natural human curiosity, and to trust in the efficiency of the state's systems to keep them safe from their enemies. Harsh punishments and the multiplicity of police forces, combined with the easy accessibility of all life's major needs, kept the crime rate extremely low.

Their journey had passed without incident when he spotted that she had stopped ten yards in front of him, on the step to an apartment building, fumbling in her bag for the key. She was clearly not the fumbling type, so this was for his benefit. She didn't make eye contact, but put the key in the lock and pushed, swinging the door all the way open, releasing it to close slowly against its spring mechanism. Richard slipped inside without breaking his stride, not even needing to touch the door.

He saw the steps to his right and started climbing. She had gone straight ahead and called the elevator. They reached the landing at the same time. Without a word she went to one of the apartment doors and he followed.

CHAPTER FORTY

The apartment was in almost complete darkness, with just the distant glow from one of the streetlights casting a ghostly haze in the left corner. The intruder alarm started to beep, and she tapped a six-digit code into the control unit which Richard couldn't even see on the wall, let alone distinguish which buttons were being pressed. She brushed past him in the darkness and pulled the blinds down on both windows. The darkness was now total until she switched on the lamp next to the two-seater sofa.

The room was spartan. With a little more furniture, it might have looked like a house builder's show flat. The walls were painted off-white and had no pictures. The room was long, but not deep, and there were three doors in the wall opposite the entrance.

"Please. Sit." She pointed to the sofa. As he sat, he noticed the large utilitarian clock above the entrance door, reminiscent of a train station. He watched as she took off first the red headscarf and then the black jacket. The dark glasses had thankfully already disappeared. She seemed hesitant. Visitors were clearly a rarity, and this sterile environment betrayed no personality, and certainly no femininity.

"Would it be possible for me to have a bath?"

She initially seemed to welcome the interruption of her thoughts, but then her brow furrowed into a deep frown. "Sorry. There is no bath. Only douche – I mean shower."

"A shower would be great."

She pointed to the middle door. "Would you like a coffee?"

"No, thank you. I've had quite enough coffee for one day." German coffee was about ten times stronger than American coffee, and extra mental stimulation was something he could do without for the rest of the night. She didn't reply, just headed for the left door, opening it to show the tiny kitchen.

Richard decided just to go for it and opened the middle

door. He could see why there was no bath. The room was scarcely big enough for the tiniest shower cubicle he had ever seen. He found the light switch, which activated the humming extractor fan, and closed the door behind him. There was no lock on it. He looked at the shower, trying to work out how the controls functioned. It was not obvious to the non-German mind, so he would just have to experiment. He was struck by a horrible thought. In this clinical, functional, quasi-military environment, would there be any hot water? He took off all his clothes and piled them on the toilet seat – the only alternative to the floor, which seemed a liberty in the apartment of a woman he didn't know. He clambered into the cubicle, banging the door against his elbow as he closed it, and turned the water on. A freezing jet hit him full in the chest, confirming his worst suspicions. He didn't jump – there was no room – but within a few seconds the water had heated to a perfect steaminess. He stood still, letting it run through his hair and all over his body for a good minute. It felt soothing, particularly on the bruises on his arms and legs that he had picked up in the underground tunnels. He opened his eyes, looking for soap. He had seen several women's bathrooms in his lifetime, but this was the first without bottles. He noticed a thin sliver of a soap tablet, the type that could only be found in the US in the so-called 'nostalgia stores'. He remembered from his childhood how it worked and lathered his hair and body as well as he could, doing his elbows more damage in the process than all the interrogations he had suffered. He rinsed the bubbles quickly as he felt the water temperature dropping and managed to turn off the flow before it undid the benefit it had achieved.

He opened the cubicle door and contorted himself onto the tiny patch of floor between the shower, toilet and wash basin. He hadn't thought to look for a towel when he entered and was painfully aware that there was no lock on the door. There was, however, a pink towelling robe hanging behind the door. It was his only option. It almost fitted, and as he caught sight of himself in the small mirror above the wash basin, he spotted the clash of his curly chest hair against the pink fabric. He hesitated before opening the door. What awaited him? This was too elaborate to be a trap, but then what was the likelihood that the Gestapo was going to help him escape from Germany? He had stopped dripping and couldn't stand here for ever, so he stepped back into the main room.

Her laugh was instantaneous. Embarrassed, she put her hand in front of her mouth, but couldn't stop her shoulders shaking, or her eyes sparkling. All the careful suppression of spontaneity seemed to evaporate. Richard was stunned but quickly saw the funny side and grinned. She became animated as she stood up from the sofa, almost skipping into the kitchen. She came back with a slightly dusty bottle and two small glasses.

"I think we both need a drink. I hope you like schnapps. This is all I have. Sit, please." She didn't pat the sofa in the clichéd way of the movies, but it was the only piece of furniture in the room that you could sit on, so he joined her.

"Schnapps is great," he lied. His only previous experience of German schnapps had been one Christmas when his grandmother had taken him to see his German teacher in her apartment. Like all fourteen-year-olds, he had seized the opportunity to drink alcohol with relish. He had seen in old films how you threw your head back and downed it in one, and he nearly choked. When the coughing fit subsided, he still had the fierce burning sensation in his nose. That was far more uncomfortable than the two ladies laughing at him. Richard watched with relief as his hostess took a sip, and he did the same.

"Thank you. And thank you for helping me."

"You are innocent." It wasn't a question, just a simple statement of fact, as if risking her life to help him escape her employers and her country was the only natural thing to do. He thought he was quite good at understanding women, but this was way beyond him. The precision of a soldier, the efficiency of a bureaucrat (and a German bureaucrat at that), the giggle of a schoolgirl, the social skills of a nun, and a home which betrayed no personality – unless it betrayed a complete lack of personality. She stood up without warning, went into the bathroom, and returned with his discarded boots and clothing, which she took into the kitchen. She returned to her seat next to him on the sofa.

"What happens tomorrow?" Richard asked.

"I'm not sure yet. I will get a call early in the morning, and I will be told where to take you. That's all I know. The less anyone knows, the better for everyone." That was obviously the end of this particular line of conversation. The uncomfortable silence descended again, and he was desperate not to let that happen.

"Have you been in the Gestapo long?"

"Three years. I was originally commissioned into the SS, then transferred three years ago."

"Are there many women in the Gestapo?" He saw the brief hint of a smile.

"No. Not many."

"Your parents must be very proud."

Her look darkened visibly, and her eyes dropped. "I suppose so."

He had no way of knowing why he had just hit a nerve. Family was another subject better avoided.

"Was it what you always wanted to do?"

"No. But you can't always choose your destiny. I am proud to serve the Fatherland in whatever way I can." As well as helping escaped prisoners out of the country, obviously.

"Will you get into trouble?"

She looked at him quizzically. "What do you mean? If you're found here, I will be shot."

"I mean because of my escape."

"No. I was not to blame. I was not there. Others were responsible for you at that time."

Another uncomfortable silence. "Look, I don't even know your name."

"Linden." She hesitated before continuing. "It's Hanna."

"That's not a very common German name, is it?"

"What do you mean?"

"I just meant it's an old-fashioned German name." Was he digging himself an even deeper hole? Anything but the awkward silences. This woman held his life in her hands, and he had no idea what to make of her.

"It was my mother's choice. My father didn't mind. He had just wanted another son, so he chose my brother's name and probably didn't pay much attention to what my mother suggested. My mother was a, how do you say, a fan of Hanna Reitsch."

"The astronaut?"

The slight smile returned to Hanna's face. "Yes, that's right. I was born just after she died, so there are a few women of my age called Hanna."

"And you have two brothers?"

She looked troubled – clearly uncomfortable talking about personal things, but he was determined to make some sort of connection. "Yes. I had two brothers."

Richard thought he detected a slight sigh. It was as if he had extracted the confession of a secret that had been closely guarded for a long time but was now being given up quite easily. He waited for her to carry on.

"My older brother had some difficulties. He couldn't be controlled, either at home or by his teachers, so he was taken to a special educational establishment. We heard he had died. A cerebral aneurysm. He was fifteen, so I must have been ten at the time."

Richard had heard rumours of these 'special education establishments'. Little was known for certain, but it seemed that the Nazis had ways of removing troublesome individuals from society, and that they very rarely returned to everyday life. This approach to social engineering stretched all the way back to the start of the Hitler era in 1933. The reported incidence of mental illness, physical disability and other conditions inconsistent with the Aryan ideal had always been extremely low, and everyone knew that it was better not to probe the reasons behind this too closely, either within the Reich, or abroad.

Hanna seemed to have frozen next to him on the sofa. Her hands were clasped in her lap, and he noticed that the knuckles had gone white. Gently, he put his hand on top of hers. He was surprised how cold they were. She looked him in the eye for a second, then cast her eyes down again, and carried on.

"I was a twin. My brother and I were very close." He heard the faintest catch in her throat, but she continued. The words didn't come easily. It felt like a story that had been mentally rehearsed a thousand times but never spoken out loud. "He was not very competitive, but I was. My father adored him, especially since Michael went away, which happened when we were eight. I was jealous. I wanted my father to love me as much, but whatever I did, I just got patted on the head. It was Erich he took fishing and on long walks. It was Erich he played football with. My mother could see my resentment, but there was nothing she could do about it. She knew the place of the woman in the German home – cooking, cleaning and children. She had tried to do more when she was a girl, and I got the impression it was beaten out of her. I think she called me Hanna because she secretly hoped I could break out from the traditional role of women, in the way she hadn't been able. She tried to teach me cooking and everything while my father was out with Erich, but she knew I had no interest. She told me stories of famous women from history and what they had achieved, especially Hanna. At school we only heard about the mythical heroines, in the *Nibelungenlied*, and things like that. Mother told me about Catherine the Great, Queen Elizabeth of England, Joan of Arc, Magda Goebbels, Cleopatra of Egypt."

She paused again and took a deep breath. He twisted round to face her, folding his right leg underneath him.

"Then one day, I shall never forget it, Erich and I were playing in the woods behind the apartment block we lived in. It was just before our twelfth birthday. I was racing him up the big tree. He wasn't really interested, but I think he did it to humour me. I always beat him, but this time I got my foot caught in one of the branches and he got ahead of me. I was furious and started screaming with anger and frustration because I couldn't get my foot out. He stopped and came back to help me. If it had been me, I would have just kept going to the top to make sure I won before turning back. But Erich wasn't like that. And it was humiliating to have to be helped, so just before he got back to me, I made one final effort and managed to get my foot out. But I lost my balance and fell out of the tree. Erich tried to catch me, but I pulled him down with me. He hit his head on a rock."

She stopped. She was still staring into her lap, but he could see a single tear rolling down her cheek. Gently he cupped his hand under her chin and raised her face. Her eyelids were about to overflow, and her glistening blue eyes stared deep into his as he wiped away the single tear. She looked like a little lost girl. He stroked the top of her hair, moving his hand to the back of her head. She let him pull her head onto his chest where she started sobbing. He wrapped his right arm around her shoulders and started to rock her gently. She twisted her body slightly and put her right hand on his left thigh to support herself. Richard felt himself going hard. He was embarrassed, but more than that, he was terrified of her reaction. She must have felt the movement of the bathrobe because the next thing he knew she was stroking the inside of his thigh. Gingerly he kissed the top of her head. She moved her hand and slowly, deliberately, ran a single finger along the length of his now fully erect penis. The nervousness left him. This unimaginably complex situation now felt like the most natural thing in the world. She lifted her head towards his and closed her eyes. The tears were gone as they kissed. Richard slipped his hands down her back and fumbled to find the zipper on the dress. She caught both his hands in hers, firmly pushed them back into his lap and quickly undressed herself. He couldn't take his eyes off the fit, slender body which emerged, removing any doubt that the blonde hair was completely natural. She threw her clothes to the floor as she removed them, but even so they fell in a neat pile. He expected a move to the bedroom, but she came back to the sofa and pulled open the cord on the bathrobe that was barely holding the ridiculous pink garment together. Her powerful hands pushed his shoulders back into the side of the sofa as she sat astride him and kissed him fiercely on the lips. It was clear who was in charge, and Richard was more than happy to follow wherever he was taken.

CHAPTER FORTY-ONE

Richard woke to find himself lying on the living room floor, his nakedness covered by a blanket. He remembered that this was where they had ended up during their love-making last night, but now he was alone. The railway clock over the door showed a few minutes before eight. He heard a rustling sound coming from the bedroom and stood up, modestly wrapped himself in the blanket and walked towards the open door where Hanna was finishing making her small bed. She heard him coming towards her, turned sharply and looked at him accusingly. He got the message and walked back to the sofa as his mind processed what he had seen. Above the bed was a framed picture of Adolf Hitler. It was one of the standard authorised images of the Führer that were sold like icons throughout the Reich. On the small bedside table there were another two framed photographs. One was a family group – father, mother, boy and girl of about ten. The blonde hair was much longer than today, but it was instantly recognisable as the young Hanna. The other picture was a typical military group photograph of about twenty young faces and identical uniforms, surrounding an older figure. Hanna was the only woman in the photograph. The background was dominated by a full-scale replica of the Mars Lander.

She seemed nervous, tidying things that were already immaculately ordered. She jumped, visibly startled, as the doorbell rang. She looked at Richard and pointed to the kitchen. Gripping the blanket that was still wrapped around him, he tiptoed in and pulled the door almost shut. Hanna cleared her throat before walking over to the apartment door and picking up the entry phone.

"*Ja?*" She pressed the button to open the door to the street, hesitated for a second, then hung up the phone. She waited by the door. Richard could see her standing there through the small opening in the kitchen doorway. Her hands were clasped in front of her, knuckles white, muttering under her breath, like an actress about to step onto the stage for a first night. He heard the faint, single knock on the apartment door. She stepped forward to look through the spyhole, then opened the door, standing behind it so that the visitor had to step into the empty doorway. A tall, dark-haired man walked inside and stood still as she closed the door behind him. Neither wanted to speak first.

"Wo ist er?"

Richard was about to step out of the kitchen, when something in his subconscious made him think better of it.

"Come out here, please."

He was right. She had switched back into the heavily accented English that he had first heard yesterday evening in the street.

He came out of the kitchen and took a good look at the visitor. The tight curls of his hair were just visible around the edges of the workman's cap, which he didn't remove. The pointed beard and full moustache seemed more suited to a university lecturer, or Bolshevik revolutionary leader, than to the workman's clothes he was wearing.

"Here, put these on." The new arrival handed the holdall to Richard, who glanced at Hanna, looking for confirmation. She nodded sharply and Richard returned to the kitchen, gripping his blanket with the one hand he still had free. The clothes in the bag seemed to be a twin set of those the man was wearing – thick checked shirt, heavy dark-blue workmen's trousers, a synthetic donkey jacket with fake leather collar and a peaked cap. He was relieved to find the appropriate underwear, but the boots were too small. He looked around, and the ones he had stolen from the railway workers' hut were visible in the top of the sack where yesterday's clothes had ended up. He swapped the two pairs and decided not to mention the fact. When he was fully dressed, he returned to the living room, folding up the holdall as he went. The tension between the two Germans was palpable as they stood in silence, a couple of feet apart, watching him walk in.

"They are good fit," the man said. Having taken the folded bag from Richard and stuffed it in his pocket, he continued. "I'm

Alex. We go now." Hanna reached for the door handle as the tall man turned towards it. Richard looked at Hanna, unsure how to take his leave of her. The need to follow the visitor out of the apartment replaced his hesitation, and with a final look into her bright blue eyes, he walked out. As he started down the steps, he heard the door close behind him. He wondered if he would ever see her again.

CHAPTER FORTY-TWO

The tall man walked down the two flights of stairs at a measured pace. He carried on towards the front door, holding it open just a fraction longer than if he had been leaving alone. He turned immediately left onto the street. This was the way Richard had arrived yesterday evening, but it looked completely different on a bright and bustling morning. After about two hundred yards they walked across a road where the pedestrian crossing was already on green. Then they took the next street to the left, followed quickly by another left and then a right. Richard realised they were now on the road they had crossed a minute or two earlier.

They walked for about twenty minutes, Richard a few steps behind Alex. The streetlife of the Berlin morning paid them no attention. Mothers with young children congregated in coffee shops, and the Wurstmann restaurants they passed were doing brisk business; newspaper vendors were preparing for the end of their morning shift, and shops selling every imaginable commodity were well into their stride. He noticed the tattered remnants of posters advertising the Olympic Games and welcoming the honoured foreign guests. One of these posters had been torn almost completely away, laying bare the instruction to report anti-social elements to the special free-phone number. This seemed not to be a tourist area of the city, but one of the inner residential parts with nothing much to interest visitors. He noticed a policeman walking towards him on the same side of the street. He was sauntering quite casually, nodding to the occasional passer-by. As he passed, the policeman paid absolutely no attention to Richard.

The bearded man turned off the main road into a side street, where the apartment blocks were only occasionally interrupted or supported by a small supermarket or a magazine vendor's kiosk. After about fifty yards he turned sharply into the doorway of a bar, walked the length of the counter, turning right at the end, then right again into the gents' lavatory. The bartender didn't appear to notice the two men passing in single file a couple of feet in front of his nose and continued to polish the beer glass with the cloth tucked into the string wrapped around his apron. The two old men sitting on separate tables by the window had also paid them no heed. As Richard entered the toilet, there was no one in front of him. He jumped slightly as the door was pushed shut behind him, and he turned to face the tall man with the beard.

"Stand here." He was being directed at a roller towel located to the side of the facility's only hand basin. As he stood there, the man pulled a camera out of his pocket. It was a small silver model, not large enough to hold the standard films, so presumably one of those new electronic devices which were starting to appear in high-end stores in the USA.

"Look straight at the camera and don't smile." Alex took six shots – three with flash and three without. "Okay. You wait here for a while. I will be back as quick as I can." Richard had visions of spending a couple of hours in this toilet, but then the man opened the door and gestured him outside. As they passed the end of the counter, a lonely small beer was standing unattended. The photographer picked it up and walked to the heavy brown curtain at the back of the bar. He pushed it aside to reveal a partitioned area with five tables, each encircled by two or three uncomfortable-looking wooden chairs. He placed the glass of beer on a table against the opposite wall, next to which was an almost identical brown curtain. With a final whispered, "Stay here," the man left the way he had come, leaving Richard alone, without even the noise of traffic to keep him company.

Richard sat and considered his position, trying to ration the sips he took of his beer as he had no idea how long it would have to last him. He wasn't wearing a watch and there was no clock in this part of the bar. Who were these people working on his behalf? What was their motivation? What were they planning to do with him, and where would he end up?

After what seemed like an hour, or perhaps two, his thoughts were interrupted as the curtain leading back to the main body of the bar was pulled aside. A pale face, surrounded by straggly curls of brown hair, poked in and scanned the tables briefly, deciding that this side of the curtain was preferable to the one he was coming from. He sat down at the first table and tried to look calm. Small beads of perspiration sat on his brow. After a few moments, the new arrival wiped his sleeve across his forehead before resuming his rigid pose, staring into the nothingness in front of him. He started as the curtain behind him was pulled back again. A look over his shoulder took in the figure of a middle-aged man wearing a greenish jacket over his shirt and tie, balancing his plate and glass of beer in one hand, while he closed the curtain with the other. He placed his late breakfast, or early lunch, on the furthest table from Richard, and started to eat from the small mountain of bread and cheese piled on his plate.

A few minutes later, a slight commotion of muffled voices was audible from the main area of the bar, and the man without the beer looked furtively around himself again, his glance resting momentarily on the second brown curtain next to Richard's table. The first brown curtain was pulled open, this time with a theatrical flourish, as a uniformed policeman stepped through it.

"Papiere, bitte," he announced to no one in particular, but stood decisively by the nervous man with the straggly hair. The policeman's colleague didn't enter but blocked the way back to the bar area. As Richard panicked internally, the other man tried to remain calm under the policeman's stare and started rummaging in his pockets. He stood up to access the back of his trousers, and with a power that belied his small frame, he barged the policeman in the middle of the chest with his shoulder. As the policeman was tumbling to the floor, the man with the shaggy hair leapt over to Richard's table, ripped the curtain aside and pushed open the door behind it. The policeman on the floor turned his head to watch the man's escape but made no attempt to stand up. His colleague pulled the sidearm from its holster in slow motion, took careful aim through the open doorway, and fired a single round from where he stood. The explosion from the pistol was immediately followed by a sharp cry of pain, and the sound of a trash can crashing to the ground. The first policeman got back to his feet and casually dusted

himself down as his colleague returned the gun to its holster, saluted the room and said,

"Sorry for the disturbance, gentlemen. Please enjoy your meal."

The two policemen then left the bar in the direction taken by their fugitive, who could be heard groaning where he had fallen. The other customer turned back from the spectacle to his plate of bread and cheese, as if this was an everyday occurrence of little interest. Or perhaps an occurrence to which it was unwise to pay too much attention. Richard wondered if he should close the door, but just at that moment, the bartender poked his head through the first curtain. Certain that both his paying customers were still intact, he went over to the back door, pulled it shut and closed the curtain over it. He then returned to his bar, closing the other curtain behind him. Richard looked over to his fellow customer, but the man was again engrossed in his diminishing plate of cheese, with a level of concentration most people reserved for books and newspapers.

The next hour or so passed without incident. The middle-aged man finished his meal and departed, leaving Richard alone again with his thoughts and the last remnants of his flat beer. The procedures for dealing with those sought by the authorities were clearly ruthlessly effective, but once again he had evaded them. If they had been looking for him, he would now be back in custody, or worse. Either the communications between the regular police and the Gestapo and military were not as efficient as they were reputed to be, or the Gestapo were too embarrassed to own up to their loss.

The other side of the bar had now fallen silent, or at least quiet enough that none of its sounds penetrated the heavy curtain. Richard took this to mean that the Saturday morning rush, if one man with a plate of bread and cheese could be considered a rush, was now over. Then the curtain opened briefly again, and the man with the Bolshevik beard entered, sitting opposite him at the table.

"Put this in your pocket." Reaching into his own pocket, Alex extracted a piece of white plastic exactly the size of a credit card, and placed it face up on the table in front of Richard. The right-hand side was taken up with Richard's photograph. On the left was the name SORENSEN, <u>Olaf</u> Karl, and underneath this a miniature of the Norwegian flag, blue and white Nordic crosses on a red background with the black swastika in a white circle dominating the upper left quadrant. Next to the flag was a gold circle inlaid into the plastic, and underneath it an alphanumeric code starting MNW followed by a string of fifteen numbers. The whole card was coated in a thin layer of plastic which shimmered with a rainbow effect when tilted, showing alternately the Reich eagle and a swastika.

"That's your identity card. It won't get you through any serious security checks, because the fingerprint and eye scan belong to someone else, but it will allow you to use the trains in Berlin." Richard turned the card over. The back contained nothing but a set of instructions in small black print, the top half in German, the bottom half in what he assumed was Norwegian. He couldn't see a fingerprint, but didn't want to appear stupid.

"Will it be enough to get me into the American embassy?"

"That's not an option, unfortunately. All the foreign embassies are in a special zone just next to the Brandenburg Gate. It's one of the most heavily guarded parts of Berlin, which is saying something." He continued before Richard had the chance to protest. "Have you ever used one of these cards?" Richard shook his head. "It's very simple. You touch it on the yellow circular card reader, and that identifies you to the system. So, if it's a train station, it lets you on and off the platform and charges your bank account with the fare. In shops and restaurants it pays your bill, and so on. Simple. It doesn't even matter which way up the card is, and it doesn't even need to touch the yellow reader, just come very close to it. Most of the time someone will just check the photograph, which is fine. In some places, like airports or government buildings, you will also need to verify your fingerprint or retina, and you must not do that."

Richard nodded. "So, who is Olaf Sorensen?"

"You don't need to worry about that. He is someone the police are not looking for, or you would get arrested the first time you use it. Also, there are very few people in Berlin who can speak Norwegian. Do you know any German?"

"A little, yes. Enough to get by."

"Good. It's better if you don't speak English, because your

accent is clearly American, and the only Americans in Berlin are diplomats or trade delegations."

The bearded man put his hands palm down on the table in a business-like manner. "Ready?" He had switched into German.

"*Ja.*" Richard couldn't remember the last time he had spoken German and hoped it would come back to him quickly. An image of his childhood German teacher, Frau Henkel, and her late-night visit, flashed into his mind. The man stood up, pulled the brown curtain aside and opened the back door. As they stepped out into the alley, Richard looked for signs of the earlier excitement. About ten yards from the door, he thought he could see a faint reddish-brown smudge on the cobbles which could have been blood, but you would really have to be looking for it. The line of trash cans would have passed a regimental inspection.

They came out of the alley into another residential street, turning right back towards the main road where they turned right again. After no more than fifty yards, Richard saw the large white *U* on its background of a blue light box hovering over the street. As they got closer, he could read the name of the Heinrich-Himmler-Strasse station. At the bottom of the stairs, they turned left into the echoing, white-tiled corridor with its framed advertisements, propaganda posters and network maps. Richard noted how different the smell was from the New York subway – a mixture of strong antiseptic and sweet-smelling polish in contrast to the vomit and urine which usually characterised the network in his home city. Halfway along the corridor they came to another flight of steps to the right. Waist-high posts of stainless steel stood at the sides like silent sentries, the raised yellow circle on the top tilted at an ergonomic angle but carrying no instructions. Richard copied Alex, who held a plastic card over the circle, which emitted a short shrill beep. His own identity card evoked exactly the same sound, which echoed along the empty corridor.

Separated by about five paces, they descended the staircase, which took them onto a platform with train lines running either side of it. Alex stopped by one of the wooden benches which ran intermittently down the centre of the platform. He stuffed his hands in his pockets, sat down, leaned back and crossed his legs

– a study in nonchalance. Richard walked past him, avoiding eye contact, and sat on the next wooden bench a few feet away. He consciously adopted a very different pose – hunched forwards, forearms resting along the length of his thighs, head bowed, carefully studying the random mottled pattern in the textured concrete slabs of which the platform was built. After a few minutes, a rumble started on Richard's right. It turned into a clattering as he felt the draught from the tunnel stroke gently against his face, and finally an echoing metallic roar when the train entered the platform. He turned his head as it passed, looking beyond his companion, who was rising slowly to his feet. Richard was surprised that the underground trains were yellow, despite the number he had been within inches of in the last twenty-four hours.

He followed his guide and watched carefully as he lifted the stainless-steel knob, at which a pneumatic hiss was instantly followed by the rapid sliding-apart of the double doors. Once inside the carriage, Alex turned to the left and sat facing the platform, so Richard turned to the right and took one of the seats with his back to the platform. Opposite him were two brightly coloured diagrams. The first, a long strip, showed the current line, number two, in its red colour. To its side was a network map on which he could plainly see his red line running across the schematic of Berlin.

The driver started his safety mantra, addressing a completely empty platform:

Einsteigen, bitte. ... Zurückbleiben."

After about half an hour, including one change of line, they left their destination station through a similar network of stairways and corridors. After making the necessary acknowledgment to the yellow circle with their identity cards, they emerged into the bright sunshine of a leafy street, across the road from an imposing university building.

They set off through what appeared to be an affluent and very quiet suburb. After walking for about ten minutes, Richard was surprised to see the entrance to the Dahlem Dorf underground station – the stop before the one where they had alighted. They carried on for another five minutes before turning off the main road. They were now in a residential area whose dwellings evolved from large, almost palatial villas, through their smaller cousins, detached houses and finally into apartment blocks. It was at one of these that the bearded man turned sharply and descended the stone steps from street level towards the basement flat. Richard looked around, confirming for himself the emptiness of the street, before following.

The man had let himself in with his own key and held the door open for Richard to enter. He pointed in the direction of the major room before closing the front door.

"Sit down, please," he said. He gestured towards a faded sofa facing towards the window which functioned as a source of natural light rather than as a view, overlooking as it did the wall supporting the street's pavement. It was the first time either of them had spoken since leaving the bar. He heard a toilet flush nearby, and then the steps of a man approaching.

"Richard, this is Günter. He will be looking after you for a couple of days." As he entered the room, Günter was still tucking his shirt into his trousers. Less-than-average height, compensated by larger-than-average girth, his scruffy dishevelled state was in marked contrast to the man Richard had been tailing all morning. His thick stubble was several shades darker than the sparse brown hair, which looked like it had been piled onto his head like an ungenerous portion of spaghetti on a plate.

"*Guten Tag.*" Günter stretched out the huge hairy hand he had just retrieved from the back of his trousers, and Richard shook it, without any outward sign of the momentary hesitation in his mind.

"I will see you again when the arrangements have been made. Until then, do exactly as Günter tells you." With that, and a mutual nod of acknowledgment between the two Germans, Alex departed with as little ceremony as he had arrived, leaving the awkward silence behind him.

"Thank you for helping me." This appeared to be a statement for which the German didn't have a prepared response. He grunted an acknowledgement, then regained the initiative.

"Coffee?" Richard nodded with genuine enthusiasm and followed the German into the small kitchen so that he wouldn't have to remain at the mercy of his continued generosity, and in case the coffee formulation was in need of improvement. When they returned to the main room, coffee in hand, they settled onto the sofa while the German explained the procedure. Günter would shortly be leaving to carry out his regular job, which meant that Richard had to spend a lot of time in the apartment on his own. He had to remain invisible, not answering the phone, not opening the front door, or doing anything else that would betray his presence. The building was not under surveillance, so they didn't anticipate any problems. But if any of the neighbours suspected something, they would report it to the authorities, as expected of all good Germans. Apart from that, Richard could do anything he liked in the apartment.

"I have to get ready for work now." He plodded back into the bathroom, and Richard could hear the various sounds of running water, an electric razor and tooth cleaning. When Günter emerged, he was virtually unrecognisable. Clean-shaven, hair combed, and in a smart business suit and polished shoes. Richard noticed that his bearing had also changed to correspond to the work uniform: an upright stance, shoulders back, and the direct eye contact that had been missing previously.

"Help yourself to anything you fancy. I'll bring back fresh bread and milk when I return tonight. I'll be back around nine. Any other questions?" Richard couldn't think of any that would be worth asking, so shook his head. "Fine. I'll be off then. See you about nine."

Richard was standing in the middle of the living room where he had taken his leave of Günter. He looked all around, passing his gaze slowly in a circle, stalling momentarily at the few items of potential interest, like a malfunctioning lighthouse. A sudden feeling of isolation overtook him, and he stood rooted to the floor. This was worse than prison. Sitting around all day not knowing what to do would send him mad. He needed a structure. His regular routine back home had revolved around writing, but it was a long time since he had written anything. However, even if he could find paper and a pen, in the current situation writing anything down was probably not the wisest way of passing the time. He decided an exercise routine to regain some of his strength might be a better investment of his time.

CHAPTER FORTY-THREE

By the time it went dark Richard had cooked himself two meals and read most of the books he had found in a suitcase on top of the wardrobe, starting with Adolf Hitler's *Mein Kampf*. This was the revised 1955 complete edition, which contained the additional three parts that had been originally published separately as *Nach dem Kampf – After the Struggle*. Richard had slogged through most of the original while studying German many years ago, but his fluency in the language had improved dramatically since then and he found the new elements much easier to read. The first of these contained the Führer's reminiscences on his tactical brilliance, which had single-handedly won the war. The second new section concerned the rebuilding of Berlin and the other major cities of Germany, which he had carried through with the Reich's chief architect Albert Speer. After the victory celebrations of 1942, Hitler had decided that his political work was complete, and that what was now needed was a consolidation phase, for which he considered his old friend and comrade, Josef Goebbels, the best equipped. This had allowed Hitler the opportunity to return to his true vocation as an artist and architect. The final part of *Mein Kampf* was titled *My Political Testament*. For the most part, this was a restatement of the original work, rationalising the benefits for mankind of a world run by the Aryan master race and their honorary cousins, the Japanese. The decadence of the United States was to be tolerated and exploited, at least for the moment, as it provided economic opportunities for the Reich to fund its master plan. But the Germans had to plan for the eventual self-inflicted downfall of America, as it would inevitably be brought to its knees by the perfidious influence of the Jews. That Germany would continue to thrive was inevitable, and the thousand-year Reich would probably exceed its nominal destiny. But even after the empire's eventual collapse, future eras would still be able to marvel at its grandeur and magnificence, visible in the ruins of its monolithic constructions in Berlin and beyond.

It was with relief and an aching neck that Richard returned the Nazi bible to the suitcase, exchanging it for the other Hitler volume. He recognised the picture on the cover but couldn't place it at first. The painted alpine scene managed, in an impressive if amateurish way, to capture the magnificence and scale of a landscape, which dominated the few insignificant human specks dotted around the foreground. It was only when he realised that the frame was actually part of the painting that he recalled where he had seen it before. This was a view captured by Hitler through the huge picture window of the study in his alpine retreat in Bavaria. It had been used, alongside da Vinci's *Mona Lisa*, to advertise the art exhibition in the Naziland theme park in Cuba. The contents of this volume of Hitler's paintings were an eclectic mix, ranging from church and street scenes from across Germany to watercolours of the monumental buildings throughout Europe and a series of illustrations to Wagner's *Ring Cycle* of operas.

The third book in the suitcase was an old catalogue of the stamps of the Third Reich. This held little interest for him, so he flicked quickly through its pages. To his mind, the selection of events for philatelic commemoration showed little imagination. Hitler's birthday on April 20th featured every year until the eightieth in 1969, and all the major anniversaries of the founding of the party, the seizure of power and the Final Victory were commemorated in Germany and many of the other countries. The football World Cup and Olympics also featured strongly, especially when they were held within the Reich. Alongside art and architecture, space exploration provided another recurring theme. The last German issue featured in the book was the fiftieth anniversary of the first manned landing on the moon in 1961. This prompted Richard to flick back to the early 1990s, where he soon found what he was looking for. Hanna Reitsch was commemorated in 1992, the year she had died, aged eighty. In addition to the value featuring her death, other denominations detailed her other achievements: the first woman to fly a jet fighter; the first to pilot a rocket plane; the first non-stop circumnavigation; the first woman in space, and finally the first woman on the moon.

Before embarking on the fourth and final book in the suitcase library, Richard was in urgent need of coffee. His hand was hovering over the switch on the electric percolator when he heard the knock on the door. He froze instinctively, before checking over his shoulder that he was not in the line of sight of anyone who might be looking through the window. Carefully he stepped behind the kitchen door, which would also hide him from the kitchen's small window. The knock was repeated, quickly followed by the insistent hammering of a fist.

"We'd better give it a minute before we break in. What do you reckon – knock the door in or break the window?"

Richard felt a sickening pain in his stomach. Two men in broad daylight, openly discussing the best way to break in, weren't after the television set.

"The door looks pretty solid. The window would be easier, but one of us would have to squeeze up to it to get in. And then someone will have to board it up. Knock again, I think I can hear something inside." The second voice sounded younger and better educated. The hammering on the door resumed, followed by a brief silence.

"Go and get some cloths from the van so we don't shred ourselves climbing through the window." The grunt of acknowledgment was followed by laboured steps climbing back up to street level. Richard assessed his options. There were two of them, but he probably had the element of surprise, as well as the kitchen's selection of knives and frying pans. Being taken into custody was not an option. The sudden sound of music shattered the quiet. He recognised the opening bars of *Horst Wessel*, the popular marching song which was the official anthem of the Nazi party.

"Schmidt. ... Yes, we're there now. There's no one in, so we're about to do a three-ninety. ... Isn't there someone closer? We're almost at the end of our shift. ... Okay. Send the address through to the van's nav system. And make sure you put this on the file. I don't want the shit for not finishing a job." The second set of footsteps making its way up the stairs was followed a couple of minutes later by the engine of a small van coming to life before driving off.

large rocks in the belt of debris orbiting the sun between Mars and Jupiter had broken out of its orbit and was heading towards the sun. Its path was calculated, and the German scientists realised that it was on a collision course with the Earth. It was estimated that the impact would be more dramatic than the one which had caused the extinction of the dinosaurs, even though the rock was still not close enough to be detected by the biggest observatories in the Americas or Australia. The survival of the human race was at risk. Fortunately, the German space program had invested heavily in providing a defence against just such an eventuality. A massive arsenal of nuclear missiles and high-powered laser guns was in orbit around the Earth, and these could be aimed at any point in the skies to tackle this type of threat. Three days before the projected impact, as soon as the asteroid had come into range, one of the largest nuclear missiles was launched. It scored a direct hit, and the rock broke into around a dozen large chunks. Ten of these would crash harmlessly into the sun, but two were still heading for the earth and would cause considerable damage. The following day, the larger of these two chunks was destroyed by one of the smaller nuclear missiles. The final threat was resolved when the remaining rock was vaporised by the laser battery positioned in stationary orbit over the north-east coast of the United States. The operation was so completely successful that the millions of people, including Richard, who had gazed skywards on the night of the projected impact, didn't see a single shooting star.

This story so dominated the news of 2019 that other events received little coverage, either at the time or in this documentary. There was mention of the trade dispute which had started early in the year. As far as Richard remembered, some major American corporations had invested heavily in research and development and were trying to break into high-technology markets traditionally dominated by the Germans. The German version of the story identified the problem as an attempt by the USA to create copies of technologies developed by Siemens and other organisations, which were protected by international patents. The dispute between the two countries had started to escalate, and for a while it looked like it might get out of hand. Each side had imposed sanctions on the other. With the significant imbalance of trade between the two countries, it was the German companies which suffered most from this, as their largest external market disappeared virtually overnight. The luxury car market in the USA was turned on its head, as more than three-quarters of all sales were typically Mercedes, Daimler, BMW and Porsche, giving General Motors, Ford and Chrysler a short-lived boost for their models at the top end. Boeing and Grumman also benefited, but to a lesser extent. The German government didn't permit the export of what they referred to as 'strategic technologies', which, as well as all the rocket-powered hypersonic aircraft, included the latest generation of jet engines. As it happened, at around the time the asteroid crisis had been resolved, the trade dispute petered out, and commercial relations reverted to normal, with a slight easing of restrictions on both sides of the Atlantic.

Elsewhere, the year also brought other frictions. The Japanese Empire had to deal with significant internal difficulties. Richard knew from US coverage of the story that the Chinese uprising had actually resulted in major concessions from their Japanese overlords. The tension between these traditional enemies was generally considered the world's most likely flashpoint.

On a more positive note, 2019 had seen the coronation of King George VII of England, allowing a demonstration of that country's famous talent for pageantry. The death of King William towards the end of 2018 had generally been seen as a welcome relief for the old man, who had valiantly struggled against poor health for most of his life. Few had expected him to survive the thirty-two years that he had reigned since the death of his father Henry. He had managed to consolidate the position of love and respect which the monarchy had previously considered its right in England, without turning it into a focus for anti-German sympathies, as had nearly happened in 1950, when the assassination of Edward VIII was followed by calls for the restoration of his brother, George, from exile in Bermuda.

The coronation day had provided a rare coming together of the nations of the world, such as was only usually seen at a sporting level. Representatives from all parts of the former British Empire were delighted to attend, either revelling in their current independence, or drawing comparisons between life under their former masters and their current overlords. Even the Emperor of Japan, keen to display confidence in both his country and his personal rule following the recent difficulties, attended with his spectacular personal guard of samurai warriors. The United States president was also happy to visit the country where his grandfather had been ambassador in the first months of the European War.

The final few minutes of the programme were devoted to the sporting highlights. The lead item was a painful one for Americans generally, and for Richard personally. He had been present at the Yankee Stadium on that fateful day when the Germans had beaten the USA at baseball. This match had been arranged towards the end of the year as part of a series of sporting spectaculars to demonstrate that there were no hard feelings after the confrontations earlier in 2019. As a result of this national sporting disaster, huge emphasis was placed by the American press on the so-called return fixture, where the USA would take on the German national soccer team in Berlin's Olympic Stadium and gain their revenge. It was a sign of the emotional impact of this humiliating loss at their national sport that the hype took such a hold in the four days between the two fixtures. In a sober mood, no one would have considered such a challenge realistic, and so it proved. The four-nil defeat would have normally been taken in their stride by the Americans, but because of the symbolic significance which they had heaped on it, the final score only served to compound the catastrophe.

Günter seemed to have relaxed, so Richard took the opportunity to try to find out more about his host.

"So why do you do this, Günter? Why are you helping me?"

The German looked puzzled. "That's not important."

"I think it's important to you. You don't know me. You don't know anything about me. And yet you're taking terrible risks to help me. Why?"

"It's best if we don't talk about it. The less you know, the less you'll be able to tell anyone if you're captured."

"I don't want to know anything personal about you, or anything about the organisation. I just want to know what makes a man like you help someone in my position. Is that a secret?"

The German sighed. "It's because of my family."

"What about your family?" This was like pulling teeth, but Richard persevered. Years of experience had demonstrated that it was the ones who were reluctant to talk who often had the best stories to tell. And a lot of these were even better because they hadn't been heard before.

"The twins. We had twins. Siegfried and Adolf."

"Were they identical twins, Siegfried and Adolf?"

Günter shook his head sadly. "Anything but. Unfortunately."

Richard thought he had lost him and was about to interrupt the German's memories, but he started again just in time.

"It was as if the two brains had been divided up wrongly. Siegfried was incredibly bright. When he was two, he could do sums in his head. Not ordinary sums, but big ones. He was too good for us. We had to use a calculator to check his answers, but he was never wrong. If you gave him three five-digit numbers to multiply together, it took him less than four seconds."

"Wow! That's amazing." Richard had never felt at ease around children, but marvelling at them was usually the fastest way to connect with the parents.

Günter carried on as if he hadn't heard. "But Adolf had difficulties. He had difficulty walking, and he couldn't form his words properly. Siegfried could understand him, and told us what he was trying to say, even though it only sounded like grunts and moans to other people. Siegfried was heartbroken when they took his brother away. He refused to do his sums for the scientists who came to see him. Then, after two weeks, we were allowed to visit. It was a really nice place. There were lots of children, all around Adolf's age – he was three by then, and he seemed really happy. Siegfried felt better after that and let the professors do their experiments. He was really looking forward to visiting Adolf again."

"What sort of experiments?"

"Oh, I don't know. I don't understand all that stuff. They put wires on his head and asked him lots of questions, gave him sums to do, and lots of puzzles. They showed him all sorts of pictures. On the screen you could see the different bits of his brain lighting up as he was doing different things. They seemed really pleased with him."

"And what happened with Adolf?"

Before answering Günter dropped his head forward slightly and pinched the bridge of his nose. "The second time we visited Adolf he was completely different. The nurse said it was the drugs they were treating him with. He didn't even recognise Siegfried. In the car on the way back, Siegfried didn't stop crying. When we tried to go back two weeks later, we couldn't get a permit. And then we were told he'd been moved to a special facility on one of the islands in the Baltic, and that we wouldn't be allowed to visit until he moved back to the mainland."

"So, what happened then, Günter?"

"We got a letter from the Reich Education Office. Siegfried had been awarded a place at the country's top academy for gifted children. Most children went there when they were ten, but there were a small number of places for five-year-olds. Of course, we were happy for him. But then we started to hear stories about this academy. The children were encouraged not to visit their parents after the first year, and most of them lost touch completely."

"What did you do?"

"We were trying to work out what to do for the best when we heard about Adolf." Günter's head tipped forward again, and his voice became little more than a hoarse whisper. "It was a cerebral aneurysm. Instantly fatal. They said he hadn't suffered at all. It was a huge shock, because he had been doing so well. Telling Siegfried was the hardest thing. He took it really badly. We decided the best thing for him was to keep the family together, and we said we would send him to the local school. That's when the trouble started."

"What do you mean, trouble?"

"Just little things at first. My salary didn't get paid. And on the same day we got a letter from the Education Office, encouraging us to reconsider the offer, for the benefit of our son. I wrote, explaining the reasons. The next thing was the Party Organiser at the office. He said he'd received reports of subversive comments. And things had gone missing in the office, and they wanted to know if I'd taken them. The next letter from the Education Office said we had a duty to the state to ensure that the talents of such a gifted child wouldn't be wasted."

"How did you know these things were linked?"

"We didn't at first. It seems so stupid now, but we thought it was just a coincidence. Then the neighbour called me at the office and said I had to come home at once. She had seen them take my wife away in handcuffs, and the police had let her in to look after Siegfried. I called the police station to find out what was going on, and they said I needed to go to there, with a lawyer. A woman from the Child Protection Department turned up at the apartment at the same time as the lawyer. When I got to the police station, they let me see my wife straight away. She had been beaten, but not badly – there were no broken bones. She was accused of murder – someone I had never heard of. I stayed with her while the lawyer went to talk to the inspector." Günter took a handkerchief from his pocket and blew his nose loudly. "It was about two in the morning when the lawyer came back. He said it had probably been a case of mistaken identity, and we could go home while they cleared it up. When we got back to the apartment, there was no sign of Siegfried. All his clothes had gone, and his two favourite toys. On the table was the release form for sending him to the academy. That was when we realised."

"So, you signed?"

"What choice did we have? The next morning, before seven, the doorbell rang. Outside was the woman from Child Protection, who wanted the signed form, and a policeman who wanted to ask more questions about the murder. We handed over the form, and they both went away."

"What happened to Siegfried?"

"We never found out. We heard nothing more from that day to this."

"And what about your wife?"

"After that we never stopped arguing. About nothing really. Then she left me. They let us have a quick divorce, without the usual penalties, because of what they called the 'extreme marital stress' resulting from the death of Adolf."

Richard felt guilty at having made Günter relive this dark period of his life, but he found it strangely reassuring that the control exercised by the state didn't happen completely unchallenged, however futile that challenge turned out to be. He left his host to his thoughts and the television as he tidied the kitchen.

CHAPTER FORTY-FIVE

Richard was woken by the television's morning laughing-baby spot. He padded into the kitchen and made them both breakfast, while his host was in the bathroom. They ate sitting side by side on the sofa.

"What time are you going to work today?"

"I'm not. It's Sunday."

"Oh. I'd completely lost track." Richard hesitated before continuing. "Günter, how much do you know about medals?"

The German's head turned slowly away from the television to face Richard.

"Some. Why?"

"I've seen one I don't recognise. I just wondered what it was."

"There are thousands of the things. The most common is the Iron Cross, and there are about twenty different versions of that."

"This one was white. Four arms, with bits between each of them."

"What period?"

"What do you mean?"

"Before the Nazis or not is a good place to start."

"Current. Or at least it was awarded in the last ten or twenty years."

The hand rubbing against the stubble sounded like a particularly slow piece of sandpaper.

"Could be medical. Or the fire brigade. If it was white, it's unlikely to be military. Who was wearing it."

"I've no idea," Richard lied.

"That's not much to go on. Alex might know."

"It was for hanging round the neck."

Günter's eyebrows raised noticeably, and he twisted his body round to look Richard in the face.

"Were there eagles between the arms? And small swastikas underneath each one?"

"That sounds like it. What is it?"

"It's a special award for foreigners. Non-Reich foreigners. Special friends of the government."

"It was gold, apart from the white enamel."

"Can't have been. The neck badge of the Order of the German Eagle is only awarded in silver and bronze. And the medal, of course, but that's on a normal ribbon pinned to the jacket. It's mostly given to Japs. The emperor might have a gold one, come to think of it. That would make sense."

"You want more coffee?"

The body turned back towards the television, draining the last dregs from the cup on the arm of the sofa.

"Yeah. Thanks."

There was a loud knock at the door. Günter's look was enough, and the American scrambled behind the sofa, picked up the sleeping bag, folding it roughly around his discarded clothes and shoes, and disappeared into the kitchen. Once the kitchen door had been pushed almost shut, the German stood up from the sofa and walked over to the front door, looked through the peephole and opened it. He closed it quickly behind Alex, who followed Günter's gaze and walked into the kitchen. Richard felt ridiculous, like a naughty child, hiding behind the door, hunched over the screwed up sleeping bag that he was holding in place with both his wrists as his hands gripped his shoes.

"We're moving you today. Go and have a shower and a shave – you need to look presentable."

As Richard disappeared into the bathroom, still clutching his bundle, Alex handed him a plastic shopping bag with a new set of clothes.

Ten minutes later he came back into the room to find Günter and Alex in earnest conversation on the sofa. As Richard appeared, they stopped talking and Günter stood up, reaching out his hand.

"Good luck" he said in the best English he could muster, before going into the kitchen.

"That should be okay." Alex surveyed Richard quickly from

top to toe and the approving nods seemed more optimistic than the comment.

"Where are we going, Alex?"

"Out of Berlin, Richard. At least you are. You don't have a handy phone, do you?" Richard shook his head. "Good. And you'll need this." As Alex handed him the identity card, Richard glanced at it, wondering who Rainer Hermann really was, if he even existed, and how long it would be before he went the local police station to try to explain how he had lost his most precious possession.

Richard cast a final glance at the clock on the table. It showed half past eight. He climbed the steps to street level first, and turned left down the side street, hands stuffed into his pockets, shoulders hunched, and head tipped forward under the black felt peaked cap that would have looked so out of place on any other continent. He walked slowly until Alex passed him, then picked up speed slightly.

Richard followed Alex down into the underground station he remembered from his previous expedition, using Herr Hermann's identity and bank account to gain access. As there was no way to avoid the system recording their details, he assumed Alex was also travelling on a fake identity, since the journey would inevitably eventually show up as a problem, and the two men would be inextricably linked to each other. They travelled to the centre of Berlin, changing twice.

It was a crisp but sunny morning. The walk, which took them along the bank of the Spree, would have been pleasant but for the ever-present threat of arrest and a return, probably all too brief, to the Gestapo's prison cells.

"While there's no one about, I need to explain the plan, Richard. Lots of art gets shipped around the Reich, and we use this as an escape route. From here you go to Linz, which is the hub of the art network. From there you travel with more art to London."

"I have to get a message to the American government as quickly as possible. How will I be able to do that, Alex?"

"We're working on getting you aboard an American ship. You'll be able to use the radio as soon as it's outside the Reich's territorial waters. Before then you won't have any opportunity."

As the two men crossed the bridge, Richard resisted the temptation to look up at the array of classical architecture to his left, watching instead the silver sparkle of the sunlight on the black ripples of the river's surface. German cultural policy encouraged every citizen to admire the artistic marvels of the Reich, and Berlin's Museum Island shared top billing in that respect.

The majority of their fellow walkers broke left to enter the famous Pergamon Museum, named after the ancient altar, excavated in the 1870s, which it had been built to display. Richard followed Alex, who continued before taking the next left and climbing the imposing symmetrical staircase to the mock ancient temple that formed the entrance of the Old National Gallery. Their arrival had been timed to coincide precisely with its opening at ten o'clock, so they attached themselves to the queue just as it started to move. The bulk of the visitors spread out to left and right, or ventured upstairs after touching in on the yellow entrance disc. However, Richard and Alex walked down the narrow passage at the side of the main stairwell, along the signed route to the museum's café.

The bored, middle-aged woman in the apron and paper catering hat was surprised, and clearly a little irritated, to see customers so early in her shift. She closed the door of the cabinet she was still loading with the morning's supply of cakes and pastries, brushed her hands on the apron, and stepped along the counter to where Alex was waiting. His companion had already been directed towards the table in the far corner of the café. She gave her customer the obligatory, and patently insincere smile of greeting, then prepared his two coffees before returning to her display.

Alex placed the two coffees and a couple of paper napkins on the table, and took the seat opposite Richard, facing in towards the counter and the empty tables of the café.

"In about fifteen minutes the door behind me will open. You go straight through it and follow the instructions of the man on the other side. The items from the exhibition which has just finished are being shipped back to the art depository in Linz today, and you'll be packed into one of the crates. It isn't comfortable, but it is safe. After you get to Linz, another of our people will open the crate and get you out of there. That will be early tomorrow morning, so you'll find it more comfortable if you don't drink the coffee. I suggest you go to the toilet now, because this is the last chance you'll get." Richard noticed that the toilet was over to his left and quickly followed up on Alex's suggestion.

A couple of minutes later he returned and sat opposite Alex again.

"Now put the identity card underneath the napkin, without anyone noticing, including the cameras." Richard fished the small piece of plastic out of his pocket and, holding it in place under his flat palm, he rested his hand on the table. He slid the card underneath the small white square of paper with his thumb, while Alex watched the empty tables for any sign of movement or trouble. The German then picked up the napkin and put it into his trouser pocket. Apart from the clothes he was wearing, Richard once again had nothing.

They sat opposite each other in silence, Alex taking occasional sips of his coffee. When Alex noticed the startled look in Richard's eyes, he had to whisper sharply to him to break the spell of panic.

"Just walk away. Say nothing."

Richard stood up sharply, making the chair screech along the floor. He turned to look over his shoulder, but the woman behind the counter was paying no attention to anything but the coffee machine she was polishing, and there were still no other customers. Richard walked towards the crack of the door opening set into the back wall of the café. As he reached it, he pushed it open and walked through.

He sensed rather than heard the presence of the person who closed the door and leaned against it, standing directly behind him. Richard turned round and came face to face with a short, stocky individual sporting a bushy Emperor-Franz-Joseph moustache, which looked out of place on a face that couldn't be more than twenty-five years old. The mouth beneath the moustache broke into a wide grin.

"Welcome to the shipping department, mein Herr. Artworks and refugees crated and dispatched at very reasonable rates. You can call me Fritz."

Richard tailed behind Fritz as he walked the length of the corridor, opening the door at the far end, before turning sharply and descending the flight of stairs to their left. Richard found himself in a huge cellar with whitewashed walls and very bright ceiling lights, which created a glare like the side of a snowy mountain. The central expanse of the room was empty, except for a small, shiny forklift truck parked in the middle. Fritz led him over to the far wall, against which an array of wooden crates was standing. Just beyond these neatly regimented crates were two empty ones, surrounded by packing materials – white cloths, straw and polystyrene blocks. Leaning almost unnoticed against the wall, between the empty cases and the wide brushed-aluminium workbench, were two paintings. Richard recognised one of these from the lid of expensive boxes of chocolates he had often seen in the New York department stores just before Christmas.

"The stuff you're interested in is over here." Fritz was pointing to the far side of the workbench, where there was a jumble of much less uniform crates, in a variety of shapes and sizes. Most of these were already sealed, but in those few which were not, he could see works of sculpture ranging from white marble through to bronze, together with an Egyptian mummy case in the shape of a large bird. The next crate contained a huge eagle, its wings fully extended, carved in unblemished white marble, in the unmistakeable style of the early Nazi years. The eagle was standing on the blasted stump of a tree, which left a three-feet-high gap beneath its six-foot wingspan. "I'll pack the bottom with straw – that's the best thing in case you have to pee – but after I've hung sheets over the wings, I'm going to have to fill the rest of the spaces with polystyrene blocks. The crates are not airtight, so you'll be able to breathe, but there's no air circulation, so it won't be pleasant, especially after twenty-four hours. And because of its size and shape, this will be the first item to go into the container, so it will be the last out. But as long as the train doesn't crash, you should be all right."

Richard waited for his cue, then threw the overcoat into the crate and climbed in after it. He wrapped himself around the eagle's perch and then lay motionless as Fritz continued with his work, as if packing refugees and marble sculptures into shipping crates was all part of the average day.

"Right, I'm putting the lid on now. Please stay quiet until someone lets you out at the other end. Hopefully, it will be one of our people! Even if it goes very quiet, you may have a guard standing near to you, so you aren't allowed to sneeze or snore. Good luck!"

Richard tried to relax, knowing that the next twenty-four hours were probably going to be the most boring of his life. If he was lucky.

Linz – October 2024

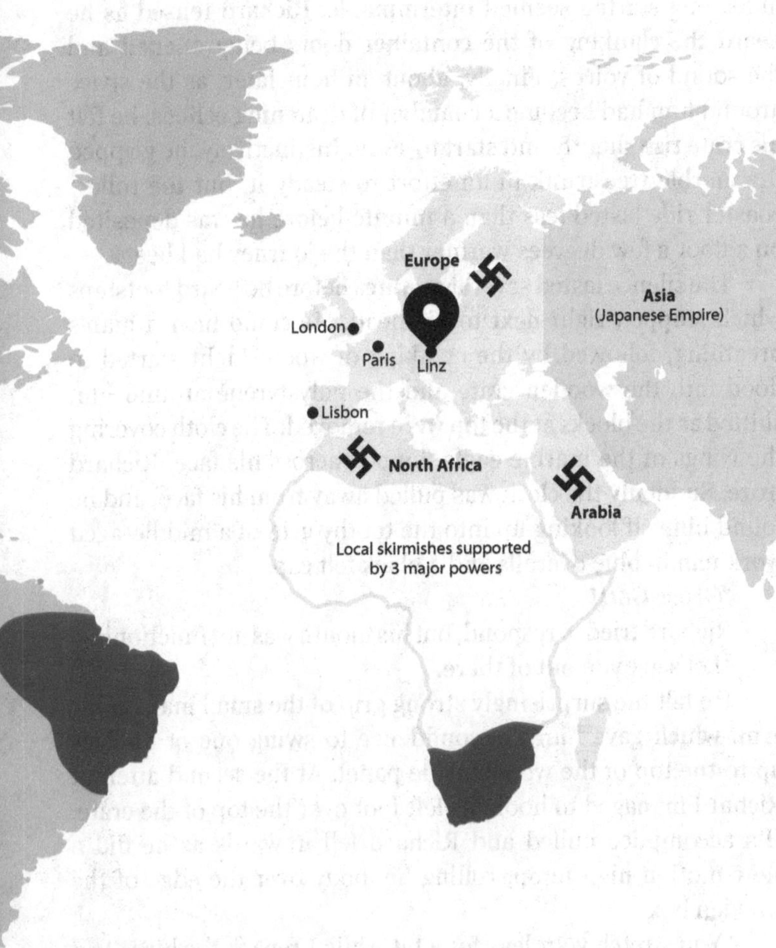

CHAPTER FORTY-SIX

After a final jolt, the train came to a halt. The wait until the unloading started seemed interminable. Richard tensed as he heard the clanking of the container doors being opened and the sound of voices. Finally, about an hour later, as the space around him had become a chamber of deafening echoes, he felt his crate rise slightly and start to sway. Instinctively, he gripped the marble tree trunk in an effort to steady it, but the roller-coaster ride lasted less than a minute before he was deposited on a floor a few degrees warmer than the journey had been.

The silence lasted several minutes before he heard footsteps which stopped right next to his head. He could hear a man's breathing, followed by the creaking of wood. Light started to flood into the wooden crate and the polystyrene around him shifted as the blocks at the top were removed. The cloth covering the wings of the marble eagle flopped across his face. Richard froze. Suddenly the cloth was pulled away from his face, and he found himself looking up into the toothy grin of a middle-aged workman in blue overalls and a black felt cap.

"Grüss Gott!"

Richard tried to respond, but his mouth was not functioning.

"Let's get you out of there."

He felt the surprisingly strong grip of the small man on his arm, which gave him the confidence to swing one of his legs up to the top of the wooden side panel. At the second attempt Richard managed to hook his left foot over the top of the crate. His accomplice pulled and Richard fell upwards as he did a slow-motion high jump, rolling his body over the edge of the wooden box.

"You stretch your legs for a bit while I repack the bird. And put this on." The man pulled an identical set of blue overalls from what had appeared to be a well-maintained beer belly. Richard dressed and watched as his latest protector quickly completed the packing job which union rules would no doubt say required two men and three times as long. But then they didn't have unions in Germany. Like Jews, communism, unemployment, cancer and, if you believed the official statistics, serious crime, unions were one of the many plagues that the Nazis boasted they had managed to eradicate.

While stuffing Richard's coat into his own overalls, the man looked his new twin up and down, deciding he had passed this latest test.

"Right. Now we just walk out of here. Follow me and keep your head down. Touch this card to the scanner the same way I do, and don't speak." He handed Richard an identity card. A glance at the photograph confirmed that it looked nothing at all like him.

They left the huge expanse of the white room and proceeded down an echoing corridor towards a guard post. This consisted of a small cubicle of plastic glass, in which sat a solitary figure in a grey uniform, complete with peaked cap and, as Richard saw when they got closer, a look of complete boredom. The guard glanced up momentarily as the two blue overalls approached but showed no real interest. Richard's companion touched an identity card to the shiny metal pillar which reached just above waist height, and the double glass gates swung apart. Richard followed suit.

The loading bay was empty except for an unmarked white van. As they approached the vehicle, the man slowed, allowing Richard to catch up, gripped his arm and whispered.

"When you get in the van, don't look down, and try not to tread on the man lying on the floor."

Richard opened the nearside door while the short man walked round to the driver's side. He climbed up onto the seat, placing his toes as gingerly as he could manage on the floor of the cab, and looking determinedly out of the window. The driver got in and muttered something under his breath in heavily accented German, which Richard couldn't catch. The answer was a brief grunt from between Richard's feet. The engine started and they drove towards the gateway.

They carried on for about a mile in silence, rising above a substantial town. Richard could see a hill, on top of which stood a small but imposing white church with two towers capped by black turrets. Below them to the right the silver-grey ribbon of the Danube flowed. Beyond it the buildings with their steep, red-tiled roofs clustered around a couple of small onion-domed churches and a larger one with a spire, which seemed to form the focal point of the town. The near side of the river was dominated by a giant square tower, reminiscent of those he had seen in Berlin, which dwarfed the buildings around it. The town centre looked to be a few hundred years old, while the areas further afield were characteristic of the architecture of the so-called Victory Era, when a huge quantity of buildings had to be built very quickly. This was particularly the case in those towns and cities which were of special significance to the Nazis, so Linz was probably the chief beneficiary of this localised building boom. Its growth, from the third or fourth city of the former country of Austria to the major cultural focus of the German Empire after Berlin itself, had taken only ten years to complete. As the town where the Führer had spent much of his youth and nurtured his early artistic ambitions, it had become a key place of pilgrimage. It ranked alongside Hitler's birthplace at Braunau am Inn, the sites in Munich associated with the birth of the party, and the huge parade ground in Nuremberg which still hosted the annual rallies. Linz was now home to the greatest art collection the world had ever seen. The Art Museum was the world's largest, but even so it was only ever able to display a small fraction of its collection. It was nominally the owner of all of the Reich's art, so even those pieces which never actually moved from the Louvre Museum in Paris or from the Trafalgar Gallery in London, were technically on loan from Linz. They had just left the Reich Art Depository, the storehouse for all artworks which were either not significant enough to merit permanent display, or which were on the merry-go-round of the art-exhibition circuit which had Linz as its hub. Looking down towards the town, Richard recognised the massive central hall of the Art Museum just on the other side of the river, close to the bridge. It seemed a long time ago and a world away from the miniature replica in Cuba, where he had watched the queues clamouring to get close to the *Mona Lisa*.

They pulled into a rest area just off the main ring road

around the city and parked in the far corner under the shade of several trees, out of sight of the patrons of the café. Richard exchanged clothes with the man who emerged from the floor well of the van, before the driver jerked his head slightly to the side.

"You see the man over there? He's your contact. Good luck!"

Richard walked round the front of the van in the direction of the man in the light-coloured overcoat leaning against the tree. As he got closer, the man glanced up. The gaunt face looked strained, and Richard estimated that this probably added ten years, making him early thirties at most.

"Cigarette?" Richard panicked, wondering what code word he needed to use in reply, but the man tapped the open packet of cigarettes in his hand to indicate that this was no more than a simple offer.

"No thank you. But I do need a toilet."

"I can believe that. Let's go inside and get a coffee. You can call me Adolf."

They ended up sitting at a corner table, ignoring each other like an old married couple. Adolf was reading his newspaper while Richard stared absent-mindedly out of the window. Within fifteen minutes he was almost completely recovered. He promised himself he would never again take for granted the basic comforts of everyday life that few people are ever deprived of – water, coffee, toilet facilities, fresh air, enough room to stretch your legs.

"If you're ready, it's time we left." Richard snapped back from his reverie and nodded. He drained the last of his coffee and immediately regretted it as the cold, gritty liquid hit the back of his throat, leaving a lingering, bitter taste. They walked to the middle of the car park, where Adolf started to open the driver's door of a green Volkswagen Paris. Richard climbed in the passenger side. When they reached the clogged ring road, they came to a virtual standstill almost immediately. Adolf was apologetic.

"The rush hour here lasts from around half past seven to nine on a Monday. We're not going too far, so it shouldn't take long." Adolf seemed to be more forthcoming than most of those who had so far helped on his quest, so Richard decided to risk a question.

"That warehouse contains a vast amount of priceless art, doesn't it?"

"Yes, that's right."

"Then why was it so easy to get out? Why is the security not much tighter?"

Adolf laughed and his face broke up into even more creases. "Good question. The security is very tight, but it's focused on the art. No one is checking up on the people who go in and out, just the pieces, and they all have micro-beacons inside them. When you left, the facility was officially closed. Nothing goes out of there except between nine in the morning and five in the evening." He paused to concentrate on changing lanes before continuing. "It would be a higher risk for incoming pieces to have to wait until it opens, so it's still possible to deliver art when it's closed. The guys who met you there made a delivery. The only concern of the authorities is that they didn't take anything out. The main part of the art store doesn't contain anything small. Anything that can be put in your pocket is kept in a different area, and the people who go in and out of there are all searched."

"Right. But how did two people manage to get out when only one had gone in?"

The driver chuckled. "That's a clever little trick we've developed. Did you notice how strong your driver was?" Richard nodded. "Well, he can hold a crated painting on his own and make it look like there's someone on the other side as well. Then all he has to do is scan two identity cards, and two people can come out. It's a bit like a magic trick."

"But very dangerous."

"Not as much as you'd think. If they get caught, it will be going in. And the one guy was just doing his mate a favour because he was tired. They would both get in trouble, for sure, but no one would actually get shot. That only happens if you get caught coming out." Silence returned as they stared at the stagnant river of traffic in front of them.

Six cars behind, two men sat in identically silent poses. They were dressed in the standard uniform of travelling salesmen but didn't have the confidence-inspiring faces which would make you buy soap powder or vacuum cleaners from them. The driver started to drum the steering wheel nervously and his companion distractedly chewed the rogue edge of a rough nail. They knew exactly how much this operation depended on them not losing their target. They had radioed in the Volkswagen's registration number and location, so the traffic surveillance cameras should have already picked it up, but the coverage of Linz was restricted to the major roads and the old city centre, and almost completely lacking in the other residential areas. If their target stopped again, they would be able to locate one of their rain-soluble transmitters on it, otherwise they had to depend on the old-fashioned method of tracking by sight with its doubly-increased risk – the chance of losing the target, and the heightened possibility of detection.

For no apparent reason, the traffic started to move again, crawling at first, but steadily accelerating to the sixty kilometres per hour that everyone knew was the tolerated maximum when the signs along the road indicated a limit of fifty. In urban areas the prosecution rate for speeding beyond this was virtually a hundred per cent, and while the fines were bad enough, it was the humiliation of having to retake the driving test that proved the real deterrent. The pass rate was around three out of four, and if you failed, you had to wait three months before being allowed another attempt, for a significantly increased fee. And driving without a licence was virtually unheard of. Every vehicle had its individual tracking beacon which recorded its route and speed every time it was driven, and this was all logged against the individual's identity card which had been used to activate the ignition. Unfortunately for the pursuers, this data was of such volume that it would only be available the following day. The vehicle logs were uploaded during the night, when the state computer system had adequate capacity. If they lost their target now, the trail would probably have gone completely cold by the next morning.

Adolf pulled off the road and parked behind a modest hut at the edge of a wooded area. The door was not locked, and they both went inside, where Richard was briefed on the next stage of the plan.

At two o'clock, after Richard had managed a few hours' sleep, they set off again, returning the way they had come around the ring road. They turned off, and after a few hundred yards, they pulled into a large car park. To judge by the signposts dotted around it, this facility was for the benefit of those who chose to explore the hills surrounding Linz on foot. A forlorn café sat at one end of the concreted area, its windows all shuttered for the winter. A poster advertising Austria Delight ice cream flapped against one of its wooden walls in the gentle breeze. The only other building was a low bunker on the opposite side of the car park. Adolf parked a few yards away from its entrance and got out of the car, retrieving a large plastic shopping bag from the trunk. This second building also appeared to be closed up, but a sharp push was all it took for the iron grille barricading the entrance to swing open. The inside of the toilet block was damp and pervaded by the stench of stale urine. There was no visible sign of any recent human visitors, but a sharp scurrying under the blanket of dead leaves betrayed the presence of smaller inhabitants immune to the smell. Adolf handed the white bag to Richard who stood glued to the spot for a moment, wondering how best to get changed in this most unsavoury of environments.

"Now I'll leave you. Good luck with the rest of your journey. The taxi will be waiting for you outside when you've put the uniform on." With that Adolf reached his hand out for Richard to shake and disappeared back through the opening, a much-relieved man.

Richard looked into the bag. He pulled out the smart green overalls and hung the peaked cap on the top corner of one of the cubicle doors, before laying the plastic bag on the floor. He briefly examined the patches sewn onto his uniform. The embroidered number 17703 stood out against the white strip of cloth over the left breast pocket. Each shoulder had the metal letters *RKSD* sewn across the top. The overalls were a perfect fit, and he had no difficulty pulling them over his clothes. Richard stuffed his hands into the trouser pockets. In the left one was a cheap watch showing the time as half past two. He had the impression the rain had eased slightly as he nervously stepped outside.

The Volkswagen had gone, and an ivory-coloured Mercedes taxi was sitting with its engine running. He walked over to it, opened the rear door and got inside. Unsure what to say, he stayed silent, and the taxi pulled off. The meter was running and had already gone beyond a fare of three marks. Since he had no money, and Adolf had assured him he wouldn't need any, he resolved not to worry about it and spent the rest of the journey staring out of the window at the rain-soaked townscape. He thought he caught a glimpse of a gunmetal-grey strip running through the city far below him just about where the Danube should be and wondered why the river was universally associated with the colour blue.

After another ten minutes, with the meter approaching six and a half marks, Richard saw the low white expanse of the Reich Art Depository nestling in a clearing. The driver took the next exit, quickly passing onto a road festooned with warning signs prohibiting access to anyone without official business with the *Reichskunsthauptlager*. As they approached the red-and-white pole blocking the road ahead of them, the guard in the small cubicle at the roadside leant forward and peered into the back of the taxi. He required no further reassurance before activating the switch which opened the barrier and waved the vehicle through. Once the driver had cleared the guard post, he spoke to his passenger for the first time.

"I'll drop you outside the main reception. You just go inside and stand in front of the person at the desk. From then you'll be told exactly what you have to do. It's better if you don't talk to the other guards."

"What name do I use?"

"No names are used. They know who you are from the number on your overalls, and you're expected for this job, so there won't be any problem. If you need to use a name, make one up. That's what everyone else will do." As the driver finished speaking, they came to a halt beside a flight of five white concrete steps which led up to a door in a plate glass wall, through which Richard could see what looked like a standard office reception desk. Seated inside were four or five other men wearing uniforms identical to his own. He was about to open the taxi door and take his leave when the driver turned round and pushed a clipboard between the front seats under Richard's nose.

"Make it look like you're signing for the fare, then get out. Good luck." Richard moved the pen over the paper and handed the contraption back. By the time he opened the door, an identical vehicle had pulled up alongside them and the man in the back was putting his signature into the driver's notebook. This spurred Richard on to make his way up the steps to the reception desk.

He felt stupid standing silently in front of the woman who was sitting there in a white shirt and plain black tie. When he entered, she had glanced up then looked at the clock. Richard peered over the raised edge of the desk and watched as she wrote his number and arrival time, 14.51, onto a form which already had several lines filled out, and space for a dozen more.

"Take a seat until all your colleagues have arrived. Then you will go to the briefing." She spoke in the slow, deliberate German, with all the difficult word endings removed, that was reserved for unskilled foreigners. Any benefits this simplification had were more than offset by her strong Austrian accent. Richard turned away from the desk to find himself the least conspicuous seat among those who were already waiting.

As he sat down, the receptionist was processing the man who had followed Richard through the door. Just as she opened her mouth, he beat her to the prepared speech, repeating it word for word, this time in all its correct grammatical glory. She glared at him and nodded sharply towards the row of chairs which lined the wall of the reception area. The silence of the room was only interrupted when she repeated her introduction for the benefit of new arrivals.

At two minutes to three she noted the number of the latest arrival and stood up. Turning on her heel, she said to no one in particular,

"Follow me." The other fourteen men all stood up and followed as the woman made her way out from behind the desk, displaying the tight black skirt which looked like it had been fitted several cream cakes ago. At the end of a sterile corridor, the group entered a windowless room, in which fifteen chairs stood ready in three neatly regimented rows of five.

"Sit down, gentlemen. The briefing will commence shortly." At this she returned through the door, closing it behind her. In silence the fifteen sat themselves down, the first movers securing the back two rows, and waited. Even the comedian decided against making any further comment, much to Richard's relief, as he was now sitting alongside him in the middle of the second row.

Everyone in the room stiffened to attention as the loud military stride became audible in the corridor outside. The door snapped open, and a few of those sitting around him jumped up smartly, clicking their heels together. With only a couple of seconds' delay, the remainder of the squad shuffled and scraped to their feet. The man who entered was an imposing figure in an immaculate black uniform. Tall and slim, the silver-grey hair under his peaked cap and the piercing blue eyes marked him out as one of the Aryan master race, even before the silver SS runes and the *Totenkopf* skull symbol were visible on either side of his collar.

"Sit down gentlemen." The German scanned the group in front of him. "This is shipment number T2437. You need to remember that number. T is for the Trafalgar Gallery in London. Twenty-four is the year. And this is the thirty-seventh shipment of the year from Linz to London. T-two-four-three-seven. This shipment will leave at sixteen hundred hours by train. The train has six carriages which contain the artworks. These are designated *A*, *B*, *C*, *D*, *E* and *F*. Two of you will be assigned to sit inside each of these carriages, which will be locked before we depart. One of you will accompany myself in the cab of the locomotive with the driver. Two of you will accompany the guard in the rear van of the train. These two employees of the Reichsbahn are the only people apart from ourselves who are working on this shipment." The pause was dramatic. As he again scanned the rows, all eyes were focused on him. "The total journey time to London is fifteen hours, including one stop for a comfort break and interim inspection. The location of this stop is known only to myself and one official of the railway company. If we are attacked, there are rifles in locked compartments in each of the carriages. The control which opens these compartments is with me in the locomotive. When we board the ferry to cross to England you will get a meal break, while the army guards the shipment. So, before I hand out your carriage assignments, are there any questions?"

No one spoke.

"Good. Remember that no names are to be used. You identify yourselves to me by the final two digits of your uniform number. Only speak when the job requires it and only speak in German." He unbuttoned the top of his uniform tunic and took a single folded sheet of heavy official notepaper from his inside pocket. Slowly he read out the list of uniform numbers and their workstations, starting with carriage *A*. Richard managed to suppress the urge to look down and remind himself of the number on his uniform, and prayed that he didn't end up in the front of the train with the officer. As it happened, guard 17703 was assigned to carriage *E*, at which he tried not to show his relief, and wondered who 06442 would turn out to be, with whom he was destined to spend the next several hours.

The group trooped through the building to the siding where the train was parked.

"Stand by your carriages. *A* is at that end." The SS officer pointed in the direction of the locomotive and started to march towards it.

Richard walked in the opposite direction and stood alongside the next to last carriage, waiting for the officer to work his way down the train towards him, checking off the uniform numbers of the guards as he locked them inside. Richard's travelling companion turned out to be a short individual with extremely dark hair. Judging by his complexion, Richard guessed he was probably Spanish and was therefore unlikely to speak English. As they climbed inside, Richard quickly took in his surroundings. The bulk of the carriage was taken up with huge cages filled to the brim with wooden crates, all identified by individual bar-coded labels in a uniform pink colour. The narrow passage which ran between the cages and the wall of the carriage along one of its lengths contained two fold-down seats. In the middle of this passage, making it almost impassable at that point, was a tall, narrow wall cupboard with a keypad lock, above which shone a bright red bulb. Attached to the ceiling of the railway carriage were three dark hemispheres – the video surveillance system with which he was already familiar from the underground trains in Berlin.

As the door closed behind them, even before the heavy clunk of the key turning in the lock, his companion scampered to the other end of the carriage and pulled down one of the seats. Richard settled himself into the seat alongside the carriage's only access door.

They could hardly feel the gentle jolt as the locomotive finally started its overnight journey towards London. A few seconds later, the white overhead lighting switched to a dull blue glow, which made it impossible to sleep or read while on guard duty. The gentle swaying of the carriage, and continuous rattling of the rails beneath it, exerted an almost hypnotic influence, inducing a trance-like state. The hours of the night passed quickly as the train gobbled up the hundreds of miles towards the French coast.

London – October 2024

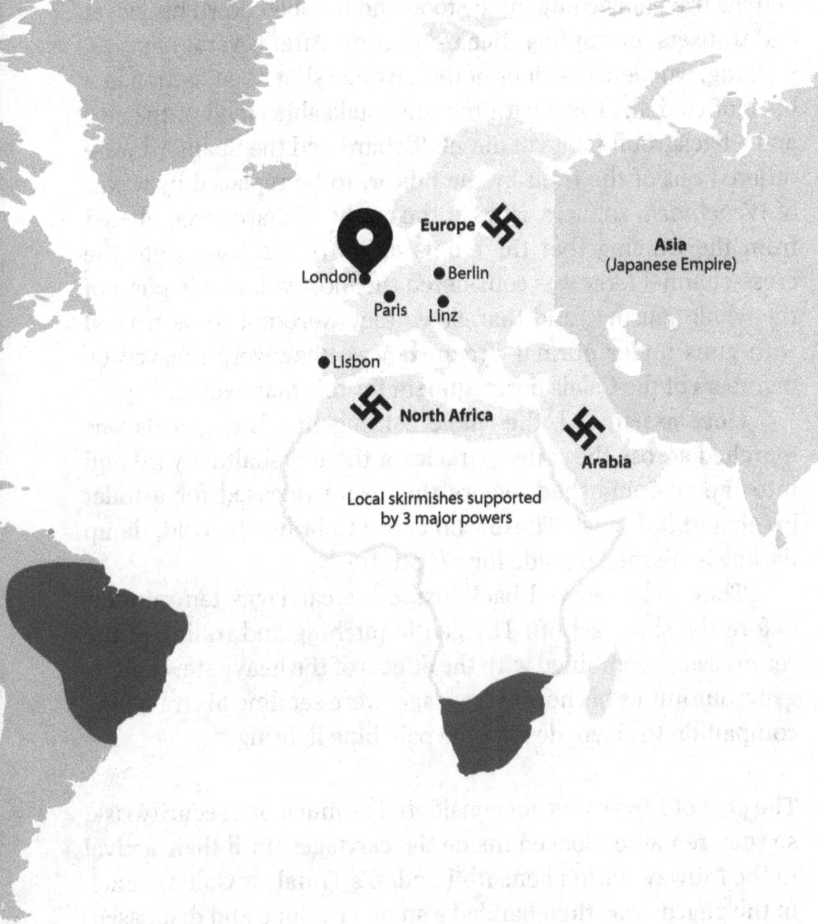

CHAPTER FORTY-SEVEN

As the train slowed, the clanking outside the carriage got louder. Horns and heavy machinery could clearly be heard once they had come to a complete stop. The white lights came on again, and his travelling companion stood and brushed down his jacket and trousers, prompting Richard to copy. After several minutes, the long, wooden side door of the carriage shot open, letting in a blast of cold air, laced with the unmistakeable smell of the sea, and a background note of diesel. Richard and the Spaniard were ordered out of the train by the officer, to be replaced by a pair of *Wehrmacht* soldiers, rifles at the ready. Richard remembered from the briefing that the embarkation of the train onto the cross-channel ferry was considered the most vulnerable point of the whole journey, and that, since they were not to be trusted with guns under normal circumstances, they were relieved by members of the Calais port regiment for this manoeuvre.

Once assembled, the whole contingent of art guards was marched across the railway tracks of the marshalling yard and into the customs shed, where they were released for a toilet break and hot meal. Those who chose to brave the cold, damp darkness stepped outside for a cigarette.

They were secured back inside the carriages ten minutes before the ship cast off. The gentle pitching and rolling of the sea crossing, combined with the effects of the heavy stew and its generous lumps of chopped sausage, were sending his travelling companion to sleep, despite the pale blue lighting.

The port of Dover was not considered as much of a security risk, so they remained locked inside the carriages until their arrival in the railway station beneath London's Trafalgar Gallery. Each of the guards was then handed a small envelope and dismissed. Richard followed his companions from the gallery basement out into the misty dawn and broke away from the group as quickly as he could. Two left turns later, he found himself in front of the gallery's main entrance, at the edge of a large square dominated by a huge statue of Hitler surrounded by bronze lions. He sat on a bench at the side of the square, just beyond the splash zone of one of the two fountains, and ripped open his envelope. Inside were two stiff green cards, each bearing the black outline of a plate with a knife and fork to either side, a hotel card marked 'Room 412', an itinerary slip instructing him to be back at the gallery at 18.00 that evening, and a plastic London Temporary Travel Permit with its familiar small gold square. On the back of each was stamped the number 17703.

"A lot of the places round here will try to rip you off. That card entitles you to a full cooked breakfast. Let me show you somewhere that does a really good one."

Richard looked up into the face of a man of about fifty with intelligent grey eyes. He was roughly Richard's height and build, and wore the standard worker's uniform of blue overalls, black boots and a black jacket with a fake-leather collar. He smiled before continuing.

"It's better if we don't speak English, as your accent would give you away. Follow me."

They walked up the steps out of the square towards the art gallery and turned right past the elegant spire of a large white church. After a hundred yards they crossed the road and entered the huge façade of a major railway station. Inside the Traveller's Café they sat in the far corner, underneath a fan heater which sounded like its bearings were long since due an overhaul.

"Full English breakfast for my friend, and a mug of tea for me." The waistline of the man in the white apron who took their order could have been designed to inspire confidence in the establishment's cooking. As soon as the waiter left in the direction of the kitchen, the workman asked Richard to hand over the envelope and again checked the details on the cards. He laid one of the green pair on the table between them, and Richard returned the remainder to his jacket pocket. "Once you've eaten, we're going somewhere you can stay for a few hours. I can't take you on to your next contact until this evening."

Richard's breakfast arrived. Two fried eggs, pale rashers of bacon, sausages unlike any he had seen in Germany – short, fat and greasy, with a palette ranging from the dull grey, through every shade of brown to a singed blackness where the cook had forgotten to turn them – all swimming in twin seas of watery tomatoes and small beans in a vivid orange sauce. His companion identified the small grey pieces as mushrooms but declined to explain the thick black disks speckled with white lumps of fat. Richard felt hungry and apprehensive in equal measure, but the need for a decision was taken away by the shouting and screaming which started outside the café's main door. Like everyone else facing the same way, Richard turned to see what was going on. About thirty policemen in their dark blue uniforms, brandishing pistols or rifles depending on their rank, had swarmed onto the station concourse. They were forcing the civilians against the walls. Those who moved too slowly were accelerated by the butt of a rifle. One woman, who had slipped to the floor, was kicked before being dragged towards the largest of the groups, which was now facing the wall, hands on heads, legs spread apart.

"Quick. Follow me and keep your head down." The panic was starting to spread into the café. Everyone was focused on the group outside, and no one seemed to notice as the workman grabbed Richard by the lapel of his overall and dragged him towards the kitchen at the back of the café. They crouched behind a tall, wheeled rack stacked with used dishes and considered their next move. On the other side of the door, they could hear the police entering the café. Suddenly the swing door they had just used crashed open, the noise immediately cancelled out by a single gunshot. The look of shock and horror was frozen into the man's eyes for the split second before his face started to disintegrate as he fell to the floor. His legs were jamming the door open, and the momentary silence was shattered by the screams flooding in from the café.

"The door at the back. It leads into the hotel. It's the only other way out of here."

Richard and his English companion ran as well as they could in their crouched position, weaving between the ovens, refrigerators and washing-up sinks towards the door. They burst into a white-walled corridor. Before passing through the door at the end they slowed to walking pace. The hotel lobby was a picture of calm, in sharp contrast to the mayhem a few feet away. They followed two hotel guests out of the main entrance and immediately turned right, heading for the side street. The police vans, eerily quiet with their blue flashing lights, stood unattended on the station forecourt. A screeching of tyres on the road in front of them made them pause. Richard reached his arm across his companion's chest and gently shepherded him back towards the hotel entrance as a large official car crunched to a halt and three figures emerged. The two in black leather coats were struggling to keep up with the slim blonde woman, who was yelling in German, demanding to see the officer in charge. Richard recognised Hanna instantly, but she was completely oblivious to his presence. The three new arrivals rushed through the façade into the station concourse. Richard and the Englishman walked other way, turned right past the empty car, its doors still hanging open, and headed down the narrow street. After a couple of hundred yards, at the bank of the river, they stopped.

"You look like you've seen a ghost," said the Englishman.

"You saw that woman?"

"The one screaming at the police? You could hardly miss her."

"She's Gestapo. She helped me escape from the prison in Berlin."

The Englishman was silent for a second. "Shit. You know what that means, don't you?"

"Yes, I do. It was a set-up. Do you have any way of warning the other people who helped me?"

"I'll try. But if she's been tailing you, it's probably already too late for them. At least the London end of the operation is still safe. And we need to get you out of sight as quickly as possible."

They backtracked a few yards and entered a small public park bounded on one side by the river and on the other by a series of tall white buildings.

"See that small arch on the left? That's a water gate. The river used to go up to there until the Embankment was built about a century and a half ago." The workman quickly got the message that Richard had other things on his mind than a guided tour of the city's sights. A few moments later he nodded in the direction of one of the tall buildings. "We're going up there. Just past the Savoy Hotel."

Richard followed, and they emerged into a narrow street which was completely deserted. A few yards further on there was a small church on the opposite side of the road, looking forlorn and completely out of place.

"You can hole up in there for a few hours. It's disused, so no one will disturb you." The man checked behind him as they crossed the road. Bending to tie a shoelace, he slipped his hand into the slats beside the dark oak door and extracted an ancient cast iron key, with which he hurriedly unlocked the door, hustling Richard inside. While the Englishman struggled to open a second door, Richard moved forward into the body of the church. The dark gloom was only relieved by light seeping through the filthy stained-glass windows, enabling glimpses of a ceiling which must once have looked spectacular.

"In here."

Richard stepped back towards the entrance to find his latest guide pointing him up a narrow staircase.

"This is the tower. You'll be safe here for a few hours. There's some food and a thermos of coffee. I'll be back for you around five this afternoon."

He climbed the stairs to a small room where a window slit looked out onto the street they had just used. He settled in to wait as he heard the scraping of the key in the lock of the main door.

Richard opted for the cheese from the tin of food, leaving the dark piece of cake for later, and washed it down with a cup of the weak, milky coffee from the vacuum flask. The exhaustion caused by the journey through the night and the morning's escape suddenly overcame him as he lay down on the floor, serenaded by the pigeons somewhere above in the bell tower.

Richard had just finished the cake and the final remnants of the coffee when he heard the scraping of the key in the door again. He lay silent until the Englishman poked his head into his hiding place. He was almost unrecognisable in his suit and tie.

"Here. Put these on, then we're ready to go."

He threw Richard a bundle of clothes, into which he

quickly changed, leaving his numbered uniform on the floor. They exited the small church, leaving the door unlocked, and made their way towards the river where they turned left under the bridge and continued along the bank. After a few minutes they reached a station of the London Underground.

"You know how to use the Travel Permit?" Richard nodded and they entered.

The tube train journey took less than fifteen minutes. When they returned to the surface the two men stared in silence at the departure information boards on the concourse of the main railway station. Finally, the Englishman announced under his breath,

"Go with her. Good luck."

Richard looked straight at the young woman in a long, beige raincoat, who was walking towards him. As she got closer, she smiled, dark brown eyes matching her long hair. She thrust her arm through his as she continued towards the far end of the station. They each used their cards to pass through the barrier, but as soon as they were on the platform, she took Richard's plastic travel card from him.

"We need them to think you got off somewhere else."

On platform three there was a train already in position. After a couple of minutes, a shrill beeping started. The doors hissed shut and the train motor clanked into life just before the first jolt of forward movement.

"We're getting off at the first stop. It takes just over two minutes."

Richard peered out of the window as the railway tunnel gave way to the grey of London's East End. The first stop was Bethnal Green, an unmanned station watched over by a single camera and three cats. The two of them descended the steep steps and squeezed through the exit barrier together, using just her identity card. This was not enough to trigger any alarms, and they stepped into the street in silence.

"This is where I leave you. Follow the man standing against the wall. And good luck."

Without changing pace or looking around, she turned right, leaving him facing to the left. The man leaning against the brick wall about twenty yards in front of him was wearing a workman's jacket covered in brick dust, and a flat cap. He folded his newspaper, tucked it under his arm, and launched himself off the wall with an arch of the back. Richard kept his distance and followed as the man passed the sign proudly announcing Weavers Fields and entered the park area to their right. The central crossing of the footpaths was dominated by a statue which carried a dedication plaque from the Prime Minister of the time, Sir Oswald Mosley. It commemorated Reinhard Heydrich, the first Reich-Protector of England. Exiting the park, the builder crossed the road before turning left into a side street. It was easy to identify which of the old dwellings had been modernised and upgraded by the upwardly mobile young, and which were in their original state.

Richard was no more than twenty yards behind the man at this point, and as he turned the corner, he saw that the builder had stopped near the bottom of a flight of stone steps which led up to the dwellings to his right. Richard slowed and as he passed, he heard his instructions.

"Up the steps, third door – the white one." The man's accent was noticeably English, with the precise speech and the lack of those modernisms which had increasingly come to characterise the American variant of the language over the last twenty years.

As Richard climbed, he could hear the footsteps of his latest guide continuing purposefully down the street. He approached the white door, and it opened in front of him. He walked straight in and stopped immediately inside the door to allow the person behind to close it.

CHAPTER FORTY-EIGHT

She was a petite brunette, and a slight glimmer of trepidation was visible in her bright, green eyes. The pleated grey skirt reached to just below the knee and the smart green jacket hinted that she had just returned from work. The door closed almost silently behind him, and his latest custodian started up the stairs, beckoning him to follow. As he passed through the door into her bedroom, it too closed. She walked over to the window and looked briefly outside to left and right.

"This is the safest room. They can't make out what's said, provided we keep our voices down." She sat on the edge of the bed and pointed to the wicker chair hiding in the corner, out of sight of the window.

"I've heard some of your story, but I'd like to hear it from you. From the beginning." She folded her hands in her lap and fixed him with a concentrated stare. A very different interrogation technique from the Gestapo, but no less intimidating, and probably no less effective.

He settled in for what he thought was going to be a lengthy monologue, but when he mentioned who had sent him to Cuba, her eyes were a picture of total astonishment. She jumped to her feet.

"What do you know about Samuel Levy?" The cool, controlled façade evaporated momentarily. She regained her composure and sat back down as a sign for Richard to continue.

He thought for a moment before answering.

"Major figure in the Jewish community in New York. His grandparents managed to get the family out of Germany just after *Kristallnacht* in 1938, when Samuel's father was about fifteen." He looked into her green eyes. She had leaned forward, the lines across her brow betraying the intense concentration. "His grandfather was a tailor, and after a brief stay in England, he moved the family to New York, where he and his son set up their own small business on the Lower East Side. Samuel was born in New York in 1950. His first wife died in an accident, and he remarried. His second wife is about twenty years his junior. He had two children from each marriage and a number of grandchildren." Richard hesitated. "What else can I tell you?"

"Just wait here for a moment." Without a word of explanation, she went downstairs. He heard the telephone by the bed ping, but he didn't dare to pick up the receiver and try to listen in. Strain as he might, he couldn't catch any of what she said. It was a good five minutes before she returned to continue the conversation as if it hadn't been interrupted at all.

"What do you know about the grandchildren?"

"Nothing. Sorry."

"Do you know how many there are, at least?"

"No idea. But when I was in the house, I saw three young children there. A couple of boys were playing in the kitchen, and I saw a sick girl with an oxygen cylinder – she looked about ten years old – who called the old man grandfather." That answer seemed to satisfy her, so Richard prepared to carry on with his tale, but she got in first with her next question.

"So, Richard, what is your plan from here? You can call me Victoria by the way."

"Well, Victoria, I need to get back to America as quickly as possible."

"And why is that – apart from the obvious desire to escape the Nazis?" He thought he detected a wry grin.

"When I was in the Gestapo prison in Berlin, I saw something." Richard hesitated. "I think the Nazis are trying to manipulate our presidential election."

"You mean they want to stop the Jewish candidate?"

Richard thought back to the photograph of Heinrich Goebbels on the wall of the Gestapo doctor's office in Berlin. "It's much more complicated than that."

The silence following his answer lasted an uncomfortably long time. When Richard looked up, he caught her gaze studying his face intently. Her eyebrows knitted slightly when she was concentrating, but the earlier signs of nervousness had disappeared.

"Tell me about the Gestapo woman."

Again Richard hesitated. The question hadn't been asked with any tone of accusation or malice. Slowly he told her the little he knew, and the conclusion he had drawn from this – that he had been used to betray the underground movement's escape route.

"I guess the raid at the train station messed up her plans. I've never seen a woman so angry. Do you know what happened to the other people who helped me, Victoria?"

She shook her head.

"So why are you helping me?"

This time it was Victoria who hesitated. "We need something delivering to New York."

The doorbell rang.

"Get under the bed and don't make a sound."

Richard could hear what he assumed was a neighbour popping round for tea. It was about an hour before Victoria came back to the bedroom, and Richard crawled back to his chair.

"So, where were we?"

"What is it you want me to take to America?"

She was looking straight into his eyes as he asked the question, but her gaze immediately dropped to some invisible point on the floor between them.

"It's not what. It's who."

Richard was even more puzzled. He was the one who needed help with the practicalities of escape from this alien world, with its all-seeing, all-knowing, all-conquering regime that would have no hesitation in liquidating him.

"You already know her, Richard."

His thoughts turned immediately to Hanna. She was the only other woman he knew in the Reich. A few days ago, he would have believed that she could want to escape the regime – after she had assisted him, but before he realised her ulterior motive and true loyalties.

Finally, Victoria continued. "It's Rebecca Levy. Samuel Levy's granddaughter. You saw her when you visited his house in New York. The girl with the oxygen cylinder."

"How? Why? I don't understand. Why is she here? She's Jewish."

"I don't know the full story. I just know it's vitally important she gets back to America." Her tone was reproachful, but Richard felt he had every right to ask. His escape was going to be difficult enough on his own. What chance would he stand of evading the Nazis with a sick Jewish girl in tow! And wasn't it Samuel Levy who had got him into this whole mess in the first place?

"This makes no sense at all. Tell me everything you know, or I leave right now." It was a bluff, but his instincts told him that Victoria was desperate for his help, and that he was her only chance of fulfilling this extraordinary mission. She delayed before answering and took a deep breath.

"I work in the Health Administration Office. We manage all the non-medical decisions of the medical service. That ranges from the financial management of hospitals and doctors, the administration of patient records, and the decisions of who is entitled to what treatment." At this final point she glanced up to see if there was any reaction.

"Accident and emergency care is available to all, of course, and cancer treatment is done as routine provided it's diagnosed early so that it can be cured. But when it comes to the expensive procedures, there's a formula to determine who does and does not get treated, and that is managed by the Health Administration Office. So those who need expensive procedures to extend their lives are assessed by us on the basis of their value to the Reich and the lifetime cost of their treatment." She glanced up at Richard again before continuing. "Senior party officials are top of the priority list, of course, followed by others who make a substantial contribution, such as the greatest artists and writers. Heroes are also given priority, but as their contribution is all in the past, they fall into the next group. Does that make sense?"

"I understand what you're saying. I wouldn't go so far as to say it makes sense. What happens to the vulnerable in your society? How do you work out the value of children, or of the mentally ill?"

"We don't have the mental health problems you experience in America, and children are given high priority. They are the future of the Reich."

"But only the German ones, presumably?"

"No. Not just the Germans. Race does play a part in the decision, and Germans do get the highest priority in practice. In theory the same treatment is available to all the Germanic races, but the actual Germans are higher up the list."

"I'm sorry. You've lost me there. What's the difference between German and Germanic?"

The bureaucrat in her sighed almost imperceptibly as she went back to the basics. "The Germanic definition was introduced after the victory when it became necessary to classify the citizens of the Reich into bands. Peoples who had been enemies were conquered and absorbed into the Reich, but it wouldn't be appropriate to give them the same rights and privileges as the victors. Initially there was a simple classification into the Conquerors and the Conquered, but over time it evolved as more subtle distinctions were required. Generally, the classifications exist at the level of country, but it is possible for individuals to be granted a status that differs from their nationality."

"It sounds very complicated."

"Like any system which has evolved over time, it does tend towards complexity, but managing the classification of people is an area of Nazi expertise." Richard searched her face but couldn't detect any hint of irony.

Victoria continued, "The top Germanic band is defined as the full citizens of the Fatherland - those countries within the borders of Germany before the start of the war. The next band was originally the major allies of Germany at the start of the European War - Italy and Finland. Spain was included as a country with a special relationship and compatible system of government when it chose to join the Reich in 1942, and England negotiated the same status as part of its incorporation into the Reich."

Richard pondered for a few moments before responding.

"Okay, I can see the logic of how it works. If it costs the same amount to operate on an eighty-year-old grandmother as it costs to operate on the five-year-old child of a party official, no one here is going to argue with that. Unless it's your grandmother." Richard paused for effect but couldn't see any.

"But what does all of this have to do with me?"

"Because of my job, I get to process all the transfers of patients between hospitals and other institutions. Two weeks ago, I noticed something very odd. There was a Johanna Sarah Schmidt in the Josef Mengele Hospital in Oxford for a heart and lung transplant. She was being transferred to a special facility in Carlisle. I have come across the name before. Johanna Schmidt is the cover name used for someone whose identity is secret. This type of heart and lung transplant is a very expensive procedure. With most patients there's a need for them to take anti-rejection drugs for the rest of their lives, so that the new organs are not attacked by the body's immune system. A procedure has just been perfected which genetically modifies the organs before transplant, so that they match the DNA of the recipient and are not at risk of rejection. This washing technique is very expensive and currently reserved for the highest party officials and very few others."

"Very interesting. So, what do you think is happening?"

"It gets even more odd. She was being transferred to Carlisle."

"Yes, you said that."

"No one ever leaves that facility in Carlisle. Officially they either stay there for long-term care, or they die from incurable conditions. But there are rumours that the patients transferred there are used in experiments and then disposed of." There was a glint of fear in Victoria's eyes.

"That sounds like what they did to some of those Jews who didn't get out before the war started. If they find any Jews today, isn't it logical that that's where they'd send them?"

"I suppose so. But you wouldn't carry out one of the most expensive procedures in one of the Reich's best hospitals before sending them there. The Oxford hospital is second only to Berlin, and in some areas it's the best in the world. That's where the research is going on into PCR – post-cryogenic revival."

"You mean bringing Hitler back to life?"

"Exactly. Volunteers are frozen in precisely the same way the Führer was, so that the techniques for resuscitation can be perfected before they are used on him."

"Tell me more about the girl."

"Some rich foreigners come to the Reich for operations that they can't get in America, because our techniques are more advanced. Most of them go to a special hospital outside Berlin, and the relevant specialists go to that hospital to operate. A small number come to England. Most of them are cryogenics, who are beyond the capabilities of current medical science to cure. There's a special storage facility for them linked to the Oxford hospital. I can only think that the little girl is in England because it would be unthinkable to operate on a Jew in Berlin."

"How did you find out who she is? All you knew was that her identity was secret."

"I mentioned what I had found to a colleague in the organisation. Two days later he got back to me and said the girl was related to a friend of our organisation in the USA. I don't know how he found out, or what had happened, but he wanted me to try to save her. I went into the system and changed the transfer documentation to send her to a hospital in the south of England which often takes children. While she was in transit, I went back into the system and changed her name. She is now in a Southampton hospital under the name of Joanna Smith. So far no one has asked any awkward questions, but she is almost ready for discharge. We need to get her out of there soon, before people start wondering why her parents aren't arranging to take her home."

"What do you expect me to do about it? I'm going to have enough difficulty getting myself back to the USA. And I don't think I exactly owe Samuel Levy any favours. If it wasn't for him, I'd be safely back home in New York."

"We can get you both as far as Portugal. Our contacts in Lisbon will be able to help you get out of the Reich."

Richard doubted he had any choice. Unauthorised travel was virtually impossible, and this wasn't a country where you went to a friendly official to request a passport or buy a plane ticket.

"It's late and I need to go to work early tomorrow. Should I make the arrangements for you and your new daughter?"

Richard nodded.

Victoria took a pillow and a blanket out of the top of the wardrobe, and he followed her back down the stairs into the room directly beneath her bedroom. As an afterthought she nodded her head back in the direction they had just come from.

"There are some men's clothes in there which should fit you. Have a look tomorrow and see what you can find. And I've left you food in the kitchen." Victoria dropped the bedding onto the sofa and drew the curtains before switching on the light. "I'm afraid it's not very comfortable, but it should only be for two nights at most."

"It's fine. Thanks."

"Try not to move around too much or make any noise. I don't often have visitors, and the neighbours are nosy. Obviously, I'm supposed to notify the Residence Department if anyone stays here."

"I'll be as quiet as a mouse."

"Good night then."

He settled down into the sofa. She was right. It was uncomfortable, and he turned himself this way and that for a few minutes in a vain attempt to find a tolerable position. Eventually he just decided to lie still and stared at the blackness where the ceiling must be. By the time the pub at the end of the street disgorged all its customers, he was fast asleep.

CHAPTER FORTY-NINE

He panicked as the slightly cold hand clamped over his mouth left him desperate for breath. He opened his eyes, but could only make out the vague, dark outline hovering above him. Richard's mind raced, trying to work out where he had gone to sleep the previous evening. The cold and pain in his back gave the momentary impression that he was in the cell in Berlin, but there the light had rarely been switched off. As he tried to push himself up, the hand was released. He took a deep, relieved gasp just as it all came back to him.

"Sorry to wake you, but I have to leave now." Victoria was starting to come into focus. He wondered if she could see him better than he could see her.

"What time is it?"

"Just before six. I need to get in early to start the paperwork to get you and the girl out of the country."

"Thank you," was all he could think to say. She didn't respond, just left the room, pulling the door almost closed behind her. A couple of minutes later he heard the front door shut and her heels clicking down the steps on the other side of the window. He wasn't tired but tried to get back to sleep.

When he awoke it was completely light. The rumble in his stomach was insistent. He reached across the floor to the pile of clothes he had discarded the previous evening and dressed as silently as he could. Then he crawled off, staying below the level of the windows, to find the kitchen and the food he had been promised.

By the time the kettle boiled, he had also managed to find the supply of tea bags. He left the tea to stand, while he ventured towards the fridge. He pulled open the door and was pleasantly surprised. Along with a varied selection of fresh fruits and vegetables, he found the milk and orange juice. Everything else was in the sealed square plastic boxes which had been the basis of an explosion of so-called 'social selling' in the States about thirty years ago. He took the milk over to the tea, which looked well beyond help.

He started to explore the plastic boxes. One contained examples of that other English delicacy, the sandwich. These seemed to account for both the main course and the dessert as one was filled, although the word was a slight exaggeration, with some sort of ground paste which smelt like meat, or possibly fish. The other was much more recognisable as strawberry jam. He didn't even have to fold back the top of this one to check what it was, as a trickle had leaked out onto its partner. Victoria was clearly not used to feeding hungry men, or perhaps the English just ate less than the Americans. From its position he had guessed this was intended for him, but he decided to explore the other boxes, if only to satisfy his curiosity rather than his hunger. The bacon, sausages and cheddar cheese came as no surprise. The small pie, completely encased in dark brown pastry, would have baffled him if a quarter hadn't already been sliced out of it. He guessed that the pinkish meat inside was probably pork, and not of the highest quality, but he thought better of examining the jelly-like ingredient which provided a sort of buffer between the meat and the pastry casing. If that could be attributed to English eccentricity, the next plastic box went several steps beyond. It looked like a hosepipe that had been chopped into one-inch lengths and was suspended in a thick substance similar to the one in the pie. It was the greenish tinge and the strong smell of fish which made him decide that this item was definitely off today's menu. He made a mental note to ask what this was when his hostess got back home. He wanted to be sure of his facts to avoid being laughed at when he related this particular anecdote. The next box proved to be much more appetising. Curry and a brightly coloured rice were neatly separated on either side of the box. This was obviously restaurant production. He had heard stories of inhabitants of India, Hong Kong and some other parts of the old British Empire who had decided to escape the prospect of serving their new Japanese masters at the end of the war. Many had travelled to the United States, but they were turned away by a country still reeling from the effort of trying to integrate ten million Jews.

Rather than return to the Japanese Empire, they had sought permission to go to England to rejoin their imperial colonists. The Nazis had no objection to this, and the conscience of the Americans, embarrassed at having to turn away the oppressed in search of refuge, resisted the demands of Tokyo for their return. And the result of this reverse colonisation had ended up here in Victoria's fridge. And it smelled good. Much better than any of the other options.

Richard placed the cup of tea on the floor, returned all the plastic boxes to the fridge except the one with the sandwiches, and sat with his back propped against the kitchen door. The tea was hot, which with the current state of his mouth and stomach was the priority. And the jam sandwich did a pretty good job of masking the taste of the one that preceded it. With his immediate needs dealt with, there followed a careful crawl to the bathroom, reminiscent of particularly heavy nights during his student days. For the next half hour he ran through the exercise routine he had developed before reverting to his preferred way of killing time. With the benefit of daylight he managed to make the combination of blanket, pillows and sofa a lot more comfortable than it had been the night before.

The siren seemed part of a dream, until its screaming got too close and too loud to dismiss as unreal. Richard's stomach knotted until the note changed as the vehicle passed and sped off into the distance. Once the silence returned, he concentrated to check that there was no activity in the immediate vicinity before shuffling back into the kitchen. The clock now showed four, and Richard hoped the pork pie wouldn't be missed. Judging by the taste, he was probably doing Victoria a favour. Finally, he remembered her promise of clothes and spent the next couple of hours rifling the wardrobe.

CHAPTER FIFTY

It was completely dark by the time Victoria returned home. Richard asked how the escape plan was progressing.

"We still need to make the detailed arrangements, but basically we'll go to the hospital in an ambulance that we'll borrow and take her from there onto a boat to Portugal." Richard noticed that she used the word *'borrow'* completely without inhibition.

"So, is this something you do a lot? Is this the objective of your group?"

"The objective of the group is to support the return of England to English control." The fluency of Victoria's answer bore all the hallmarks of a campaign slogan, though it was unlikely she often had the opportunity to articulate it. "One day the time will come when it is possible to strike back against the Nazis and throw them out of our country. That time is not now, but it will come. And when it comes, the Children of Arthur must be ready."

Richard had to bite his lip. Victoria's expression was that of the zealot, speaking the words of a deeply held faith. Ridicule would have been totally inappropriate, however silly the group's name seemed to him.

He decided not to probe any further. "When will we hear about the plans – the ambulance and the boat?"

"Tomorrow. I hope." She hesitated before looking straight into his eyes. "You're not having second thoughts, are you?" She sounded concerned, an impression reinforced by her gently putting her hand on top of his as it rested on the table. Richard didn't move away.

"Of course not. I need to get to America as quickly as possible, and that's not something I'm going to manage on my own. I need you as much as you need me." Her smile betrayed more than relief, and Richard continued. "So, what made you join the Children of Arthur?"

"It was a man. George. I'd never been interested in politics before. There's not much opportunity to get interested. And I was not unhappy with my life, so I didn't feel any need to rebel. Most people are like that. It's not only that rebellion is very dangerous. Most people are quite content with their lot in life and don't want to put that at risk. The state tries to keep us happy and generally makes quite a good job of it. The freedoms that are denied are not missed by most people. We never go hungry, and we don't get bored."

"The old principle of bread and circuses," Richard said. Victoria looked at him, puzzled, so he explained. "It was the way the Romans kept their empire in check. One of the emperors said that all it took to keep the Romans in line was bread and circuses. By which he meant food and entertainment. So, food was plentiful and cheap, and every major town had an amphitheatre with theatrical events or, even better, gladiators. After the war that was Goebbels's big idea. Hitler and the generals won the war. It was Goebbels's job to make sure they won the peace. He studied all the great empires in history, looking at what they got right and wrong, and trying to understand how they eventually failed. He then put together a package for Hitler on what it would take to ensure that the Reich would last for the thousand years they wanted."

"I've never heard that." Victoria squeezed his hand and smiled at him, willing him to go on.

"Well, the Nazis are hardly going to explain to their people how they're being manipulated. But it's something that gets studied a lot in the States. In a way, it's the ultimate marketing case study. It started with the rebuilding of Berlin immediately after the war. With that and the construction in other cities, there were jobs for everyone. Then they started to focus on making consumer goods for export to America. Once all the construction work was finished, the focus shifted to the space programme. Putting men into space and then getting them to the moon and Mars focused the whole empire. Thousands of people were directly involved, and everyone wanted it to succeed, so anyone who felt like complaining or protesting about the government couldn't find an audience. Alongside that there was lots of sport and state-sponsored circuses and other entertainments. That's also why executions are done in public."

"Wow! I'd never thought of it like that. But you're right. Nobody dares to complain openly, but most people don't seem to want to. They're all focused on getting the latest gadgets and getting on with their careers. And beating Scotland and France at football."

"That was another of Goebbels's ideas. Hitler apparently wanted to arrange the conquered areas of Europe into large blocks so that they were easier to administer. Goebbels thought that breaking the empire down into small units was a better idea. If the English and the Scotch were in separate countries, the ancient animosity between them would stop them cooperating against the Germans. The same applied to the Poles and Russians, Greeks and Turks, and so on. That's why international sport is so important for the Reich. On the one hand it creates unity, when the Reich can beat all the Americans and Asians. On the other hand, it maintains the internal divisions, to prevent any serious alliances that might be able to threaten the power of the Germans in the centre."

"So do you think the Reich will last for a thousand years, Richard?"

"A thousand years is a long time. So far they've managed just over ninety, and there's no sign of a problem. The next big test will come when Hitler actually dies, if he ever does. He's still the figurehead, and there's no sign of what would replace him if he wasn't there. And because he doesn't actually do anything, it's easier to maintain him as an ideal. If mistakes are made, it's obviously not his fault, just the person who's running the government at the time. On his behalf, so to speak. I don't know." Richard's stomach made an embarrassing growl.

"Let's eat."

Richard followed Victoria into the kitchen and watched as she concocted something out of the tins and packets he had found earlier in the cupboards. As they ate, he asked how she had got involved.

"How did George bring you into the group?"

He thought he saw the beginnings of tears before she cast her eyes down again.

"He was a great man. He was married, so we only ever met in secret. He was so full of energy, and he believed anything was possible. He managed to get people to take great risks for the cause. But eventually his luck ran out, and he got caught. He was killed trying to sabotage a train bringing in tanks. His wife was arrested. We think she ended up in one of the labour camps in Russia. There was no known link between George and me - he had always been very careful about that - so I was never suspected. Since his death, I have tried to keep the London operation going, so that what he did wasn't in vain. But we haven't tried anything really dangerous since that operation three years ago."

"What did George do for a living?"

"He was a careers advisor. At seventeen you get to choose what you do as a career."

"Isn't that decided for you?" asked Richard.

"The quotas do have to be filled, but that's not usually a problem."

"Quotas?"

"Of course! There have to be enough doctors, teachers, engineers, scientists, computer people, firemen and everything. But these jobs are highly paid and highly valued within the system, so they are always over-subscribed and competition for them is fierce."

"When you say, 'highly valued,' this includes them getting higher priority in your medical system?"

"Yes, of course. For them and their families. So, a girl's parents will always want her to marry a doctor, a teacher or an engineer, because of the way the state looks after their families."

"So, the cleverest men get the most beautiful wives," Richard said.

"And what's wrong with that?"

"Nothing. I'm sure Darwin would approve."

"Darwin? The Father of Eugenics?"

"That's the one. Though he called it 'natural selection'. It's the Nazis who started to actively manage the process, which is when they changed the name to 'eugenics'. So how did George get involved with the resistance?"

"In little ways at first. Just on his own. Most people aren't really aware of the organised resistance movements. There are rumours, of course, but it's a criminal offence if you know someone is involved in anti-Reich activities and you don't report them. And any acts of sabotage that get reported in the press are always put down to 'enemy agents.' The government won't acknowledge the existence of groups like ours."

"So how did you two meet?"

She hesitated for just a moment.

"I came back from lunch early one day and found a colleague on my workstation, amending the records on my computer. When I challenged her, she panicked. After I had calmed her down, she explained that she was trying to protect someone who worked for the resistance. She knew that they were both lost if I reported her, so she took the chance of telling me what had happened. George had been involved in sabotaging a chemical factory. It had gone wrong, and his hands had been burned. The Gestapo were looking for the people who had done it, and the fact that he had chemical burns would make him an automatic suspect. She was trying to change the records to show that he had been in a fire. Any amendments to medical records could only be made by doctors or me, which is why she needed my computer. It turned out this wasn't the first time she'd changed records on my computer, so I would be under suspicion myself. At the very least, I would be guilty of breaching security by letting someone discover my password. I let her get on with it and tried not to think about it." As she paused, Richard noticed a faint smile appear on her lips. "Then, about a month later, he came round to the house one night. I suppose I should have seen it coming. I was compromised, so I would be easy to recruit. And I was in a position that would be of great use to them. It all went from there. The woman in my office applied for a transfer. It was risky to have two operatives in the same office, and also a waste of resources. I have no idea where she ended up, and I've never seen her since."

"What kind of things did you get involved in?"

"George wouldn't let me get involved in anything dangerous. Even before we were seeing each other. He said I was too valuable. Strategic, he called it. The dangerous work was for the 'soldiers', which is how he liked to consider himself. So, I mostly worked with the computer systems – finding out information, changing records. Stuff like that."

"That sounds dangerous to me!"

"I suppose so, but it's not like planting explosives on railway tracks and detonating them when a train goes past." She hesitated. "It's something I'd rather not talk about."

Richard put his hand on top of hers. "It must be difficult. And very lonely."

For a few moments neither of them moved. Then suddenly she pulled her hands away and stood up. "I need a drink. Do you want one?"

She came back from the kitchen with a small bottle of whisky that was just over half full, and two glasses with ice cubes rattling around in the bottom. She sat down and poured, sliding one of the glasses over to Richard.

"Prost!"

"Cheers!"

They both sipped their drinks in silence for what seemed like an eternity.

"This is scotch, by the way. The people are Scottish. They get very annoyed when anyone gets that wrong."

Richard laughed but said nothing.

"Tell me what you're going back to in the States."

"I work in New York as a journalist. What do you want to know?"

"Everything. New York is such an exotic place. We get some American films here, and most of them are set in New York. Is it really full of gangsters?"

He laughed again and started to feel relaxed for the first time in months. He had almost forgotten what it was like to have a normal conversation.

"Actually, these days most of the crooks wear suits and work in offices. There are some gangsters, but they are mostly Italians. Most of my work is as a crime reporter. I once even wrote a book about one of the major mafia families in New York."

"Do you have family in New York?"

"Not any more. My grandmother died recently. My father and mother were killed in a car accident when I was a baby, so I don't remember them."

"Wife, girlfriend, brothers, sisters, cousins?"

"No. None of those. I'm an only child."

"Sounds lonely." She took hold of his hand again.

"At least we have that in common."

She downed the rest of her whisky in one gulp. "Richard, how long is it since you slept in a proper bed?"

CHAPTER FIFTY-ONE

Richard was woken from a deep, dreamless sleep by an insistent ringing. When he came around, Victoria was sitting up in bed next to him, speaking on the phone. It was still dark, but he could see the red numbers on the alarm clock showing a couple of minutes before six. She was talking about a friend who had been taken ill in the night. Richard lay still so that he didn't make any sound which might betray his presence to the person on the other end of the line. After about a minute, Victoria hung up.

"Is your friend really sick?"

"No. Nothing like that, silly. It's code, because all the phones are bugged. It's all arranged. We go tonight."

"Does that mean we have to move straight away? Or do we still have time?" He slipped his hand back under the bedclothes.

"God, Richard! You're freezing!"

"I have an idea how we can deal with that."

She reached over to the clock and reset the alarm to nine.

At ten she returned from the quick trip to the shops which sat beneath this row of elevated apartments. She had the ingredients of the traditional English breakfast that Richard had shown so much interest in. After they had eaten, Richard left the house first and was nearly at the bottom of the stone steps before Victoria caught him up and slipped her arm through his. He looked up at the sign on the other side of the narrow, cobbled road and wondered why the name Voss Street seemed familiar. It felt good to be wearing normal clothes again, even though they would have been a better fit on a man who hadn't spent months in a Gestapo jail. Victoria didn't show any emotion that Richard could detect while watching him put on her long-dead lover's clothes.

Two left turns took them onto the High Street and under-neath the apartment's front windows. Richard reckoned they must either be above the small grocery shop or on top of the take-away which offered a range of Chinese cuisines from Peking to Cantonese via Szechuan. Victoria set off at a determined pace towards the knot of tall buildings he could see in the near distance. Apart from housewives struggling home with their shopping and, as often as not, a couple of small children, Richard noticed other purposeful groups heading in the same direction. The excited chatter reminded him of the crowds of spectators on the way to baseball matches in New York, but the coloured scarves and hats were completely absent, and games didn't happen in the middle of the day on Thursdays.

As they got nearer to the city, the crowds of pedestrians continued to thicken. Richard tried to keep his head down to avoid attracting any unwanted attention. After about an hour they passed beneath an archway and turned slightly to the left. Richard couldn't take his eyes off the odd bridge, which looked like it had been designed as a background to a Gothic ghost story. The soot-black twin towers, with their pinnacles borrowed from a medieval castle, flanked an elevated walkway enclosed in a lattice of metalwork. On their right the imposing grey walls of the massive castle, which had guarded this entrance to London for nearly a millennium, dominated the crowds. Richard looked up at the flagpole rising above the four towers and wondered if the swastika would still be there in another thousand years.

Suddenly the crowd veered off to the right, congregating from all directions around the castle. He noticed Victoria look at her watch and perform a brief mental calculation, after which she turned sharply left onto the road across the bridge. The crowd on the bridge was thinning, but still substantial, and Richard had to bite his lip to avoid apologising to the men, women and children they were buffeting against as they navigated the stream the wrong way. Once across the bridge, they resumed their walk along the opposite bank, where the throng heading for the castle got less and less, but more and more rushed as the stragglers dashed to reach their destination. Richard noticed that the cargo ships which were lined up along both banks of the river mostly flew flags which incorporated the black hooked cross, though he felt strangely encouraged by the sight of two which were proudly bearing the stars and stripes.

Checking her watch again, Victoria slowed noticeably as the oncoming mass rapidly thinned to nothing.

A sudden gust of wind struck the back of his neck, and Richard felt a shiver run down his spine. Just at that moment, a cheer went up in the distance behind them. Victoria caught his confused glance, and checking that there was no one in earshot whispered,

"It's the last day of the month. The executions have started."

London was cold, but there was none of the rain he had always heard was compulsory. The people hurrying along the windswept streets looked slightly less well off than those he remembered from his walks through Berlin.

After the best part of an hour, they turned onto one of the bridges. Three-quarters of the way across, Victoria stopped and leant against the massive stonework. Richard peered down at the dark grey river, before raising his eyes to look east at the distance they had just covered.

"What's that?" When Victoria looked at him, Richard nodded in the general direction of the financial district, the famous 'City', which had been the true heart of the British Empire before the war. "The very tall building."

"That's the Millennium Tower. Or the 'Icicle' as we call it." Among the monumental square buildings which it dominated, this one really stood out, especially when the sun, low in the autumn sky behind them, caught its outline. It seemed to be twice the height of the next tallest building and looked to Richard like a piece of broken glass, a dagger, stabbed upwards into the heart of London, reaching up to scratch the clouds. One side was nearly vertical while the other converged with it in a series of jagged steps. Its translucent white construction played tricks with every change in the light, and under complete cloud cover it almost disappeared from view.

Victoria carried on talking, more to stop him speaking than to satisfy his curiosity. "It houses the local offices of the Reichsbank. Gold reserves are stored in the basement in what is supposed to be the most secure vault in the world outside Germany. The rumour is that the top section is the government's main communications centre. The very top of the building houses a huge antenna which listens in on all radio communications across the country. That's also where they process all the data from the navigation satellites."

"What do you mean?"

"It's an open secret that everyone's movements are continuously monitored through their cars and handy phones. You know that program on the phone that tells you how to get to anywhere from where you are now?" Richard shook his head. "I'll show you how it works later. But basically, every phone, and the mapping device in every car, sends out a signal to the navigation satellites once a minute. That allows the government to track everyone's movements."

"Why don't people just switch off their phones?"

"That's forbidden. Everybody over the age of ten has a phone, and they have to be left on all the time. You can set them so that they don't receive incoming calls, if you don't want to get woken in the middle of the night, but you can't switch them off. There isn't even an on-off switch, so the only way you can stop it working is to take the battery out."

"What if the battery runs down?"

"It doesn't. Unless you're on the top of a mountain. The batteries are continuously recharged through wireless technology. And if you somehow manage to break your phone, you get a new one for free, and all your phone numbers, addresses and everything are loaded back onto it for you."

"Sounds like a great system."

"It is. Except that they always know where you are. But you can find any information you want through it: when the next bus is due; which restaurants have tables free; weather forecasts. You can book seats in a cinema or theatre. And it's the cheapest and fastest way of communicating. You just type a note onto the screen, and it's sent to the other person immediately. You don't need to write letters anymore."

"But what do you do when you don't want them to know where you are?"

"You have to steal a phone from someone who isn't going to notice it's gone for as long as you need. But even that's starting to get more difficult. The newest phones have voice recognition systems, so they know if the wrong person is using it. And if you report your phone as stolen, you automatically get one of those, in case it happens again."

Richard looked up at the top of the glass tower. As the sun momentarily found a gap in the cloud cover, he noticed the glint of gold.

"It all sounds very sinister."

"It is. But as they always say, if you have nothing to hide, what's the problem?"

"What if you're having an affair?"

"They don't care about that. And only the state is allowed to use the information. If you want a divorce, you're not allowed to use the navigation data in court. Because officially, it doesn't exist."

A pleasure boat passed noisily underneath them. The open top deck was completely deserted except for the large pennant flag with its swastika surrounded by a stylised red sunburst and the stark black letters KdF. Victoria noticed Richard's curious glance towards it.

"London is the second most popular tourist destination, after Paris. But at this time of year, even the hardy Germans aren't usually up for the trips down the river." Richard turned and leaned his back on the parapet to look across the bridge to the western side of the city, where the boat was heading. In front of it, just before the river bent to the left, Richard could see the landmark clock, in its mock Gothic tower, at the near end of the former parliament building. The tower at the other end had been left in its broken-tooth shape as a reminder of the devastation caused by war. The last air raid on London in September 1941 had been immortalised in one of the most famous films made about the war. *Operation Big Ben* told of the daring sortie that Hitler had personally sanctioned in order to speed up the peace negotiations following the death of Winston Churchill. By using a British Wellington bomber captured during a raid on Kiel, the crack Luftwaffe crew had managed to fly up the Thames unchallenged in broad daylight. Precision low-level bomb aiming equipment, developed specifically for this attack, had enabled the damage to the ultimate symbol of British democracy, with only the minimal loss of civilian lives in the surrounding area.

The untold part of the story, as Richard had heard it, was

that the bomb had hit the wrong tower. The attack, symbolically carried out on the second anniversary of Britain's declaration of war on Germany, had apparently been because the new Prime Minister, Lord Halifax, had held out for better terms than Hitler anticipated. 'Von Halifax', as the newspapers dubbed him at the time, because of his original opposition to the war, secured a personal guarantee from Hitler that much of the fabric of English life would remain untouched. The monarchy itself was the subject of a plebiscite vote six months later. By the time the people voted, the old king and queen had taken their family and moved to Bermuda, where they enjoyed the protection of the United States government. The previous king, who had spent the five years since his abdication in exile, returned in triumph. Hitler's first ever visit to London had been timed to coincide with the long-delayed coronation of Edward VIII and Queen Wallis. It took place in the late summer of 1942, when the Führer received from the reinstated king the tribute due to the overlord of all Europe.

"Okay, we're off."

Victoria's sudden switch from bored tour guide to focused underground activist took Richard by surprise. At the end of the bridge they turned right, quickly walking past the imposing building surmounted by a green dome. Two armed guards were standing to attention on either side of the archway, through which he caught a glimpse of a magnificent courtyard lined on three sides by a queue of people in heavy coats.

They paid no attention to the man looking in the shop window as they passed. He followed them into a student café a hundred yards further down the road known as the Strand and sat down next to Victoria at the uncleared table. Richard managed to hide his surprise. Introductions were clearly going to wait, as the two started halfway through the conversation he assumed they had begun on the phone that morning.

"The vehicle is waiting for us in an old barn. It's about a mile from the nearest train station. Everything we need will be inside. Did you manage to make the rest of the arrangements?"

"The transfer letter is in my pocket," Victoria said. "It's dated for tomorrow, which means we can't use it before midnight. But that suits us anyway, as all the administrative staff will have gone home."

The waiter came to the table, an empty round tray tucked under his arm. Like virtually everyone else in the establishment, he was in his early twenties, scruffily dressed in the worldwide uniform of a student. As he put the tray onto the table and started to load it with the used cups and plates, Victoria and the man both surreptitiously placed their handy phones onto it.

"Three coffees, please." It was the man who spoke. The student took his tray back behind the counter without a word, returning with the drinks a couple of minutes later. He put the tray down on the table, and paid no attention as Victoria picked the three plastic identity cards from it, while he arranged the chipped mugs of coffee fastidiously on the table. The man placed a folded wad of money onto the empty tray. Richard thought he counted five ten-Reichsmark notes. The chalked scribble on the blackboard behind the counter showed that coffee cost half a mark.

They drank their coffees slowly, the English pair talking about the weather and sport. The man complained to Richard about the unfairness of the results in the recent European championship football match. One of the Berlin teams had beaten one of the London teams by virtue of a penalty awarded as the result of a blatant mistake. Richard nodded at what seemed the appropriate points in the story, trying to give the impression that he understood, or cared, or even both.

It was dark by the time they finished their drinks at just before half past seven, and they took the opportunity of a large influx of new customers to escape onto the street. The trio retraced their earlier steps. As they crossed the bridge, Richard looked to his left at the receding bank of the river. The tops of the dark bank buildings could just be discerned thanks to the red aircraft navigation lights which dotted the sky. In contrast, the white shaft of the government bank was fully illuminated by the spotlights shining up at it. On its top Richard could now see the clear outline of a shape which had become familiar to him during his stay in Europe – a gold-plated eagle, wings spread, holding a wreath containing the swastika.

"Call me Michael, by the way." The man kept his hands tucked firmly in the pockets of his coat.

"What happens with the phones, Michael?"

The Englishman laughed. "That café is part of the university. The building above it is student accommodation. That means it's not as closely monitored as other buildings in the city. So the students have a number of sidelines which they can use to supplement their incomes. A lot of them rent out their rooms to couples having affairs. If the police want to track our movements this evening, they will assume that Victoria and I were using one of those rooms. The tracking system only works in two dimensions. They know our phones are in the building, but they have no idea which floor."

"So are the identity cards another sideline?"

"Exactly. Three students taking a train outside the city at night isn't going to raise suspicion. And because we're driving from there down to the south coast, no one can make the connection, as we aren't carrying handy phones. As long as we swap them back before midday tomorrow, it will be as if nothing had happened."

They reached the end of the bridge and walked towards the huge railway station. The train left from platform one, the furthest from the station entrance. The ten minutes before its departure gave them ample time, avoiding the need for unseemly haste through the crowd milling around in the enormous concourse. One after another, they used their plastic cards to click open the barrier and boarded in the middle of the train. It left precisely on time, making brief stops at the first four stations, before hurtling through a series of increasingly suburban halts.

"This is our stop," Michael announced to his two travelling companions. They were the only passengers to alight before the train made its way on through the countryside.

Michael led the way off the platform and through the automated barriers which they again operated with their plastic cards. They soon left the dense housing and lights of the small market town behind them. In the middle of a deserted street, Michael collected the identity cards and stuffed them into an inside pocket. After about twenty minutes, they eventually turned off the latest in a sequence of side streets and walked down an unlit path. The dark shape looming at the end was dimly visible in the orange glow from the surrounding residential areas. As they approached the unlit building, Michael held up his hand to bring the procession to a halt. They stood in silence for what seemed more than the fifteen seconds it really was, before Michael walked to the side door, which he opened with a loud click. Once Victoria had followed Richard inside and closed the door behind them, Michael turned on the light. Taking up virtually all the space inside the small barn was the shape of a large vehicle, its rough outline visible under the tarpaulin which hid its detail from view.

Michael took a corner of the large sheet in both hands and pulled slowly but firmly, revealing the ambulance beneath. He knelt down by the front wheel and rummaged on the floor. The key was on a simple metal ring with no identifying marks. In the back the stretcher and wheelchair were folded and propped up against the bench seats, which made the inside of the vehicle surprisingly spacious. Michael returned to the driver's door, opened it, clambered up into the seat and started familiarising himself with the controls. Once he was satisfied, he pushed the key into the ignition and climbed back out again. In the meantime, Victoria had retrieved three uniforms from somewhere inside. Since these pulled comfortably over the clothes they were wearing, there was no need for any of them to undress. Michael looked at his watch.

"Half past nine. Are we ready?" Richard looked at Victoria who nodded. "Right then. Victoria, you sit in the passenger seat and Richard, you get in the back after we've opened the barn doors."

Michael edged the ambulance slowly out onto the pathway without turning on the lights. Leaving the engine running, he alighted and closed the doors behind them. He drove as quietly as he could for another hundred yards, peering through the windscreen to plot his route between the tall hedges on either side. As the hedges cleared, the path started to drop, and they approached a proper metalled road ahead of them. Michael turned on the ambulance's headlights just as he turned off the track onto the deserted road, and set off at a sedate pace, heading south.

CHAPTER FIFTY-TWO

In the back of the vehicle Richard felt completely isolated, and the brightness of the interior light removed any thought of trying to sleep. After a couple of hours, he was thrown sharply against the side of the ambulance as they turned off the road and stopped. The back door opened, and the bright white light switched to a pale blue. Richard was relieved to see Victoria in its dim glow, dressed in her baggy green uniform which did nothing to flatter her figure.

"We're nearly there, Richard. We have to wait here for a few minutes so that we arrive just after midnight. At this time of night there shouldn't be any traffic, so we won't run into any problems. When we stop you need to get out with the wheelchair. Try to make it look like you know what you're doing when you unfold it, and don't make eye contact with anyone."

Victoria returned to the front of the ambulance for the last few minutes of the journey, and the interior light switched back from blue to brilliant white as the door closed behind her. Five minutes later they slowed and came to a stop. Again it was Victoria who opened the back doors. His eyes adjusted quickly to the return of the pale blue light, and Richard grabbed the two handles of the wheelchair in one hand, dragging it behind him as he reversed out of the back of the ambulance. He almost missed the step, but recovered just in time, landing the wheelchair on the ground outside the hospital's main entrance, unfolding it with a sharp outward flick of both wrists. He felt very proud of this first-time demonstration of medical skill, until Victoria leaned across him to push the locking clips into place. Without a word she walked towards the building, passing under the concrete archway with *Magda Goebbels Hospital* in bold silver lettering. Richard followed dutifully behind, keeping his head down.

They walked through two sets of motion-activated sliding

doors into the main reception area, which was bathed in the now familiar bluish tinge of night lighting. The man in a security guard's uniform sitting behind the large, curved desk looked up nonchalantly from his book. He was visibly surprised to see two ambulance staff walking towards him.

"Good morning. We're here to pick up Joanna Smith. Is she ready?"

The guard said nothing but started to study the large logbook spread out in front of him.

"There's nothing here about a pickup. You'll have to wait till the nurse gets back."

Richard hoped the guard hadn't spotted the panic he could sense in Victoria's response. "We can't wait. We're on a very tight schedule."

"She'll only be a minute. She just popped to the toilet and asked me to sit here until she got back."

Even before he finished speaking, they could hear the rhythmic clicking of heels approaching their position. Victoria seemed to recover her composure.

"These guys are here for a pickup."

"There's no pickup scheduled." The nurse who appeared looked to be about forty and was wearing the rank insignia of a ward sister. "We don't do night-time pickups here."

"We're here for Joanna Smith. She's being transferred to the South London," said Victoria with all the authority she could muster.

"Why would she be going to South?"

"I have no idea, Sister. My job is just to take her there." Victoria pulled the papers out of the inside pocket of her uniform and held them out. The nurse walked past Victoria, refusing to take any further part in this conversation before she was back in her rightful position behind the desk. The security guard stood to let her retake her seat and shuffled off to the side. Once back in place, the sister reached out her hands for the documents, which she studied intently.

"This is most irregular," she muttered to herself, ensuring that the three people around her could all hear.

"But the papers are in order."

"They appear to be. But I will check."

Richard hoped that no one else could see the small beads of sweat that appeared on Victoria's brow as the nurse started to operate the computer terminal on her desk. She tapped away, referring frequently to the details on the documents. The procedure seemed to take an eternity. Eventually, without looking up from the screen, the nurse picked up the telephone. Victoria put out a hand onto the wheelchair to steady herself.

"John, it's Susan. Sorry to bother you. Can you go to registry for me? I need the records of Joanna Smith so she can be transferred. ... Yes, I know. But it's all in order. Just nobody bothered to let us know. ... Thanks." She put the phone down and turned to Victoria. "She's on Hindenburg. Bed seven. Take my drug key." The nurse unclipped a small key on a long plastic chain from her belt and stretched her arm out towards Victoria. "Hindenburg is down that corridor, then turn right."

"Thank you." Victoria nodded to Richard to follow, and they set off in the direction the sister had indicated.

Hindenburg ward was a collection of eight beds, only three of which were occupied. In the far corner a shape lay under the bedclothes, completely obscured from view, but far too large and snoring much too loudly to be a young girl. Two beds closer to them an old lady was sitting up, the large hospital headphones clamped to her ears. She showed no sign of life, let alone wakefulness. On the other side of the ward, in the bed closest to the window, Richard could see the pale face of a girl, with a halo of dark curly hair down to and beyond the white sheet, which gave the impression that the head was not connected to the slight body below it. Victoria checked the clipboard at the end of the bed and removed the record sheet attached to it. Richard had no understanding of medicine but interpreted the fact that all the graphs on the page were climbing steadily as a good sign. He moved back into the doorway to keep lookout as Victoria roused the girl. He could hear her loud whisper behind him, punctuated by what he assumed was a gentle shaking. After a few moments Richard turned round to see the girl sitting on the edge of the bed, rubbing her eyes with the backs of her hands, while Victoria emptied the few items out of the bedside cabinet into the container on the back of the wheelchair. Even in this light, the girl looked frail. He was concerned about her chances of coping with the rigours which Richard imagined to be ahead, based on his own trials of the last week.

Victoria gently lifted the girl from the side of the bed and lowered her into the wheelchair. Despite the pain evident from the sharp wince as she was moved, the girl didn't make a sound. Victoria looked towards Richard and pointed to the blanket folded at the end of the bed, while she herself moved towards the small wooden cupboard over the bedside cabinet and took out the key she had been given by the sister.

With a final check along the corridor, Richard moved towards the wheelchair, picked up the blanket, and crouched down to put his head at the same level as the girl's as he covered her up. Her blank stare didn't flicker as his head came into view, and his attempt at a smile remained unanswered.

"Follow me." Victoria marched officiously out of the ward and down the corridor the way they had come. As they emerged into the reception area, Richard turned left, pushing the wheelchair towards the exit, and halted just far enough away from the door not to trigger its mechanism, while Victoria completed the transaction with the sister, returning the drug key and signing the logbook.

"We can't find her medical file. Registry only works from nine to five. We'll forward it on in the morning." Victoria nodded her assent.

By the time the hospital's entrance doors slid apart to release them, Michael was holding open the rear door of the ambulance, and the wheelchair ramp was already extended. Victoria subtly moved Richard aside and then pushed the wheelchair up into the blue glow of the ambulance's interior. Michael expertly stowed the ramp and closed the door behind them, before he and Richard returned to the front seats.

The exhilaration which Richard felt was not reciprocated by Michael, who looked even more tense than he had all evening. Richard felt he ought not to interrupt the driver's concentration as he drove quickly, but within the speed limit, down the dark road. As they pulled out to overtake the only other vehicle on the road, Richard looked to his left to see who else was passing through the Hampshire countryside at one o'clock in the morning. He just had time to re-read the warning sign on the back of the van as they drove past it. It really did say *Caution Bears.*

In the distance he could see a rapidly brightening glow of artificial lights on the horizon. He started to make out the tell-tale outlines of hangars and the control tower before the shapes of the aircraft themselves became discernible. The ambulance pulled into a large parking area about half a mile from the airport where they pulled up just a few feet behind a heavy goods vehicle. Michael immediately turned out the lights but again left the engine running. They waited in silence. After a couple of minutes, a man walked towards them from the truck. Michael wound down the window to its full extent before reaching inside the top of his green ambulance service overalls, extracting a large, overstuffed envelope which he handed through the window. The man counted the wad of notes. Michael addressed Richard for the first time since their visit to the hospital.

"This is where we leave you. By the way, he is called Joseph. Now go round to the back of the ambulance. And good luck."

Michael was gripping the steering wheel as if his life depended on it, which Richard took as a sign that a handshake was not in order. He opened the passenger door and walked round to the back of the ambulance in total darkness. He reached for the handle on the ambulance's back door but hesitated a second before opening it. As he pulled it towards him, a pool of bluish light spilled onto the tarmac.

"Get inside quickly and close the door behind you. Then take off the overalls." The gentleness of the tone belied the strictness of the command, but Richard did as he was asked. As the door closed, the light changed back to the harsh brilliant white.

"Rebecca, this is Richard. He is going to look after you." Richard turned slowly to face the girl who had just been introduced to his back. Victoria had changed her out of the white hospital gown into the clothes she had taken from the bedside cabinet, and over it all a bright red coat.

"He's from New York, just like you." Richard sat on the side bench seat and smiled at Rebecca for the second time. This time there was a glimmer of a response.

"She's been sedated," Victoria continued. "Most of the drugs she was given were to keep her quiet. You should take these two with you." Richard looked at the small brown bottle and slightly larger cylinder that Victoria was trying to press into his hand.

"The tube is antibiotics. You should give her one of these at night and one in the morning after food. There's enough left for three days. The bottle has painkillers in it. They are very strong so if she needs them, only give her one, and never more than three in a day. Got that?" Richard nodded. He jumped slightly as he felt the cold on the back of his hand where the girl had reached out to touch him. He turned to see her smiling. It could have been a trick of the light, but he had the impression that there was more colour in her cheeks than when they had left the hospital an hour earlier. He smiled back and she released his hand, slumping back into the wheelchair.

"She's exhausted, poor thing. She'll be all right after she's got enough sleep. But for the moment you'll have to carry her."

"Where are we going?"

"Didn't Michael tell you?"

Richard shook his head.

"You're flying to Lisbon with the circus. Because of the animals the plane has to stay low so that the cargo hold doesn't depressurise. And it's heated. This is an established smuggling route. They have been well paid to get you to Portugal. The circus people have an arrangement with the customs in Lisbon, so their cargo is never checked. Someone from the Portuguese resistance will meet you after you arrive. One more thing." Victoria put her hand in her pocket and pulled out a small wad of banknotes, which she handed to Richard. His natural instinct was to decline the offer, but after a moment's consideration, he realised there was no practical alternative. He pocketed the money with just a simple word of thanks.

She turned her gaze from Richard to take a last look at the little girl. "Take care of her. And get her safely back to her family. Is there anything else you need to know?"

Richard suppressed the desperate urge to ask the stream of questions running around in his brain and shook his head.

Victoria's tone changed as she turned back into the efficient administrator she was for most of her life. She was not cold, just not warm, and the memories of their night together seemed to belong to a distant age, a lifetime ago. "Pick her out of the chair. You're going to have to get used to it sooner rather than later."

He felt Victoria's concentrated gaze evaluating his performance, as he worked out how best to get his arms around the sleeping girl and avoid the sharp pain he had seen on her face the last time she had been picked up. She moved easily as he wrapped one arm behind her back before slipping the other underneath her legs and gently lifting. He was surprised how light she was, and how hard the bones felt beneath the thin flesh. As he rested her against his chest, her head snuggled naturally under his chin and her arm wrapped itself around his neck, even though she showed no sign of being awake. Victoria opened the door of the ambulance behind him. He steadied himself as the change in the light momentarily disturbed his balance, before backing gingerly out of the vehicle. When he stepped onto the tarmac, he felt a rough hand grip his arm.

"Hurry. We're running late."

As Richard turned, he saw the man who had taken the envelope. He smelled strongly of sweat and garlic, and his accent sounded vaguely eastern European. He led them away from the back door of the ambulance. Looming in front of them was the shape of a large van. Richard realised why it looked familiar. The words *Caution Bears* split down the middle as the man pulled open one side of the door. Richard froze until the man pushed him in the middle of the back, not hard enough to make him move, but forcefully enough to make it clear this was not a request.

The inside of the van was in total darkness. He could feel the straw under his feet as he stumbled inside and imagined he could hear a rustling and grunting coming up from the ground just beside him. Taking care not to jolt the sleeping girl on his shoulder, he took another tentative step.

A light shone from behind him, and Richard's peripheral vision caught the movement of the black shape to his right as the bear shifted its position. As the light moved, he was reassured by the faintest glint of its reflection from the cage bars.

"Sit down against that wall, and don't get close to the bars," Joseph said.

Richard let himself down to the ground one knee at a time

before shuffling himself into position with his back against the wall. A couple of seconds after the slam of the door, the engine juddered into life, and they moved off.

It was only about five minutes before the van came to a halt again. Richard could hear the clanking of gates and the discussions about paperwork as they negotiated their entrance to the airport. When the rear doors opened again after a few minutes, they were in the airport's cargo area. Bright eyes were staring at him intently from behind the cage bars, but something inside Richard told him this was a look of curiosity rather than anger or hunger. The girl on his shoulder hadn't moved or made a sound during the brief journey. Richard was suddenly overcome by the pain of cramp in the back of his left leg. He staggered jerkily and gingerly to his feet and the bear mirrored his movements, letting out an irritated growl as the head on top of its eight-foot body thumped against the five-foot roof of the van. Richard stepped towards the van's doorway, and with just a brief glance to either side, jumped down onto the tarmac.

A few yards to his left three men were huddled. Richard immediately recognised Joseph, but not the other two who were wearing peaked caps on top of their uniforms. The circus man looked up momentarily. The eerie quiet of the night was suddenly broken by a crunch of gears. Richard stepped to one side to peer around the van in the direction of the new noise. As he turned, the sight took his breath away. Less than ten yards in front of him was the cavernous gaping mouth of the Blohm & Voss Pelikan, the cargo hold of the world's largest aircraft.

Joseph moved towards him while the other two men turned to face Richard. He could now clearly see that the one in just a shirt was wearing the uniform of a pilot, while the other had on the jacket of a customs official, the English flag on his shoulder overshadowed by the spread eagle clutching the swastika as if about to drop its bomb load. Richard followed as Joseph started to marshal the trucks into the aircraft. For the first time he could see into the nearside of the cargo hold. Tucked against its left wall, partially shrouded in tarpaulins, were two battle tanks, one green and one in sand-coloured camouflage.

An hour after their arrival at the airport, the vehicles had all been secured. The roaring of the lions had subsided as soon as their late-night snack of several pounds of beef had been thrown into their transporter. The look of fear in the whites of the elephant's eyes, its legs securely lashed to stop it running into the sides of its van, must have made quite an impression on Richard, because Joseph had to pull him away as they finished their work.

"It's mostly down to her that we have to fly. She hates travelling by boat, and it can take up to three days to get to Lisbon. These transport planes are never full, so we get a good rate. And fortunately, we get to fly up front."

Richard joined the circus troupe as they trudged towards the stairway. At the top of the steps, they picked their way carefully behind the last of the leather crew seats. He squeezed Rebecca closer to him, determined not to brush against any of the dozens of switches and levers that were passing inches away from his shoulders and elbows. Immediately behind the crew area was a pair of benches against the side walls. These, and two further rows of seats running across the width of the hull, provided space for about twenty passengers. Richard strapped himself into a seat with his one free hand, pulling the seat belt to its full extent in order to pass it over Rebecca's body as well as his own.

As the first pair of the eight huge jet engines burst into life, Richard heard the co-pilot asking the control tower of Southampton airport for permission to taxi. It struck him as strange that these two Englishmen were speaking German to each other. Once they were cleared to roll, the pilot powered up the second pair of engines, which made any conversation between those who were not wearing headphones completely out of the question. The aircraft reached the end of the runway and halted. All the remaining engines were switched on in rapid succession and the noise inside the extended cockpit became deafening. He felt a lurch as the brakes were released, and the girl on his shoulder shifted uncomfortably. He wondered whether she could possibly be sleeping through this unbearable noise. As the plane picked up speed the vibration started. The coiled wires on the intercom handpieces hanging from the cockpit roof danced wildly in unsynchronised directions, and he felt as if his teeth were being shaken from his head. From his seat, Richard could see directly through the front window. The white lines, picked out of the darkness by the aircraft's lights, were flashing ever more quickly underneath them until they suddenly disappeared as the pilot rotated the nose into the air. One second later, the noise level dropped sharply and suddenly. Richard's final view of England was the orange lights beneath the aircraft as it banked gently. He could clearly make out the dividing line between the orange coast road and the blackness of the sea. He later had no recollection of how he had managed to sleep through the noise and buffeting as the aircraft flew low across the Bay of Biscay and the north of Spain. His next memory was the solid thud of sixteen wheels hitting the concrete of Lisbon airport's runway in the moments before dawn.

Lisbon – August 1941

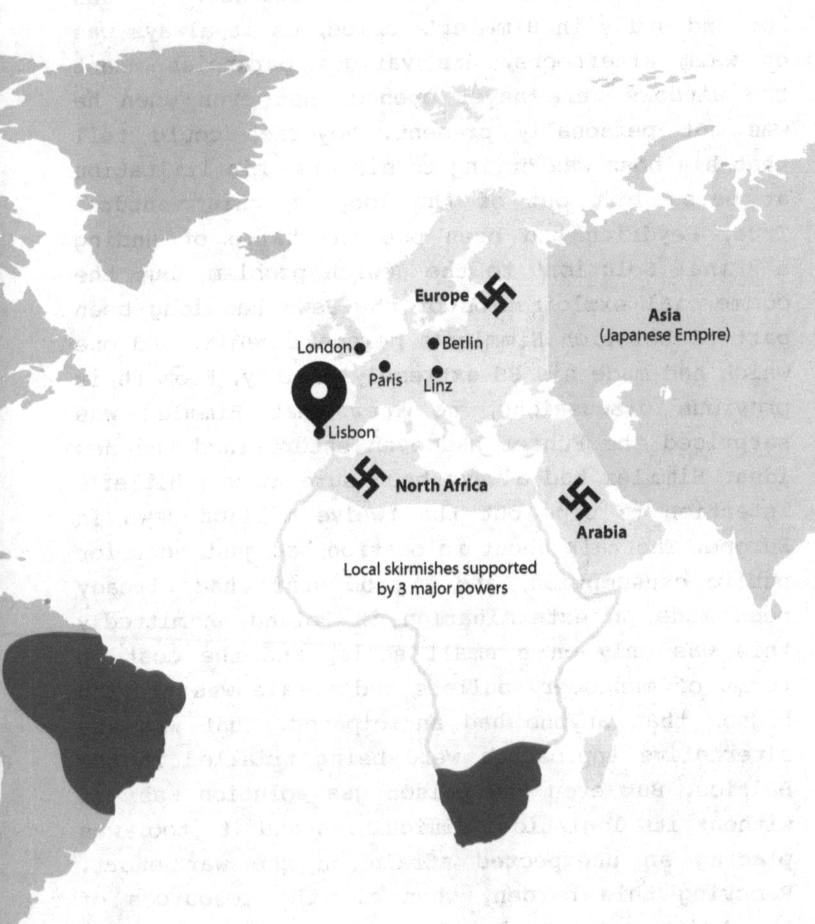

CHAPTER FIFTY-THREE

"What did the Führer say, Herr Heydrich?" It was hot and stuffy in Himmler's office, as it always was on warm afternoons. His various paranoias meant the windows were never opened, not even when he was not personally present. Heydrich could tell that his boss was trying to disguise his irritation at being left out of the loop on this venture. True, Heydrich had been put in charge of finding a 'Final Solution' to the Jewish problem, but the commercial exploitation of the Jews had long been part of Heinrich Himmler's personal remit, and one which had made his SS extremely wealthy. From their previous discussions, he knew that Himmler was surprised the Führer had even entertained the new idea. Himmler had always been sure it was Hitler's intention to wipe out the twelve million Jews in Europe. The talk about relocation had just been for public consumption, and a good start had already been made on extermination in Poland. Admittedly this was only on a small scale, and the cost in terms of manpower, bullets and morale was proving higher than anyone had anticipated. That was why alternative approaches were being trialled in the Baltics. But even the poison gas solution was not without its logistical difficulties and it, too, was placing an unexpected strain on the war effort. Removing this burden, when all the resources of the Reich were needed for the on-going invasion of the Soviet Union, would clearly bring military benefits, but at the cost of a major compromise to the ideology.

"He has given very clear parameters for the

negotiation, Herr Reichsführer. The Americans can have the Jews, if they do not want us to find another way of removing them from Europe, but they must take them all, and they must pay for each one."

"How much?" Himmler's mind was working through the twelve-million-times table, wondering where all this money would be directed.

"That is not a major issue, sir. We have a target value for each individual, but it is the principle which is important, so we would settle for just a token payment for each one, if that was where the negotiation ended up." Heydrich was struggling to suppress any visible sign of the joy he felt at being able to treat his superior's concerns so flippantly. He looked straight into Himmler's eyes before continuing. "The second key item is a complete stroke of genius from the Führer. He was concerned how we could keep track of these Jews and decided that the Americans would have to register them, so that they knew where they all were in the future. While he was working through this idea, he hit upon his master plan. Because the Americans believe that the Jews create economic wealth, the USA will benefit in the long term from taking them. It is, therefore, only right that we should share in the benefit. So, in future, the USA will have to pay the Reich a percentage of the profit from every Jewish business."

Heydrich stopped to let the full significance of Hitler's idea sink into the mind of his superior.

"Brilliant. *Judensteuer!* A Jew tax!"

"Exactly. But that creates a major challenge. Politically I cannot see how that would be acceptable to the American people. We expect that their government will want to keep it secret. That also suits the Reich. It avoids giving the impression that, by placing a value on the Jews, we are acknowledging they are valuable. We anticipate that the secrecy will suit everyone."

"But all of this only works if America stays out of the war."

"Yes, and that is the other major area for discussion. The American people do not want war, especially when that means joining forces with the communists. But their president is edging them ever closer towards it. Roosevelt is breaking every international law by ordering his ships to attack our ships without declaring war, and he is planning all this with Churchill. Roosevelt and Churchill are the only reason the two countries want to fight us, because neither is our natural enemy."

"How much has Roosevelt already been told?"

"He has been told that Germany does not want to fight America, but that Japan does and is confident of a rapid victory. Some American analysts think the Japanese have advanced weapons, and we have been encouraging that view. They now believe we keep sending our top scientists to Tokyo to share ideas. Roosevelt knows we can stop Japan attacking America if we choose. So, in return, America must agree to stop all support for Europe immediately."

"But the American president will never agree to that because of his relationship with Churchill," Himmler said.

"Exactly. And that leads to the final part of the plan. While I am meeting the former US ambassador to Britain in Lisbon, one of our agents will assassinate Winston Churchill."

Himmler was silent a long time before responding.

"I don't believe it! Just sending someone to London to kill Churchill won't work. This has been discussed several times already."

"That was my view also, Herr Reichsführer. But someone had proposed this plan to the Führer a month ago, and he believes it will work. He has decided that now is the time to put it into action. When Roosevelt hears of Churchill's death, he will tell his envoy Kennedy to agree to America staying strictly neutral."

"Amazing. When do you leave for Portugal?"

"Tomorrow morning, Herr Reichsführer."

CHAPTER FIFTY-FOUR

The armour-plated black Mercedes pulled up directly outside the main entrance of Lisbon's Avenida Palace Hotel. The whole of Lisbon's substantial community of spies would recognise the car as belonging to the German embassy, but none of them was yet aware that its occupant was SS-Obergruppenführer Reinhard Heydrich, the overall head of the Third Reich's security services. The true details of this visit had not leaked, and the cover story of another attempt to entice Portugal's President Salazar to join the German cause, was as credible as it was futile. The wartime traffic in goods, information, secret agents and refugees, which was so enriching the less scrupulous elements of Lisbon society, was not generating any substantial revenues or benefits for the government or the vast majority of its people. However, having spent three years as neighbours to one of the most brutal civil wars in history, and the last two as an outsider spectating on its larger brother raging its way across Europe, the Portuguese people had no appetite for a war. Their leader was also convinced of the benefits of avoiding it.

The tall blond man who emerged from the car, a slim leather case clamped under his left arm, would have been instantly recognisable from his widely circulated image had he been wearing his uniform. But the business suit, combined with the fact that he was believed to be permanently in or between Berlin and Prague, created an adequate disguise.

The equally blond, though not quite as tall man was sitting on the sofa facing the hotel's main entrance. He struggled to his feet, the stick provided to assist him in such manoeuvres languishing, as it always had, in the bottom of his Berlin wardrobe. This slight delay allowed the hotel's duty manager to reach his new guest first. His greeting was unceremoniously brushed aside as the tall man spotted his subordinate, whom he had never previously seen out of uniform. No words were needed as the former navy man led his boss up the staircase, turning left at the top and stopping outside the third door on the left to retrieve the key from his pocket. The head of the Nazi security apparatus stopped a few inches behind him and surveyed the corridor. At the far end a man he didn't recognise, in an unseasonal beige raincoat, had snapped to attention as the two men stopped in front of the door. Turning on his heel, Heydrich confirmed the presence of his counterpoint at the other end of the corridor. This second man painted a completely different picture. The lack of a coat betrayed the slight bulge under the left side of his jacket, but his nonchalant seated pose in no way reflected the presence of the fifth most important man in the Reich, whose life he was well used to protecting.

The sharp snap of the lock brought Heydrich's attention back to the room, and he followed von Graber inside. The curtain, which had been drawn across the single window when von Graber had first checked the room at six that morning, was more effective at keeping out the light than the stifling heat of a Lisbon summer. Heydrich's security detail had insisted on all the car's windows remaining closed for the brief drive from the airport, and for once he had chosen not to object. The stuffiness of this room was a different matter. He marched towards the curtain, flinging it open before deftly releasing the catch on the sash window and pushing it up to its full extent. The low hum of traffic, which started like a radio being turned on, belied the proximity of the main road just below. Heydrich leaned against the wall to survey the scene outside, looking briefly like one of the thousands of minions he employed across the Reich to stand and watch.

"Did you have a good flight, Herr Obergruppenführer?" Heydrich ignored the question, but in truth, any flight which he didn't personally pilot was an experience more unnerving and uncomfortable than he would ever be able to admit. But the Führer had made it very clear that he didn't want his top people taking unnecessary risks. Rudolf Hess's flight had been the last such escapade that Hitler had sanctioned, and that was clearly a special case. Hess had insisted his plan would only work if he flew to Scotland alone, and he was probably right. The two of them went back a very long way. The relationship which the Führer had with Hess was quite unlike that with all the other Nazi leaders. Apart from the Führer, only Willy Messerschmitt had known about the plan, because someone had to provide a suitable aircraft and flight briefing. But even Messerschmitt was unaware of the flight's key role in the plan for bringing the war with Britain to an end, by having Hitler's representative on the spot for when the time came.

"When does the American arrive, von Graber?"

"He is already in Lisbon, Herr Obergruppenführer. His plane arrived from London last night, and he went straight to the United States embassy. He is due here at two o'clock, one hour from now."

"Good. Very good. You will translate."

"I am sure he will bring one of his own people as well, Herr Obergruppenführer."

"That's as maybe. But when he becomes aware of the sensitivity of what we are discussing, he may choose to send anyone else away. That is what we shall assume."

"Very well, Herr Obergruppenführer."

"The room has been checked?"

"Yes, Herr Obergruppenführer. I checked it for listening devices myself just before your arrival. But we will need to close the window before we start."

"Even better. It will be good to watch him sweat. I take it you are fully conversant with the details of our discussion. There can be no ambiguities. The American must understand exactly what we are telling him."

"You can rely on me, Herr Obergruppenführer."

Heydrich stared at his aide in silence. Since that first meeting, when the young navy man had told of his reservations about the Abwehr intelligence department, his new boss had indeed found him to be completely reliable. But this meeting was likely to prove pivotal in the outcome of the war. And the details of the proposal were so secret that less than a dozen people in the whole of the Reich were aware of them.

"Good. Very good. We will start off by asking about their relationship with Japan. Until Foreign Minister Ribbentrop mentioned it to them a week ago, they had no idea Japan was considering an attack. They will have spent the week checking that out. We have made sure their FBI will hear the rumours about the long-range weapons under development."

"I hadn't heard anything about their plans to drop plague bombs on San Francisco, Herr Heydrich. Do they really think they can make that work?"

"I have no idea, von Graber. They have asked us for some technical assistance on airships, but the Americans have no way of knowing how advanced they really are. Still, that is something we need not concern ourselves with today, so long as the Americans believe it is possible. Then, as a next step, we need to convince them that Germany can persuade the Japanese to transfer their interest to the Soviet Union instead of the United States. The scale of our victories so far on the Eastern Front should make that easy. The Japanese must now be thinking that Russia will prove a far easier target than America. What is the latest you have heard from Tokyo?"

"The emperor seems to like the idea of attacking Russia instead, sir, but there is some resistance from the Imperial Navy. They want to exploit the power of their aircraft carriers and think they will lose face if they have to abandon their plan. It was the navy that persuaded the emperor to move away from their original intention to attack Russia. They believed America isn't geared up for war, so it would be an easy victory."

"I see. We should remind the Japanese that Germany made precisely that mistake in 1917. So, when we have explained all this to the American, we will talk about the Jews. Today we need to give them food for thought and get agreement in principle. Then we can come back to the subject in more detail tomorrow. We will explain our dilemma. How are we to achieve the Führer's stated intention of removing all the Jews from Europe? Our initial efforts to persuade them to emigrate before the outbreak of war were only a limited success. We have no idea how much the Americans know about our current thinking, so we need to make sure they realise we are serious. The photographs will help."

"Will they believe we are prepared to shoot or gas several million Jews, Herr Heydrich? Such a massive undertaking hardly seems credible."

"I know. But the Führer has been true to his word so far. And many doubted him before."

"But surely they won't be able to agree to that today?"

"No. Of course not. Today we aim to get agreement on the basic friendship pact. This means the United States will stay out of the war in Europe, and, in return, Germany will agree to support the United

States if it is attacked by the Soviet Union or Japan. And don't forget that the Americans hate the communists almost as much as we do. The Jewish question will be a separate protocol to the treaty. For today this protocol will just commit the United States to considering how it can assist Germany in achieving its objective of a Jew-free Europe. The actual agreement and details will be dealt with later."

"But you think they will sign the basic treaty today? What about the so-called special relationship between Roosevelt and Churchill?"

Heydrich looked at his watch. "I agree, that is the major stumbling block. However, I believe we have the matter well in hand."

"But will they trust us? I mean, the last friendship pact we made was with the Soviet Union."

"I think the Americans will understand that was a special case. And never underestimate personal motivation, von Graber. Kennedy is a very ambitious man. Once he understands how we can help him personally, I think we will be able to count on his enthusiastic support. If that's all, von Graber, get me a coffee."

CHAPTER FIFTY-FIVE

CHURCHILL AIRCRAFT CRASHED STOP PREMIER
FEARED DEAD STOP KING INFORMED STOP
EMERGENCY CABINET MEETING CALLED END

Joseph Patrick Kennedy's face went white. The silence in the small conference room of Lisbon's Avenida Palace Hotel was compromised only by the ice cubes in his drink rattling against the glass as his hand started to shake. He put the glass down and tightened his grip on the note his aide had just brought in. The tall blond man sitting across the table from him was completely expressionless. The former American ambassador to Great Britain consulted his watch. Half past three in the afternoon, or more importantly, half past ten in the morning in Washington DC.

"You will have to excuse me, Herr Heydrich. I need to make a phone call. May I suggest we reconvene at four thirty?"

Heydrich stood up sharply from the table and nodded his agreement. Despite his fluency, he hadn't spoken English until now.

"Please give the president the Führer's very best regards, Mr Kennedy." He remained standing and watched the American walk unsteadily out of the room. Not for the first time — not even for the first time that day — he marvelled at the genius of their leader.

Lisbon – November 2024

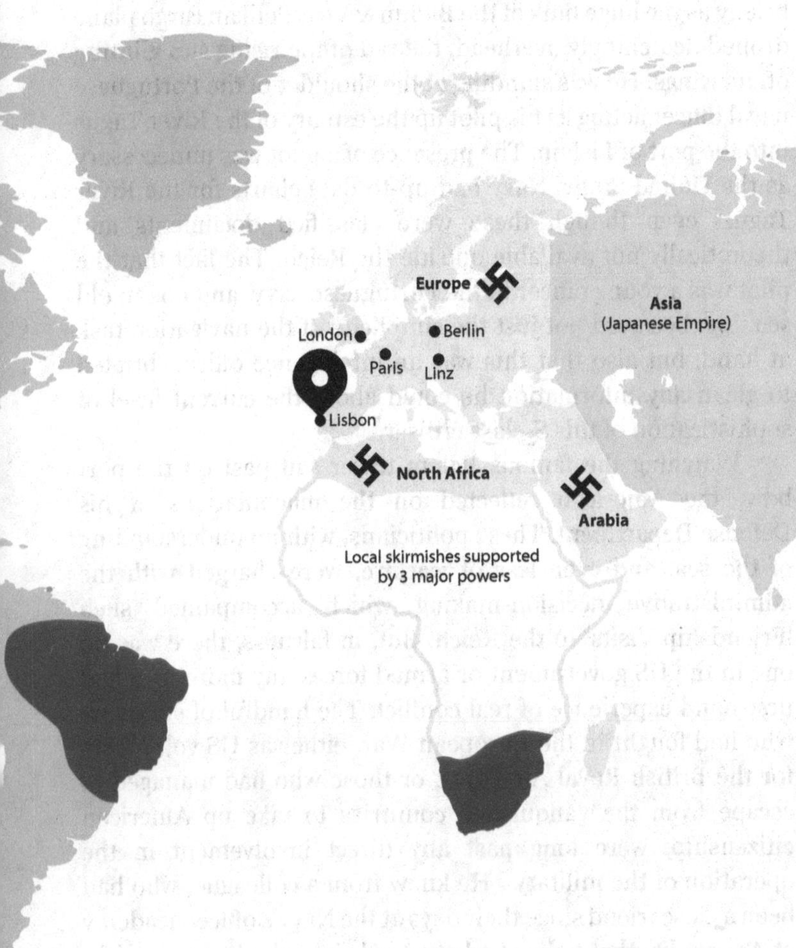

CHAPTER FIFTY-SIX

Captain Brian Callaghan of the United States Navy glanced up briefly as the huge bulk of the Blohm & Voss Pelikan cargo plane droned deafeningly overhead, the red of the rising sun glinting off its wings. He was standing at the shoulder of the Portuguese naval officer acting as his pilot up the estuary of the River Tagus into the port of Lisbon. The presence of a pilot was unnecessary as the United States Navy had up-to-date charts for the River Tagus, even though these were classified documents and theoretically not available outside the Reich. The fact that the pilot was a young officer in the Portuguese navy, and not an old sea dog, betrayed not just the simplicity of the navigation task at hand, but also that this was an intelligence officer, briefed to glean any information he could about the current level of sophistication of this S-class cruiser.

Watching the famous Belem tower sail past on the port bow, the American reflected on the machinations of his Defense Department. These politicians, with no understanding of the sea, and even less of warfare, were charged with the administrative decision-making which accompanied such 'Friendship Visits' to the Reich. But, in fairness, there was no one in the US government or armed forces any more who had first-hand experience of real conflict. The handful of survivors who had fought in the European War, either as US volunteers for the British Royal Air Force, or those who had managed to escape from the vanquished countries to take up American citizenship, were long past any direct involvement in the operation of the military. He knew from a colleague, who had been a close friend since their days at the Navy's officer academy at Annapolis, that policy had changed since the last such visit. His friend had captained the USS *Cuba*, the fast destroyer which had entered Hamburg eighteen months earlier, flanked by two fully armed escort vessels of the German *Kriegsmarine*. His friend's ship had represented the pinnacle of current American military hardware, bristling with the latest in armaments and satellite technology. There were two basic options: attempt to intimidate the Germans with your sophistication and firepower or keep them in the dark about the latest developments. His current command, the USS *Arizona*, definitely fell into the latter category. Last refitted eight years ago, she was due to be mothballed at the end of her current tour of duty. In her forty years on the high seas she had never fired a shot in anger at anything larger than a fishing boat caught smuggling. Captain Callaghan had seen the reports of last year's reciprocal visit of the destroyer *Hermann Göring* to New York. This was not even in the top level of what the German navy had to offer, when compared to the reputed speed and sophistication of the Bismarck-class cruisers, to say nothing of the sheer power of the Adolf Hitler-class aircraft carriers. But even this minnow of the German fleet could boast nuclear power and nuclear armament, both of which were only available in the submarine fleet of the US Navy. It seemed the defence planners had this time decided on discretion, inviting the Germans to guess what the Americans were currently developing, rather than seeing it for themselves.

His own men took over and manoeuvred the *Arizona* into her final berthing position on the quayside, while the captain escorted the pilot onto the deck, where they joined the majority of the crew, already standing at attention in their dress uniforms. The two officers took their positions, and the combined German and Portuguese military band on the quayside started to play. Senior officers of the German and Portuguese navies, together with the mayor of Lisbon and the German military governor of Portugal, processed up the gangplank for the formalities on board. The band continued to work through its repertoire – *Yankee Doodle Dandy* and the *Horst-Wessel-Lied* – as the parties exchanged greetings. This was followed by the three countries' national anthems, for the complete duration of which all those in uniform maintained their regime's standard forms of salute. The German government had long since given up any real hope of getting visiting military or dignitaries to perform the Nazi salute on such occasions, but they still always made a formal request, forcing their guests into a formal refusal.

Captain Callaghan was looking forward to the next two days. The non-stop round of parties and special events was a far cry from the mundane routine of sea patrols, and he knew his men felt the same way. He had always envied the social life his brother enjoyed in the diplomatic service, but, even on all his brother's travels, he had never yet set foot inside the German Empire. The captain just hoped that his men wouldn't disgrace themselves when allowed ashore. They had all been briefed on the treatment they could expect from the Nazi military police if they were to step out of line, but there were enough men aboard who relished the prospect of a fight for that to be a virtual certainty.

The US navy captain and his party stepped ashore to be whisked off to the first of several official receptions at Lisbon town hall. He left the ship in the capable hands of his Executive Officer, Lieutenant William Benedict, whose immediate task was to make the final preparations for the next party of official visitors. This group consisted of Nazi dignitaries and their wives, plus the press, including a television news film crew from the German Channel One, representatives of the major newspapers of Germany, Portugal, Italy, France and England, as well as a number of magazine journalists. The most presentable members of the crew had been carefully briefed on how to handle interviews – no politics, either American or Reich, and no military details, which basically left just the everyday life of an American sailor as the only topic of interest still in bounds. Following standard practice for such occasions, both sides had agreed that, as far as the press were concerned, none of the crew was Jewish. The one Jewish officer and nineteen men in the ship's complement of three hundred and sixty would not be allowed ashore and so formed the backbone of the skeleton crew which would guard the ship when the rest of the sailors were granted shore leave at the end of the day's formalities.

CHAPTER FIFTY-SEVEN

The virtual silence which followed their landing had woken Rebecca. Richard took the opportunity to shift her from his left shoulder, which felt like it had been irreparably damaged, onto the other side. She was now peering out of the front window of the aircraft, neither saying a word nor paying any attention to the people sitting around her. Richard looked forward, trying to discern what had caught her attention. He could make out nothing against the harsh white glare reflecting off the concrete of the airport's apron area, except for the slow progress of the flight of steps making its way towards them. It was weaving along the clearly marked pathways between the aircraft parking bays, even though none of these was occupied or showed any sign of impending activity.

"I'm hungry."

It was the first time he had heard her speak. Before Richard had time to think up a response, the man in front of them turned round to face her.

"Won't be long before we get breakfast. We've just got to unload the animals first. Do you want to watch?" Rebecca nodded, her hunger temporarily forgotten.

They climbed down from the aircraft, and Richard happily relinquished control of the girl to Joseph, who carried her while masterminding the unloading. Eventually he returned Rebecca, before crossing through the line of circus vans towards the airport official looking on from his small, prefabricated hut. Richard recognised the uniform as identical to the one in Southampton, except this time the eagle was about to drop its swastika onto the red and green flag of Portugal. He watched the transaction between them and wondered if it was the same overstuffed envelope he had seen changing hands the night before.

Joseph waved them over as he walked towards the cab of

the long truck. He opened the door and climbed in beside the driver, reaching down to lift Rebecca out of Richard's arms so that he too could get into the cab.

"Now, young lady, it's time to find some breakfast for you." Then, speaking over her head, he continued, "Your contact will be waiting for us there. It's about four kilometres from here." As if on cue, the driver eased the huge vehicle into gear, and it led the procession of circus people and animals towards the perimeter fence.

CHAPTER FIFTY-EIGHT

Richard must have been attuned to this secret life by now. As they sat over plates of cold meats, cheese, eggs and sardines, he had been certain that Joseph would indicate the stocky man in the brown overalls, who was sitting on his own against the window, as their next contact. When the Portuguese man stood up to leave, Richard also stood, lifted Rebecca back onto his shoulder, and without a word to the circus people, followed the man outside into the still heat of an autumn day.

The man climbed into a small, unmarked van, while Richard opened the right-hand door. He carefully placed Rebecca between the two of them on the bench seat, and the driver turned his face towards her with a huge grin. She smiled back and he tickled her under the chin with his bear-like paw. Richard expected the worst and was relieved as she giggled. Still without speaking a word, the driver set off. Richard and Rebecca watched in fascination as the life of Portugal's capital unfolded before their eyes. Men in brightly coloured shirts shouted across the narrow streets to each other, while wizened old ladies in black looked on disapprovingly. They drove past a bustling street market where everything imaginable was changing hands, from huge fruits to simple, shabby clothing, car tyres, and spare parts of every conceivable shape and size. Rebecca pointed through the front window as she caught sight of a vendor selling brightly coloured birds, housed in cages which were themselves mostly the colour of rust and looked uncomfortably small for their occupants. Eventually they came to a halt at the foot of an anonymous apartment building.

"We're there," the driver said as he opened his door and jumped down into the road with hardly a glance. His German was functional rather than fluent and clearly spoken without any relish. Richard opened the passenger door and stepped down onto the pavement, reaching back inside the van to pick up Rebecca.

"Please follow me."

A large carrier bag bearing the logo of a local grocery store in his hand, the Portuguese led the way towards the entrance, where he punched a four-digit code into a control panel before pushing the door open. Richard caught it as it swung back towards Rebecca's head, while the man set off in the direction of the block's solitary elevator. As they caught up with him, he was jabbing at the call button with his oversized thumb, showing increasing signs of frustration and desperation. He muttered something under his breath, before turning to face Richard with a dramatic shrug of his shoulders. He spun on his heel and stomped off three steps to a doorway which led to the building's well-trodden flight of stairs, up which he started to huff and puff with a noise more indicative of exasperation than effort. Richard picked Rebecca up onto his shoulder again and followed. The floor numbers were painted in huge bold red figures on every landing, starting with two. They reached number five and the van driver stopped outside the fourth door on the right, extracted the bunch of keys from his pocket, and opened it.

The apartment was dark and stuffy, permeated by a smell of stale sweat. Felipe Jorges, if the name on the apartment's doorbell was to be believed, put the bag of groceries on the floor in the kitchen. He then led them through to a side room which contained a small bed, piled high with boxes full of magazines, which he proceeded to move onto the floor.

"The girl sleeps here." They trooped out of the room behind him as he led the way back into the small kitchen. The sink was piled with unwashed dishes and wine glasses that betrayed either a recent party or a solitary drinker who washed up once a week.

Richard nodded in turn at the dumb show of kettle, refrigerator, cupboard with plates, drawer with cutlery and other cupboard with the remnants of Felipe's collection of glasses.

"Now I explain to you the plan." Felipe sat on one side of the small table and indicated Richard should take the seat opposite. Rebecca sat on the sofa by the window and settled down to sleep.

"There is a US warship here on a friendship visit. You will be on it when it leaves tomorrow night."

"How do we get on the ship? Won't the Germans be guarding it?"

"We've worked all that out. This afternoon I'm going to the reception at the town hall, where I'll finalise the arrangements with one of the American officers. You just have to stay here until tomorrow and make sure no one sees or hears you."

"Why are you doing this, Felipe?"

"Because I've been told it's vitally important that we help to get you back to America."

"No, that's not what I mean. What makes you work for the resistance?"

"Oh. That's a long story." He turned away from Richard's expectant face and padded into the kitchen. A couple of minutes later he returned, holding two glasses full of the local wine, identifiable by its slightly green tinge. He looked into Richard's face, on which the same expression was still fixed. Felipe must have accepted it was there for the duration, so he started to explain.

"The Nazis took away everything that mattered to me. They left me with nothing to live for. I will do anything I can to pay them back for that. However small. However dangerous."

"What did they do, Felipe?"

The Portuguese sighed heavily as he moved towards the armchair.

"My wife was knocked down by a Nazi officer. She was in the hospital for three days before she regained consciousness. The local police took a statement, and she told them what had happened. The officer was drunk and swerved to avoid a cat. He ended up running into her while she was standing on the pavement. Then he drove off, leaving her there. Somehow, she had managed to remember the registration number of the car. The next day one of the German police came and asked the same questions. He tried to bully her into changing her statement. She refused. That was the Thursday. I was there again on the Friday. I left her bedside for a couple of minutes to talk to the doctor. He said she was going to make a full recovery. As I was going back into the ward, I passed a German officer in the corridor. It struck me as odd, because there's a special hospital for Germans on the other side of Lisbon. When I got back to her bedside, she was dead."

"Oh, my God! What did you do?"

"There was nothing I could do. The doctor said that she had had a cerebral aneurysm, and that it was a result of the accident. He denied that he had told me she was getting better. The police arrested a Portuguese man for running her down, and he's still in prison."

"Isn't there someone you can go to? To get justice?"

"Justice isn't a word you often hear inside the Reich. Not unless it suits the Germans."

"So that's when you joined the resistance?"

"No. Like most people I decided there was nothing I could do against the power of the state, so I just carried on with my life. I knew that if I did anything, they wouldn't just punish me, they would punish our daughter as well."

"*Sippenhaft.* Your family shares the guilt for anything you do."

"That's it. And it's very effective. The only people who can take risks are the ones who are only putting themselves in danger."

"So, what changed?"

"My daughter's boyfriend got involved in something. They say he was smuggling arms into Portugal for so called 'enemies of the state'. Of course, he denied it, but once the Nazis think you're guilty of something, then you're guilty, and that's the end of it. He was arrested and held at Gestapo headquarters in Lisbon for a week. Then they came here in the night and arrested my Manuela. They took his parents too, and his sister, as well as the families of the other two members of what they called his gang. The three of them were hanged after a show trial. Then all the family members were put on a train for one of the labour camps in the east. Probably Poland or Russia."

"That's horrific. Where's your daughter now?"

Felipe took a deep breath before continuing. "They told me she had been shot while trying to escape. As far as I know, Rodrigo's family are still in the camp, but it makes no difference as nobody ever comes back." Felipe took another few sips of his wine in silence before standing up and putting the glass on the table.

"Okay, Felipe. What do we do while we're waiting?"

It took Felipe a while to understand what he was being asked, and a few seconds more to realise that he didn't really have an answer.

"I don't know. Eat. Drink. Watch television." Struggling for something else to say he continued, "I have some things for you. I may as well give you them now." He opened the door of the big cupboard which filled most of the side wall, and pulled out an old plastic holdall, which he placed triumphantly on the table between them. As Richard hadn't touched it by the time he sat down again, Felipe tipped its entire contents onto the table. There was a street map of the city, a tatty old English-Portuguese dictionary, a small wad of Reichsmark notes held together by an elastic band, and two credit-card-sized pieces of plastic. Richard reached for these and looked at the photographs on them. One showed a man of roughly Richard's age while the other was a young girl, but there the similarity ended. He looked questioningly at Felipe.

"Those are just so you can get the bus. Don't worry about the photographs. These are Portuguese identity cards, so if anyone asks for them, you're already in trouble. But they won't be reported stolen, so they're safe. Do you know how to use them?"

Richard had already noticed the small gold square embedded in the cards, just as they had been in Berlin and London, so he nodded.

"Good. I need to go now."

Felipe disappeared into what Richard assumed was his bedroom. A couple of minutes later he emerged, a waiter's uniform clearly visible under his coat.

As Felipe closed the apartment door behind him, Richard looked at his watch. He was not hungry, and Rebecca was fast asleep, so he decided it would be safe to catch up on the sleep he had missed during the night.

CHAPTER FIFTY-NINE

The blonde in the Gestapo uniform poked her sharp fingers into his shoulder then started to shake him. He tried to shrink away from her and turn over, preferring his prison cell to another session of drugs and questions. Her shaking became more insistent, and against his will, Richard opened his eyes. The glare of the light silhouetted the head hovering menacingly a few inches from his face. But the stern cropped hair had disappeared, replaced by the softer outline of tight curls through which the light diffused, capturing the tiny dust motes in a freeze frame.

"I'm hungry now."

Richard stood up and led the way into the kitchen.

"Okay. Let's see what we've got." Without a word, Rebecca started methodically emptying the contents of the grocery bag onto the kitchen floor.

"Is there anything there you like?"

She looked at the floor and pondered, as if seeing the items for the first time.

"Bread, bananas, tomatoes, cheese. I don't like fish out of tins. And we aren't allowed to have sausages at home."

"Well, at least we won't starve. So, what else aren't you allowed to eat, Rebecca?"

"Just sausages. And pork. And bacon, of course, but that's a type of pork. Do you eat pork?"

"I'll eat just about anything. What's your favourite food then?"

"I don't know. Since I got ill there are lots of things I haven't been able to eat."

"Like what?"

"Eggs. They make me sick now. And donuts. I used to like donuts, but it's ages since I had one."

"How about cheese and tomato sandwiches?"

Richard was surprised at how much the little girl ate. He thought her face already had more colour than when she had got off the aircraft that morning, and the fragile girl from the hospital had been totally transformed in a few hours. He retrieved one of the bottles of pills from his coat pocket and made her take one with the last of the orange juice they had found in the refrigerator.

"So, what would you like to do now, Rebecca?"

"Go home."

"No. I mean until Felipe comes back. He will be gone several hours. Do you want to watch TV? Are you tired?"

Rebecca frowned as she concentrated. "I don't know. What do you want to do?"

For the first time Richard realised how much this unlikely pairing had in common. He had no idea how to answer the question. He, too, just wanted to go home.

"Let's see if there's anything on the TV."

Rebecca sat herself on the sofa, watching as Richard tried to get the old television set to work and to understand how the remote control functioned. The third channel he found was showing a cartoon in which words were replaced by crashing noises and the sounds of its main characters, a cat and a mouse, chasing each other round a house. Thankful for the respite, Richard left Rebecca on the sofa. He returned when he heard a man's voice replace the soundtrack of fast music and crashes, to find the girl lying fast asleep. Her head seemed to be jammed alongside her shoulder at an impossible angle, so he picked her up and carried her into the small bedroom where he lay her on the bed and folded the covering over her.

To kill time, he started to study the map from the holdall, easily identifying their current location, the harbour and the main landmarks of the city centre.

CHAPTER SIXTY

"Get out. Now. We've been betrayed."

Felipe was on the point of collapse as he burst through the door into his apartment.

Richard rushed into the bedroom and shook Rebecca until she woke up. She resisted instinctively and momentarily but then sat upright.

"What's happening, Richard?" For the first time there was real fear in her eyes, reflecting what she could see in his.

"We have to leave right now. Put your coat on."

Rebecca got off the bed and picked up her coat. The hospital nightgown was hanging out of the pocket and Richard pulled it away, stuffing it into the holdall.

"Ready? Have you got your shoes on?" Rebecca nodded and he shepherded her towards the bedroom door.

"Where are we going?"

"I have no idea, Rebecca. I haven't worked it out yet." If she acts like an adult, she deserves to be treated like one.

They entered the living room just as Felipe was hanging up the phone. "They know you're here, and they know about this place." He was still sweating profusely. Richard didn't ask what would happen to him as he had a pretty clear idea, and he didn't want to upset Rebecca. Felipe was rummaging in the bottom drawer of the cupboard.

"This might help. It's all I can do for you now." Felipe handed Richard a sealed small brown envelope, little larger than an identity card. Richard slipped it straight into his pocket and looked at Felipe for an explanation.

"It should be self-explanatory. I don't actually know what it is. This was given to me as the last resort. I hope you can make good use of it. Now you must go. Take the elevator down to the second floor and then walk the rest of the way. Go out of the back door and stay in the shadows. It's a rabbit warren down there, so you should be able to give anyone the slip."

"Thank you, Felipe. And good luck."

"It's you that needs the luck now, Richard. You and Rebecca. God be with you." With this final greeting Felipe closed his apartment door.

The elevator arrived surprisingly quickly, and as they got in, Rebecca pushed the button marked two very hard. Richard jabbed repeatedly at the door close button. The screech sounded very loud, and the descent seemed impossibly slow. Richard fished the two identity cards out of the holdall. He put them in his coat pocket and took out the small envelope, which he ripped open. Inside were a key card for the Avenida Palace Hotel and a blank business card with a single handwritten line: *925SE*. He slipped them back into the envelope, which he returned to his coat pocket. Just as they reached the second floor Richard heard a sharp crack from somewhere above them. Rebecca looked up into his eyes questioningly, but he couldn't hold her gaze. He took her hand as the elevator door slid open.

The rear stairwell was deserted, amplifying the clatter of their footsteps. As they pushed the door into the courtyard behind the building, the cool evening air hit them. Richard had to think quickly. Whether to risk that the less-than-perfect identification cards had already been linked with the fugitives – meaning that boarding a bus or train would automatically result in it being raided by the police at the next stop – or to walk three miles from the outskirts of Lisbon into its centre with a sick girl. The sound of approaching sirens convinced him to risk using the cards. The area would be swarming with police within a few minutes, and as soon as they realised that the apartment block no longer contained what they were looking for, they would fan outwards from it and very quickly overtake two pedestrians.

He saw a bus on the other side of the street, so they ran across to the stop. Their luck held as the bus was heading into the city centre. He knew a bus or a tram was a far better option than a train – though the system recorded you getting on, it had no idea where you got off as you simply opened the doors and climbed down. The closed-circuit television, which recorded all movements on all of Lisbon's buses, would make it possible to identify where they had got off, but this would probably not be processed for several hours. With this in mind, Richard sat tight as they reached the square known as Rossio, dominated by the statue of a king standing on top of a huge white column. He looked out of the window again a minute later, watching as the large railway station and then their destination, the Avenida Palace Hotel, passed by on the left-hand side.

It was reassuring to note the complete lack of any police presence. At least any visible police presence. One person alighted at the railway station stop, and one passenger joined the bus at the following stop in the next square which contained another tall monument, this time in the shape of an obelisk. As they pulled away Richard whispered to Rebecca,

"We're getting off at the next stop." She reached across the aisle to press the red button. The indicator on the second electronic display lit up, confirming in Portuguese and German that the bus would indeed stop at Saint Joseph's church on Liberty Avenue. Richard's heart missed a beat as a smartly dressed man, carrying just a newspaper, moved from the front half of the bus to join them at the door. As they alighted and turned right to retrace their route, the other man turned left and continued down the avenue.

His journalistic experience had given him years of practice entering hotels where he had no business. The key was confidence. Just walk in as if you have the right to be there, and on no account hesitate. Even if you have no idea where you're going, you must keep moving with apparent purpose, not looking around or back. If you come to a dead end, it's much safer to hesitate while heading back towards the entrance rather than away from it. No one pays any attention to people leaving a hotel, just to those going in. He didn't need to tell Rebecca to keep quiet and stay close, because she already was. He just said, "Look happy," and squeezed her hand tightly as they stepped through the open entrance.

They strode confidently across the lobby of the Avenida Palace, avoiding eye contact with either the reception desk to the right or the concierge's station to the left. They headed directly for the main staircase, rather than the bank of elevators or the famously ornate bar area which reflected the glitz and glamour of Portugal's *belle époque* in both its decoration and its prices.

Once they reached the top of the main staircase, they were in a completely deserted corridor with deep-pile carpets and extravagant wall decoration. Richard hesitated before opting for right or left. The sign on the wall showed that all the rooms to the left were conference or meeting facilities bearing the names of historical figures ranging from the explorer Vasco da Gama to the eighties tennis star Carvalho, while those to the right were bedrooms. The rumble of a group about to exit one of the conference rooms forced his hand, and Richard pulled Rebecca to the right. There were about six rooms on either side of the corridor, and outside one of them was a chambermaid's cart – a common sight in the late mornings, but unusual at this time of day. They walked towards the end of the corridor and Richard slowed as he passed the room in which the chambermaid was working. A quiet singing could be heard, interrupted by the turning on of a tap. Satisfied that she was not about to leave the room, Richard started to explore the cart and soon found what he was looking for. On the side nearest the wall, out of sight of passing guests, hung the clipboard carrying the printout of that day's room cleaning schedule. Around ten of the room numbers were ringed in red ink, including 206, the number on the door beside him. Half of these had been crossed through. Richard took a deep breath and hoped that German logic had combined with the relaxed Portuguese attitude to life. If these were the late checkout rooms which were not needed that day for arriving guests, that would explain having a chambermaid on the evening shift. He memorised four of the ringed numbers which had already been crossed through and headed for the closest of them. At the end of the corridor was a stairwell. They went up one floor and moved along the corridor. Outside room 308 Richard stopped. They stood in silence for a moment. The hum of the air conditioning was just perceptible above the silence, before it was absorbed into the deep carpet of the hallway. Richard put his ear to the door but could hear nothing. He knocked loudly. If someone answered, he would trust to his instinct to come up with some excuse – his daughter had lost her doll, or some such lie. Still no sound. He took the key card out of its brown envelope and tried it in the door – slide into the slot and pull out quickly. A pinprick of red light flashed twice as the silence of the hotel was broken by a shrill, accusing bleep. One more attempt, this time pulling the card out slowly. The bleep sounded even louder this time as Richard thought he could hear movement further down the corridor towards the hotel's centre. Third time lucky?

The steady green light was followed by a reassuring click. Richard twisted the handle and pushed open the door. He signalled Rebecca to stand against the wall just inside the room and wait as he stepped silently inside, dropping the holdall to the floor to prop the door open. He poked his head quickly into the bathroom and the bedroom which led off this sitting room and rushed back to collect the girl and their bag, closing the door gently behind them. He slid the master key card into the slot by the door, and the desk and bedside lamps came on, rapidly followed by the television. He frantically hunted round for the remote control to do something about the ridiculously loud volume. Rebecca calmly stepped over to the set and pressed the on/off button, immediately restoring the silence. Richard turned round at this sudden change and, seeing the girl by the television, his face broke into a broad grin. She looked back at him with that cheeky, but captivating, smile.

"Are we safe now, Richard?"

"For the moment, yes, Rebecca. For the moment."

The receptionist ignored the red number 308 which flashed up on his console as he preferred to give his full attention to the pretty young lady he was checking in. The log printer in the duty manager's office chattered out the single line:

    Room 308. Unreserved. Servicing confirmed
    19.48 Occupied 20.36.

The duty manager was in the wine cellar with the head barman, trying to locate a case of premium French champagne that had gone astray. The log would wait until his handover meeting at eight the next morning.

Richard helped Rebecca put on her nightdress and covered her with the red coat.

"No one must know we've been here, so we need to keep the room perfectly tidy. Okay?"

She nodded, rolled over and closed her eyes.

Richard sat in the chair at the desk and took out the card which had been with the hotel key. He knew that looking at it again was unlikely to yield any new information, but he needed something, anything, to provide the inspiration to help him decode it. He turned the card over, held it up to the light, strained his eyes to find microscopic traces of other writing, but finally resolved that it was as simple, and therefore as complex, as it appeared: *925SE*.

He had instantly assumed that it referred to a meeting place to be used in the event of an emergency. On that basis 925 would be a time, meaning SE had to be a location. He had never been a great lover of puzzles, considering them just an opportunity for people cleverer than himself to show off. He stared at the card for an hour but made no progress.

He stood up to stretch the tension out of his arms, legs and neck, and checked on Rebecca, wondering what thoughts and dreams were going through that young head as he watched the peaceful sleep of the innocent. Resolving to stay calm and start again, going back to first principles, he took the street map of Lisbon out of the holdall, found a piece of notepaper and a pen, and sat himself back down at the desk, ready to doodle himself to a solution.

He studied the south-eastern corner of the map, then that quadrant of the city centre, before reviewing all the street names and metro stations for the right combination. Nothing.

A new thought entered his head. How would he be recognised? Then it struck him. There was something fundamental he had been overlooking. This had been intended for Felipe. The thought of Felipe made him shudder. A good, simple man who had decided to work against the Nazis, despite the risks and the frustration that there was probably little practical damage he could ever do them. Another addition to the list of people who had risked and possibly lost their lives to help him for reasons Richard himself could hardly fathom. He owed it to all of them to succeed. As well as to Rebecca. A defenceless, sick child whose only hope lay with him. A fate neither of them had chosen, but that was where they now were.

He started again with this new perspective but made

no further progress. He took another look at the map. In the bottom corner was a compass rose with the single letter N on the top of the most prominent point. N for north, in English, and clearly also in Portuguese. Frantically he grabbed the dictionary and looked up the points of the compass. North – norte, south - sul, east - leste, west - oeste. N, S, L and O. No E. So, the south-east idea, on which he had expended so much time and effort, was a complete red herring. He checked the ends of the dictionary for a section on abbreviations, to see if SE had some other significance in Portuguese. Again, he drew a blank. His head and eyes were aching, so he moved over to the armchair to give them a brief rest. He would just close his eyes for a couple of minutes.

CHAPTER SIXTY-ONE

He woke with a start as something soft brushed past his hand. Rebecca was standing next to him in her hospital nightgown, looking at one of the many paintings on the wall of their hotel room.

"Good morning, Rebecca. Did you sleep well?"

"Very well, thank you. How about you?"

"Not that well. I spent most of the night trying to do a puzzle."

"I love puzzles. What sort of puzzle was it?"

Richard levered himself stiffly out of the armchair, and picked the card off the desk, handing it to the little girl.

"Nine two five S E" she read it out slowly and deliberately. "Is it a secret meeting place?"

"I think so."

"Meet at S E at nine twenty-five. Where's S E, Richard?"

"That's what I spent most of the night trying to work out."

He looked at his watch in a sudden panic. It was already after seven.

"Get dressed, there's a good girl. We're going to have to get out of here before anyone finds us."

"And we need to be at the meeting place by nine twenty-five."

Exactly. But before that someone was going to have to work out where the meeting place was. Rebecca put her clothes back on and smoothed the bed covers, while Richard went back to the desk to try to pick up where he had left off with the map and his sheet of doodles.

When she had finished, she studied him carefully, hunched over the desk, his head in his hands.

"Can I help?"

"I wish you could. I really do." Polite adult speak for 'No. Go away and leave me alone.'

Silently she stepped away from him and worked her way round the other paintings and etchings on the walls. She had loved looking at the paintings in her grandfather's art books after she got sick and couldn't easily move from her chair. Many of the books were foreign, and she had tried to work out what the words underneath the pictures meant. Against the long wall of the hotel room was a group of four drawings of some of the major old buildings of Lisbon.

"S E."

"Yes, that's right, Rebecca. S E."

"S E."

"Yes, Rebecca."

"S E."

"I'm busy, Rebecca. Let me get on with this. We don't have very long."

"S E." She was almost shouting at him in frustration. "I've found it."

Richard spun round in the chair to look at her.

"Look, Richard. The church."

Richard followed her arm, pointing at one of the pictures on the wall. He walked over to her and peered at the inscription. '*Sé – duomo da Lisboa.*' Lisbon cathedral. He looked at his watch. It was just coming up to eight o'clock.

"That's it. You're a genius, Rebecca. Well done. Let's go and have a look at a cathedral."

Richard grabbed Rebecca's nightdress and all the items he had been working with on the desk and stuffed them back into the holdall. He screwed up the piece of paper with his notes on and threw it into the waste-paper basket. Holdall in one hand, Rebecca in the other, he looked out of the security peephole, opened the door a crack to listen for any movement in the corridor, retrieved the passkey, and took one last look at the room to check they hadn't left anything behind. As he turned to leave, something made him stop. He picked the scribbled page out of the waste-paper basket and put it in his pocket.

"Ready for a nice morning walk?"

"Can we have breakfast on the way?"

"I'm sure we can manage that. How are you feeling today?"

"Very well, thank you. The pain has almost completely

gone, and I have no difficulty breathing any more. I haven't felt this good in months."

He opted for the direct route and took the main elevator to the lobby. If they had taken the stairs, they would have passed the night duty manager who wanted to check on room 308 before clocking off from his shift.

Despite the darkness, the city was full of its morning bustle. For once they had the luxury of time and space, and Richard felt almost like a tourist, off to see one of the major sights of an exotic city. The young girl at his side would confirm that impression for the benefit of passers-by. From the mental map he now had of the centre of the Portuguese capital, he had already selected a route from the hotel to the cathedral which he felt would give them the best combination of remaining inconspicuous and having a selection of cafés to choose from. Richard was relieved that the girl showed no sign of tiredness even after half an hour, meaning they didn't have to risk their identity cards on the public transport system again.

The sky was starting to lighten as they entered the busy Praça do Comércio square, and Rebecca tugged on his arm. He looked down and she pointed at the building on the corner. A welcoming orange glow was emanating from a large café with tables inside as well as outside under the impressive arcade. Just under half of them were occupied with a complete cross-section of society. Richard approved of the choice and decided to add fugitives to the existing clientele of labourers, businessmen and tourists. He moved to go inside and felt a slight resistance in his arm. Rebecca wanted to stay at one of the outside tables, but Richard continued, and she quickly gave up her objection. They passed through the black façade with the huge glass windows and their gold leaf inscriptions, into a spacious interior with nearly twenty tables, mostly designed for two customers, but with one or two larger ones. The single customers seemed to be sitting or standing at the bar on the left-hand side. Opposite the entrance was a low counter over a glass display case showing off a bewildering array of local specialities, ranging from sliced meat and cheese sandwiches to cakes and pastries. Richard selected a table over to the right, against the side wall. From here he could keep an eye on the only entrance door, but without being readily visible to those passing by. While he remained standing next to the counter, he pointed to the selected table, and Rebecca went to sit herself on one of the chairs, watching him. He smiled at the girl, failing to notice the middle-aged woman behind the counter who was waiting to serve him, until she said something he didn't understand. His puzzled look was clearly something she encountered every morning, so the sweeping movement of her hand along the length of the display cabinet invited him to order.

"Einen Kaffee und eine kleine Orangensaft, bitte." He looked into the case. Tucked away in the bottom corner was a huge zinc tray of the small custard pies for which Lisbon was famous. He pointed at them.

"Wieviele?" It still sounded odd to hear German spoken with a Portuguese accent.

"Vier."

"Alles?"

"Ja."

She pointed to his table and Richard nodded and went to sit down, stuffing the holdall as inconspicuously as he could into the small gap between the table and the wall. They sat opposite each other in uncomfortable silence until the waitress brought over the coffee, the orange juice with a drinking straw and the small plate with the four pastries, which she deliberately put closer to Rebecca, giving the young girl a conspiratorial grin. Rebecca responded with one of her special smiles. The waitress slid the bill under the sugar bowl, before bustling cheerfully back to her station behind the counter. Rebecca looked at Richard with a smile of thanks.

"We can talk while the tables around us are empty, but we need to keep it quiet. And no names."

Rebecca took a long drink of her orange juice before speaking. She put the glass back on the table, wiped her mouth and whispered, "Who are we going to meet?"

"I really have no idea. Perhaps there will be no one there. We just have a time, but no date, so perhaps no one will come today."

"So, we would have to come back tomorrow?"

"Exactly." Richard took a look around all the tables to ensure no one was paying them any attention before continuing. "I hardly know anything about you, Rebecca. Tell me about yourself."

"Like what?"

"Have you always lived in that big house in New York?"

The little girl frowned, which made her nose wrinkle. "I think so. I don't remember any other house."

"What about school. Where's that?"

"It's about a mile away. We go in the car every morning and come back the same way."

"Do your brothers go to the same school?"

"Jacob does. But Salomon is older, so he goes to a different school."

"Who else lives in the house?"

"Martha. Grandpappy. And Mummy and Daddy, of course."

"What does your dad do?"

"You mean for a job?"

"Yes, Rebecca. That's what I mean."

"He works for a bank, so he's away a lot."

"Is it an international bank then?"

"No. It's in New Zealand. But daddy is in charge of America. He goes to New Zealand a lot. Every time he comes back, I get a stuffed animal. They have very strange animals there. And birds that don't fly." Richard kicked himself that he had never made the connection. He knew that David Levy was one of the most important figures in the world of New York finance but hadn't realised he was Samuel Levy's son. Since the end of the European War, New Zealand had managed to fill the gap left by the absorption of Switzerland into the Reich and had turned itself into the centre of confidential banking, both for the world's governments and for those rich enough to need to avoid their domestic taxes.

The localised silence returned as the chatter from the other occupied double tables in the room continued. Richard took a sip of the coffee – strong, hot and black, just what he needed any morning, but particularly this one. A movement in the doorway caught his eye and he looked up. He felt his jaw drop as a uniformed local policeman entered. Rebecca saw his reaction and turned to look at what had caused it. This brought Richard back to his senses, and he looked away from the door to a non-existent point above the girl's head. Rebecca took another sip of her orange before starting on the second of the pastries.

The policeman walked towards the bar area, greeted the owner with a gruff *"Bom dia"*, and leaned against the bar while the coffee he hadn't ordered was poured and placed in front of him. He was slowly casting his gaze around the room, reviewing each table in turn. Just before he worked his way round to Richard and Rebecca, a loud laugh in the doorway broke the spell. He turned his head to watch as four garishly dressed middle-aged ladies trooped in. To Richard's relief, they sat at the first table inside the doorway, keeping the policeman's gaze off his own quiet table. Richard turned towards the food counter to gauge the reaction of the waitress. Every new customer he had seen had gone up to her or to the owner to order, but these four were clearly expecting table service. Having defiantly delayed long enough to satisfy her own pride, but not so much as to cause serious irritation, the waitress picked up a small order block and pen and walked slowly towards the table. The ladies kept changing their order. In response to questions the waitress pointed towards the display case, answering in Portuguese to requests posed in German. In the end, the local won her minor victory. The Germans' desire to sample the local delights prompted one of them to accompany her back towards the case to point out a selection of the goods on offer. As this representative of the group moved to the counter, she got close enough to Richard's table for him to notice the plastic card hanging from a red, black and white ribbon around her neck. Inside a sunburst effect of red lines was the three-letter inscription of the state travel operator, KdF, below which was a colour photograph of the lady. He couldn't make out her name, printed in small type immediately below, but the bottom line of the badge was clearly visible – the name MS *Magda Goebbels* picked out in white block capitals against the red stripe. He looked across to the table to confirm that the other three ladies were wearing identical cruise-ship lanyards.

Richard turned back to Rebecca. Unable to speak, she was now waiting for him to indicate whether she was allowed another of the pies. He picked up one of the two remaining and grinned at her. Joyfully, she picked up the final custard tart and polished it off far more quickly than he did, before finishing the last of her juice and wiping her hands and face.

As the waitress returned to the Germans' table with a tray laden with coffee, sandwiches and pastries, Richard wondered how overweight these four would have been without the miracle slimming drug he had seen advertised on the television in Berlin.

He looked at his watch then checked the bill on the table. Eight Reichsmarks fifty. He fished a pale blue ten-mark note out of his pocket and left it under the saucer. Rebecca recognised her cue and slid off the chair.

They kept their heads down and started to walk past the policeman as casually as they could manage. They were forced to stop right next to him as a group of six sailors crowded in through the doorway, heading straight for the bar. Their leader stopped in his tracks as he noticed the uniformed policeman, towering over the girl in the red coat, but after a moment's hesitation, he led his shipmates towards the alcohol. Richard noticed the ribbon which bore the inscription *Danzig*, in the old gothic script which had fallen into disuse during the war and nowadays was only to be seen on the cap tallies of the German navy.

Once the doorway cleared, they made their way out into the bright sunshine. An antique tram clattered past as they stepped outside the door, and Richard turned left out of the square. It was five minutes past nine, and he estimated their destination was a leisurely ten-minute walk away.

They rounded the third corner on Richard's route, and the ancient white cathedral loomed in front of them. Around a dozen people were sitting on the steps which the American pair casually walked up, towards the movable bilingual sign in front of the closed heavy doors. *Cathedral opens 9.30. Entry free.* Therefore, a meeting time of nine twenty-five must mean outside the church. Richard turned to look out from the top of the steps, trying to identify the most likely meeting place. To his right was a maze of narrow streets. Directly in front was the steep hill they had just climbed, while over to the left was the main road. He noticed the sign for the tram stop about twenty yards along it. The man standing there was staring straight at them. He carefully folded his newspaper, tucked it under his arm, took three deliberate steps backwards and leaned against the iron railings on the stone wall, never once taking his eyes off them. Richard squeezed Rebecca's hand, walked down the cathedral steps with her and crossed the road to the left.

The two men stood awkwardly a couple of feet apart, just staring at each other. Rebecca looked up at each of them in turn without speaking. The contingency planning hadn't got as far as deciding on a password.

"Do you have the time please?" It was the Portuguese who asked this question, in German.

Richard looked at his watch. It read twenty past nine. He turned his wrist, so the watch face was visible to the other man and replied, also in German, "Nine twenty-five. Precisely."

"Are you planning on visiting the cathedral?" The question was now in English.

"Yes. My friend Felipe recommended it. But I don't understand why it is called Sé."

"Okay, Mr Johnson. I think we can dispense with the formalities. I am Jorge, like your American George." At this point he smiled down at the girl patiently holding Richard's hand. "The big castle on the hill is named after me. And you must be Rebecca. I've heard a lot about you." Rebecca brought out one of her smiles, precisely on cue as usual.

"Let's go and have a look around the cathedral," Jorge said. "It will be open in a few minutes." They crossed the road together and climbed back towards the entrance. Those sitting on the steps were starting to stand up, dust themselves off, and form a group around the doors. Richard resisted the temptation to look around. He assumed that Jorge would have a friend watching his back, checking to see if Richard and Rebecca had been followed.

Once they got inside the cathedral, Jorge started explaining to Richard the details of the revised plan. Rebecca strolled along behind the two men, making sure she was never more than a few feet away from them, marvelling at the strange carvings and the beautiful windows all around her. She had never been inside a Christian church before but instinctively knew that she was surrounded by symbols which would be as meaningful and important to believers as those she had so often seen inside her synagogue. She was particularly fascinated by the huge stone cases with the sculptures of men lying on top of them. As they reached the far end of the church, the two men stopped beside one such memorial and continued talking. No one was paying her any attention, so Rebecca decided to take a closer look at this one. Just as she stepped behind the head of a man holding a particularly large sword, Richard looked up and panicked – the girl was nowhere to be seen. But before he had time to decide what to do, Rebecca reappeared.

"Is he buried in there?"

"Yes, I suppose he is."

"Is his dog in there with him?" The question puzzled Richard, but Jorge burst into laughter, which provoked a few brief, disapproving glances from those nearby. As Richard looked at him in disbelief, he pointed at the foot of the tomb, where a large dog of indeterminate breed was sitting at its master's feet.

"Let's shake hands and then you leave the cathedral before me, so that I can check whether you're being followed. We'll meet later as arranged." Jorge shook hands with Richard and patted Rebecca on the head. She had retaken her usual place and was standing by his side. "Goodbye, young lady. And good luck to you both."

Richard held Rebecca's hand as they walked back down the aisle of the cathedral and stepped into the bright morning sunlight. He hesitated at the top of the steps – how were they to pass several hours inconspicuously in the city, now that they had nowhere to lie low? Jorge had confirmed that the hotel was probably still safe for them, but hotel rooms and corridors are virtually deserted around lunchtime and therefore don't provide good cover.

"Do you fancy going to see George's castle?"

"It's not really his castle, is it?"

"No, of course not. But it is a real castle. It's just up the hill." Richard pointed along the road to their right.

"Okay. And then can we eat?"

CHAPTER SIXTY-TWO

It was after six by the time they returned to the Avenida Palace Hotel, having toured the old town and the castle on foot, and taken a long, slow lunch in a family-run restaurant. This time Richard decided to take the elevator, and they worked their way down through the floors searching for a chambermaid's cart. As fate would have it, the only cart was exactly where they had found it the evening before. Richard managed to quickly glance at the work schedule – this was the only unbooked room in the whole hotel, and it was still being cleaned. At the other end of the corridor a manager appeared out of one of the conference rooms. Richard noted which one it was and led Rebecca in the opposite direction. He turned the corner, then stopped immediately.

"We can't stay here. We'll go and hide in that conference room for a few minutes until the chambermaid has finished doing 206, and then we can go in there." Rebecca nodded her understanding, and Richard poked his head around the corner to check that the corridor was clear.

The manager had come out of the third door on the left, and as Richard reached it, he noticed the name plate on the door, while pulling the pass key from his pocket. He tried the key in the lock. This time the door of the *Reinhard Heydrich* room clicked open first time, and he ushered Rebecca inside, quickly closing the door behind them.

The room had a single large window looking out onto the busy street below. The furniture was modern and functional, laid out like a small classroom, with a large desk and chair at the front with three rows of four chairs tightly arranged in front of them. Against the wall opposite the window were three small cupboards. Richard slumped into the teacher's chair and looked at his watch again, while Rebecca started to explore, opening the cupboard doors and looking at the pictures on the walls, taking care not to stand in front of the window. As she arrived back at the front desk, Richard asked her,

"Find anything interesting, Rebecca?"

"Not really. The cupboards are mostly empty. What's the Treaty of Lisbon?"

Richard couldn't hide his surprise. "It was when America decided not to fight against the Nazis in 1941. Why?"

"It was signed in this room. The thing over there says so."

Richard looked where she was pointing. On the far wall was a small brass plaque with an inscription. He got to his feet and walked round the desks towards it. Unusually the plaque was in three languages – German, Portuguese and English.

In this room the Treaty of Lisbon was signed by SS Obergruppenführer Reinhard Heydrich on behalf of the German Reich and Presidential Envoy Joseph Patrick Kennedy on behalf of the United States of America on 17th August 1941.

Richard felt a shudder down his spine. This insignificant hotel conference room had witnessed a meeting which defined the course of world history. No one would ever know what might have happened if the United States had decided to continue its support when Great Britain stood alone against the Nazis in 1941. And this was where the fate of the Jews of Europe was decided, when his government had agreed to collaborate in their enforced exile.

"Come on, Rebecca. The room should be ready by now." Richard carefully opened the door and first listened, then looked, for activity in the corridor. It was empty and silent, and the chambermaid's cart had gone. Side by side, they walked quickly towards room 206. Richard once more managed to get the key to work first time, dropping the holdall just inside the door. The hotel computer recorded the entry into room 206 using the passkey, but as it was not inserted into the slot by the light switch to activate the room's electricity supply, the occupation of an unreserved room was not printed out.

Once inside the room, Richard looked at his watch again.

"Listen, Rebecca. I have to go out for a bit to meet Jorge again. You stay in here. I'll be as quick as I can. Then we can get out of Europe. Okay?" He could see the fear in her face as she stood at the end of the bed and looked into his eyes, unblinking and silent.

"Don't worry. You'll be fine. It's safer for you to stay here this time. But don't touch anything. Is that okay?" She nodded slowly, but he could see she didn't mean it. As an afterthought he said,

"I'll leave you the key. When I get back, I'll give a secret knock, and you let me in. What knock shall I give, Rebecca?" She thought for a moment then knocked on the end of the bed next to her, two loud followed by two quiet.

"Very good" he said, more patronisingly than he meant to. "See you soon." He handed her the room key and stepped quickly to the door, trying not to give her any time to object.

The corridor was still empty. He closed the door without looking back and marched down the stairs into the hotel lobby. He turned right on the main road for the quick walk to the café in the Rossio square where he had arranged to meet Jorge and the driver who had insisted on seeing the American for himself.

CHAPTER SIXTY-THREE

Rebecca gradually became aware of a flickering red light playing on the white frame of the window. Then it was joined by a pulsing blue light. Then another. She got out of the chair and moved over to the window to take a look outside. What she saw scared her. White police cars and large green vans, all with flashing blue or red lights, were pulling up outside the hotel in silence. She could see policemen in a variety of uniforms getting out of the vehicles and lining up on the pavement, facing the hotel entrance. Rebecca dashed into the bathroom, then opened the wardrobe and cupboard doors in turn. Finally, she lifted the blankets at the side of the bed, but it had a solid base. There was nowhere in the room that she could hide.

CHAPTER SIXTY-FOUR

In the growing gloom Richard walked out of the square and thrust his hands back into his pockets. As he rounded the slight bend in the road, his heart sank. On the opposite side of the street, just over fifty yards in front of him, a sea of flashing red and blue lights illuminated the roofs of the police cars and vans parked outside the hotel. The bright-coloured flashes created an eerie stroboscopic effect on the faces of the crowd which had gathered on this side of the road. Every instinct, honed through the adventures of the last week, told him to turn away. But he slowed his pace and merged cautiously with the growing group watching the activity. The policemen were paying no attention to the crowd.

To his side he heard a loud laugh which sounded somehow familiar. A few feet to his right he recognised the group of four German ladies from the café that morning. They were approaching the crowd from the other side. He edged closer to them, sure they hadn't paid him and Rebecca any attention that morning, desperate to hear what was going on in a language he could understand. One of the ladies asked no one in particular what was happening. A small, elegantly dressed Portuguese man in the crowd started to explain to them in broken German.

"They are looking for that kidnapped girl. The one in the newspaper." Richard was close enough to see as the man pulled the evening paper out of his coat pocket to show the ladies. He couldn't make out the headline, but it clearly related to the photograph underneath it – a head shot of Rebecca which covered three column widths. In the picture she looked pale, tired and sickly. He looked across the road to the hotel. He was not sure exactly which was room 206, but the lights were on in every visible window on the second floor, and a slow ribbon of light was working its way along the third with dark shapes looming within. There was no way Rebecca could have escaped as a cluster of policemen around the hotel entrance were checking the papers of anyone trying to enter or leave. Taxis attempting to pull up outside the hotel were being waved further down the street to disgorge their fares. Richard watched as the staccato ribbon of light on the fourth floor was completed, and the search of the top floor commenced. There was no way he could get into the hotel, and if he missed his rendezvous, it was going to be impossible for him to get out of Lisbon in the near future, or maybe ever. He absolutely had to get his message to Washington, and if Rebecca had been found, there was nothing he could do for her now.

With a heavy heart, he started to retrace his steps in the direction of the railway station. Then, out of the corner of his eye, he noticed renewed activity immediately in front of the hotel. A number of more senior officers, some Portuguese and some German, had started to move towards the entrance. Richard watched as a senior Portuguese officer came out of the door, triumphantly clutching their holdall. He was immediately confronted by a Gestapo officer. Her short blonde hair was clearly visible beneath the black peaked cap. Hanna. She relieved the Portuguese policeman of the bag and climbed into the back of a marked police car, its lights still flashing. The siren was turned on for added effect as it pulled away from the kerb. It was clear from the reaction of the crowd that this was the highlight of the spectacle so far. That meant that Rebecca had not been brought out of the hotel.

After the departure of the most senior officer, the activity level subsided rapidly. The lights in all the hotel rooms went out one by one, starting with the recently illuminated top floor and progressing downwards. As the guests were allowed back in, room lights started to come back on in a random pattern. An empty tourist coach attempted to pull up in front of the hotel. The policeman, who was about to wave it on, was tapped on the shoulder by his superior, who told him to let it park. The police started to get back into their cars, which pulled away one by one, the Germans driving off in one direction and the Portuguese in the other. The two policemen standing either side of the main entrance were receiving a briefing from their officer before he too escaped in his waiting car. The watching crowd also sensed that the show was over and started to thin.

Richard walked away from the crowd before crossing the main road and doubling back towards the hotel. In front of him the driver of the coach was unloading suitcases onto the pavement and, as Richard got alongside, he was buried deep in the bowels of his vehicle. On impulse, Richard reached out and grabbed a very large red wheeled suitcase which was standing upright and unattended. He pressed the knob to extend its handle, and dragged it behind him towards the hotel entrance, expecting at any moment to hear the shout that would result in his arrest. He was so flustered that he didn't notice as one of the police guards moved to intercept his path. He was about to walk into the officer, but the man was quick enough to see what was happening, and moved smartly aside, the door handle in his hand, as he held it open for the hotel's non-paying guest.

Richard kept his head down and walked straight towards the elevator. The lobby was crowded with people milling around before returning to their rooms, absorbing the last of the unscheduled excitement of their evening in Lisbon, which would give them a story to tell for years. Richard had the elevator to himself and pressed the button for the second floor, almost crushing his foot as he brought the suitcase to a standstill at his side.

The corridor was as deserted as it had been previously, and he strode confidently towards room 206. Two long pieces of blue-and-white-striped police crime-scene tape created a cross blocking the door. He walked past to give himself a moment to think what to do next and stopped at the end of the corridor. There was nothing else for it. He returned to the room, took a deep breath, and knocked, two loud, two quiet. The noise echoed horribly in the silent corridor. He put his ear to the door but could detect nothing. He tried again, with the same result. He waited as long as he dared, before starting towards the main staircase in defeat.

He was wondering whether to drag the suitcase down the stairs, to pick it up, or just to abandon it, when a sudden thought came to him. He turned round and went down the other end of the corridor. He stopped in front of the door bearing the plaque *Reinhard Heydrich* and knocked, two loud, two quiet. Nothing.

After a few seconds he tried again and put his ear to the door. He thought he could hear something inside, so he knocked again, the same sequence twice in quick succession. The door started to open.

A vertical strip of darkness appeared in front of him. He pushed the door open wider and pulled his suitcase inside. The door clicked shut behind him and he reached his hand out, fumbling along the wall for the light switch. In the silence, he heard a slight creak to his left, just as he found the switch and turned the light on. The room appeared empty.

"Rebecca?" The creak returned as the cupboard door to his left burst open and Rebecca crawled out and bounded towards him. Richard bent down to her level and held out his arms to hug her. She threw herself at him and flung her arms around his neck.

"Clever girl. I thought I'd lost you." He felt the gentle shaking on his shoulder and realised she was sobbing. Girls crying had always been one of Richard's greatest terrors. He stood up straight, but Rebecca clung on to him, hiding her face in the collar of his coat.

"It's all right, now. We've nearly made it. We've got to get out of here quickly. We have a ship to catch." As he managed to put her on the floor, Rebecca was rubbing her eyes, avoiding looking at him and saying nothing. He wondered how to bring back the cheerful, positive girl he had grown so fond of.

"Listen, I need your help. We need scissors. Any ideas?" Without a word she turned away from him and opened the next cupboard. It was half full of office stationery including paper, drawing pins, and all the things you needed to run a meeting. Including scissors. He used them to lever open the lock on the large red suitcase. With a loud crack the hole on one of the ends of the zipper broke apart, leaving the small padlock in place on the other. He opened the case and tipped its contents into a pile on the floor. It was a woman's suitcase, full of clothing, toiletries, shoes and a small library of German magazines. Richard piled the clothes back inside, leaving everything else on the meeting room floor.

"Let's go, Rebecca. Have you ever ridden in a suitcase?"

She looked at him in that scornful way children have of

responding to particularly lame jokes.

"Unfortunately, you're famous. Your picture is on the front of the newspaper, and all the police in the city are looking for you. The only way we're going to get out of this hotel is for me to pull you in this suitcase."

Rebecca looked at the suitcase lying open on the floor with the pile of clothes thrown untidily into it and shrugged. She handed him the room key from her pocket and went to lie down, pulling the clothes around herself to make it as comfortable as possible. While she was doing this, Richard scooped up all the other items from the suitcase and dumped them into the cupboard where Rebecca had hidden. He zipped the suitcase shut, stood it back up, and pulled it from one end of the conference room to the other.

"How does that feel, Rebecca?"

"Bumpy."

"Does it hurt?"

"Not yet."

"Okay, we have to go. Keep very quiet. I will talk to you when I can. Ready?"

"Yes."

Richard cast a final glance around the room. They hadn't left anything behind – they no longer had anything but each other – and the room bore no obvious immediate traces of their presence. He listened at the door before opening it. The corridor was still empty, so he pulled the suitcase outside, reached back inside to turn the light off, and let the door swing shut behind them. He continued to the end of the corridor, quickly learning how to control the overweight bag as he followed the route which Jorge had confirmed still led directly to the railway station next door. They passed no one as they crossed from the hotel into the station. Richard turned away from the sign pointing to the platforms and dragged the suitcase onto the escalator and out into the street.

CHAPTER SIXTY-FIVE

It took a little over five minutes for Richard to pull his suitcase to the meeting point. As soon as he turned into the narrow, dark alley, he could see the van parked a hundred yards away. It reminded him of Felipe except, when he got closer, he could see that the vehicle was a dark colour, with a gaily painted display of fruit and vegetables filling most of the side panel. He was still a few feet away when the driver's door opened.

"You're late. Another five minutes and I'd have had to go without you. Where's the girl?"

Richard laid the suitcase gently onto the sidewalk and unzipped it. He helped Rebecca as she struggled out onto the pavement, looking a little the worse for wear. The Portuguese driver opened the side door of his van and pointed to where Richard and Rebecca had to squeeze between the wooden crates filled with strong-smelling fruit. Once they had arranged themselves to his satisfaction, he stacked other crates over the top of them, completely obscuring their view. The door closed, and Richard heard the driver position himself beside the wheel, then the thud of the suitcase as it landed in front of the unoccupied passenger seat.

Throughout the drive to the docks, Richard tried to shield his own and Rebecca's heads from what he thought was the inevitable collapse of the precarious arrangement of fresh produce above their heads. When they came to a halt, Richard could hear every word of the discussion between the driver and the sentry guarding the entry to the port. It sounded reassuringly good natured, and they were soon on their way without any further formalities.

A couple of minutes later, the van came to a halt again, and the side door was slung open. Footsteps approached, then silence for a few seconds.

"Are they in there?" The answer must have been visual,

because Richard heard no response to the question, which had been asked with an unmistakeable American accent.

"Mr Johnson, I want you to stay there for a few moments until we manage to distract the guards." Richard didn't respond as the boxes over his head started to shift. Gradually the grey expanse of a warship became visible as the space beside them was cleared. Suddenly it went dark again as something coarse hit him gently in the face.

"Okay, you need to get yourself and the girl into these two sacks. Then my men will carry you aboard. It's vital you don't move once inside the sacks or make a sound." Richard reached out and grasped Rebecca's hand in a way he hoped was reassuring. He fumbled with the sacks until he managed to separate them and find the opening in the smaller of the two. While the unloading continued around them, Richard managed to get first Rebecca and then himself inside them. He felt someone grab his ankles.

"Hold tight!" He was slung across a shoulder, like the proverbial sack of potatoes he was now imitating, and felt the exaggerated bounce in the sailor's steps as they mounted the gangway onto the ship. The grip was transferred from his waist to his shoulders as he was lowered and another man grabbed first his ankles, then his waist. As soon as he was laid down, the top of the sack was pulled apart, and he found himself face to face with the cap insignia of a United States Navy officer. The sailor left Richard to extricate himself from the sack, while he turned his attention to Rebecca, who had just been placed beside him.

"Come with me, you two. We need to hide you before the Germans start their inspection of the ship."

Richard and Rebecca followed the officer through the maze of corridors, until he led them through a door, which the plaque indicated was the officers' mess.

"Sir, if you can lift this end of the table, we need to slide it to one side." The red carpet under the table lifted to reveal a wooden floor with a virtually invisible hook. The sailor pulled up this section of the flooring to reveal a compartment beneath. Richard and Rebecca clambered inside, and the flooring was replaced above their heads. As the grinding of the table moving back into place started, Rebecca reached out in the total darkness to find Richard's hand.

After what seemed like an hour, the grinding sound returned, and within moments the sailor had opened their hiding place.

"You can come out now. We're underway."

As soon as they left the territorial waters of the German Reich, Richard sat with Captain Callaghan, who typed his message into the cipher machine.

"That's all we can do for the moment, Mr Johnson. I suggest you and the girl get some sleep while you can. You can use my cabin."

Tenerife – November 2024

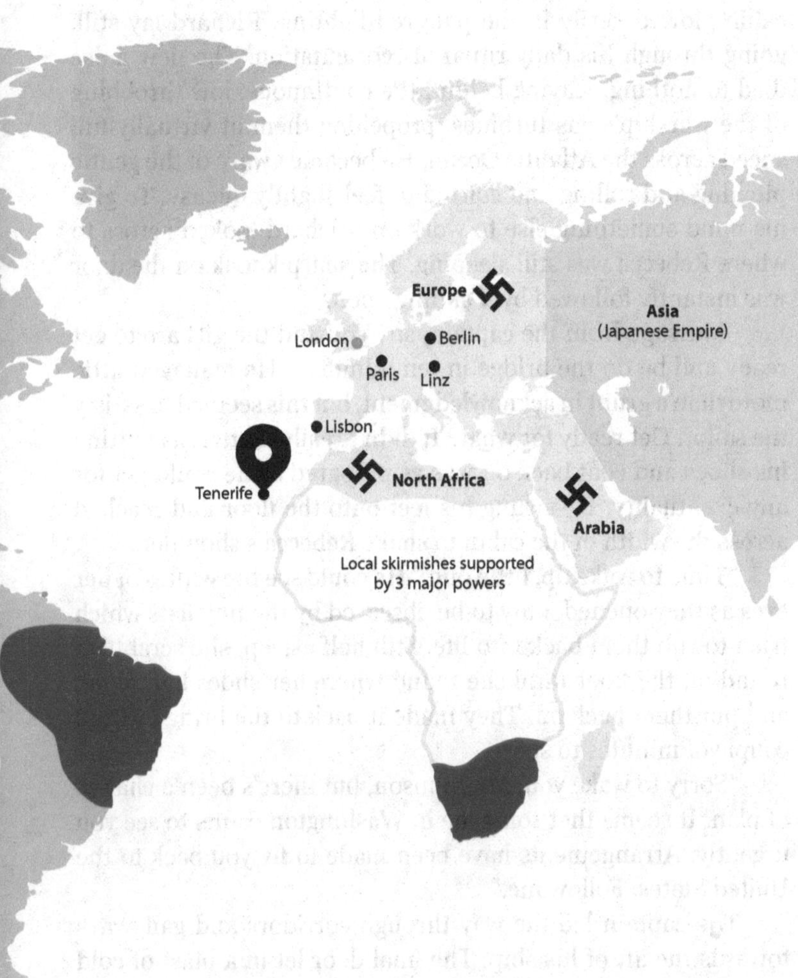

CHAPTER SIXTY-SIX

The clattering roar of a powerful engine woke him. The captain's cabin glowed eerily in the pale red lighting. Richard lay still, going through his daily ritual of reorientation. The new noise died to nothing, leaving behind the continuous, low throbbing of the warship's gas turbines, propelling them at virtually full speed across the Atlantic Ocean. He became aware of the gentle pitching and rolling and started to feel slightly queasy. To give his mind something else to work on, Richard looked across to where Rebecca was still sleeping. The sharp knock on the door was instantly followed by it sliding open.

"Message from the captain, sir. You and the girl are to get ready and be on the bridge in ten minutes." He managed little more than a grunt in acknowledgment, but this seemed to satisfy the sailor. Get ready for what? It didn't really matter, as putting his shoes and coat back on was as prepared as he could get for any eventuality. He swung his feet onto the floor and reached across the width of the cabin to shake Rebecca's shoulder.

"Time to wake up, little one." He could see the whites of her eyes as they opened, only to be obscured by the tiny fists which tried to rub them back into life. Still half asleep, she scrabbled round on the floor until she found where her shoes had fallen and put them back on. They made it back to the bridge with a couple of minutes to spare.

"Sorry to wake you, Mr Johnson, but there's been a change of plan. It seems that someone in Washington wants to see you urgently. Arrangements have been made to fly you back to the United States. Follow me."

The captain led the way through corridors and gangways towards the aft of his ship. The final door let in a blast of cold damp air, and the crashing sound of waves being sliced by several hundred tons of metal. The three of them stepped out onto the wet deck. As they rounded the superstructure and entered the wide, open space at the rear of the ship, they were confronted by the looming black insect shape of a helicopter. A man in a large white helmet reached out from inside to help first Rebecca and then Richard aboard. As soon as the door closed behind them, the roar restarted, and within a few seconds they were airborne.

Even with the huge headphones clamped over his ears, Richard found the noise of the small machine's engines deafening as it flew south at full speed. Once again, Rebecca astonished him by being able to sleep peacefully in the most extreme of circumstances. The few words that the helmeted man said indicated that the flight would take around four hours, until they reached the United States military base on the international island of Tenerife.

CHAPTER SIXTY-SEVEN

For the last few minutes of their flight, they had a clear view of the bright orange sun rising rapidly above the horizon to their left. They dropped back into the pre-dawn gloom, and Richard looked down onto the dark outline of the island growing out of the sea beneath them. He could make out the circular space marked 'H' a few yards away from a runway, at the end of which the slender shape of a Grumman C4 jet glowed under the strong white lights. He had only ever seen these expensive, small aircraft in the livery of the country's largest corporations, so finding one in the markings of the United States Air Force was quite a surprise.

The moment they bounced onto the ground, the helicopter airman unclipped the coil of wire from his helmet, slid the door open and jumped onto the tarmac, turning to pick up Rebecca. Conversation was impossible with this level of noise, so Richard made the obvious assumption, took off his headphones and ran behind him towards the small jet. The airman deposited Rebecca at the bottom of the steps at the rear of the aircraft and gave Richard a cursory salute as he sprinted back to his own machine. Rebecca checked with Richard before starting up the steps.

The interior was laid out more like an office than a jet. The silence was overwhelming, and the aircraft looked deserted, until the closest of the seats swivelled to face them.

"We meet again, Herr Johnson."

She was wearing a dark tracksuit, her blonde hair completely covered in a black woollen hat. The Lüger pistol was pointing upwards, straight into the middle of his chest, at a range any amateur would find easy, let alone an officer of the Gestapo. The voice showed none of the hesitancy it had the last time she had spoken English in her Berlin apartment.

"What do you want, Hanna?"

"You, of course. You don't really think we're going to let you get back to America, do you?"

"Rebecca, get off the aircraft."

As the little girl walked backwards towards the doorway, it was as if the German was seeing her for the first time. She shifted her aim, and Richard moved sideways to shield the girl from the pistol. Just for a second, he noticed a flicker of doubt on the woman's face. Richard held her stare as Rebecca made it to the top of the steps and he heard the clatter of her footsteps as she dashed down them.

"It's you we're interested in. The girl's not important."

"So, what are you going to do now? You can't just walk off an American military base."

"I got onto it, didn't I? And I don't think there's any of your famous cavalry on Tenerife."

"Why, Hanna? What's going on here?"

"You're being used, Richard. It's as simple as that. Your side was using you when they sent you to Cuba. And we've been using you to find out how people escape from the Reich. But all that's finished now. It's over. You've outlived your usefulness."

"And *J S*. What was all that about?"

"Honestly, I have no idea. We just needed to check whether you knew anything about it, which you obviously don't. So that's all sorted as well."

"What happens now?"

"That's up to you, Richard. You can agree to come with me to the other side of the island, or I'll just shoot you here."

"In cold blood?"

"Shot while trying to escape. You can't deny that you're trying to escape, can you, Richard?"

She stood up and stretched her gun arm straight towards him. The flash and bang sent him reeling. He crashed against the cabin wall and fell to his knees. White smoke was swirling around him, but he could make out the shape of Hanna, still standing, three feet to his left. Her left arm was shielding her face and the right was hanging limply at her side. As far as he could make out, it was still holding the pistol. He sprang like a sprinter from his crouched position, his full weight hitting her in the middle of the body. Together they smashed into the swivelling chair which tipped over. The pistol scudded across the carpet, ending up underneath one of the fixed seats against the window. Behind his ear he heard another pistol cock and instinctively he released his grip from Hanna's throat.

"We've got it from here, Mr Johnson." A strong hand gripped him above the elbow and helped him back to his feet. The smoke had virtually cleared as Richard turned to face the two American military policemen. In the doorway at the top of the steps a medic with a huge green satchel waited for the nod from the policemen, before rushing towards the door to the cockpit. Richard replaced him at the top of the aircraft's steps. At the bottom, on the tarmac, he could see the man from the helicopter, the visor on his white helmet now raised. His hands were resting on Rebecca's shoulders.

"Clever girl you've got there, sir."

Richard nodded and reached out for Rebecca's hand. The airman pulled him away from the bottom of the stairway as the policemen marched down the steps, the first dragging Hanna by the handcuff chain between her wrists, while his colleague followed at a safe distance, his pistol drawn. As the second policeman came level with Richard, he stopped.

"You'll be ready for take-off in a few minutes, sir. Just wait until the medic has finished with the pilots."

The second pilot in his immaculate Air Force uniform didn't look any the worse for wear as he buckled Richard and Rebecca into their seats for take-off, while his superior brought the four powerful engines behind them to life.

"As soon as we're airborne, you can tip these seats back and get some sleep. It's a nine-hour flight to New York."

New York – November 2024

CHAPTER SIXTY-EIGHT

Rebecca had snuggled back into Richard's shoulder, unwoken by being lifted out of the cab. Richard thought back to the frail, pale child he had first seen in this very house three months earlier, and then again in England just three days ago. There was no comparison with the rosy-cheeked bundle of health he was about to deliver. Slowly and silently, he climbed the steps to the front door of the large brownstone house. He rang the doorbell and took a half step backwards.

The old housekeeper was the one who had opened the door to him on his only previous visit. The beaming smile, which now brightened her whole face when she realised who had arrived, was in sharp contrast to the dour persona which had greeted him the last time. Without a word, she stepped aside, unblocking the hallway. He recognised the door to Samuel Levy's study on the right. Just as he started to wonder which of the other doors to head for, the one directly ahead opened, and a flood of family came towards him, deferential, grateful, but only interested in what he had in his arms. As her mother took her hand, the girl stirred and opened her eyes. Her father stepped forward, level with the shoulder of his wife, and the girl turned to him and smiled. Richard noticed his distinct family resemblance with the old man and also with Rebecca, the younger Mr Levy providing the missing link between grandfather and granddaughter which he hadn't spotted during their journey together.

As the father moved forwards, Richard for the first time caught sight of the old man, standing alone, framed by the kitchen door, his face a picture of joy and relief. The girl's mother moved in to repossess her child, and all eyes moved away from Richard to follow them, except the grandfather, who made sure that he had caught the journalist's eye before moving into the kitchen ahead of the crowd. Richard stepped slowly behind the shuffling group, breaking away to the right as he entered the kitchen, to follow Samuel Levy. While the rest of the family celebrated around their returned child, the old man slipped, unnoticed, into the study. Richard recognised the door as the one he had first seen Rebecca through.

The image of this room from his last visit was one of those which had repeatedly haunted him during his time in the cell in Prinz-Albrecht-Strasse, but the gloom had been replaced by bright lights. The religious items seemed much less prominent than Richard remembered, and the chair on the visitor's side of the huge mahogany desk felt much more comfortable as they both sat down.

"I cannot begin to thank you, Mr Johnson. You have no idea what it means to an old man to have a grandchild restored to him. All the money in the world is nothing compared to family."

Richard was at a loss how to respond. The slight glimmer of a tear in the man's eye confirmed his sincerity, and Richard couldn't bring himself to resent what he had done for Rebecca on anyone's account. But he could not reconcile the relief and joy at the reunion he had just witnessed with the fact that the man opposite had deliberately put Richard's life at risk. And the confusion remained as to what it had all been for.

"She's a lovely girl."

"Isn't she just! When she got ill, we were devastated. We consulted the best doctors in New York, and they all told us nothing could be done. We had almost given up hope when the German doctor came to see us. But you know all about that."

"Actually, Mr Levy, no I don't. I know about your granddaughter's treatment in England, but I have no idea how or why that came about."

"Oh. I see." The old man was visibly surprised. Richard saw his opportunity and pounced. This was the only chance he was ever going to get.

"That's how you can thank me, Mr Levy. Let me know why I was abducted after you sent me to Cuba. Why I was tortured in Berlin. What all this has to do with the election." Richard paused. He watched the furrows on the old Jew's forehead deepen as he struggled to reconcile his twin obligations of duty and gratitude.

"It's too late for me to do anything about it now," Richard

continued. "And I suspect no one would believe me anyway. It's just for my own satisfaction, Mr Levy. So, I can make sense of the people who died trying to help me."

"Okay, Mr Johnson. But on the strict understanding that this remains within these four walls."

"You have my word."

Samuel Levy raised his considerable bulk from the ornate chair and shuffled out from behind it. Slowly he opened the bottom door of the bureau on the opposite side of the study and poured over-large measures of bourbon into two glasses.

"What do you know about *J S*, Mr Johnson?"

"It's one of the biggest secrets our country has. It's a key element of the Lisbon Treaty – the deal we made with the Nazis that kept us out of the European War."

"Very good, Mr Johnson. But you don't need to worry about betraying that secret to me. I know exactly what the *J S* is. I am one of the very few people in our country who administer it. And you're right. I doubt there's a bigger secret anywhere."

"Actually, that's as much as I know. The Gestapo tortured me to find out what I knew, and I think they eventually realised, that I had learned more from their questions than I had known before I was taken to Berlin. In fact, before the interrogation, I'd never even heard of it."

Samuel Levy returned to his desk and placed the drinks carefully onto the leather coasters. He looked the journalist in the eye, as if trying to read his true intentions. Finally, he sighed to himself and sat down.

"Okay then. At a meeting in Lisbon in August 1941, SS General Reinhard Heydrich persuaded the presidential envoy, Joe Kennedy, that the USA should stay out of the war. Kennedy managed to convince President Roosevelt, and the rest is history. As part of this deal, the Germans allowed all the Jews in Europe to emigrate to the United States. That much is common knowledge." He hesitated until Richard nodded his confirmation.

"But there was more to this agreement. Firstly, the US was not *allowed* to take the Jews, it was *required* to take them. Some went to Madagascar, as you know, but the majority came here. The Nazis managed to convince Kennedy that Hitler wanted them – us – all dead, and moving all the Jews out of

Europe was the only alternative. Kennedy and Roosevelt knew that would be unpopular, but by a mixture of threat, bribery and moral blackmail, they were persuaded. One of Kennedy's aides had been given a tour of the Sachsenhausen concentration camp where the Nazis were testing the most effective techniques for liquidating eleven million people. They thought we weren't worth a bullet each, so they developed poison gasses to do the job more cheaply. But they still had the problem of disposal. Eleven million bodies are not easy to get rid of – not even for the Nazis. It was Heydrich's job to find this 'Final Solution', as they called it. He managed to convince Hitler that it would be enough to just get us all out of Europe.

"Meanwhile, the Nazis discovered that the Japanese were planning an attack on the United States which would have brought them – us – into the war. Hitler thought this was a good idea, but his generals managed to persuade him that America's intervention could cost Germany the war, as it had in 1917." Samuel Levy took a sip from the crystal glass and seemed hypnotised by the movement of the ice cubes inside it. "Hitler agreed that Heydrich should try to make a deal to stop the Japanese attack, keep America out of the war, and get all the Jews out of Europe. Heydrich was ruthlessly efficient, and Kennedy was equally ambitious, which made the perfect combination. I like to think that they deserved each other. It's no coincidence that they both ended up running their respective countries. And while the motives of both of them were despicable, I suppose we should be grateful for what they agreed. I dread to think what would have happened if America had ended up in the war and the Nazis had set up their extermination programme." Again, the old Jew hesitated, but this time only for a moment.

"And there was a final part to the deal, Richard. The Third Protocol. The emigration of the Jewish population of Europe came at a price. In addition to a nominal sum per head, the US had to pay to Germany, in perpetuity, a proportion of the profits of all Jewish businesses. The Jew Tax. In German that is *Judensteuer*. But it is only ever referred to as *J S*. And I, for my sins, I am responsible for calculating the amount of tax we have to pay to the Germans every year. I have a small team of accountants who do all the detailed calculations, and one official in the Treasury Department manages the payment and keeps the transactions out of the government's published accounts. The only other people who know are the treasury secretary, the United States' ambassador to the German Reich, and the president."

"Not the FBI?"

"No, Richard. I'm pretty sure no one in the FBI has the slightest idea about the *J S*. Why do you ask?"

The old man stopped, staring at his folded hands on the desk in front of him. Richard felt that Samuel Levy was not even aware of his presence in the room. He thought it was only the Catholics who believed in confessions, but that was exactly what this sounded like.

After a few moments, the old man continued. "Not surprisingly, the US government insisted on keeping this agreement secret. There is a list, in a safe in the United States Treasury, of all the people who know of the existence of this Jewish tax on our side of the ocean." Levy ran his fingers through his beard before continuing.

"When Jimmy Sullivan was killed in Cuba, we had to find out if the *Judensteuer* story was about to come out. We knew that he was investigating Isaiah Horowitz, and we've been worried about him for a while. We didn't think Isaiah knew anything about the Jewish tax, but the fact that *J S* was cut into Sullivan's hand meant we had to investigate."

"But why me, Mr Levy?"

"You were chosen because you know your way around tricky situations, and you speak German. That's quite a select group. Because you're a journalist, it doesn't look strange if you go snooping, and as you have no Jewish links, we thought you couldn't be traced back to us. So, we called in a favour from your editor. And now your name needs to be added to that list I mentioned."

"So why do you think Jimmy Sullivan was killed, Mr Levy?"

"I'm really not sure, Mr Johnson. He must have found out something that Horowitz couldn't afford to get out. That could either be to do with his wife, or something about the election. He is Senator Goldberg's most important fundraiser, after all. Frankly, as long as it had nothing to do with the tax, I don't care."

The journalist thought for a moment.

"Can you tell me where I can find Mr Horowitz? And his wife?"

Samuel Levy scratched his beard for a moment before opening his desk drawer, retrieving a notebook, and writing two addresses on a piece of paper, which he handed over.

"Be very careful, Richard. He is a dangerous man." The journalist nodded as he took the paper.

"So where does Rebecca fit into all this, Mr Levy?"

"Ah, Rebecca." The look of sadness in his eyes, before he cast his head down under Richard's direct gaze, was unmistakeable. "The weakness of an old man. What else could I have done? Do you know the story of Faust, Richard?"

He shook his head.

"I did a deal with the devil. The Nazis were her only hope. They offered to save Rebecca, but at a price. They wanted me to pass over all the details of the tax calculation. They are convinced we're cheating them, but they needed my cooperation to prove it. I was desperate, and anyway, I was sure I could outwit them. In any case, the figures we give them are accurate, so I agreed. What else could I do? But then they captured you, and you told them it was me who had sent you to Cuba. I thought I had managed to keep the two separate. The two things were completely unrelated. But the Germans assumed I had double-crossed them, which is when they decided Rebecca had no more value." The old man sagged into his chair, overcome by the heavy weight of the memory.

"For a month we assumed she was dead. But you know all that." The old man stopped, lost in his thoughts, until a renewed purpose brought a twinkle back into his eyes.

"There's someone I want you to meet." Samuel Levy stood up and slipped out of the door into the hallway. Above the silence, Richard could hear the excited chatter coming through the closed door to the kitchen, as the rest of the family continued with the reunion. It was nearly five minutes before the old man returned.

It took Richard a few seconds to recognise the now beardless German.

"My God! Alex! I thought you were dead!" The two men

shook hands enthusiastically.

"I'm glad you finally made it back, Richard. I know you didn't deliberately betray us. We chose to deal with the Gestapo woman knowing the risks, but even the slightest possibility of recruiting someone in her position, or just the chance to blackmail her at a later stage, was too good to pass up."

"Richard, the man you know as Alex is the head of our operation in Germany. Although, for the moment, he has had to take up temporary residence here." Samuel Levy made no gesture from which Richard could determine the precise scope of 'here', whether it meant the United States in general, specifically New York, or the Levy household itself.

Samuel went to retrieve the bourbon bottle as Alex continued.

"We know what Samuel did, and we understand. Any one of us would have done the same. We're all human, after all." Alex didn't turn round to the man who now put a glass beside him but continued to talk to Richard as if their host was not present. "The Nazis agreed to treat Rebecca because they knew they could blackmail Samuel and maybe do serious damage to Jewish interests in America. Rebecca was accompanied to Europe by Tom Monroe, Samuel's lawyer, and his best friend. After the operation was successful, the demands started. Firstly, they threatened Tom's life. When Samuel didn't respond, Tom's finger was delivered to this house by a courier from the German consulate. Tests showed he had been poisoned with cyanide and the finger cut off after death. That was when Mr Levy told us what he had done. The next threat was against Rebecca. Fortunately, they only knew of Samuel's political and business activities. They have no idea that there's an American anti-Nazi organisation operating out of New York. It was Samuel himself who decided there was no way out for Rebecca. That was the hardest decision any man can ever make. That we now have Rebecca back is nothing short of a miracle."

"So how did you connect me with Rebecca?"

"That's just it," Alex continued. "We didn't. I had no idea you were in Berlin, and when we were approached by the Gestapo woman to get you out, it came completely out of the blue."

"So, what is it your anti-Nazi group is trying to achieve?"

Samuel noticed the puzzled look on Richard's face and tried to explain.

"As far as the Nazis are concerned, Richard, the major role of the United States at the moment is as an outlet for their consumer goods. It's more important for us to keep them happy than the other way round. What price do you put on curing cancer, for example? It costs thirty cents for a simple urine test that's a completely reliable indicator of cancer. We have failed to reverse engineer it, and they only send us three months' stock at a time. The same applies to the cures, so they have us over a barrel. And if they decided they wanted to expand their empire further, we would be in no position to stop them. That's not going to happen at the moment, but who can tell when some ambitious leader will decide to take another shot at world domination? If they start to get trouble at home, a nice war is always the best way to refocus public attention."

"But we need to be ready," Alex said. "The time will come when we are in a position to strike back. To redress the balance. To restore democracy." His face showed the furrowed brow of concentration – a man with a mission.

"Listen to the enthusiasm of youth, Richard," said Samuel. "When my generation passes over the torch, we have to hope that the idealism will have been tempered by realism. We haven't fought a real war since 1918. Do we really want to now?"

The silence returned. Richard looked on as the two men sat, each absorbed in their own thoughts – the calm before what would likely turn into a long-drawn-out debate on the future approach to anti-Nazi policy. Neither paid him any attention as he slipped out into the hallway. Through the door at the other end, Richard could see Rebecca sitting in the kitchen, a princess surrounded by her adoring subjects. She alone noticed Richard as he made his way from the study to the front door. She gave no indication of his presence to the rest of the group as she caught his eye and just gave him a smile. One of her special smiles.

Richard closed the heavy front door behind him as quietly as he could. Reaching the bottom of the steps he turned left. The old beggar sitting on the sidewalk had his heavy coat buttoned right up to the top. His hat rocked gently on his head in time with the deep, rasping breaths. Richard slipped a twenty-dollar note between the empty enamelled cup and the cardboard sign with its Hebrew inscription.

He decided against returning to his apartment or checking into a hotel. The residential address he had been given for Mr and Mrs Horowitz was a two-and-a-half-hour train ride from Penn Station in the commuting rush-hour, so he expected it to take considerably longer on a Sunday evening. If that meant sleeping in a railway station or even a bush for one last time, so be it.

CHAPTER SIXTY-NINE

"Mrs Horowitz."

As Richard emerged from the shadows into her sightline, he watched the sequence of emotions in her eyes: panic; terror; confusion; curiosity. Only now did it occur to him that his appearance was likely to cause a scream, but she didn't, fixing him instead with a stare as hard as was possible from behind a mud facial.

"Have you come from my husband?"

The calmness in her voice shocked him. It was either resignation to the hopelessness of her position – defenceless in a soundproof room – or a tremendous strength of will. Based on what it must take to be married to Isaiah Horowitz, Richard guessed the latter.

"No, Mrs Horowitz. Your husband doesn't know anything about this. And I intend to keep it that way. That's why I had to see you here."

"What is it you want? You must know my husband is a dangerous man to cross."

"Is that what happened to Jimmy Sullivan?"

Her eyes betrayed the surprise.

"What do you know about Mr Sullivan? Who are you?"

"I know you hired Jimmy Sullivan, Mrs Horowitz, to investigate your husband. And that shortly afterwards he turned up dead in Cuba. Why Cuba, if I may ask?"

"Isaiah was there on a business trip. He has investments in a number of the casinos."

"And other interests on the island, perhaps?"

"You tell me, Mister whatever your name is. You seem to be very well informed."

"Not as well as I would like to be. I am sure your husband killed Sullivan – not himself, of course, but he had it done. That doesn't add up. If you want to get rid of a private investigator looking for girls, you bribe him or beat him up. You don't murder him. So what am I missing?"

"That's a question you should probably ask my husband. Now if you don't mind leaving, ..."

"I will leave just as soon as you tell me why it was necessary to kill Sullivan."

"If you must know, he was getting too close."

"Too close to what? The girls?"

"You don't have a clue, do you? Everyone knows about the girls. The photographs appear in the papers, for God's sake. Sullivan stumbled across the political stuff. Now go before I say something that you regret."

"How do you know this, Mrs Horowitz?"

"If you're surprised I know, why was it me you asked? Isaiah told me, of course. I am still his wife, after all. For better or worse."

"What is *J S*?"

"I have no idea. I've heard it mentioned a couple of times, but no more than that. Now, this is getting tiresome. I must ask you to leave."

"Thank you, Mrs Horowitz."

"Just make sure my husband doesn't find out about this. For your sake, young man, not mine."

Richard slipped out into the corridor and left by the fire exit he had forced an hour earlier after following his first target of the day from her palatial and very well guarded home to this beauty parlour.

CHAPTER SEVENTY

The setting in one of Manhattan's more run-down districts belied the wealth of the organisation. This supported the view of Isaiah Horowitz as a man of the people, true to his poor immigrant roots. It also kept the rent down. But most importantly, it kept the number of visitors to a minimum. The sight of white men in suits walking down this main road raised eyebrows. Those foolish enough to end up in side alleys raised their hands and left without their wallets, Breitling watches, and anything else easily convertible into the underworld currencies of cash and hard drugs.

Richard was wearing a suit, but something else was making him uncomfortable. His job had often taken him into dangerous territory, and he hadn't always escaped unscathed, despite the back up of a prestigious newspaper with good police contacts, which always knew where he was going. This time he was completely on his own. Samuel Levy wouldn't be able to lift a finger to help him, and Jack Gordon, almost the only other person in the country who knew he was still alive, was over a thousand miles away.

He walked up to the front door of number 427 and pressed the only buzzer. The voice that answered managed to sound female, young, bad-tempered and surprised all in one word.

"Yes?"

"I want to see Mr Horowitz."

"Do you have an appointment?"

"No, but he'll want to see me."

"Mr Horowitz is not in today. Call and make an appointment."

"I watched him walk through this door five minutes ago." The silence was even more bad-tempered, but hesitant. It was now or never.

"Tell him I've come from Jimmy Sullivan."

The silence returned for almost a minute. Then the door

lock buzzed.

Richard entered a narrow dingy hallway which ended after three yards in a single flight of stairs, whose carpet was frayed in all the important places. Not a corporation trying to impress visitors any more than passers-by. Richard climbed through the featureless stairwell. Three turns brought him face-to-face with the intercom voice. She was reluctant to look him in the eye and didn't need to speak. She just nodded in the direction of the corridor. As Richard turned towards it, the suited frame of a huge black man, at least six and a half feet tall, blocked it completely. He stood still just long enough for Richard to see the symmetrical bulges created by the arm and leg muscles, and the single lump level with his left elbow. When the man turned to lead the way, Richard glimpsed the brown straps of the shoulder holster and the sparkles from the grip of his pistol.

The bodyguard rapped gently on the door to the end office on the right of the corridor, pushed it open without waiting for a response, and stood facing Richard. The journalist turned and stepped inside.

The office was as unassuming as the rest of the building. The blinds were closed, enhancing the drabness given off by the grey of the walls. The older man behind the desk didn't look up from the document he was marking with a gold-plated mechanical pencil, affording Richard a view of the small balding patch in the centre of the unconvincingly black head of hair. He was casually dressed, but elegant and expensive. After a few moments he set the pencil down carefully, perfectly parallel with the document, the blotter and the filing tray on the desk, and slowly eased himself upright in the chair. Elbows on the desk, he pressed his fingertips together, as if in prayer. The cold, grey eyes stared into Richard's for much longer than was comfortable.

"And who are you?"

"A friend of Jimmy Sullivan."

The stare continued, unperturbed. "So what? Perhaps you want to join him?"

"No. This time the trail would immediately lead to you, so that's not going to happen. I just want to understand why he had to die."

"You are being very stupid," Isaiah Horowitz said. "I heard

that Mr Sullivan died because he knew too much. Just supposing I knew what that was, and just supposing I told you, that would mean you knew too much. You can see where this is going, can't you?"

"He found out about *J S*." Richard heard his own voice catch. The tension visibly flowed out of Isaiah Horowitz's neck muscles, and he put his palms down onto the edge of his desk. A man who knew his secret was safe.

"That's right. He found out about *J S*. Which has nothing to do with me. So I suggest you go and look elsewhere."

"What is *J S*?" Richard noticed the twitch in the Jew's eyebrow, and the slightest hint of a frown.

"That would be telling. And it's not a healthy secret to know. Just ask Jimmy. Now get out of here before I start to take you seriously." He picked up his pencil and continued to read the document in front of him. Richard stood, rooted to the spot, expecting the man to look up again, but he just continued to make his notes. The only movement came from behind as the bodyguard laid a guiding hand on his shoulder. Richard turned to see that the black man's other hand was wrapped round the grip of his holstered pistol. Tamely, he walked out of the office, past the relieved-looking receptionist, and down the stairs. As he reached the front door, his hand was trembling so much he had difficulty turning the catch to let himself back out onto the street.

The need to run as far away from this place as possible was only exceeded by the need for alcohol. He crossed the street, entered the seedy bar and ordered a large Jack Daniels. The only other customer was sitting on a stool by the bar and made a move to engage his new best friend in conversation, so Richard went to sit by the window to compose himself. After a couple of sips the shaking subsided, and he stared absent-mindedly across the street for several minutes, wondering what progress he had made. At least he was now convinced that *J S* was not the reason for Jimmy Sullivan's death, just something Isaiah Horowitz had known would make a good smokescreen.

He downed the remainder of his drink in one and stood up to leave. The door on the other side of the street opened, and the only other suit in the neighbourhood stepped onto the sidewalk.

The black bodyguard paused and looked both ways, but he was not interested in the traffic. He turned his body to face Richard head on and purposefully started to cross the road. For a second the journalist froze, before coming to his senses. He grabbed his coat and made his way as quickly as he could to the rear of the bar. Beyond the seating area there was a payphone attached to the right-hand wall, opposite the restroom. Richard headed for the emergency exit at the end of the corridor and crashed against it with his full momentum. The door held. He pushed it again before noticing the heavy padlock that was holding it shut. He heard the main door of the bar open, and swift footsteps moved towards him. He darted into the restroom and helped the spring-loaded door to close behind him. The inward-opening doors to the two cubicles on the left were both ajar and showed signs of having been kicked open more than once. A disgustingly stained washbasin stood opposite the nearest cubicle, just beyond the arc of the main door. In a snap decision, Richard decided the dry-cleaning bill would be a worthwhile investment, if he lived long enough to pay it, squeezed up tight against the wall by the restroom door, and held his breath. The door crashed open, coming to a juddering halt less than an inch from his head as the rubber stopper screwed into the floor did its job. The force of the push jammed the spring mechanism, and the door hung limply, directly in front of Richard's face. He would have to time his kick perfectly to disable the bodyguard for long enough to stand any chance of getting out of the bar. He braced himself for the black man's next move. The ping came as a complete surprise, followed by the rattle as nickels and dimes were fed into the payphone and a ten-digit number was dialled. Out of town.

"Frank, it's Louie. We may have a problem. Some guy's just been round here mouthing off about Jimmy Sullivan. ... No, we've no idea who he is. White, late thirties, about six foot, short light curly hair. Not a cop. ... No, he didn't mention anything about the hookers. ... Okay, will do. The boss just thought Mr Goldberg should know about it."

The handset was dropped back into the cradle and two of the coins were returned. Richard heard the first few steps away from the payphone, then silence. For the next five minutes he strained his ears but couldn't hear a sound. Finally, he decided he had to make a move and gently pushed the door away from his face. The creak made him jump and he froze again, but when it came to a halt, there was still silence. He took a deep breath and stepped round the door, hesitating again before entering the bar. The solitary drinker paid him no attention, but the barman was visibly surprised to see him. Richard walked hurriedly out through the front door, turned right and made his way as quickly as he could back to the subway.

CHAPTER SEVENTY-ONE

"Jack Gordon?"

"Yes?"

"Don't say the name. I hope you recognise the voice."

The other end of the line went quiet for several seconds.

"My God! Where have you been? I've got some stuff you left behind in a hotel room."

"Better hang on to that for a while. I've just mailed you a package. Call it an insurance policy. I have a meeting in Washington tonight, and I'd feel safer if someone else knew about it."

"Sure. What do you want me to do?"

"If you don't hear from me in the next few days, then something's gone wrong. I trust you to act accordingly."

"Sounds mysterious. Can't wait to see what it is. By the way, you remember our friend who had the accident here?"

"Of course I do. Why?"

"Well, I finally got to the bottom of what happened. Nothing at all to do with the Germans. Just the usual – money and sex."

It took Jack Gordon less than five minutes to provide the missing pieces in the jigsaw. Richard waited for his friend to hang up and listened hard. There was no second click. Last year's scandal about the tapping of the public telephones in Grand Central station had either scared the police off or had led them to develop more advanced technologies. He walked back to the centre of the concourse, circled the information desk under the famous clock, then made his way to the subway.

CHAPTER SEVENTY-TWO

"Hello, Mr Johnson. Sorry to keep you waiting. My name is Gibbs."

He was in his early thirties, about six feet tall and clean-shaven. His blond hair looked like it had been sculpted into place by a Hollywood make-up artist. The suit was smarter than any of those Richard had passed while being escorted to this interview room in the far corner of the FBI's Manhattan field office. Gibbs placed the sheaf of papers onto the desk, before sitting opposite Richard and continuing.

"I will be escorting you to your meeting with Director Stanhope in Washington this evening."

Richard couldn't help looking at his watch. Half past five and they were still over two hundred miles from the capital.

"What time will I be meeting the Director?"

"Just as soon as his schedule permits, Mr Johnson. He is a very busy man, as I'm sure you appreciate, especially with the election tomorrow. Perhaps if you could tell me what you wanted to discuss with the Director, it would be easier for all of us."

"No, Mr Gibbs. I need to speak to him personally, as I have explained. But I do have something for you."

Gibbs frowned as he waited for Richard to continue.

"Do you know about Jimmy Sullivan?"

"Yes. The man who was found dead in Naziland in Havana. It's all in your file." He rested his hand on top of the papers, as if in confirmation. "But that is a matter for the Cuban State Police, and they caught the man who did it."

"Actually, it's not as simple as that," said Richard. "Jimmy Sullivan was murdered by Isaiah Horowitz." He studied the FBI man's face as he waited for the information to sink in. "You know who Isaiah Horowitz is, I take it?"

"Of course. But that has nothing to do with the FBI. The

murder is within the clear jurisdiction of the state police."

"Not if it's all tied up with election fraud, it isn't."

Gibbs slid a yellow legal pad from underneath the pile of papers and took a slim gold pen from his jacket pocket.

"You'd better tell me what you know."

For the next ten minutes Richard explained how the private investigator, while looking for evidence that would allow Mrs Horowitz to divorce her husband, had stumbled upon a fundraising event which Horowitz had organised for the Republican Party. The donors had been treated to one-on-one time with the presidential candidate, and as many call-girls as their stamina would allow.

"What do you have in the way of evidence, Mr Johnson."

"According to Senator Goldberg's office, he spent the weekend in question in Texas. According to the logs at Havana airport, his plane landed at seven p.m. and took off again at two the next morning. And if you search Horowitz's office here, I bet you'll find the photographs that will be used to blackmail the guests."

"But what about the murder? Who committed that? Presumably not Horowitz himself."

"For what it's worth, my money's on a guy named Louie. It could even have been an accident. He looks to me like someone who doesn't know his own strength."

Gibbs clicked the pen off and laid it on top of the pad. Richard was disappointed.

"Isn't that enough for you, Agent Gibbs? You would find all the evidence you need in that office. Or if not there, in one of the casinos."

Gibbs clasped his hands together, swung them behind his head and stretched his elbows backwards to release the tension.

"No, that's fine, Mr Johnson. We've had our eye on Horowitz for a few months. Back in August he was in deep financial trouble, then suddenly he was flush again. We suspected he was creaming off the top of the election contributions but had no way of proving it. The timing fits nicely with this murder, so you've just given us enough to get a warrant. I need to brief my colleagues, then you and I can be on our way to Washington.

If you'll wait here for a few minutes. Can I get you a coffee or something?"

Richard shook his head, and Gibbs left the room. It was a quarter of an hour before he returned.

"Ready?" Gibbs had a beige overcoat slung over his arm and a slight bulge under the jacket. Richard followed him to the elevator and was surprised when he pressed the button for the top floor.

Washington DC – November 2024

CHAPTER SEVENTY-THREE

It was approaching nine o'clock when the helicopter reached Washington DC. A recent shower had cleared, leaving all the major monuments shining white under their floodlights. They passed over the Capitol and started to descend as they flew along Pennsylvania Avenue. Richard turned towards Gibbs to ask why they were in the no-fly zone.

"The director has a second office in the White House. In the build-up to the election that's where he spends most of his time."

"Is the president in residence today?"

"I believe President Kennedy is at a Democratic Party event in California this evening. He will be back in Washington tomorrow afternoon."

They touched down on the lawn of the White House, and Gibbs led the way to the entrance of the East Wing. He surrendered his weapon, before going through the body scanner. Richard watched as the gun, still in its holster, was secured in one of the small lockers inside the guard's bullet-proof cubicle.

Once through the security checks, Gibbs called the elevator and pressed the button marked two.

CHAPTER SEVENTY-FOUR

Red Donovan nodded to the *Eastern Times*'s legal counsel listening in on the second earpiece of the editor's phone.

"Let me make sure I understand you, Mr Director. Are you telling me I am not allowed to publish?"

"You know I can't do that, Mr Donovan. I am asking you to think of the best interests of your country."

"Our country," the editor corrected him. "And, generally, the best interests of our country lie in upholding the freedom of information and the power of democracy."

"Generally, that is true. I absolutely agree."

Donovan could sense the resignation in the voice of the FBI Director. There were few people who could outsmart the editor of *ET* in an argument, and Bradley Stanhope wasn't one of them.

"And that is exactly what we plan to do, Mr Director. We will give the people of our great country the full benefit of the facts, so that they can make the most informed choice tomorrow."

"But publishing now will create a disproportionate response. It's not as if this man is standing for office himself. He is just one of the financial backers of a candidate."

"Listen, Brad. I understand your concern, and to a degree I share it. But think for a moment what happens afterwards. How would I respond after the story comes out and people realise I suppressed it to avoid having an influence on the election? And, believe me, it will come out."

"Can you at least tone it down?" Bradley Stanhope knew he was a beaten man.

"I'll see what I can do. But it's not really any great surprise. Everyone knows he's a crook. Everyone knows his wife should divorce him. And Goldberg looks like he's lost the election already, even before this story breaks. I'm not really sure why it bothers you so much, Brad."

"To be honest, Patrick, what really concerns me is that someone has leaked this story now in order to influence the voting."

"And just how is that different from what you're asking me to do?"

"I'm trying to keep things on an even keel, Patrick. I'm trying to stop someone sabotaging the election. At the end of the day, I'm the one responsible for making sure this election is legal and fair."

"Rather you than me, Brad. I'll stick to writing about politicians. Keeping them honest is a hopeless cause, as far as I'm concerned."

"I just wish it hadn't happened now, Patrick. This is the worst possible timing."

"I think that's what was intended," said Donovan.

The Director latched onto the words in a flash. "Does that mean you know where the leak came from?"

The editor of the *Eastern Times* hesitated longer than he should have. He was still trying to work through in his own mind how Samuel Levy had got his hands on the story. And why he had waited until now to pass it on.

"Not necessarily. And that's not a road you want to go down, Brad. The Senate upheld my right to protect my sources two years ago, and as far as I'm aware, the law hasn't changed since then."

"I'd appreciate it if you could give some thought to what I said, Patrick."

"Well, Brad. If you've got a nice exclusive for me ... Something juicy enough to keep a major political scandal off the front page on election day ..."

"I wish, Patrick. I wish."

Donovan hung up. He liked to stay on the right side of the FBI, and his relationship with its director had been beneficial on several occasions. But he knew he would be hung out to dry if he gave in.

CHAPTER SEVENTY-FIVE

The marine standing outside the elevator on the second floor of the East Wing of the White House snapped to attention as the door slid open, his rifle moving from the cradled position across his chest to the vertical. As the journalist and the FBI agent walked past, he quickly reverted to his previous stance. Gibbs led the way to the end of the corridor where a middle-aged woman, dressed just as smartly as him, was sitting at a large wooden desk. In front of her the name *Miss Martha Van Buren* was etched in gold letters into a triangular block of highly polished mahogany. Behind her was an enormous portrait of George Washington in his general's uniform, sitting astride a white horse which the caption identified as Blueskin.

"Good evening, Mr Johnson. Director Stanhope has been called away to a meeting. I expect him to be back soon. Please take a seat." She made a sweeping gesture towards the chairs perched against the opposite wall. Her head immediately dropped back to the paperwork on her desk, very effectively silencing any question or comment that might have been under consideration. As Richard took his seat, Gibbs took his leave.

"I will see you later, Mr Johnson." He strode off down the corridor, back the way they had come. The carpet absorbed the sound of footsteps, and even the elevator door was inaudible. The clicking of the marine's heels was the only sound in this library-like atmosphere.

Richard tried to remember if there was a clock above where he was sitting. He was starting to feel self-conscious about how frequently he was looking at his watch, not that Miss Van Buren seemed to notice. He didn't recall exactly when he had arrived, but he had first checked his watch in frustration at quarter past nine. He had read the evening paper from cover to cover, and it was now after eleven.

"He won't be long now, Mr Johnson." They obviously didn't

do coffee on this floor.

"Do you think I might have a glass of water?"

The secretary finished the current sentence she was writing on the document in front of her and placed the pencil down on the desk before looking him in the eye. The next hesitation seemed to threaten dire consequences if he dared to repeat his question, which he didn't.

"There is a water cooler at the end of the corridor." She nodded almost imperceptibly in the direction to her left, away from the elevator and its marine guard.

Richard got up and turned past her desk, determined to take as long as was humanly possible to retrieve water from a cooler. Finding a gentlemen's restroom, and several further presidential portraits bearing descriptive labels from the National Archives, proved helpful in this respect. He was studying the detail on the first of the four Kennedy presidents, visualising the man in a Lisbon hotel room, when the phone on Miss Van Buren's desk rang.

He edged his way back slowly towards where he had been seated, while the secretary made grunts of acknowledgement to her caller. By the time she hung up, he was already seated.

"Mr Johnson, I'm afraid Mr Stanhope won't be able to see you until first thing in the morning. I suggest you try to get some sleep and be back here for six o'clock. Would you like me to get you a hotel room, or would you prefer to use a sofa in the basement area?"

Richard looked at his watch. It was just past midnight. Election day. He had never slept in his own office, and now he had the prospect of bedding down in one of the most important buildings in the world. Though it would never make print, this was one of those stories you saved up for the grandchildren.

"The sofa will be fine."

He waited while she locked her papers in the desk drawer, put on her coat and packed a couple of personal items into her handbag, then followed her towards the elevator. The marine clicked back to attention, but no one exchanged a word. Miss Van Buren pressed the button marked B.

Richard was surprised at the layout as they stepped through a glass door into what looked like a schoolteachers' common room, glowing dimly in the emergency lighting. Miss Van Buren led him off to the right, behind a partition of clouded glass, where two large sofas faced each other. She walked between them and crouched down very elegantly, opened the cupboard, and extracted a blanket and two pillows, which she dropped behind her left shoulder onto one of the sofas.

"I hope you will be reasonably comfortable, Mr Johnson. I shall tell the guard to wake you at half past five. The washroom is just round the corner there." She gestured behind his sofa. "Now if there is nothing else I can do for you, I shall wish you good night."

Richard nodded, and she stepped back into the main body of the room, where he could hear the glass door open and close. He removed his shoes and jacket, arranged the pillows on the end of the sofa, and settled down for what he hoped would be his final night of sleeping rough. For the first time he wondered what state his New York apartment would be in after such a period of neglect, and what mouldy delights would await his return in the refrigerator. As his head touched the pillow, he drifted off into a deep sleep.

CHAPTER SEVENTY-SIX

"Mr Johnson."

The waiter was hovering next to him, his white tuxedo shining in the brilliant sunlight. He had nothing better to do than wait for the guest to shift his gaze past the palm trees, away from the crystal blue waters of the Pacific Ocean and decide which cocktail he fancied this time. Richard licked his lips in anticipation and was surprised how rough and dry they were.

"Mr Johnson, sir. It's zero five thirty."

It took a massive effort to force his eyelids apart. In the virtual darkness he could see the giant black shape hovering over his head. "Good morning, sir. I brought you some coffee." As the marine spoke, his huge white glove placed a steaming mug on the cupboard by Richard's head. He grunted an acknowledgment and started to sit up, swinging his legs off the sofa, still entangled in their blanket. He stood up and the guard marched away to his post beyond the glass door. Richard rubbed his eyes for a few moments before trying the coffee. It was military standard rather than five-star, but its warmth, strength and sweetness were exactly what he needed. He thought back over the events of the previous day and remembered that he was supposed to be meeting with the director of the FBI at six.

The washroom was as well equipped for the current eventuality as the rest of the staff area, and after ten minutes Richard was surprised just how presentable he appeared in the mirror above the wash basin. The clock showed five fifty when he returned for a further dose of the coffee, which had cooled to a more bearable temperature. There was no other sign of life on either side of the glass door, so he decided to see if the elevator would operate without secretarial or military intervention. He pressed the call button, and the door opened immediately. Stepping inside, he pressed button two. The door slid shut and the metal box glided upwards. The opening of the door was silent, punctuated only by the click of the marine's heels as he exited. Out of the corner of his eye Richard checked – it was a different marine. As he made his way back to the previous evening's chair, the huge panelled-wood door of the office behind Miss Van Buren's desk opened. She emerged with a large diary and a sheaf of loose papers in her hand, closing the door behind her. Catching sight of Richard, her eyes flicked momentarily to the clock over his chair.

"Director Stanhope will see you now," she said, pausing only to place the paperwork on her desk before turning on her heel, knocking on the door and opening it again without waiting for a reply.

The sensation which Richard later remembered was not the change from the harsh fluorescent lighting of the corridor to the warm glow emanating from the desk lamp against the dark backdrop of the Washington skyline, nor the wafting aroma of brewing coffee that contrasted with the sterility on the other side of the door which had just clicked shut behind him. It was the carpet. He hadn't registered the carpet in the corridor, but as he crossed the line, he was immediately conscious of the plush red pile beneath his feet, which made it feel like he was wading through cotton wool.

The man behind the desk stood up and walked around it, stretching out his hand while still several strides away from his early-morning visitor. His face was familiar from several appearances on television, but he was not as tall as Richard had expected.

"Richard, a pleasure to meet you at last. I apologise for yesterday, but I was unavoidably detained." He gestured towards the large sofa with its antique-looking brown leather, where they sat down next to each other.

"Well, you've had quite an adventure, by all accounts. I'm really glad we managed to get you back in one piece. You've been causing a number of people here some headaches and long nights, but it's almost over now."

"Thank you, sir." Richard didn't understand why he had said that. He was not usually intimidated by meeting the great and the good, or not so good, and he was unaware what role the director in person, the FBI, or the government in general had played in his escape from the Nazis.

"Now, Richard, I understand you have some information which you wanted to discuss with me personally." Richard was unsure whether he could detect a hint of reproach in the voice. The smile certainly betrayed no sign of impatience or reluctance. Two old friends might sit on just such a sofa, though clearly less impressive in its quality, antiquity and historical significance than this one, to mull over old times after a well-lubricated, relaxed dinner.

"Yes, sir. I do." He was suddenly tongue-tied. He had thought through this conversation a thousand times – on the warship, on the plane, last night in the corridor outside this very office – but it no longer seemed right.

"I think the Nazis are manipulating the election and that Senator Masters, the vice-presidential candidate, is their spy. Sir."

Director Stanhope hesitated before responding. "Okay, Richard. How many people have you shared this theory with?"

"None, sir. Until now."

"And what evidence do you have, Richard?"

"I don't have any evidence of that, although it makes perfect sense. The evidence I found was that Senator Masters is a Nazi spy. When I was in Gestapo headquarters in Berlin, I found a photograph of him receiving a medal from Chancellor Goebbels. And if they can get one of their people elected vice-president today, they are just one bullet away from him becoming president."

The director nodded sombrely. "A terrifying thought, Richard, I agree." He looked serious, but neither surprised nor particularly disturbed. Richard attributed this to a lifetime's practice of not displaying any reaction as political events unfolded in front of his eyes, as they frequently did.

"Can you describe the photograph for me, Richard?"

He thought for a moment. Every time he had tried to summon it before his mind's eye since that day in Berlin, Richard had focused on the key players in the image. The background had literally gone out of focus for him, dominated as it was by the red curls of the doctor's hair, escaping from under his military cap.

"In the foreground was Chancellor Goebbels about to hang the Order of the German Eagle around the neck of Senator Masters. Behind them were two rows of Gestapo, about twenty altogether. One of them was the red-headed doctor who attended most of my interrogation sessions."

"Where was the photograph taken?"

Richard scanned the image in his mind. The background was a complete blank. He closed his eyes and tried again. Was there a smudge in the corner? Could it have been the Great Hall in Berlin? Was it even outdoors?

"I think it was sunny, which means it was outdoors. But I don't remember anything specific. No buildings. Nothing."

"Why didn't you take the picture with you, Richard?"

The journalist looked at him in surprise. The thought had never occurred to him. Not at the time, nor since.

"I guess I had other things on my mind." He didn't intend the sarcasm to come across quite that clearly, but the director laughed it off.

"Of course you did, Richard. A silly question on my part. Still, was there anyone else in the photograph you recognised?"

Richard shook his head slowly. As Director Stanhope was about to ask his next question, a sudden thought entered Richard's head.

"Maybe." The director's face tensed momentarily while Richard was searching in the recesses of his memory for any connection he hadn't made previously. "Most of the Gestapo in the picture were quite young. It looked a bit like a graduation class photo. But in the middle was an older guy. He was a bit obscured by Goebbels's arm, which is why I didn't recognise him at the time. I think it could have been the general who did my final interrogation."

Stanhope's shoulders relaxed again. "Anything else, Richard?"

"No, sir. That's definitely all I can remember."

"And who did you tell about the photograph?"

No one you would know. And certainly no one I would want you checking up on.

"Nobody, sir. You're the first person I've mentioned it to," Richard lied.

"Good. It's better for everyone that way."

To make sure his message had got through, Richard felt compelled to repeat the implications. "So, the Nazis are trying to undermine Senator Blackwell's campaign for the presidency, and then they can assassinate President Goldberg and put their own man in the White House."

"Actually, Richard, if you'd seen this morning's newspaper, you would realise that it's Senator Goldberg and his people who have made an excellent job of sabotaging their own campaign. We now know what really happened in Cuba – the murder you went there to investigate. It was carried out by one of the senator's people. We tried to suppress that information so that it didn't have a bearing on the election, but the freedom of the press has prevailed, and the story is out." While he was speaking, he walked over to his desk and returned with a newspaper, folded to highlight what he wanted Richard to read.

GOLDBERG BACKER ARRESTED

Isaiah Horowitz, the New York businessman and socialite, was arrested late last night, charged with the murder of Jimmy Sullivan, a private investigator hired by his wife. Horowitz has been a major supporter of the Goldberg campaign, and this blow to the Jewish presidential hopeful has come just hours before voting is set to start.

A tired-looking Goldberg said he had no knowledge of the accusations against Horowitz and declined to comment further.

The body of Jimmy Sullivan was discovered in August inside the Germany attraction at MicroWorld, leading to numerous conspiracy theories. It is now claimed that Jimmy Sullivan was murdered in Havana by Horowitz and the body was dumped in Naziland by his associates in an attempt to lay a false trail.

This latest scandal comes after persistent rumours of Horowitz's connections to organised crime, illegal gambling and money laundering.

Richard felt confused and completely deflated. The problem he had raced across the world to resolve had evaporated of its own accord. However, the issue with the senator still remained, and the only man in a position to do something about it had decided he wasn't going to bother. But Richard's stunned silence seemed to be mistaken for comprehension.

"Well, I'm glad we've got that straight," the director said.

As far as Richard was concerned, nothing had been straight since he had left for Cuba. That had been a mere three months ago, but it seemed much longer. A world away. A world he didn't realise he had until he lost it. A world of simple certainties: of good guys and bad guys; of straightforward, boring politics; a world order dominated by three massive power blocks in perfect balance, if not quite harmony. But his uncherished equilibrium had gone. He could not un-know what he had experienced. Even though he didn't fully understand, he knew he could never forget.

"So, what do you plan to do next, Richard?"

The question took him by surprise. Had the conversation moved on, never to return to the most pressing topic? Had he failed to get his point across? He hesitated, realising two things simultaneously. Firstly, his thoughts had never progressed past this moment. His objective had been to get to someone in a position of authority, so that this person could deal with the situation. He hadn't given any thought to what that would actually look like. Nor had he given a moment's thought to what would happen next. The second point that now occurred to him was that this question from the director might have been a threat. What kind of trap was his next answer going to precipitate him towards?

"I haven't given it any thought, sir. My only concern has been to get to Washington so that someone could deal with the situation."

"Very commendable, Richard, but as is often the case, the situation is much more complex than it appears." The director paused momentarily. "To be frank, Richard, we need your help. Your country is depending on what you choose to do next."

Richard's face must have betrayed the full extent of his puzzlement as Stanhope took a deep breath before starting again.

"I'm sure you have a very interesting story for your readers, Richard. Probably a book that would sell many more copies than *The Fall of the Ginnelli Family*. Your adventures in the Nazi empire alone would guarantee its success, even without your concerns about the election. But we need you to keep all this to yourself. For the good of the United States." He hesitated, scanning Richard's face, but seeing no reaction.

"We know about Senator Masters, Richard. We know all about him and the Nazis." He waited for this to sink in, but the shell-shocked gaze remained transfixed. "Do you know how we know, Richard? No? We know, because he is working for us, Richard. The Nazis think he is spying for them. He is actually working for us." Another pause. Richard looked into his eyes. His brain seemed to be working at half speed as it tried to process all this new information. "You must realise how dangerous a position he is in. No one must find out what is happening. Richard, his life depends on you saying nothing."

The pieces started to drop into place in his mind. The confusion blocking Richard's thoughts was displaced by the sheer enormity of the situation.

"We need your help, Richard. We need your silence. More than that. We need you to disappear."

Richard's uptake was now significantly quicker. There were two ways in which his silence and disappearance could be arranged.

"So, Richard, we have a proposition. We set you up with a new identity in a new location. You have no family ties, so this should be no hardship. And since you disappeared in Cuba, no one outside the government has heard anything from you. To be frank, no one will miss you, because you are already missing." Stanhope paused again to allow this to sink in. Richard was conscious that he had not responded to anything that had been said to him, so just to fill the gap, he came out with a single word.

"Okay."

"Good. That is for the best, Richard. And we will make it worth your while." He took a notepad and pen from his jacket pocket, scribbled something on the top sheet, ripped it off and folded it over. "Our people have estimated how much you would stand to make if you published your story. Of course, you can never do that, but it's only fair we compensate you." He handed Richard the folded piece of paper. Richard looked at it before flicking it open. The amount would have been generous without the final zero. His face showed no emotion – not because there wasn't any, but because he was drained; utterly spent. Exhaustion was finally catching up with him, and the mass of conflicting thoughts, feelings and concerns was just too much for his brain to take in. For the first time he noticed a glimmer of doubt in the director's face.

"Don't worry, Mr Director. I accept your offer. You have a deal." Richard heard himself speaking but hardly recognised his own voice. Something deep-seated within him had taken over – the primeval survival instinct, which realised this was his only chance of getting out of here alive.

"Excellent, Richard. Obviously, we'll have to change your identity, but that's all being taken care of. Fingerprints, dental records, retinal scans – the works, all now point to the new you."

Richard had always found it irritating when politicians kept using your first name in an unsophisticated attempt to forge some type of personal bond. But it sounded like he was not going to be hearing his own name for much longer, so he decided to enjoy it while it lasted.

"The Germans use complete biometric profiles with full DNA records on everyone's ID card." He didn't know why he had said that. He needed to get out; to sleep for a very long time.

"Well, I guess a regime like theirs needs to feel it is in total control of its subjects. Though you, yourself, are testament to the failings of their system." The director hesitated, but there was no response. "Right then, Richard. Our people will brief you on your new identity and finalise all the details. If you have any questions, they will be able to deal with them for you. By this evening, you should be on your way to your new life."

"Just as long as it isn't Cuba."

"No, Richard. I can guarantee that you won't be going to Cuba any time soon."

There was an uncomfortable silence until the director spoke again.

"Senator Blackwell is a good person, Richard, with the people's best interests at heart. Not an outstanding mind, but as our country's first female president, people will focus on other things. And I have every confidence she'll be quite a good leader."

The director of the FBI rose to his feet. He had the look

of a man with a great weight lifted from his shoulders. But as Richard stood up and stretched out his hand, a frown crossed Director Stanhope's brow.

"There is one more thing, Richard. An infringement of your constitutional rights, I'm afraid, but under the circumstances, unavoidable. We can't let you vote today. Now, if you'll excuse me, I have a few other matters which require my personal attention. Miss Van Buren will take care of you from here." Richard became aware that the director's secretary had entered the room. "Good luck, Richard. Your country is grateful to you." Director Stanhope turned away and stepped back towards his desk. Richard remained rooted to the spot, until he felt a gentle touch on his elbow as Miss Van Buren brought him back from his reverie.

"Come with me, Mr Johnson. I shall take you to Mr Gibbs, who will make all the arrangements."

CHAPTER SEVENTY-SEVEN

The light flashed briefly on Director Stanhope's telephone, indicating that his secretary had returned to her station.

"Miss Van Buren, see to it that I am not disturbed for the next five minutes. Not by anyone." He released the intercom switch without waiting for a reply and stood up from the desk.

The bookshelf contained an eclectic collection, including a set of quarto volumes bound in dark red leather with gold tooling to a high standard of finish. The spines identified them as the collected personal correspondence of the first dozen presidents, and no one had ever remarked on the unlikely uniformity of the twelve books. Stanhope picked volume eleven from the shelf, *James Knox Polk*, and took it back to his desk. With his thumbnail he flicked up the gilt edge of the volume, which masqueraded as a hundred individual pages while actually concealing the lock to a filing box. He noticed his hand was trembling slightly, and it took two attempts to insert the smallest key on his ring into the hole. Two turns were followed by a sharp click, and he opened the leather-bound lid. He took out the envelope, and gently prised it open without tearing the flap. He shook the single photograph onto his desk and looked into the centre of the image, slightly above the German's arm. He remembered the general very well. He had only been a colonel at the time but clearly destined for greatness. Immediately behind him was the flash of red hair, to which he had never paid any attention before. Stanhope remembered that there had been a doctor present at some of the sessions he had attended over that two-week stay in Berlin nearly two decades earlier, but he had no recollection of the individual. The building in the background was the rear of Gestapo Headquarters, which meant the spectators would be standing directly over the 'House Prison', where Johnson had spent an uncomfortable couple of months. The FBI man's eyes moved over to the right of the picture, immediately beside the head of Reichsminister Goebbels – he was not yet chancellor as Rommel was still clinging to life, if not power. The clean-shaven face looking back at him was much more youthful than the one he saw in the mirror on the occasions his full beard needed a trim. And much less American. A shudder went down his spine. It was madness to keep the picture, but he couldn't bring himself to dispose of it. Taking care not to touch the surface, Stanhope returned the photograph to the envelope, and the envelope to the box, before slotting Polk into his rightful place between Tyler and Taylor.

He took up station behind his desk and buzzed his secretary. They had an election to take care of.

CHAPTER SEVENTY-EIGHT

The rest of Richard's morning and early afternoon passed in a blur as Gibbs, in as sharp a suit as the previous evening, transformed Richard Johnson, journalist resident in New York, into Bob Jarvis, an aspiring novelist, recently moved to Seattle after a substantial legacy allowed him to give up the job of selling vacuum cleaners in the Midwest. It looked like they had thought of everything. The Illinois driving licence had a convincing photograph of what Robert A. Jarvis looked like three years previously, and the application form for the Washington state licence only required his signature. His brain and wrist ached after memorising the bank account and social security numbers, passwords, family history, addresses and telephone numbers, and practising his signature until it matched the one already held by the First Providential Bank of Seattle.

The disappearance of the *Eastern Times* journalist had raised some concern within the community. The majority view was that he must have fallen foul of the vengeance of the mafia, before moving onto more topical storylines. His assets, including the proceeds from the disposal of his New York apartment and its contents, would be held in a trust account for the remainder of the seven years before he could be legally pronounced dead. Richard hoped he could rely on Jack Gordon as his only link back to the former reality, so had decided not to mention the former policeman during the extensive interviews to validate that all loose ends had been tied up and that Richard, or Bob, was psychologically equipped for the imminent life change.

At four in the afternoon Richard, in possession of nothing but the clothes he was wearing, and Robert Jarvis's slightly battered new wallet, emerged from the White House's underground car park, past the waiting throng of photographers. The blanket over his head proved an unnecessary precaution, as the tinted windows didn't provoke any interest among the paparazzi, and they sped the few miles eastwards out of the capital to the Camp Springs Air Force Base. Their small jet was at the opposite end of the facility from where Air Force One had just parked, and the car pulled right up to the foot of the steps. The sun hadn't quite set as they shot into the sky in the direction of Chicago.

Chicago – November 2024

CHAPTER SEVENTY-NINE

The small government jet taxied off the landing runway at Chicago Municipal airport towards a discreet building out of sight of the passenger terminal. The airport vehicle, with its flashing orange and red lights, quickly drove them round to the main building's VIP entrance.

"This is where I leave you, Mr Jarvis. Your flight departs from gate eighteen in just over two hours." Gibbs took an envelope from the inside pocket of his jacket and handed it over. "This contains all the information you need when you get to Seattle. You have a reservation at the airport hotel. There are directions to your new home for tomorrow morning. The keys for the house will be waiting for you at the hotel reception. Now all that remains is for me to wish you luck. Any questions?"

Richard shook his head. He was still overloaded with all the information that had been dumped on him in the last twenty-four hours. Gibbs stood and watched as he climbed the stairs and turned the corner out of sight.

The airport was relatively empty, and most of the passengers were sitting watching the election coverage on the large television screens. The consensus seemed to be that the revelations about Senator Goldberg's involvement with Isaiah Horowitz, and the latter's use of prostitutes at his fundraising events, had dealt a fatal blow to the Jewish candidate's campaign.

Richard headed towards gate eighteen, but it was completely deserted as there were still more than ninety minutes before take-off. He sat down just long enough to check the plane ticket in his jacket pocket and the driver's licence in his tatty new wallet. He unzipped the holdall, which contained his new clothes and the bundles of cash that were enough to see him through the next few weeks and stuffed the latest envelope inside. There would be plenty of time to study that on the aircraft.

He set off in search of coffee and a book to read on the flight.

Something light – no politics, no thrillers, no murder mysteries, none of the ever-popular theories about the Nazis' plans for world domination. He finally settled on *The Great Gatsby* and checked his watch. The flight was in just over an hour, so he headed to the washroom. He was splashing his face with water when he heard the door swing open behind him. The new man took two steps forwards and stopped. As Richard turned off the tap, there was complete silence. He glanced up into the mirror. Six feet behind him stood a huge black man. Once seen, Isaiah Horowitz's heavy was not a man you would easily forget. A man of few words, he reached underneath his jacket, and Richard watched in slow motion as his hand came out, wrapped around the spangled grip of the pistol he had first seen yesterday.

"It's Louie, isn't it?" Richard didn't turn round in case it was interpreted as aggression, with the inevitable result.

"So? What if it is? What's it to you, anyway?" He seemed very uncomfortable to Richard, hardly as if he was the one holding the gun.

"Do I get a last request?"

"I ain't gettin' you no steak, or nothin'."

"I don't want a steak, Louie. I just want to understand one little detail."

"What detail's that?" Richard saw in the mirror how he switched the gun from one hand to the other. As it moved, the rhinestones on the grip caught the stark fluorescent light.

"It was you that cut *J S* on that man's hand, wasn't it?"

"So? What if it was?"

"Why, Louie? Why did you write it?"

"The boss told me to."

"Yes, but why did he tell you to?"

"I dunno. What's it to you, anyway?"

"It's not much to ask, is it, Louie? A lot less than a steak."

"I suppose."

"So why did Mr Horowitz tell you to cut that on his hand? He was already dead, wasn't he?"

"Yeah. He fell awkward. It was an accident. He banged his head after I hit him. Then I called Mr Horowitz. From the phone in the hotel room."

"And he told you what to do with the body."

"That's right. He wanted it dumping in the German place. He knows some guys who go in regular, and they took it the next night. I took his ID. When I told Mr Horowitz his name, he went kinda quiet. Then said he had a great idea. That I was to carve the guy's initials on his hands. Big, like. So everyone would see."

"Why was that a great idea?"

"I dunno. I don't ask Mr Horowitz questions. I just do what he tells me. You ask too many questions." Louie cocked the pistol. So that was it. Richard was about to die because a private eye got too close to Horowitz and just happened to have the same initials as Samuel Levy's big secret. And Horowitz probably had no idea what *J S* even was, except that it was something sensitive.

Richard expected the adrenaline to kick in one last time, but instead he was suddenly overwhelmed with a tired hopelessness. He dropped his gaze back onto his hands. The knuckles went white as his grip on the edge of the porcelain washbasin tightened. Then he closed his eyes.

He heard the crack of the gunshot, then felt the delayed thump in the middle of his back, like it had been hit by a train. Richard forced his eyes open again and saw the flood of bright red blood streaming over his hands before he collapsed to the floor, and everything went dark.

It felt as if his body was being moved roughly, and a bright light shone down onto the other side of his eyelids.

"We need to get you cleaned up."

Richard opened his eyes. Gibbs was hovering over his face, trying to force him up off the floor. He managed to sit. The body of Louie was lying beside him in a pool of blood, which was still spreading outwards from where his skull used to be. Now Gibbs was rummaging around in the holdall. He pulled out a clean jacket and pair of trousers.

"Change into these. Quickly."

Richard took off his stained jacket and trousers, dropped them onto the floor, and looked into the mirror. The only blood was on his hands, which he quickly washed off, before taking the clothes from Gibbs and redressing. The last in his long line of protectors was on a pocket radio, arranging for the local

FBI office to send a cleaner. He looked Richard up and down before handing back the plane ticket and wallet from the jacket pockets.

"You'll do. Now get out of here – you can still make the flight. You're safe now. This guy was acting on his own. Have a good trip."

Richard picked the holdall off the floor. It, too, was completely clean. But he left *The Great Gatsby* where it lay, the lines of blood spatter streaked across its cover.

EPILOGUE

Cuba – 20th January 2025

The snow was falling heavily on Washington DC as noon approached. Jack shivered. The air conditioning in his Havana apartment was maintaining a comfortable seventy degrees, but the sight of snow, even on the television, still took him back to the bitter winters of his New York beat, and the scar on his leg twinged. The dignitaries were in place; the cameras were in place; the transparent bullet-proof shields were in place. Everything was set for the inauguration of the forty-fifth president of the United States – the first woman after two hundred and thirty-six years. Jack was not a great one for politics, but the phone had not rung once this morning, so he had nothing better to do than watch history being made. He settled into the comfortable but tatty armchair. Then the phone rang.

"Jack Gordon, Private Investigator."

"Hey, Jack. It's Sam. The bookstore. That package you ordered has arrived. Pass by any time you like to pick it up. We can have a drink."

"Okay, Sam. I'll be round this afternoon."

The knot tightening in his stomach was unexpected, but Jack's instincts were good – he was still alive to prove it. This search had always been a long shot, and he never thought it would be possible to track the item down. When Sam said he'd found it, Jack hadn't really believed him, but he had to play along. Get it sent over. Take all the precautions. No point in unnecessary risks, even though it would turn out to be a false alarm. But he would soon know, either way.

He turned his attention back to the television. The chief justice handed over the bible, but Jack couldn't concentrate.

The bookstore was in one of the narrow alleyways of the old town. In the peak season it did well from passing trade. Strategically placed between two of the favourite watering holes of Ernest Hemingway, there was a steady stream of pilgrims, aching to believe that the signature, even though it was impossible to absolutely verify, you understand, might actually be genuine. And after a couple of mojitos, the true value of such a once-in-a-lifetime opportunity could get quite generous. But Sam had another string to his bow, and he needed it. His drinking matched the great author's even better than the autographs. No one was quite sure how he managed it, but if you needed something from Europe, Sam was your man. First editions of *Mein Kampf* were not technically illegal, but some of the old manuscripts certainly were, as their export was completely banned. And as for the old *torahs*, well, they weren't even allowed to exist in Germany any more. But you paid for the service.

The store was shuttered, like the majority of its neighbours. Most of the businesses in this district relied heavily on the tourist trade, so stayed open all through the weekends and closed on Mondays. Even after ringing the bell to the apartment above the shop, there was no sign of life. Jack pressed the white plastic button again, and a scrabbling could be heard inside, like startled mice. Startled mice clearing away empty bottles. The door yawned open, still on the chain, as the white beard – the final Hemingway tribute – appeared to check who was outside.

It was five in the afternoon before Jack got back to his apartment, brown paper parcel under his arm, thick head on his shoulders. He bolted the door shut and drew the curtains closed, although the last of the sunlight was still just about doing its job. The space had already been cleared on his desk, and he put the package down. His fingers were trembling as he tried to unknot the string, so he reverted to the scissors, and then peeled back the layers of brown paper and protective wadding. He stared at the book on the desk in front of him. The cover photograph showed the oversized black statue of the dictator saluting his city – *Linz: Art Capital of the Reich*. The golden-jubilee edition from 1998. The one with the special end papers. Particularly the one at the back.

Jack took the scalpel from the top drawer of his desk. He knew he should wait until he was sober, but he just had to check.

The trembling in his hand got worse as the point of the knife approached the marbled end paper. Coffee. He needed coffee. That would steady his hand.

Once he had loosened both corners, he was surprised how easily the paper peeled back. The white sheet beneath had identical stamps in all four of its corners – the words '*STRENG GEHEIM*' in bold black capitals, the eagle with outstretched wings above, a circle with an emphatic swastika below. Jack didn't know any German, but even he could tell this was not allowed out. Slowly, he slid the point of the scalpel under a corner of the photograph. Time to see what he had got for his fifteen hundred dollars.

It was just as Richard's notes had described. Two regimented rows of pristine Gestapo uniforms. One shock of untidy red hair underneath a black cap – Herr Doktor Stefan Fürst, MBBS (Oxon), MD (Berlin) – secret policemen don't often leave a clear paper trail, but medical doctors usually do. One recently deceased German chancellor placing an award round the neck of a man in a business suit and fedora. There could be no doubt. The face was turned slightly away from the camera, but if anything, that made the profile even more distinctive. The profile of the senator from Texas. The man who, if things had gone slightly differently, would have been standing just behind the first Jewish president of the United States a few hours ago. The man who had not become Vice President Masters.

Jack Gordon rummaged in the desk drawer to find his magnifying glass. Heavy and expensive, both largely due to the polished mahogany handle, it had been his first purchase when he retired from the police force and set up in business for himself. He could count on the fingers of one hand the number of times he had actually used it. The clarity which it brought to the image was startling. Between the white enamelled arms of the Maltese cross hanging from the red ribbon he could make out each of the four golden eagles clasping wreaths encircling a swastika. He moved the glass up to examine the face of the senator. There was the slightest hint of a smile. Politeness, gratitude or pride? He tracked to the right and down slightly. Reichsminister, later to be Chancellor Goebbels, was a head shorter than Masters. The profile was instantly recognisable from the portrait bust used on some of the coinage. Jack's eye was drawn slightly to the right, to the face staring past the back of Heinrich Goebbels's head, straight at the camera. A trick of the light, or the memory? The eyebrows, the shape of the eyes, the nose, the mouth. Months of training, years of looking through mug shots, a simple beard was not enough to put a good cop off the scent. He put down the magnifying glass and went back to the armchair, around which the various sections of yesterday's *New York Times* lay scattered across the floor. Jack found what he was looking for on page six of the special inauguration supplement. After the timetable of events, the statistics of the election results and the summary of the campaign promises were the details of those standing around the new president at noon. The outlines of the bodies were based on a photograph of Joseph Patrick Kennedy III's inauguration in 2017, but the numbers referred to those who had been on the podium today. Number thirteen, unlucky for some, the Director of the FBI, Bradley Stanhope. The official publicity photograph on the next page showed the beard. But the eyes were unmistakeable, and the mouth. The biography under the photograph ran to the standard two paragraphs and made no mention of Germany. And this was the guy Richard had told his story to in Washington.

Jack took the painting off the wall and turned the dial on the front of his safe. He twisted the brown envelope with its New York postmark, and manoeuvred it out, past the instant coffee jar stuffed with twenty dollar-bills, and the heavy Colt revolver. He slid the envelope's contents out onto the art book. A postcard showing the Starbucks Needle observation tower in Washington state – the unsigned inscription on the back paraphrased Mark Twain, one of Richard's favourite writers: *Reports of my death are exaggerated.* A dozen closely typed sheets of notepaper. A wallet containing two hundred and seventeen dollars, a credit card and a New York driver's licence both in the name of Richard Johnson.

He slipped the photograph into the middle of the wad of papers, into the envelope, into the safe. Then he set about repairing the back of the book.

It would only be a matter of time before Richard made contact again. He hoped.

*

AUTHOR'S NOTE

Naziland is set in 2024, but in an alternative reality. The Nazis won the war and therefore everything we know today is different.

While this scenario is distasteful, it could have happened. Indeed, at the point at which the two 'histories' – the real one and my fiction – diverge in May 1941, victory for Hitler was the most likely outcome. The German blitzkrieg offensive had overcome Poland, Belgium, France, the Netherlands, Denmark, Norway, Luxembourg, Yugoslavia and later Greece, to add to the territories gained by political manoeuvres before the actual war broke out – Austria and Czechoslovakia. The rest of continental Europe was already fighting alongside the Nazis – Italy, the USSR, Hungary, Romania and Bulgaria – or neutral – Switzerland, Spain, Portugal, Sweden. Finland was separately at war with the USSR.

The only opposition still standing was Great Britain. By mid-1941 it was exhausted, impoverished, starving and battered. The Battle of Britain had been won, delaying German plans for an invasion which depended on air superiority, and what remained of its land army had, almost miraculously, escaped from Dunkirk after being pushed all the way back to the sea by the German advances. The USA was providing support, albeit illegally, but staying resolutely neutral.

Only an unlikely combination of military miscalculation and freak weather turned the tide.

As America again considers leaving the Europeans to fight their own wars, and nationalist right-wing elements become more prominent across Europe, including in Germany, it may be timely to consider what was narrowly avoided over eighty years ago.

Peter Kelly, Cornwall, November 2025

ACKNOWLEDGMENTS

I would like to thank the following for reviewing drafts of this novel over the many years of its development: Annabel Greatorex, members of Sutton Writers especially Geoffrey West and the late John Barnes, Katy Darby and the participants in her Writers' Workshop course at City University London, Pamela Newton, Richard Williams, Katie Davey Dalsgaard.

Special thanks are due to Christine Hammacott for the cover design, map and layout.

Though it was not their intention, I owe a debt of gratitude to all those who gave me the opportunities to live and work in the locations which informed many of the aspects of the countries and societies which I have invented here, including Cold War Berlin and single-party states such as Russia and China.

And last, but very much not least, I am grateful to my wife Sam for her patience and enduring support.

Needless to say, any errors of history or language and any infelicities – almost inevitable in a work of this nature – are mine alone.

Peter Kelly was born in Manchester and studied Modern Languages at Oxford before before embarking on varied careers in advertising, retailing and management consultancy.

He has lived and worked for extended periods in Germany (including Cold War Berlin), Russia and China.

He now lives in the far west of Cornwall with his wife and her dachshund.

Naziland is his first novel.